THE

Wicked

AFTERMATH

THE WICKEDS: DARK KNIGHTS AT BAYSIDE

MELISSA FOSTER

ISBN-13: 978-1948868952
ISBN-10: 1948868954

Cover Design: Elizabeth Mackey Designs
Cover Photography: Shelly Lange Photography

WORLD LITERARY PRESS
PRINTED IN THE UNITED STATES OF AMERICA

A Note to Readers

This is the story of Tank Wicked and Leah Yates—two broken souls struggling to survive unbearable loss and learning to love again. When Leah first showed herself to me a few years ago, I knew she needed the strongest, and also the most compassionate, of heroes. What I didn't realize was just how much Tank needed her. Writing their love story slayed me, but it also put me back together with more hope than I could have ever imagined. I hope they will do the same for you and that you will fall as deeply in love with Tank, Leah, and their families as I did.

For avid readers of my Love in Bloom novels, please note that this story takes place prior to the Silver Harbor series, which includes Cait Weatherby and Brant Remington's love story, MAYBE WE SHOULD.

Set on the sandy shores of Cape Cod, the Wickeds feature fiercely protective heroes, strong heroines, and unbreakable family bonds. All Wicked novels may be enjoyed as stand-alone romances or as part of the larger series. On the next page you will find a character map of the Wicked world. You can also download a free copy here:
www.MelissaFoster.com/Wicked-World-Character-Map.html

The Wickeds are the cousins of the Whiskeys, each of whom has already been given their own story. You can download the first book in the Whiskey series, TRU BLUE, and a Whiskey/Wicked family tree here:

TRU BLUE
www.MelissaFoster.com/TheWhiskeys

WHISKEY/WICKED Family Tree
www.MelissaFoster.com/Wicked-Whiskey-Family-Tree

Remember to sign up for my newsletter to make sure you don't miss out on future Wicked releases:
www.MelissaFoster.com/News

For information about more of my sexy romances, all of which can be read as stand-alone novels or as part of the larger series, visit my website:
www.MelissaFoster.com

If you prefer sweet romance with no explicit scenes or graphic language, please try the Sweet with Heat series written under my pen name, Addison Cole. You'll find the same great love stories with toned-down heat levels.

Happy reading!
~ Melissa

THE WICKED WORLD
DARK KNIGHTS AT BAYSIDE

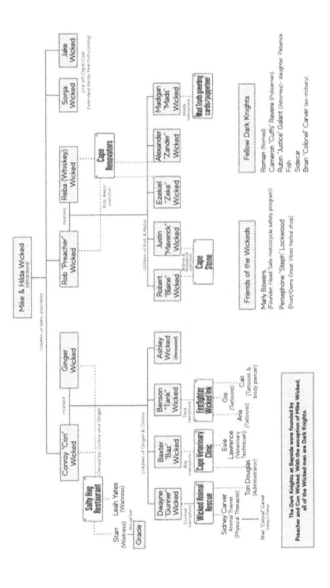

Chapter One

TANK WICKED PLANTED his boots on the pavement, took off his helmet, and cut the engine on his motorcycle. The faint sound of music pulsed in the air. He raked a hand through his thick black hair and gazed up at the Salty Hog, his family's two-story restaurant and bar overlooking the harbor. The parking lot was full of motorcycles, trucks, and cars, many of which belonged to other members of the Dark Knights motorcycle club. After the shift he'd had at the fire station where he volunteered a few times a month, he craved the comfort of the familiar.

A cool September breeze swept off the water. He turned toward the scents of the sea, and as usual, fond memories rolled in. He'd spent years watching over his two younger brothers, his sister, and their many cousins there at the Salty Hog. They'd eat dinner downstairs in the restaurant with their families, and then the kids would play outside on the grounds while their parents handled business and hung out upstairs in the bar, dancing and socializing with other Dark Knight families. He could still see his siblings and cousins running around on the docks and in the sand and grass as he and Blaine, his eldest cousin, tried to keep tabs on everyone. A bittersweet memory of his late younger sister, Ashley, trickled in. She'd been ten years old, smiling as bright as the morning sun, laughing hysterically, her long, always-tangled strawberry-blond hair flying over her shoulders as she and their cousin Madigan, an energetic brunette who was a few months younger than Ashley, chased their brothers with squirt guns. When all the boys had turned on them, the girls had run behind Tank in fits of giggles, hiding from the others. Tank had been six feet tall by the time he was fourteen and had hit his full height of six four two years later. He'd fended off the gaggle of rambunctious boys that night as if Ashley's and Madigan's lives had depended on it. He'd always been protective of his siblings and cousins, saving them from fights and getting them out of trouble, until the night he hadn't been there when Ashley had needed him most.

He gritted his teeth against the images impaling him, but there was no softening the crushing pain he'd carried since the night he'd lost the brightest light he'd ever known.

A couple of motorcycles rumbled into the parking lot, drawing him from his thoughts. He climbed off his bike as his brother Baz and their cousin Blaine climbed off theirs. Like Tank, they wore their black leather vests with Dark Knights patches over T-shirts. Tank and Baz's father, Conroy, and Blaine's father, their uncle Rob, who went by the road name Preacher, had founded the Bayside chapter of the Dark Knights about thirty years ago. Tank's other brother, Dwayne, who went by the road name Gunner, and their male cousins were also members. The club was as much a part of their lives as the air they breathed.

"Hey, man," Baz called over as they locked their helmets to their bikes. The brawny veterinarian was known as the Lower Cape's most eligible bachelor. He flicked his chin, sending his longish dirty-blond hair out of his eyes. "You just get here, or are you leaving?"

Tank strode over to them. "Just got here."

Blaine, a James Marsden lookalike with wavy dark hair, shocking blue eyes, and a playful nature, clapped a hand on Tank's shoulder. "Good, you can hang with us and we can give you shit about losing at pool last night."

Tank scoffed.

As they headed for the stairs that led up to the bar, Tank scanned the lot for waitress Leah Yates's blue Honda Civic and spotted it beneath an umbrella of trees, kicking his protective instincts into overdrive. He'd spent the summer wondering about the mysterious girl who moved with the silence of a still summer's day, as if she'd like to be invisible. He had enough resources to find out everything there was to know about her with a few phone calls. But while he'd done that in other situations when people were in trouble, Leah hadn't given any indication that she needed anyone's help, and it felt wrong to invade her privacy just to satisfy his curiosity.

"It's by the trees." Baz nodded in the direction of Leah's car as they climbed the steps. "Passed it on my way in."

"Don't tell me you're still trying to figure out whether Leah is a loner or running from something." Blaine stepped onto the second-story deck. "Listen, man, your parents keep a close eye on the girls who work for them. They'd know if Leah was in trouble by now."

Maybe he was right. Tank's parents treated all their employees like family, just as Tank did with his employees at Wicked Ink, the tattoo shop he owned. His mother had recently told him that although Leah had warmed toward customers in the few months she'd worked there, she remained tight-lipped about her personal life, and she assumed Leah was just a quiet, single girl who was new to the area and liked her privacy.

He followed the guys into the rustic bar, taking in the mass of black vests with Dark Knights patches among a plethora of other customers. His gaze moved over the women who were checking him out. He was used to the attention. Tank had female friends, but usually women either wanted to drop to their knees *for* him or run for the hills *from* him. There was rarely an in-between.

His eyes locked on Leah as she helped customers at a table across the room. She was definitely a run-for-the-hills girl, rarely making eye contact. Her features looked as though they'd been picked from a handful of people and puzzled together to create a woman as uniquely beautiful as the *Mona Lisa*. She had a mass of brownish-red corkscrew curls as wild as a lion's mane, thick brows over cautious hazel eyes, a slightly flat nose, and heavily freckled skin the color of sweet cream. Her lips were the most intriguing he'd ever seen, plump, almost perfectly bowed, and slightly too big for her face. She was thin, with slight but alluring curves, and when she spoke, her Southern drawl exuded sensuality and innocence with an edge of *please don't hit on me*. He'd seen her work her quiet magic, pulling off that invisibility cloak, slipping in to take drink orders, then gliding away, rarely capturing the attention of men the way other, more flirtatious waitresses did. But to Tank, who got feelings about people like sailors did about impending storms, she brought the roar and thunder of a five-alarm fire.

He watched Leah making her way to the bar, where his mother, Ginger, was serving drinks. His mother caught him watching her. She pushed her tortoiseshell glasses to the bridge of her nose, her eyes brightening. Her strawberry-blond hair cascaded in gentle waves over her shoulders. Tank lifted his chin in acknowledgment to the strongest, most loving woman he knew. She was everything a biker's wife needed to be, tough, fair, and able to handle—and sometimes mother—an army of belligerent bikers. Even so, he had no idea how his parents had survived Ashley's death, but they'd managed to carry on and help the rest of them figure out how to as well.

His mother pointed to a table in the corner, where Gunner was sitting with their cousins Zeke and Zander, two of Blaine's younger brothers. A brunette stood to Gunner's right, a blonde to his left, both with their hands on him, and another blonde was leaning over the table near Zeke and Zander, showing all kinds of cleavage.

Tank nudged Baz and Blaine, and as they headed to the table, he watched his youngest brother soaking in the attention. Gunner, a stocky ex-marine with short blond hair and tattoos from neck to fingers, was twenty-eight to Tank's thirty-two, and he owned Wicked Animal Rescue. Gunner said something to the girls, and the three beauties walked away, eyeing Tank, Baz, and Blaine.

"What kind of trouble are you stirring up?" Tank asked as they all sat down.

"Just deciding who I want to take home tonight." Gunner was as much of a woman whisperer as he was an animal whisperer.

"I'm thinking the brunette." Zander smirked. "Did you see the rack on her? Give me one hour, and...*Mm-mm.*" He had the same short dark hair and blue eyes as all of his brothers, but that's as far as the similarities went. Zander had no filter and enjoyed riling people up. "Or maybe I'll go for the blonde."

"Why choose?" Baz chuckled.

"Do *not* egg him on." Zeke shook his head. He'd been Zander's wrangler since they were kids. Zander had learned early on that joking around and getting into trouble could deflect attention from his learning disability. Zeke had taken it upon himself to try to keep him in line. Zeke pointed to Baz. "And women call *you* husband material?" He scoffed. "You should probably set them straight."

Baz splayed his hands, flashing his dimples. "Who am I to kill their fantasies?"

Blaine laughed. "You're about as likely to settle down as Tank is to hold a real conversation."

"Some of us have better uses for our mouths." Tank smirked.

"Speaking of which." Baz turned his attention to Gunner and Zander. "I'm always amazed at how many women you two pick up with the shit you say."

"That makes two of us," Zeke said under his breath.

"Hey, man, I keep it real. They know what they're getting *because* of the shit I say. When we hook up, I won't need to speak." Zander flashed a cocky grin. "My body will do all the talking."

Baz looked across the table at Gunner. "You do that shit, too, Gun?"

"Hell no. I'm as smooth as butter. But not everyone can be a catch like me." Gunner pushed to his feet, arrogantly showing off his heavily muscled biceps. "Six-plus feet of hard-bodied, talented-tongued business owner." He made a lewd gesture with his tongue.

"Sit your ass down." Tank yanked him down to his seat. "*Jesus.* You're animals. I need a drink." He liked giving them hell, but the truth was, every guy around that table would give their lives for each other.

"Like *you're* a saint?" Gunner said sarcastically.

"I never said I was, but I'm not an asshole." Tank had his share of women, but he didn't make a public game of it the way some of the younger guys did. He turned to flag down a waitress, but Leah was already on her way to the table, her slim hips swaying in curve-hugging jeans, her Salty Hog T-shirt straining across her perky breasts, and her eyes pointedly avoiding *him*.

She turned to Baz and Blaine. "What can I get y'all?"

Her Southern drawl drew Tank in every time he heard it. He watched her as the others ordered. Her expression morphed to a more serious one as she studied Zander's face the way she always did, like she was trying to figure him out. "Would you like a refill?"

"I'd like your number," Zander said with a wink.

Tank glowered at him.

Leah wrinkled her nose. "I'm not on the menu, but I'm happy to get you a drink."

Everyone chuckled as he asked for a refill and tried again to get her number. She turned toward Tank with her gaze trained on the order pad. "And for you?"

"Whiskey, neat," Tank said.

Her eyes flicked up to his, and in the space of a second everything else failed to exist except that thunderous roar, and just as quickly, the little color Leah had drained from her face.

"You okay, darlin'?" Tank touched her hand.

She pulled it away, stumbling backward, and scurried off toward the bar.

"Dude, are you sure something didn't happen between you two that we should know about?" Blaine asked.

Tank leveled him with a dark stare.

As his brothers and cousins joked about him scaring Leah off every time she looked at him, he watched her heading for the bar, eyes downcast, as though she wished she were invisible again. Maybe she was just a quiet girl who liked her privacy, but that didn't explain her reaction to *him*. He'd missed signs of trouble with Ashley, and he wasn't about to let that happen again. Not to her or anyone else.

LEAH FELT TANK watching her as she dragged air into her lungs and tried to calm her racing heart. She remembered the first time she'd seen the bearded, tattooed mountain of a man with piercings in his ears and nostril, coal-black hair, and eyes to match. He'd rolled into the bar with a group of Dark Knights, all of them banged up and bleeding like they'd come from a fight. She'd been curious about the intimidating and ridiculously *hot* biker who wore metal rings and leather bracelets and whose watchful eyes held so much grief it was palpable. But that was *before* their gazes had met. She'd heard her boss, Ginger Wicked, call him Tank, and later that night she'd learned just how fitting his name was. From the very first time their eyes had connected, and each and every time thereafter, he'd stolen the air from her lungs, as if she'd been run over by a tank. Only it wasn't her own suffering she'd felt. It was *him* suffocating, weighed down by an unimaginable burden. The idea that anything could be too much for such a powerful, confident man had shaken her, and even now, four months later, it was still there.

She'd always had a sixth sense. The night her father had been killed, he'd come to her in a dream, telling her to take care of her younger brother, River, and that he'd always be watching over them. She'd woken up screaming, begging him to come back. The police had shown up a little while later to notify her of his death. That was six years ago, when she'd been eighteen and River had been thirteen. She'd been raising River ever since. She'd understood why that vision and many others had come to her, but she'd never experienced anything like her reaction to Tank. When it had first happened, she'd feared he might be dangerous, but according to Starr, the waitress who had trained her, Tank was a great guy who would never hurt anyone unless they deserved it. From what Leah had witnessed since, everyone seemed to respect and trust the gruff biker who rarely said much, and though she took comfort in that, it didn't lessen her reaction to him. She'd briefly considered looking for another job, but she loved working at the Salty Hog. She'd finally learned the ropes and felt comfortable enough to joke with customers, and nothing could beat the fantastic tips she earned. Last week she'd even given up her other part-time job to work there full time. Ginger and Conroy Wicked were great bosses. They allowed her to work flexible hours, and after thirty days of full-time employment she'd be eligible for employer-paid health insurance, which would save her hundreds of dollars every month.

"Hey, you okay?" Starr asked as she sidled up to Leah, pulling her from her thoughts.

"Yeah, thanks." Leah lowered her voice. "This is *so* embarrassing. He's our bosses' son and I can't even talk to him."

"Don't sweat it. Tank's a scary-looking guy. I'll take his table, and you can take table three." She flipped her long blond hair over her shoulder and pointed to a table full of preppy guys. "I've primed them for you. They'll tip well."

"You're the best, thank you. But you can have the tip."

"Don't be silly." Starr's brow furrowed. "You're a little flushed. Are you *sure* you aren't just hot and bothered over wanting some hanky-panky with our Tanky? We both know those Wicked boys are the hottest guys in here."

"Positive." She knew the difference between lust and discomfort and didn't have time for hot guys anyway. Even if she did, there was the little issue of not being able to breathe around the only man that intrigued her enough to make her *almost* wish she could make time to figure him out.

She avoided Tank for the rest of her shift, clocked out at eight, and took her first full breath in two hours as she hurried to her car. She cranked the music and closed her eyes for a second, soaking in the little *me* time she allowed herself before heading home. With two little ones underfoot, she rarely got time alone.

As she headed home, she thought about River and the girls. For as long as Leah could remember, she'd seen two little girls and a boy in her future. She'd thought she'd eventually meet a man as wonderful as her father and bear three children, but after her father died, she'd realized River was that boy. They'd both been devastated after losing their father, and River had started hanging out with a rough crowd. When he'd come to her at fourteen and told her he'd gotten a girl pregnant—and then done it again when he was sixteen—Leah had realized she'd been wrong about the type of family she'd be blessed with. She had stepped in and adopted River's daughter Junie, and a year and a half later, she'd done the same for his second daughter, Rosie, and had never regretted it.

She pulled into the driveway of the adorable cottage she'd rented at the beginning of the summer when they'd come to the Cape and sat for a moment bobbing her head to the beat of the music. The cedar-sided cottage had two small bedrooms, one full bath, and an open living area with a bar separating it from the kitchen and the entrance to the unfinished basement. Between the two bedrooms, a recessed staircase led to the finished attic, which River used as a bedroom. The cottage wasn't in the best shape, with a few missing shingles and almost no yard to speak of, but it was *home*, and they were happy there.

She headed inside and heard River playing the guitar for the girls in their bedroom. He'd taught himself to play, and she and the girls loved it. What a difference a few years made. Raising River had been an uphill battle, but he was all heart, just like their father had been, and he loved the girls with everything he had. He took care of them while Leah worked and never acted like they were a hassle. He'd even started taking online community college classes and was determined to become the first Yates to get a degree.

For the millionth time, Leah thought about how proud her father would be of them—all four of them. She missed him every day, but she and River did their best to keep his memory alive for the girls. They told them stories about Grandpa Leo and kept his picture by their bedside.

Leah set down her things, toed off her shoes, and went to say good night to the girls. River sat on the floor between their beds, strumming his secondhand guitar, his thick curls hanging just past his shoulders. He had tighter curls than Leah, but his were softer, finer, and golden-copper, like his mother's. He lifted his face, their father's smile appearing, sparse whiskers darkening his chin. River was a good-looking guy who oozed

Southern charm. It wouldn't be long before he had hordes of women chasing after him. At least *now* he took birth control seriously.

Rosie sat beside him on the floor in her pajamas, her golden-brown curls billowing around her little face. She was holding her favorite lovey, Boo, a doll with a frilly skirt and tie that Leah had made for her from River's old shirts. Junie lay horizontally across the bed behind River, her cheek resting on his shoulder, red ringlets framing her face. In one hand she clutched the ears of her favorite lovey, a stuffed bunny named Mine. Her other arm was around River, and she was holding the silver chain he wore around his neck. It had belonged to Leo, and River never took it off.

"Mama!" Rosie popped to her feet with an ever-present impish grin and barreled into Leah's legs.

"Hey, Rosie Posey." Leah lifted her into her arms, kissing her cheek.

"Hi, Mama." Junie tangled her tiny fingers in River's hair, making no effort to get up.

Leah leaned down and kissed Junie's head. "Hi, Juju."

While Rosie was a bundle of energy day and night and the first to try to soothe anyone who was sad, Junie was a thinker and more likely to try to figure out a solution to others' issues than to placate them. She could lie in the grass playing with a grasshopper in the morning, and hours later, when Leah had forgotten all about the bug, Junie would still be thinking about it and would have come up with a hundred questions, worries, and stories about it by bedtime.

Leah sat on the bed beside her. "Did you guys have a good day?"

"Gweat day!" Rosie exclaimed, just as she did every day. She wriggled out of Leah's arms and sat next to River again.

"Wiver took us to the cweek, and he ate fwogs," Junie said with a wide grin. "He *ate* them, Mama, and he didn't get a bellyache."

Leah laughed. "Maybe River's stomach is made of steel."

"He's gwoing a fwog family in his belly. Wight, Wiver?" Junie tapped his shoulder.

"That's right, jelly belly." River kissed Rosie's cheek. "Hop into bed, doodlebug."

Rosie giggled and climbed into bed as River turned to kiss Junie.

Junie threw her arms around him, hugging him tight. "Night, Wiver."

"Night, Juju. Get some sleep, ya hear?" River stretched his tall, lanky body and picked up his guitar. His black hoodie hung open over a gray T-shirt. "I gotta go. Daryl's picking me up to shoot hoops."

"Daryl?" Leah was glad he was getting back into sports, but she still liked to keep an eye on the type of people he was hanging out with.

"Yeah. He's the guy I told you I met a few days ago when we were at the park."

"Oh, right. Be careful," she said as she tucked in the girls. A pang of longing moved through her. She'd had it a few times recently when River had gone out. He was growing up, and she had to, as her father would say, *give him the sky so he can find his wings.* "How late will you be?"

"Not too late. Probably ten or so." He cocked a grin, looking between the girls. "Farewell, my beautiful ladies." He bowed dramatically, waving his hands as he backed out of the room.

The girls giggled.

Leah finished putting the girls to bed, picked up toys and books lying around the cottage, and washed the dishes that were left in the sink. She poured herself a bowl of cereal and opened the fridge, in which she found one of Rosie's dolls holding a half-eaten cookie in its lap. She laughed to herself and reached for the milk. It was empty. She sighed and tossed it in the trash. *Darn it, River.* He was supposed to let her know if they ran out of staples so she could get them on her way home from work.

She carried the bowl of dry cereal to the couch, moving River's guitar from the cushions to the floor. Was it so hard to put a guitar away? It was an ongoing thing between them. He'd leave the guitar on the couch, and when she'd tell him to put it away, he'd give her one of his charming smiles and say something like *The girls like it there* or *I wouldn't want you to forget me while I'm out.* She sat on the couch and texted him. *Any chance your friend can take you to get milk on the way home?* She picked up the women's fiction novel she'd checked out of the library, and as she lay back to read, River's response rolled in. *No prob. Sorry I forgot to tell you we're out of it.*

"Awesome." She kicked her feet up on the other side of the couch and lost herself in the story.

LEAH STARTLED AWAKE to the sound of her phone vibrating on the coffee table. She sat up and snagged it, seeing a text from River. *Sorry, but can you come get me? I'm at the high school.*

"Are you freaking kidding me?" She thumbed out a response. *Seriously? And get the girls up? What happened to your friend driving you home?*

His response was immediate. *I didn't know they were all going to get high.*

"Shit." How could she be mad at him for being responsible? They couldn't afford to waste money on an Uber. She sent a quick reply. *Fine. Don't go anywhere, and don't let me forget to stop for milk on the way home.*

He texted back a thumbs-up emoji.

She loaded the kids into their carseats with their memory blankets and lovies—the two things that helped stave off meltdowns. At least she no longer had to worry about diapers. Rosie was a determined little girl and had been in a hurry to wear big-girl underpants like Junie.

As she drove toward the school, she reminded herself that this was a hell of a lot better than driving around at night looking for him, like she'd had to do after their father died.

"Can Wiver sit with us, Mama?" Junie asked sleepily.

"Sure, baby." She slowed to a stop at a red light and glanced at the girls in the rearview mirror, sitting in their carseats next to each other, holding hands. When they'd driven from North Carolina to the Cape, the girls had sat together and Junie had entertained Rosie so well, Leah had wondered why she hadn't thought of putting their carseats next to each other before.

She took the long way to pick up River, hoping the girls would go back to sleep, and gazed out the window as she crossed the long stretch of road over the water. It was her favorite route to and from home, worth every minute of the extra seven it took.

River was waiting for them at the entrance to the school parking lot with his hands in his front pockets, shoulders drooping. He opened the passenger door and peered inside.

"How mad are you? Lecture mad or shake your head and roll your eyes mad?"

"I'm irritated, not mad. You did the right thing, Riv."

He grinned. "You taught me well, even if it took me a while to grow up. Dad'd be proud of us." He slid into the passenger seat. He'd said things like that a lot since they'd moved and he'd started pulling his shit together.

"Wiver, sit with us," Junie whined.

"I'm already in, Junie. Let's just go," he said tightly, and Leah had a feeling it was because he didn't want to irritate her by keeping them out any longer.

"But Mama said you would," Junie pleaded in her too-tired-to-negotiate, verge-of-tears voice.

"It's fine, Riv," Leah said. "Just get in the back before she melts down."

"A'right." He climbed out and got in the back seat behind Leah.

Junie reached across Rosie for his hand after he put on his seat belt. He took it and whispered, "Sorry Mama had to get you up," but Junie's eyes had already closed.

As she drove out of the lot, Leah said, "I'm proud of you, too, Riv. It couldn't have been easy to get yourself out of that situation with new friends. Did they give you a hard time about leaving?"

"Nah. I told them I was on parole and had to get a piss test tomorrow."

She laughed. "That was kind of brilliant."

"Right? Hey, don't forget we need milk."

"Thanks." She drove to the convenience store, and as she pulled into a parking spot, Rosie woke up.

"I go in!" Rosie exclaimed. No matter what time it was, she

woke like a talking doll whose string had been pulled, bright-eyed and chatty.

"*Shh.* Don't wake Junie. You wait with River. I'll be right back."

"No! Me go in!" Rosie hollered, startling Junie awake.

"I want to go in," Junie said sleepily.

"You guys are staying with River in the car." The last thing Leah wanted was to drag them into the store. They'd beg for everything, and getting them back to sleep would be impossible.

"No!" the girls hollered.

Junie threw a whiney, crying fit, and Rosie pleaded for Leah to let *Junie* go inside, while Leah and River futilely tried to calm them both down.

"Fine! You can come in, but we're *not* buying candy," Leah snapped, and she and River climbed out of the car to get the girls. Two guys were arguing at the far end of the lot. *Great.* She quickly picked up Rosie, and her little hands shot out toward her carseat.

"My Boo!"

Leah grabbed the doll, the voices of the arguing men escalating.

"Fighting is bad!" Rosie yelled, causing the men to look over.

Leah's heart nearly stopped as the biggest man looked over his shoulder, and their eyes collided. *Tank.* She stood frozen, trying to drag air into her lungs.

"Leah. *Leah!*" River nudged her, jerking her brain back into gear. "Who's that?"

"Just my bosses' son. Let's go." She hurried inside the store.

"Did he bother you? Why'd you look scared? Because I'll go say something to him and take care of it," River said protectively.

"Mama scared?" Rosie asked.

"*No.* Mama's fine." She raised her brows at River. "I was just…" *Unable to breathe.* "Surprised to see him outside of work."

"Are you sure? Because you looked shaken up." He followed her toward the refrigerator aisle. "I'll say something after we get the girls in the car."

Leah spun around. "No, you will *not.* He didn't do anything, and he's twice your size. He could squash you like a bug."

"No!" Junie whined. "Don't let him hurt Wiver."

Ohmygod. Will this night ever end?

"Nobody's going to hurt me, jelly belly." River narrowed his eyes at Leah. "I can defend you, you know. I'm not a little kid anymore."

Leah grabbed a gallon of milk. "I know you're not, but he hasn't done anything, okay? Can we just get out of here?"

"Can we get Pop-Tawts?" Junie asked.

Here we go…

Before Leah could respond, River said, "No. But I'll make you Mickey Mouse pancakes in the morning."

"I want pincakes!" Rosie exclaimed.

River and Leah said, "*Pan*cakes," in unison.

Junie grinned. "With bluebewies?"

"You know it. Now, let's get home before Mama blows her top," River said as they headed up to the register.

Rosie patted the top of Leah's head. "Mama no blow."

Leah couldn't help but chuckle at their noisy little family. Rosie chatted about her doll wanting *pincakes* as Leah paid. When they left the store, she saw Tank climbing onto his motorcycle and quickly got the girls into their carseats. River sat in the back with them, and Leah settled into the driver's seat, feeling like she'd left the house hours ago. She couldn't wait to get home.

River turned to look out the back window as they left the lot. A minute later he said, "Do you think he's following us?"

"No. He probably lives this way. Nobody in their right mind would want to follow a car with cranky toddlers." She glanced in the rearview mirror. Tank was a good distance behind them, and the girls were dozing off.

"So did you play basketball at all?" Leah asked quietly.

"Yeah. We played for a bit. One of the guys brought his twin sister. She was cool."

"Cool, as in you like her and I need to buy stock in condoms?" Leah asked as they drove over the river, watching a truck speeding in the other direction. She hugged the right side of the road.

"She was just cool, you know? Not a pain in the butt like some girls are..."

His voice was drowned out by panic as the truck crossed the center line. River hollered, "Leah!" as the truck slammed into the side of their car with a supersonic *bang*, sending them sailing through the dark night. Their terrified screams echoed as their car nose-dived into the water so hard, Leah's head smacked something. She was momentarily disoriented, but panic took over.

"River! Get the girls! Get the girls! Get the girls!" Leah cried as she yanked off her seat belt and scrambled onto her knees. The girls were screaming and wailing. The back end of the car was up in the air, and they were slowly sinking. River's head was bleeding, and his body was contorted from the mangled metal on the driver's side of the car. Leah freed Rosie and pulled her wailing girl into the front, reaching over again to get Junie.

Tears streamed down River's face as he tugged at the latch on Junie's carseat. "It's stuck! I can't get it!"

"Huwwy, Wiver!" Junie shrieked, trying to climb out of her carseat straps.

The car jerked, and they all screamed as it tilted toward the passenger side. Thank God those windows were intact. Leah grabbed Rosie. "Unhook the seat belt! We'll get her out *in* the carseat!"

"I'm trying! Get Rosie out!" River pleaded.

Leah reached over the seat to help. "I'm not leaving without you and Junie!" The car sank deeper and water rushed in the broken driver's side window. She grabbed Rosie around her middle, yelling, "Everyone take a big breath and hold it!" River pushed Junie, free of her carseat, into the front of the car as water rushed over their heads, and they were consumed by darkness. Leah clung to Junie's shirt, trying to propel them through the broken window. Someone grabbed her and yanked them out, hauling them toward the surface, and she realized her fisted hand was empty. She'd lost her grip on Junie.

The second they broke the surface, Rosie coughed and cried, and Leah screamed, "Junie!" and Tank's face came into focus. He was holding Junie, who was also coughing and crying.

"Can you swim?" Tank asked urgently.

"Yes!"

He thrust her panicked little girl into her arms as she looked frantically for River. "River! Oh my God! Get *River!*" but Tank was already under the water.

TANK'S HEART SLAMMED against his ribs as he mentally worked through how to get the guy out. The driver's side of the car was crushed. He had to go through the passenger side and maneuver around the carseats. He tugged at the rear passenger door with all his strength, wrenching it open against the force of the water. The guy was out cold. Tank tried to pull him out, but his legs were trapped between the mangled metal and the driver's seat. Tank kicked and pulled at the metal and the driver's seat with all his strength, trying to wrestle him free. He stayed under until his lungs burned before shooting to the surface again, gulping air. He heard...*Baz?* Where the fuck did he come from? Where the hell was the fire department? He'd called 911 the second he'd seen the truck hit the car. He dove deep again, fighting with the metal and the driver's seat until they finally gave way, and he yanked the limp body free. He dragged him to the surface as fast as he could, all too aware of how much time had passed. He picked up the heavy, lifeless body and ran to shore, dropping to his knees in the grass, and tilted the guy's head back. He wasn't breathing. His eyes swept over the youthful face before him. *Jesus, you're just a kid.*

He pinched the guy's nose, administering five rescue breaths as Leah and the kids sobbed and pleaded for his life. *Come on. Come on.* He still wasn't breathing. Tank tried CPR as sirens neared. *Breathe, please breathe.* The girls wailed and screamed as CPR failed, and Tank began chest compressions. *One, two, three...Come on, damn it. Seven, eight, nine.* Painful memories of the night he'd found Ashley crashed into him. *Come on, motherfucker, breathe. Fifteen...twenty-one, twenty-two...Please, God...Twenty-eight, twenty-nine, thirty.* He still wasn't breathing. Tank gave him two rescue breaths and began another cycle of chest compressions and rescue breaths, praying for the guy's life. He started a third round, vaguely aware of chaos erupting around him and people shouting, but he refused to give up—chest compressions, rescue breaths...

"Tank, he's gone, man!" Baz grabbed his arm, trying to drag him away.

Tank threw him off and continued trying to revive the guy. Baz and someone else grabbed him by the arms, hauling him backward. "Get the fuck off me!" Tank twisted free and dropped to his knees, tears pouring from his eyes as he tried again. "Breathe, damn it, *breathe!*"

They dragged him away again, but Tank fought to get free. "I gotta save him!"

Baz got in his face. "Look at me, damn it! He's *gone*, Tank. You did *everything* you could."

Tank looked past his brother to Leah bent over the body, sobbing and shaking, and the girls, crying as the paramedics tried to check them out, and his heart shattered, knowing a piece of them died tonight, too. "I didn't even know she had a family."

"Nobody did."

A fellow firefighter, Sean Zablonski, tried to coax Leah away from the body, but she clung to it, shouting, "Get away from me!"

Tank went to help, and she lifted her tear-streaked face, setting a venomous glare on him.

"You." She pushed to her feet, sobbing, hands fisted as she choked out, "Why didn't you save *him* first? That should be *me!*" She pounded Tank's chest, hollering through her sobs, "You should have let *me* die! You should have *saved* him! I hate you!"

Sean stepped forward, but Tank gave him a back-off stare

and wrapped his arms around Leah as she shouted accusations, calling him names and spewing her grief. He crushed her to him despite her flailing fists and anguished words. "I'm sorry, Leah. I'm so sorry." He'd have given his own life for that kid.

"I *hate* you!" she seethed, throwing her whole body against him, despite his hold on her. "He should've lived."

"I know. I'm sorry." Tank held her tighter, accepting every angry, sad word, because he knew what it was like to hold it all in, the way it gnawed at a person's heart and charred their soul. He held her as her voice was swallowed by sobs, knowing her heart was breaking into a million painful pieces.

Chapter Two

LEAH LAY ON the emergency room bed with her arms around her sleeping girls, waiting to be discharged. At least that's what she thought the doctor had said. They'd been there a long time. After the doctor had checked out her and the girls, the police had questioned her about the accident. They'd said something about the other driver texting when he'd hit her. She didn't know what happened to him, and she didn't care. His recklessness was the reason someone else had come in and talked with her about bereavement counseling. She felt like her heart had been ripped from her chest, and it took everything she had to hold herself together.

Bonnie, a middle-aged nurse, walked into the curtained-off area carrying a stack of clothes. "How are we doing in here?"

Leah didn't even try to respond. Just the thought of it wore her out.

"You and your girls are very blessed. There's a waiting room full of people who are worried about you."

"We don't know anyone," Leah whispered.

"Well, honey, they sure know you. There must be twenty-five Dark Knights out there, and the whole Wicked clan."

Why were they there?

"Ginger Wicked said you work for her," the nurse said. "And Tank is wearing a path in the lobby floor. He's the one who rescued you."

He didn't rescue River. Leah closed her eyes against tears and remembered how she'd gone off on Tank, adding more grief to her mile-high pile.

"Ginger brought these clothes for you and pajamas for the girls. Would you like me to help you get them dressed?"

"She brought us clothes?" Leah had forgotten they were wearing hospital gowns.

"Yes. They're a thoughtful family. They've helped a lot of people in the community."

Leah sat up, wincing in pain. Her whole body hurt. She touched the bandage on her forehead where she'd gotten stitches.

"Unfortunately, you're going to be even sorer tomorrow. But you and your girls are safe, and that's what matters."

She knew Bonnie meant well, but she wanted to scream, *River matters, and he's not here!* Her throat thickened painfully, and she moved like an automaton, putting on the underwear, sweatshirt, leggings, socks, and sneakers Ginger had brought for her, briefly wondering how she knew her size and why she'd bothered. But thinking opened a door to misery, and she couldn't afford to break down. She needed to be strong for her girls, so she stopped thinking. They'd cried so hard for River in the ambulance on the way to the hospital, they'd worn themselves out.

Junie whimpered, eyes closed, her body limp as a rag doll, while they dressed her and Rosie. They had bruises caused by the straps on their carseats, and the sight of those bruises made Leah feel sick.

"Go home?" Rosie asked as she lay on the bed.

"Soon," Leah promised, but she didn't want to go home. She couldn't imagine being there without River.

"I want Wiver," Junie said groggily as she laid her head on the pillow beside Rosie.

"I know, baby." Leah kissed her forehead, doing her damnedest to hold back a rush of tears.

Rosie turned on her side, putting her arm around Junie, and they both closed their eyes.

"Leah, you should be discharged soon, but Ginger asked if she could come in to see you. Would that be okay?"

She nodded and leaned against the bed. A few minutes later, Ginger came through the curtains, and her compassionate expression caused another flood of tears. Leah closed her eyes against them.

"Hi, sweetheart." Ginger looked sadly at Junie and Rosie sleeping, and then she touched Leah's cheek, her gaze moving over the bandage on Leah's forehead. "My poor girl."

Leah looked down at the floor, trying not to start crying again. She opened her mouth to thank her for the clothes, but no words came.

"Oh, honey. Come here." Ginger embraced her gently. "I'm so sorry, baby girl. So very sorry."

Leah stood with her arms hanging limply by her sides, squeezing her eyes shut, but there was no stopping the tears.

"We're all here for you, honey."

But I wasn't there for River. She tried to hold back sobs, but they burst out in harsh jerks.

"That's it, sweetheart. Let it out. Cry as much as you need to. It'll help."

Her kindness was all it took to uncap the well of tears. Leah clenched her teeth against her sobs, trying not to wake the girls. But then she remembered Ginger was her boss and that River's girls needed her, so she forced all that sadness down deep, gulping in air, and stepped out of Ginger's arms.

"I'm sorry." Leah wiped her tears.

"There is nothing to be sorry about. I've been through this, honey. As you might know, we lost our youngest, our daughter, Ashley, when she was in college. I understand what you're going through."

Leah's heart broke anew. "I didn't know. I'm so sorry."

"It's okay. They said you don't have any family in the area?"

Leah shook her head. "We have no family. It was just my brother, River, and us." More tears fell, and she grabbed tissues from a box on the table. "I'm sorry. I can't talk about him."

"It's okay, honey. We've brought carseats, and if it's okay with you, we'd like to drive you home."

She hadn't even thought about her car or the carseats. "I would appreciate that."

"Okay. You and the girls can stay with us if you'd like. We have plenty of room."

Leah was astonished, but as much as she didn't want to go home, she knew the girls needed to be in their own beds. "Thank you, but we need to be home."

"I understand, but the offer stands, anytime."

The nurse came through the curtain again, and she began going over discharge instructions. "You shouldn't be alone tonight. You hit your head pretty hard and need to be watched for signs of a concussion."

"I'll stay with her," Ginger said. "That is, if it's okay with you, Leah."

"I'll be okay. You don't have to."

"Leah, it's important that you're not alone, just in case." The nurse went on to explain what to watch for. She reiterated the importance of bereavement counseling, and when she handed Leah a bag with River's wallet, phone, and necklace and started talking about his body, Leah broke down again.

Ginger put her hand on Leah's back and said, "Bonnie, why don't you and I step outside the curtain and I'll get that information for Leah. Is that okay, Leah?"

"Yes," she choked out. "Thank you."

Time moved in a slow-motion blur. Leah carried Rosie and Ginger carried Junie out of the emergency area. Tank was *right there* offering to carry Rosie when she came through the doors into the crowded lobby. But Leah clung to her. She would have carried Junie, too, if she could have. She needed them close.

Tank and Conroy flanked them on the way to the car, with Baz and Gunner leading the rest of the people a few feet behind. Nothing felt real as Ginger drove them home, followed by a pack of motorcycles. When they arrived, Tank parked behind Ginger in the driveway, and three other motorcycles parked on the street. Leah had no idea who was there or where everyone else went. Before she had even unhooked her seat belt, Tank was opening her door. She wasn't too wrung out to feel the suffocation wafting off him. Only now it felt darker, more tortured. He should hate her for the way she beat on him, but he reached for her hand and helped her out. She winced as she stood.

"My mother and I can carry the girls." His voice was deep, raspy, and authoritative, but also somehow kind.

"I need to carry one," she said softly.

He nodded and proceeded to take Rosie out of her carseat and hand her to Leah. Then he went around to the passenger side, where Ginger was talking with Conroy and their other sons. Tank picked up Junie, and she grabbed hold of the silver chain hanging around his neck, sending another spear of sadness through Leah. Junie looked tiny against him as he came to Leah's side. She realized her keys were in the car at the bottom of the river that had killed her brother. A flood of tears hit, and Tank drew her and Rosie against him. His clothes were still wet and smelled like the river, which made her ache even more.

"I don't," she said between gasps and tears, "have keys."

"I assumed that. I've taken care of it."

She looked up at his tortured eyes, and he nodded toward the house. Her front door was ajar, and a man in a black leather vest stood off to the side on the porch.

"Nobody went inside," Tank said solemnly. "That's a buddy of mine. He's a locksmith. He made you a new set of keys and stood watch until we got here."

Why was everyone helping her so much?

"Thank you," she whispered, swallowing hard as they headed up the walk. Just hours earlier she'd been thinking about how much she loved the cottage and how happy they were in their new home. It would never feel the same again.

She kept her eyes trained on Rosie as they went inside, not wanting to see the staircase that led to River's room, his guitar on the floor by the couch, his sneakers by the door, or the million other pieces of her brother that she'd never see again. She headed for her bedroom, and Tank stood in the doorway, looking at the other bedroom.

"I want them in here with me." She tossed her throw pillow on the floor and pulled back the blanket. Her bedroom was small, like the girls'. The double bed was pushed against the opposite wall, with a nightstand on one side. Her dresser and closet were on the wall to the right.

She laid Rosie on the far side of the bed and turned to take Junie from Tank, but he laid her down and pulled the covers over both of them. He grabbed the throw pillow and put it beside Junie. Then he looked around the room and said, "Can she roll over that and fall out?"

She looked up at him, hulking over her and taking up all the space. "I won't let her."

He nodded, and Rosie whimpered in her sleep, her little hand feeling around her. Leah knew she was looking for Boo, and her throat thickened. Rosie's hand landed on Junie's, and her little fingers curled around it.

Tears spilled from Leah's eyes.

"Leah."

She closed her eyes tighter.

Tank put his rough finger under her chin, lifting it so she had no choice but to look at him. "What does she need?"

"Her lovey." Her voice cracked.

He cocked a brow in question.

"It's a doll I made her. She brought it in the car. Junie had hers, too, a rabbit. They're gone." Her body shook with silent sobs, and he wrapped her in his arms again. He was so big, she felt buffered from the rest of the world. If only he could keep the pain away, too.

"Hey, sweetheart, is there anything I can do?"

Leah pushed out of his arms at the sound of Ginger's voice and wiped her eyes. "I'm fine." She needed to get rid of them so she could fall apart in private. She walked out of the bedroom, forcing herself to stop crying, and said, "You don't have to stay. We'll be fine."

Tank's jaw tightened, and he looked at Ginger.

"I have to stay, honey," Ginger said. "I promised the nurse I'd watch over you, and you or the girls might need something tonight."

She wanted to say that they'd done fine for all these years, but they'd had River...

Oh God. River.

She bit back the gut-wrenching despair and relented with a nod, willing her tears not to fall. She looked at Tank. "You should go. Your clothes are still wet."

Tank gave a single curt nod, his solemn expression unchanged.

She needed to thank him for saving them, but she couldn't bring herself to do it. She was afraid she'd go off on him again for not being able to save River, so she went back into the bedroom and closed the door behind her. She toed off her sneakers and climbed into bed with the girls, putting her arm around them. How were they supposed to carry on without River? He was their father—even if they didn't know that yet— their best friend, storyteller, and caretaker.

She buried her face in Junie's curls, giving in to the crushing pain in her chest and the emptiness in her heart, knowing that tomorrow she'd have to figure out how to tell the girls that their father, the young man who loved them most in the world, would never be with them again.

Chapter Three

TANK SAT IN his double-cab truck with a tray of coffee and chocolate milk in his lap, a bag of doughnuts on the passenger seat, and a fucking jackhammer made of knives in his chest. He'd give anything to turn back time. If only he'd followed his gut and gone to talk to Leah when he'd seen her at the convenience store last night. If she'd left the parking lot a few minutes later, her brother would still be alive. He gritted his teeth. He was just a kid. Hell, Leah must have been barely more than a kid when she'd had her first child. Where was the girls' father? Where were Leah's parents? He had so many questions, but they'd have to wait.

He gathered his things and climbed out of the truck. As he headed up the walk, he thought about the calls and texts from his family, cousins, and fellow Dark Knights that he'd fielded since the sun had risen. *He* wasn't the one who needed support.

He knocked on the front door, and his mother answered, looking tired. Her hair was tousled and her navy blouse was wrinkled. The sadness in her eyes pulled Tank back to the days after Ashley died, swamping him with the weight of a lead coat.

"Hi, sweetheart."

"Hi, Mom." He handed her the tray of drinks and kissed

her cheek as he stepped inside. "How are they?"

"The girls are still sleeping, and Leah's in the shower. I don't think she got much sleep. I heard her crying on and off all night. Poor thing."

He set the bags he was carrying on the bar between the kitchen and living room, wishing he could take their pain away.

"I heard your truck roll in around three. Were you out there all night?" She put the tray of drinks on the bar. "Did *you* get any sleep?"

"Yeah. I had to take care of a few things. Then I went home to shower, and when I came back, I caught a few hours of sleep in my truck." If only he could scrub off the guilt of being unable to save River. He'd gone over every second of the rescue hundreds of times, and he knew there was nothing he could have done differently. If he hadn't gotten Leah and the girls out first, he could have lost them, too. But that didn't change the guilt that stuck to him like a second skin. He glanced at the bathroom door. "Has she said anything?"

His mother shook her head. "I told you she was a private girl."

She took both of his hands in hers, holding them tight, looking into his eyes with the plea he'd seen too many times. He knew what she was going to say before the words left her lips.

"Honey, I know you want to help Leah and the girls, but they aren't the only ones who suffered a loss last night. I think you need to take some time and let yourself grieve, too."

He pulled his hands free. "I'm fine. *They're* not."

"Tank—"

"*Mom,*" he said firmly. "I'm not going anywhere. If anyone knows what she's going through, it's me."

She crossed her arms. "Benson, you are so damn stubborn."

She only used his given name when she was infuriated or frustrated. "Wonder where I got that from."

He went into the kitchen, and she followed him in. Several of the girls' drawings were displayed on the refrigerator, hung with magnets. One picture had Junie's name printed at the top and four people drawn as circles with eyes but no mouths. Each had two lines coming out of the bottom for legs and out of the sides for arms. Above each figure was a name. River had the biggest circle with the longest legs, and he was drawn next to Junie. Then came Rosie and Leah, who was almost as big as River but not quite. Another drawing had Rosie's name printed above a mass of crayon scribbles. Their names were written around the scribbles with arrows pointing to different parts.

"Isn't that the sweetest?" his mother said. "I used to hang up your drawings, too, and believe it or not, there was a time that you could only scribble, too. It was nice of you to bring breakfast." She opened a cabinet and withdrew plates. "They don't have much. Can you grab two sippy cups?"

He glanced in the cabinet and saw three mismatched plates and, above them, a handful of plastic cups with lids, mugs, and glasses.

"The ones with lids," his mother said with a teasing grin.

Leah came out of the bathroom wrapped in a towel as they were setting plates along the bar. Her eyes were red and puffy, her wet curls trailing down her back. There were bruises down her left arm and shoulder, and she'd replaced the bandage on her forehead. Her lips turned down at the corners in a heart-breaking frown. She looked even younger and more vulnerable than usual. Tank had the urge to wrap her in his arms and hold her, to give her every ounce of strength he had.

Her gaze moved over the drinks, pastries, and doughnuts he'd brought, and then those sad eyes met his, but that scared-rabbit look he'd grown accustomed to had been replaced with one he was more familiar with. It was the vacant stare of a person lost in a world that had once been as clear and familiar as glass and had been broken into jagged shards that would never feel whole again.

Tank reached into the bag he'd put on the counter and pulled out the girls' lovies, which he'd retrieved from the wreckage last night and had washed for them. Leah's eyes widened as he closed the distance between them and handed her the bunny and the doll.

Tears slid down her cheeks. *"How...?"* she asked with a thin voice, as if she were barely breathing.

"The girls needed them." She didn't need more details than that. If it had meant flying to the moon to get them, he'd have found a way.

She clutched the lovies to her chest and mouthed, *Thank you*, then went into the bedroom and closed the door.

God, he wanted to follow her, to sit on the bed with her and the girls, and pull her onto his lap so she wouldn't feel alone in her grief.

His mother touched his arm. "Are you okay?"

He stared at the bedroom door, imagining Leah looking at her girls and tears streaking her freckled cheeks. "Do you remember that feeling of being unable to breathe after Ash died?"

"Of course, honey."

His throat thickened. "I'd hold my breath if it meant Leah could breathe."

"Oh, *Benson*," his mother whispered, leaning her head

against his shoulder.

He hugged her.

"There are arrangements that need to be made and difficult conversations to be had," she said softly. "It's about to get harder for her."

"I already took care of things. I'll talk with her. Why don't you go home and shower, get some rest?"

Her brow furrowed. "I don't know, honey. You might be a grown man, but you'll always be my baby boy, and as your mother, it's *you* I need to put ahead of everyone else. I'm afraid this might drag you under."

"I'm *staying*. I couldn't save her brother, but I'll be damned if I won't save her and the girls from whatever grief I can."

"What about work?"

"Gia and Cait are handling the shop for a while." Gia Galant and Cait Weatherby were two of his three trusted employees. They'd worked for him for several years, and they could handle anything that came up. "I've got this, Mom. I wouldn't put myself in a position to help if I was going to fall apart. That would only make things worse for them."

"I know that here." She touched her temple. "But it hurts here." She put her hand over her heart.

He pulled her into his arms. "I love you. Now, grab coffee and a Danish and get outta here and get some rest. Dad'll be glad to see you."

"I'm proud of you, sweetheart. You're a good man." She kissed his cheek. "Tell Leah I'll be back with dinner later." She grabbed breakfast on her way out.

While he waited for Leah to come out of the bedroom, he surveyed the living room. There were toys lined up against the side wall and a few others on the cushions of the love seat beneath the window. A guitar lay on the floor by the couch. He wondered if Leah played. There was a stack of kids' books on the coffee table, two novels, a tiny pink hairbrush, and a Barbie doll. The girls' sandals and sneakers were by the door, along with larger ones and a pair of men's flip-flops and sneakers.

Tank's gut clenched, and his gaze moved over the pictures on the walls. He crossed the room and peered into the open bedroom. Sunlight streamed in through two windows with white curtains that had scribbles all over them, as if the girls had been given Sharpies and allowed to decorate. Two twin beds had the most interesting, colorful patchwork blankets he'd ever seen. One had pink bows sewn in, and the other had purple bows. Two framed pictures sat on top of a nightstand between the two beds. The closet doors were open, and inside was a dresser and a few hanging dresses and coats. Toys littered the floor along with tiny shoes, rain boots, and a basket of sparkly costumes and whatnot.

He picked up one of the pictures from the nightstand and studied it. Leah looked to be around eight or nine, wild-haired and bright-eyed, and he assumed the grinning toddler was River. They were on the lap of a handsome light-skinned Black man, who was sitting on porch steps. His head was shaved, and his beard and mustache were a shade darker than Leah's reddish-brown hair. They shared the same full lips, slightly flat nose, and freckles. He had one arm around Leah, the other around River, and the kindest eyes Tank had ever seen.

Tank felt a tug on the back of his jeans and looked down. Rosie was grinning up at him with apple cheeks and a mass of tangled curls, holding the doll he'd retrieved from the wreckage.

"Who you?" she asked in a chirpy little voice.

He crouched to look her in the eyes, and his legs hit the

beds. "My name is Tank. I'm a friend of your mommy's. Where is your mommy?"

"Sleeping." She cocked her head. "You swimmed."

His chest constricted. How much of last night did she remember? "That's right." He didn't know what Leah had told her, so he tried to change the subject. He held up the picture. "Who is this?"

She pointed to each person as she said, "Mama. Wiver. Gwampa Leo." She touched Tank's nostril piercing, then ran her tiny fingers along the tattoos on his arms. "You dwawed?"

God she was cute. "Something like that. Do you see your grandpa a lot?"

She shook her head and pointed up to the ceiling. "He watchin' us."

Jesus.

She took the picture and put it back on the nightstand, then grabbed the other one, showing it to him. "Dis Junie's."

The picture was taken outside. Rosie's grandfather was standing with one arm outstretched a few feet away from a lanky teenage Leah, as if he'd just nudged her. He was smirking, and Leah was laughing. She had her arm around a much younger River's shoulder, leaning on him. Her body was slightly angled, legs crossed at the ankle, her other hand on her hip. River held up one palm to the sky with an expression that said, *What do I look like? A leaning post?* Both of them had wild, spiral curls, though River's hair was lighter than Leah's.

Sadness moved through Tank.

Rosie put the picture back and grabbed Tank's pinkie, leading him into the living room, to the front window. She pointed to a picture on the windowsill. "Dat's Wiver's."

In the picture, Leah was sitting on a chair holding Junie,

who looked to be about two, on her lap, and beside her, River sat holding a tiny baby, who must have been Rosie, grinning like he couldn't be happier. Junie was leaning over the baby, with a fistful of River's hair, and Leah had her arm around the back of River's chair, peering over Junie's head at River, who couldn't have been more than sixteen or seventeen.

Where the hell was the father of those babies?

Rosie tugged his pinkie. "I hungwy. I get Wiver." She toddled over to the recessed staircase between the bedrooms and started climbing them.

It took Tank a second to realize that must be River's bedroom, and he intercepted her, lifting her right off the steps. "I'll get you breakfast."

She petted his beard as he carried her to the bar and put her on a chair by the plate of doughnuts and pastries. She looked up at him and wrinkled her nose. *"Pincakes!"*

He didn't know a single kid who would turn down sweets for breakfast, but this little one seemed to know exactly what she wanted. "Sure."

She turned, sliding on her stomach off the chair, and ran to the cabinet beside the stove. She pulled out a large plastic bowl, then opened the pantry door and held the lowest shelf as she stretched on her tippy-toes, reaching for the too-high box of pancake mix. Tank snagged it and put it on the counter. Rosie ran to the fridge. She grabbed the door handle with both hands, planting her feet together, and tugged with all her might.

Tank chuckled at the determined tyke. He put his fingers on the top of the refrigerator door and said, "Pull harder."

Her tiny brows knitted, and when she tugged, he pushed it open, earning an elfish grin. She grabbed a plastic container of blueberries and put them on the counter with the bowl. Tank scooped her up and set her on the counter, too, and together they began making pancakes.

They were stirring the mix when the bedroom door cracked open, and Junie's little face peered out.

"We make pincakes!" Rosie called over to her.

Junie stepped tentatively out of the bedroom, closing the door behind her. She held her stuffed rabbit by the ears. Her expression was solemn, her brow furrowed as she walked over and climbed onto a chair at the bar, watching them.

"Dis Tank." Rosie patted his arm. "Mama's fwiend."

Junie's expression didn't change.

Tank pushed Rosie to the back of the counter so her legs were straight. "Don't move."

She wiggled her toes, giggling.

He drew his brows together, and she stopped wiggling. He turned to Junie and leaned his forearms on the bar. "Hi."

She stared sullenly at him, and his chest constricted. Did she understand what she'd seen yesterday? Or was she just as wary of him as Leah was?

"Is your mama still sleeping?" He took her silence as a yes. "Would you like to help make pancakes?"

Her eyes darted to Rosie, then back to Tank.

"I could use some help figuring out how to do it right."

"Help, Juju!" Rosie exclaimed.

Junie eyed Tank for a moment before she climbed down and went to Rosie, reaching for her hand.

"How about I put you on the counter with your sister?"

Junie nodded, and he lifted her, putting her on the other side of the bowl. She picked up the bowl, scooted over so she was pressed against Rosie's side, and put the bowl in their laps.

Okay, then. He held up the blueberries. "Go to it."

The girls looked at each other, and then Rosie grabbed a blueberry and ate it.

"They're for the *pancakes*," Junie said, putting a few blueberries in the bowl as Rosie grabbed a handful.

"Here." Rosie opened her hand toward Junie, and blueberries rolled out onto their legs.

Rosie giggled, and the edges of Junie's lips twitched, as if she wanted to smile but wouldn't let herself. They scrambled to pick up the berries, and Rosie popped two into her mouth as fast as she could, while Junie held hers in her fist, looking at the bowl.

"Hey, Twitch." Tank waited for Junie to look up at him. He winked, then plucked a blueberry out of the container and put it in his mouth.

Junie's lips twitched again. He nodded, and she looked at the blueberries in her hand.

"*Twitch.*" Rosie giggled. "Eat 'em!"

Junie brought her hand to her mouth, smiling as she ate them.

Tank grabbed a small bowl from the cabinet and put half the blueberries in it. "These are for you two to eat. The rest are for the pancakes."

"Mickey Mouse pancakes," Junie said, sullen-faced again.

"I don't know, Twitch. I might need some help with that."

Her lips twitched into an *almost* smile again.

"Think you girls can help me?"

They nodded eagerly.

As the girls put the rest of the blueberries in the pancake mix, Rosie chattered endlessly. She reminded him of Ashley when she was young, full of joyous energy. Tank couldn't understand half of what Rosie said, but her cheery little voice was fucking adorable, and Junie seemed to understand her, because every few seconds she'd nod or say something. They were like tiny lights, flashing on and off in a dark time. Tank's mother's voice whispered through his mind. *Food fuels your body, but children nourish your soul.* He was starting to see what she meant.

He hated knowing that Junie and Rosie probably had no idea that River was gone, and when they did, it would likely steal some of that light. He wanted to scoop them up and protect them from the truth.

The bedroom door opened as they were cooking the pancakes. Tank was holding Junie, who had a death grip on the silver chain around his neck, and Rosie was sitting on the counter beside the stove, yammering about Tank having *ear holes* like her mama, which he figured out meant that he wore earrings.

"Mama!" Rosie yelled something about making *pincakes* as Tank's and Leah's eyes collided.

He held his breath at Leah's confused expression, hoping he hadn't overstepped. Her gaze softened as she walked toward them in jeans and a pretty sweater, her half-dry hair tangled, sheet prints on her cheek. The urge to hold her hit hard, and it took everything Tank had not to reach for her.

LEAH TRIED TO pull her thoughts together. Where was Ginger, and what was Tank doing there? She didn't know what to make of the man she'd tried to keep her distance from cooking pancakes with her girls. He was so big, he made her kitchen feel too small. He looked fierce in his black T-shirt and leather vest with Dark Knights patches, and at the same time, with Junie in his arms, he looked like a gentle giant. Junie had one arm around his thick neck, and she was holding his silver chain, like she used to hold River's, which sent Leah's heart reeling.

"Down!" Rosie exclaimed.

Leah watched him set Junie down and lift Rosie off the counter with his massive tattooed arms. He patted their heads with his enormous inked hands.

"My Boo!" Rosie toddled over to the other counter.

Tank grabbed their lovies and handed them to her girls, causing Leah's heart to squeeze. "How about you give your mama a good-morning kiss? Then you can have your pancakes with the chocolate milk I brought."

The girls ran to Leah, pulling her from her stupor, and she hugged them both. Tank put two plates on the bar, and the blueberry Mickey Mouse pancakes brought tears to Leah's eyes. She stuffed them down deep as the girls climbed onto their chairs.

Leah cut their pancakes and said, "What do you say to Tank?"

"Thank you!" Rosie exclaimed, while Junie said it quietly.

"I couldn't have done it without your help." He winked at the girls, then handed Leah a plate of pancakes.

"I'm sorry I fell asleep," she said softly, taking the plate. "You didn't have to stick around or do any of this."

"I got you coffee, but it's probably cold by now," he said without responding to what she'd said. "I can microwave it for you."

"It's okay. I don't drink coffee, but I appreciate the thought.

I'll pay you back for breakfast."

"How about you sit down and eat something instead?" He nodded to the bar.

"I'm not hungry. Do you want them?"

He turned and picked up a plate with a *huge* stack of pancakes on it. "I'll replace the box. The girls insisted we make some for me, too."

"He eats like a pig," Junie said.

"*Junie*, that's not nice," Leah said.

"*He* said it." Junie looked at Tank with a serious expression.

He was leaning against the counter, his long legs practically stretching all the way across the floor to the bar as he stabbed his fork through a stack of six or seven pancakes. He gave Junie one curt nod, which seemed to be his go-to response, and devoured a big bite, snorting like a pig, causing an outburst of giggles.

Leah put her plate on the counter, and Tank set his down beside it.

He turned his back to the girls, hulking over Leah's shoulder. "You need to eat something." His tone was gruff but quiet.

"I can't."

"I get it. Your stomach feels like it's inside out, and every time you aren't focused on the girls, you see River and you want to crawl under a rock."

It was like he'd looked inside her and knew exactly what she felt.

"I've been there, Lee."

Even with his gruff tone, *Lee* sounded intimate and tender, and that made her want to bury her face in his chest and disappear.

"But from what I've seen, your littlest has enough energy for sixteen people. You're going to need some fuel. Do you want something else? I saw some yogurt in the fridge."

She shook her head, staring at the counter.

"Danish? Doughnut?"

"No, thank you."

"I can go out and get something. What do you like to eat? Pizza? Sandwiches?"

"I'm fine, really. I've taken care of myself for a long time. I'm not going to starve, and I'm sure you have better things to do than babysit us." She felt the heat of his stare boring into her for so long, it felt like he really *could* see inside her. When she finally met his gaze, her breath caught at the emotions looking back at her. He still exuded that suffocating sensation, but it no longer scared her, because now she felt it as her own, too. She felt gutted, like she might never breathe right again, and Ginger's voice came back to her. *I lost my youngest, my daughter, Ashley, when she was in college.* Tank had lost his sister—he really did understand.

"Nothing is more important than being here for you and the girls."

Nobody had been there for them like he was, and she wasn't sure how to respond, so she went with the truth. "I appreciate that." *More than you could know.* She didn't want to sound ungrateful, but she needed to talk to the girls about River before they started asking questions, and she didn't want an audience. "But you should probably finish your pancakes and go. I just…I need some space."

He held her gaze, worry swimming in his dark eyes. "You sure about that?"

She nodded, even though she wasn't really sure.

He finished the stack of pancakes in three bites, and then

without a word, he washed his plate and the other dishes, despite her telling him not to. He dried his hands on his jeans and looked at the girls with the warmest expression. Leah melted a little inside. Nobody other than her and River had ever looked at them like that.

He put his palms on the counter in front of the girls, leaning in, and spoke in that gruff and tender tone. "Rosie, you are a master blueberry eater. Twitch, thanks for helping me learn how to make mouse pancakes."

Twitch?

Junie's lips twitched, but they didn't quite make it into a smile.

"You leavin'?" Rosie asked.

He nodded, and Rosie shook her head, whining, "No go!"

A wave of regret moved over his face as he went around the counter, and Rosie's arms shot up. He scooped her up, and she threw her little arms around his neck.

"No go!" she pleaded again.

"*Rosie*, Tank has things to do." Leah didn't have the energy for extra tears.

Tank hugged her little girl tighter. "I'll see you soon, kiddo." He whispered something in Rosie's ear, and she grinned as he set her on her chair. Junie looked sullenly up at him, and he kissed the top of her head; then he whispered to her, and her lips twitched into a smile. "Your mama's gonna walk me out. You girls stay here, okay?"

They nodded, and Leah followed him out to the porch. "What did you say to them?"

"I said if they need me, all they have to do was look out that window."

"Tank, you can't tell them things like that. They're kids.

They'll believe you, and throw a fit when you're not there."

"I never make promises I don't intend to keep," he said firmly. "Listen to me, Leah. There's a bag inside by the door. It has your purse in it and a few toys that were in your car. Your purse was soaked. I didn't go through it but thought you might want it. There were two blankets that looked like they were handmade. I washed them, but I didn't want to put them in the dryer. They're hanging on a line at my place."

It was all she could do to keep from crying. He'd already done so much, and he'd gotten their memory blankets, which she'd thought were gone forever.

Tank kept his eyes trained on her. "I need to ask you something. Rosie showed me pictures of her grandfather. I assume that's your father, since you look just like him. She said he's watchin' you from above. Has he passed on?"

She nodded.

"What about your mother?"

"I never knew her, and River's mother took off when he was just a baby."

His jaw clenched. "The girls' father?"

She shook her head, unable to even think about explaining that right then.

"Do you have *any* other family that can come help you?"

She shook her head again. "It's just us, like I told Ginger. But we're fine. You've done way more than enough. I just need to figure out how to tell them about River."

"I'll help you with that if you'd like."

His kindness brought more tears. She blinked them away. "It's okay. I can do it."

His face tensed, like he wanted to push but wasn't going to. "When you're ready, arrangements need to be made for River."

"I know." She felt like she was going to cry again and tried to swallow past the lump that lodged in her throat. "I did it for my father."

His brows knitted. "I'm sorry to hear that." He pulled a cell phone and a business card from his pocket and handed them to her. "You can't be without a phone. This one should do for now. I put my number in it in case you need anything, and that's my buddy Lenny Covington's card. We call him *Saint*. He's a fellow Dark Knight, and he owns the best funeral home around. I've already spoken to him. All you need to do is make a phone call and he'll take care of everything. If you're not up to it, tell me what you'd like and I'll handle it. If you need anything, at any time, call or text me."

"Tank…" She looked at the phone and the card. She'd forgotten about her phone, and she'd been dreading the thought of finding a funeral home and having to go in and explain her loss to strangers. "I don't know what to say."

"You don't have to say anything. Just know that you don't have to shoulder this alone."

There was a knock at the window, and they both looked over. The girls had their faces pressed against the glass. Rosie was smiling. Junie wasn't. Rosie waved. Tank lifted his chin in their direction. Rosie kissed the glass, earning an extraordinarily rare grin from Tank, revealing his dimples.

"Is Junie always this serious, or does she understand what happened last night?"

I think she senses things the way I do was on the tip of her tongue, but she didn't need for him to think she was crazy on top of everything else. "She's a thinker. Thank you for taking care of them. I didn't mean to fall asleep this morning."

"You needed it, and you're going to need more. I'm not

going anywhere, Leah, and this isn't the time to prove you deserve an award for being a strong mom. Your girls are a reflection of how incredible of a mother you are."

She tucked his praise deep inside her. "I couldn't have raised them without River." Her eyes dampened again. "Please tell your mom and your family that I appreciate their support. I'd better get back inside."

"My mother is stopping by tonight with dinner. Is there anything you or the girls are allergic to?"

"No, but she doesn't have to do that."

"The minute you started working at our family restaurant, you became one of us. I think whatever drives this world knew that you'd need the strength of family, and that's why you found us. She'll bring dinner, so if you and the girls have favorite foods, let me know." He nodded in the direction of the girls watching them through the window. "Being with them will help. They sure brightened my day, and I appreciate that."

He took a step away, then turned back. "I don't claim to know shit about kids, but if you believe in heaven and all that, you might try telling them that River had a really special job to do up there with their grandfather. Maybe think of something he did with them that was meaningful and wrap that into the explanation." He shrugged. "It might bring them comfort."

Tears sprang to her eyes. *God, this is so hard.*

"It's okay if they see you cry." The muscles in his jaw bunched. "Parents are allowed to be sad, and it might even help them deal with their own grief."

"You don't give yourself enough credit," she said as tears slid down her cheeks. "I think you know a lot about kids. Thank you."

With a nod, he headed to his truck, and Leah went inside.

"Mama!" Rosie waved her over to the window. "He watchin' us."

Tank was standing with his back against the truck, hands in his pockets, as if he intended to stay right there. Rosie waved, and Tank lifted his chin in what Leah now knew was his standard greeting.

She had no experience with a guy like Tank or a family like the Wickeds, and she didn't know how she should feel about the big biker parked outside her cottage. But she didn't feel quite as alone with him standing there, which might make telling the girls about River a little easier. She sat on the couch, her gaze drifting to River's guitar, and Tank's advice seemed like a nice way to say what needed to be said.

"Hey, Posey, Juju." She patted the cushions beside her. When the girls sat down, she put her arms around them and said, "I need to tell you something."

Chapter Four

LEAH SAT ON the floor organizing the girls' toys. She'd stayed as busy as she could to keep from crawling into bed and hiding there. The cottage had never been so clean. She dusted, vacuumed, scrubbed, and even forced herself to call the funeral home. That had been difficult, but she'd gotten through it thanks to Tank paving the way for her. She was supposed to pick out an outfit for River to wear and take it to them, but she couldn't bring herself to go up to his bedroom. She glanced at his guitar on the floor by the couch, unable to put it away. *I wouldn't want you to forget me while I'm out.* She vowed to remember every little thing about River, and to make sure the girls did, too.

She listened to them gabbing animatedly as they played, as if she hadn't told them River was gone just eight hours earlier. Junie wasn't quite herself, which Leah had expected, but other than Rosie asking *Wiver with Gwampa?* about once an hour, they were in pretty good shape. She was grateful for that, but it also made her a little sad, because the three of them were the only people who would remember him. It also made her even more determined to keep River's spirit alive.

The sound of car doors closing sent the girls scrambling to

the window. Tank had been out there all day. Leah had tried to convince him to leave, but she was secretly, guiltily thankful that he'd insisted on staying. It helped to know he was there. When she felt like crying, she looked out at him, and it gave her strength. The girls had invited him in to eat lunch with them, but he'd said he preferred to eat outside and invited the girls to eat with him on the porch. She knew he was giving her the space she'd asked for, and she appreciated that as much as she appreciated him letting the girls eat with him. She'd taken advantage of that time and locked herself in the bathroom for a good cry.

"Who dat?" Rosie asked.

Leah went to the window and saw Ginger and Conroy talking with Tank. "That's Miss Ginger and Mr. Conroy, Tank's mom and dad. They're the nice people I work for."

"I say hi!" Rosie ran out the front door.

"Wosie!" Junie ran after her.

Leah followed them out, and her heart stumbled. The girls ran to Tank, each wrapping their arms around one of his legs, as if he were a security blanket. His giant hands palmed their heads. Rosie chatted animatedly, and Conroy crouched in front of her, his happy expression exposing his dimples. He tickled Junie's belly, saying something that brought that new twitchy *almost* smile to her face.

The girls in the bar called Conroy a silver fox, because he looked like a movie star, with a long, straight nose, dimples, wavy, collar-length silver hair, and bright blue eyes. He was a tough biker, like his sons, but he had a playful side, like Gunner, and he was warm, like Baz. Tank was such a master at keeping his emotions in check, she'd thought Conroy's dimples and height were the only traits he'd inherited. She'd seen him go hours without saying more than a few words, his watchful eyes keeping tabs on the people around him. But now she knew that beneath his intimidating exterior, he possessed his father's warmth and his mother's caring nature.

"Mama!" Rosie ran to her as she approached. "Dey bwing dinner!"

Tank looked over as she lifted Rosie into her arms, and those devastating dimples appeared, softening his hard edges. Her stomach fluttered in a way that she hadn't felt in so long, she almost didn't recognize it for what it was, and it made her a little self-conscious.

Rosie wriggled out of her arms and ran to Ginger, reaching for her hand. Junie hadn't moved from Tank's side.

"Leah, sweetheart." Conroy embraced her. "I'm so sorry for your loss."

He held her longer than she expected, like her father used to, and she choked up. "Thank you."

"I hope you don't mind that I came with Ginger. I wanted to see how you and the girls were doing."

"I don't mind. But I feel bad for taking up your family's time."

His brow wrinkles. "Darlin', nothing is more important than family, and you're family to us. Starr and the others send their love and condolences, as do our other boys and the rest of the Dark Knights. Whatever you need, we're here."

"Thank you. I know I need to get back to work, but if I could just have next week off to—"

"Honey, we're giving you six weeks of paid full-time leave," Ginger said. "You and the girls need time to heal."

Leah was at a loss for words. "But...I can't...That's too long."

"We insist," Conroy said. "Now, I want to know if someone let our secret out about me and Ging spoiling kids. Is that why you've been hiding these cutie pies from us?" He ruffled the girls' hair.

"Oh no, it wasn't like that. I didn't mean to make you feel that way."

"He's just kidding, Lee," Tank reassured her. "At least about hiding them. They do have a reputation for spoiling kids."

"There's nothing wrong with a little spoiling. You turned out pretty well." Conroy clapped a hand on Tank's shoulder. "Now, how about we serve up some dinner?"

They carried everything inside and emptied the cooler they'd brought onto the counters. The girls climbed onto the chairs by the bar, and as each dish was unpacked, Junie and Rosie cheered. "Woni 'n' cheese! Tatoes! Jell-O!..."

"That's a *lot* of food," Leah said with awe, taking in the dishes of homemade macaroni and cheese, an entire roasted chicken, stuffing, mashed potatoes, vegetables, salad, biscuits, celery with peanut butter and raisins, a bowl of cut fruit, Jell-O, and a tray of cookies.

Tank came up behind her, and his chest brushed her shoulder. "This is what happens when the Wicked women cook."

"Ginger, you made all of this?"

Ginger laughed. "Me and my sister-in-law Reba and her daughter, Madigan. You know them from the restaurant."

"Yes, of course. But you didn't need to go to all this trouble. Please thank them for me." She'd had a hard time keeping all the Wickeds straight when she'd first started working there. Especially since they acted like one big family. But eventually she'd learned that Conroy and Preacher were brothers, and Ginger and Conroy were Tank, Baz, and Gunner's parents, while Reba and Preacher were the parents of Blaine, Justin—who went by the road name Maverick—Zeke, Zander, and Madigan.

"It wasn't any trouble at all. We made an afternoon out of it," Ginger explained. "We weren't sure what you and the girls liked, and we figured that whatever you didn't finish, you could eat another day."

"That's so nice of you. I don't think I've ever seen this much food in one kitchen," Leah said.

"Not even on holidays?" Conroy asked.

Leah shook her head. "I never really learned to cook like that."

"Maybe one day you and the girls can come over and cook with us," Ginger suggested.

"Can we, Mama?" Junie asked excitedly.

Before Leah could answer, Rosie exclaimed, "I cook *pincakes*! Tank a piggy!"

Ohmygod. Leah was mortified, but everyone else laughed, even Tank, whose laugh was deep and rumbling.

"I heard you made delicious pancakes." Conroy tapped the tips of Rosie's and Junie's noses, earning giggles from both of them.

It was good to hear Junie laugh. Leah imagined if her father had lived, he might act like Conroy was with the girls, too.

"I meant what I said about you and the girls coming over to cook with us," Ginger said. "I'd really enjoy it. I used to cook with Ashley all the time. I started when she was about Rosie's age."

She talked so easily about her late daughter, Leah wondered if she'd ever be able to talk that easily about River again.

"Please!" Junie and Rosie begged.

They were so excited, Leah couldn't say no, and even though she felt weird about it, she was kind of excited about it, too. "Okay, one day."

The girls cheered.

Tank touched Leah's back. "Do you have any more chairs?"

"No. Just these. I can eat on the floor with the girls."

"A picnic!" Junie exclaimed, and ran into her bedroom.

Rosie toddled after her. They returned a minute later with their bucket of plastic picnicware and a red-and-white checked picnic blanket.

As the girls set up their picnic, Ginger said, "They're so cute. I miss having little ones around."

"Our kids loved picnics when they were little, too," Conroy said.

"It's hard to imagine Tank as a little boy," Leah said, surprising herself that she'd said it out loud.

"He was a *big* little guy," Conroy said. "Always watching out for the other kids. Especially Ash. He gave the guys hell when she was in high school." His expression turned thoughtful. "She was lucky to have him."

Tank's jaw tightened. He went into the kitchen and began gathering plates. Leah wanted to go to him and ask if he was okay, but Ginger nudged her and said, "Someone's up to something."

Junie was whispering to Rosie, and Rosie was grinning from ear to ear, nodding. Rosie ran to Tank, taking his hand as Junie took Conroy's, and they led them into the living room. Rosie pointed to the picnic blanket. *"Sit."*

"*Rosie*, be nice." Leah shook her head. "I'm sorry."

Ginger laughed. "Are you kidding? Your girls are wonderful."

Junie looked up at Conroy and Tank with a hopeful expression and said, "Will you have a picnic with us?"

"I wouldn't miss it for the world." Conroy lowered himself to the floor.

She looked at Tank, and he said, "Sure thing, Twitch."

Junie beamed at him as he sat beside their tiny blanket.

"Picnic!" Rosie clapped.

Leah and Ginger filled everyone's plates, and for nearly two hours, the living room was filled with laughter and chatter. The girls wanted to know why Tank and Conroy drew on their arms, and Conroy told them that every tattoo had a story. The girls prodded them through five or six stories before moving on to a dozen other topics. After dinner, Ginger refused to let Leah do the dishes, urging her to relax instead, but relaxing gave her mind time to wander into sadder territory.

Conroy lifted one girl into each of his arms and walked around the living room, asking about the pictures on the walls. Rosie said, "Wiver's with Gwampa! He watchin' us!"

Conroy looked up at the ceiling and said, "Hello, Grandpa. Hello, River. I'm sorry I didn't have a chance to know you. But maybe I can through these lovely little ladies."

The girls started talking excitedly about River.

Leah teared up and turned away, overcome with mixed emotions.

Tank put a hand on her back, leaning closer and lowering his voice. "You okay?"

"Yeah. My girls never knew their grandfather, and your parents are so nice, with the food, and the stories, and tonight was just…" Her voice was lost to tears.

He drew her into his arms as he'd done last night, moving his hand soothingly up and down her back. "Tonight you got to remember what it's like to have a parent around. That's a good thing, darlin'."

She was surprised that he already felt familiar, and although she wanted to stay right there in his protective arms, she didn't want to give anyone the wrong impression. She stepped back, wiping her eyes. The girls were showing Conroy their bedroom, and Ginger looked over, smiling warmly as she set a plate of cookies on the bar.

Tank touched Leah's hip. "What can I do for you, Lee?"

Didn't he know that short of bringing her brother back, he'd already given her more than she could ever ask for? "I can't think of a single thing."

LATER THAT NIGHT, Tank headed over to the tattoo shop to check in with Gia and Cait. They gave him hell about looking exhausted and needing to take better care of himself. What else was new? He hadn't slept well since Ashley died. After catching up on shop business, he headed home to get the blankets he'd hung out to dry for Leah. He drove down the narrow-wooded lane to his four-bedroom home nestled on a private wooded lot, with just enough lawn for a game of football with his brothers and cousins. He'd gotten a steal on the place. Preacher and Reba owned Cape Renovators, and Zeke and Zander worked with them. They'd helped Tank renovate the interior and build a two-story deck off to the side.

He didn't care much about where he rested his head at night, but he liked his privacy, and the house had become his sanctuary. He liked the open floor plan, the cathedral ceilings, and the rustic feel of the hardwood floors, the exposed stained rafters, the brick fireplace, and the views of the surrounding woods through two walls of patio doors. He went around back and took the blankets down from the laundry line. He'd been in a rush to get back to Leah and the girls when he'd washed them and hung them up to dry, but now he saw that they were made of tiny onesies, baby socks, hats, and other cute pieces of clothing. There were bibs and bows, and each blanket had one of the girls' names sewn in with colorful fabric. He wondered if Leah had made them. As he carried them inside, thinking about Junie's serious expression and Rosie's impish grin that never seemed to falter, Leah's beautiful face sailed through his mind, and he felt a tug deep in his chest.

How was it possible that he *missed* them?

He headed into his bedroom to grab a sweatshirt and a few books, then went to the kitchen to make a thermos of coffee. His house was too quiet and empty. It didn't have the warmth of Leah's much smaller cottage. Who knew toys strewn about and the pitter-patter of tiny feet and chirpy voices could make a house feel more like a home?

And why the hell am I thinking like that?

He drove back to Leah's and parked out front, wondering what Leah and the girls were up to. It was only eight forty-five. Were they sleeping? They had to be exhausted. He picked up a book, but his eyes kept trailing back to the house. His phone rang, and Baz's name flashed on the screen.

Tank put the phone to his ear. "Hey, brother."

"Hi. How's Leah?"

"She seemed a little better tonight. Mom and Dad came over with dinner. I think it helped."

"They can make the shittiest times feel better, can't they?"

Tank laughed softly. "Yeah. She and the girls laughed a lot."

"I'm glad to hear it. It fucking sucks to lose a sibling."

"No shit. I hate that they're going through this. You should see the girls. They're the sweetest little things. Rosie is just like Ash used to be, all bubbly and shit. And Junie...*man*. She's intense. She's not talking much, like she's trying to figure it all out." He gritted his teeth. "She's too fucking little to need to figure out this shit. And Leah's so torn apart. I just want to hold her and let her know that even though every minute feels like hell right now, she's going to be okay. She's got no one, man. The girls' father isn't in the picture, Leah's dad's dead, and she never knew her mom. It's just her and the girls."

"Sounds like she's got you."

Tank looked up at the house. "Yeah, but I'm sitting out here in my truck feeling like I should be in there."

"Wait. You're still at her place?" Baz sounded concerned.

"I just told you she's got nobody. You know how grief is. She could wake up at two in the morning and need someone to lean on. I want to be here in case she needs me."

"Well, she must be pretty special. I haven't heard you sound like this...maybe *ever*," Baz said.

"She is, but it's not like that. I just want to help."

"Tank, I know you. It might have started that way, but that's not what I'm hearing."

Very little got past his most intuitive brother. "Yeah, well, now's not the time."

"Right. Do you want me to come hang out with you? We can shoot the shit so you're not alone?"

Leah's front door opened, and she headed toward his truck with a pained expression.

"No thanks, Baz. I gotta run. Leah needs something." He

ended the call and climbed out of the truck. "What's wrong?"

"I hate to ask you this, and you can say no, but the girls want to know if you'll say good night to them. I tried distracting them with stories and songs, but—"

"I'm happy to, and you don't need to be sorry. That's what I'm here for. Whatever you and the girls need." As they headed up the walk, he said, "I'm sorry if I'm causing an issue with your kids."

"You're not. They like you, and I'm glad you're here." She touched his arm and stopped walking, looking a little troubled. "Thank you for giving me Saint's number. He made everything so easy, but, Tank, he said the cost was already taken care of. Did you do that?"

He nodded, and her eyes filled with tears.

"I'm grateful, but you didn't have to do that. I'll pay you back."

"There's no need to pay me back. It's a gift for you and the girls—and for your brother, who I never had the honor of knowing."

"Thank you." Tears slid down her cheeks, and she hugged him. She stepped back and wiped her eyes. "We're not having a service or anything. It'll just be me and the girls saying goodbye. Your mother said she'd drive us to the cemetery."

He remembered the hailstorm of emotions that the finality of Ashley's burial had caused, and there was no way he'd let Leah and the girls go through that with only his mother by their side. "Would you mind if I show up? I'd like to say goodbye to him, too."

The tension in her face eased. "I'd like that. We should go in before they come looking for us."

They went inside, and when he walked into the girls' room,

the girls sat up.

"Tank!" Rosie exclaimed.

"You came," Junie said.

"Of course I did. I made you girls a promise, and Wickeds always keep their promises."

Junie scrunched up her face. "What's a Wicked?"

"That's my last name. Yours is Yates." He sat beside her as she lay down, holding her bunny against her chest. "What's your bunny's name?"

"*Mine,*" she said.

Tank laughed. "I know it's yours, Twitch, but what's its name?"

"Mine *is* his name," Junie explained.

Tank looked at Leah, and she shrugged one shoulder. "Well, little darlin', I like a girl who claims the things she loves."

"My *Boo!*" Rosie waved her doll at him.

"That's a great name, too, little bird."

"I no *bird,*" Rosie said. "I a girl."

"Yeah? You seem like a bird to me with your cheeky smile and constant chirping." He winked, and Rosie giggled. "You girls had a pretty big day. It's time to close your eyes and dream about happy things. Okay?"

They nodded. He brushed Junie's curls from her forehead, and she reached up and hugged him. "I'm going to be right outside, okay?"

She nodded as she lay back down. "You gonna be here in the mornin'?"

How could one question turn his insides to mush? "I'm going to be here whenever you need me." He pressed a kiss to her forehead. "Get some rest." He went to sit with Rosie, who was beaming up at him, which made him laugh. "You look wide-awake." He felt around her neck with his fingers, and she giggled. "Where's your *off* button? Hey, Twitch, how do you turn your sister off?"

Junie giggled.

"Okay, Cheeky, time for you to go to sleep so Boo can rest up for tomorrow." He kissed her forehead, and Rosie threw her arms around him, pressing her tiny lips to his cheek. He tucked her blanket around her and pushed to his feet. "Sleep tight."

As he left their room, Leah mouthed, *Thank you*, the relief in her eyes palpable.

He could take down six men single-handedly, but as he headed outside feeling all warm and squishy, he knew he was no match for the debilitating power of those three girls.

Chapter Five

LEAH DRESSED AFTER her shower and peered out the front window again, hating herself for being disappointed that Tank wasn't there. She'd seen his truck outside when she'd woken up at three o'clock in the morning from a nightmare about the accident. She'd been *this close* to asking Tank to sit with her on the porch, because she'd just needed to be near someone who understood what she was going through and could tell her everything would be okay. But she hadn't wanted to burden him and had curled up around her pillow and cried herself to sleep. Now she was glad she hadn't turned to him, because his truck had been gone when she'd gotten up at six thirty. The girls were busy playing in their room for now, but she prayed they wouldn't ask for him. It wasn't like he owed any of them a darn thing, but he'd promised the girls. *He promised me.*

A knot lodged in Leah's chest.

It was bad enough that she kept expecting to hear River's voice. She couldn't walk past the stairs to his room without expecting him to peer down and tease her about something. She knew better than to lean on anyone, despite how sincere Tank had seemed. River was family. The girls were *his*. He had a stake in their well-being. Tank was just a nice guy who had rescued them and probably felt bad because he couldn't save River.

I'm such an idiot.

She made her bed and went to the bathroom to get the dirty clothes hamper and peeked into the girls' room. Rosie was sitting on the floor in her underpants playing with plastic animals, and Junie was lying on her stomach wearing only her pajama pants, drawing a picture. Why did little girls like to take their clothes off?

"I playin' zoo," Rosie said.

"What happened to your pajamas?" Leah asked.

Rosie pointed to a pile of pajamas on the floor.

Leah picked up the pajamas and tossed them into the hamper. "I'm going to run down to the basement to do laundry."

"'Kay, Mama!" Rosie said.

Junie rolled onto her side, looking up at Leah. "Is Tank comin' soon?"

The knot in Leah's chest tightened. She was walking on eggshells with her own emotions and couldn't deal with letting the girls down without losing it, so she said, "I guess we'll see."

Junie's brows knitted, and she went back to drawing.

"Tank comin'," Rosie said. "He pwomised."

"Wickeds always keep their pwomises," Junie said softly.

Leah wanted to say, *Apparently not as well as Yateses do,* but she bit her tongue and headed to the basement to do the laundry. She heard the girls run into the living room giggling. She was glad they were happy, but their brains were like Fort Knox. Junie would spend all day picking apart Tank's absence, and eventually she'd have a hundred questions, to which Rosie would have a hundred answers, all rationalizing Tank not showing up.

Didn't he know how fragile they were? They were used to

River making them a priority, and now he was gone. *Forever.* Tears welled in Leah's eyes as she threw the laundry in the washer. They didn't need another disappointment. This was her fault for letting Tank get close to them. It had felt *good* to let him help. *God*, how could she have been so selfish? So wrong about him? Tears spilled down her face as she started the machine. She'd survived her father's death and done well by River. She and the girls had each other. They didn't need anyone else. They would get through this. Somehow...

She noticed the dryer door was ajar, and when she pulled it open, she saw River's clothes inside, and her heart broke all over again. She looked up at the ceiling, tears streaking her cheeks. She was furious at God, at herself, at Tank for not saving River. She wanted to scream. *What the hell are you doing to us? What's next? Are you going to take me away from them, too?* Her legs gave out, and she sank to the floor, giving in to the crushing reality that they were now truly alone.

The girls squealed and giggled as they ran across the floor, bringing her mind back to them. She loved being a mom, but it was so fucking hard sometimes. Trying desperately to regain control of her emotions, an impossible task, she forced herself to her feet and pulled River's clothes out of the dryer. She pressed his shirt to her nose despite knowing his boyish scent was gone and folded them for what she knew would be the last time, placing one of his favorite shirts, a hoodie, and jeans on top for his burial. This was so fucking unfair.

She dragged air into her lungs and wiped her tears. She had to hold her shit together for the girls. Once she was able to swallow past the lump clogging her throat, she put on the happiest face she could muster and trudged upstairs with the laundry basket of River's clothes. As she closed the basement door, she heard a car door. She looked across the living room, through the front window, and saw Tank heading up the walk with his arms full of grocery bags. She hadn't misjudged him after all, which brought tears of relief. God, she was a mess.

She wiped her eyes as she opened the door. "Hi."

"Hey. Sorry I'm so late. I would have been here forty-five minutes ago, but I stopped to help a lady with a flat tire, and I had some club business to take care of. I've got more groceries in the truck." His brows knitted. "Are you okay?"

Groceries? How could she have doubted him when he was so good to them?

"Yeah." *I was just having a mini breakdown.* "I didn't sleep very well. I'm just tired."

Sorrow rose in his eyes. "Maybe you can catch a nap later. I'll watch the girls."

"Thanks, but I'm okay. You didn't have to bring us groceries."

"It's not a big deal," he said as he stepped inside.

The girls came out of the bedroom giggling. Tank winced, and Leah followed his gaze over her shoulder, and her jaw dropped. Junie stood in her pajama bottoms, Rosie in her underpants. They had ink all over their arms, bellies, and noses.

"We dwawed!" Rosie held out her arms.

"Every picture tells a stowy," Junie said. "Like Tank and Conwoy."

Rosie pointed to the ink on her nose. "Nose hole!"

Tank stifled a laugh.

Leah put one hand on her hip, trying to stifle her laughter. "Are you *allowed* to draw on yourselves?"

The girls looked at each other. Junie shook her head with a serious expression. Rosie shrugged, grinning like a goon.

Leah looked up at Tank, who towered over the three of them, holding five bags of groceries, tattooed from fingers to neck. How could one man have such a tremendous impact on their lives so fast?

"Am I in trouble?" Tank arched a thick dark brow, looking like a kid caught with his hand in a cookie jar.

"*Big* trouble." Laughter bubbled out before Leah could stop it, which made the girls and Tank laugh, too.

Tank set the groceries on the floor and knelt, motioning for the girls to come to him. He put his arms around them, pulling them in close. "I don't know about your mama, but I want to hear the story behind each and every one of those drawings."

The girls burst into chatter about the pictures they'd drawn, and Leah's breath caught. River would have said something just like that, turning a not-so-bad parenting moment into a chance to learn more about the girls. She watched Tank with them. He looked different, gentler, with laughter glittering in his eyes. She had a feeling they were having just as big of an impact on him as he was on them.

TANK HAD BROUGHT enough food for an army. Through giggling baths, a chatty and delicious breakfast, and finishing the laundry, Leah kept imagining River being there with them and the things he might say or do. Tank had somehow sensed her thoughts, and he stayed close by with supportive comments and warm embraces. When he'd seen River's clothes in the basket, she'd told him about needing to take some to the funeral home, and he'd offered to do it. He'd also taken the rest of

River's clothes up to his bedroom so she wouldn't have to. She came out of the girls' room after putting away their clothes and found them playing on the living room floor. Tank was standing by the side window, leather-booted feet planted hip-distance apart as he thumbed out something on his phone. His eyes darted to her and the girls every few seconds, watching them as closely as he watched over his family and friends at the Salty Hog. He caught her looking at him, causing an unexpected flutter in her chest. He pocketed his phone and closed the distance between them.

"Are you wiped out? Want to catch a nap?" he asked quietly.

"No. I'm okay, thanks." She lowered her voice. "I just miss River. I keep expecting him to walk into the room."

"That happened to me for a long time after Ashley died. I think getting out of the house would help. How about we take the girls on a little outing? Would that be okay?"

"Sure, but you don't have to spend all your time with us. We're not your responsibility. Don't you have a girlfriend or a job you need to tend to?"

His brows slanted. "Have you ever seen me bring a girlfriend to the Hog?"

"No, but…" She shrugged.

"There are no *but*s. I'm not here out of obligation, darlin'. I don't leave the special people in my life alone. End of story. So what do you think? Are you up to an outing? Gunner's got a litter of puppies at the animal rescue, and I know two little girls who might get a kick out of seeing them."

"I don't have carseats."

"I do."

You have carseats? He glanced at the girls, but she continued looking at him, trying to put the pieces of the thoughtful man she was getting to know together with the harsh man she'd thought he was. But it was like they were pieces from two different puzzle boxes, and she'd had the wrong impression all along.

THE GIRLS WERE so excited to see the puppies, they wore their zip-up animal-print hoodies with ears on the hoods. Rosie's had cat ears, and Junie's had dog ears. Tank and Leah buckled the girls into the carseats in Tank's truck, and as Leah started to climb into the front seat, she saw their memory blankets, clean and folded on the seat. Blinking away bittersweet tears, she turned to Tank, waiting to close her door, and threw her arms around him. "Thank you. You can't imagine how much this means to me."

His arms circled her. "You just showed me."

Their eyes locked, and that flutter in her chest strengthened. She shifted her eyes away and climbed into the truck, glancing over the seat at the girls.

"Look what Tank found." She handed them their blankets, and they squealed, hugging them along with their lovies, and thanked Tank profusely as he settled into the driver's seat with one of his *very Tank* silent nods of acknowledgment.

Junie and Rosie talked nonstop. Leah had warned Tank that they were a handful when they were excited, and as he drove through the gated entrance to the Wicked Animal Rescue and Wicked Veterinary Clinic, she wondered if he was regretting the offer yet, although if he were, he wasn't letting on.

"Piggies!" Junie shouted as they passed a pen with piglets in it, and Rosie started *oink*ing like a pig.

"That's right, Twitch." Tank stopped the truck so the girls could watch the pigs. "Sometimes Gunner rescues farm animals."

"Gunner is a funny name," Junie said.

He chuckled. "I guess it is. Gunner is my brother. His real name is Dwayne, and my other brother Baz's real name is Baxter." He looked at Leah, as if he wanted her to hear what he said next. "And my real name is Benson. We're all part of a club, and we use our nicknames instead of our real names. We call them our road names."

"Like *Twitch*?" Junie asked.

Tank nodded. "Yes. Exactly."

"Can I be part of your club?" Junie asked.

"I be in it!" Rosie chimed in.

"It's not a club for kids," Leah explained quickly. She should have warned him that when Junie was comfortable with people, she asked a lot of questions.

"Why not?" Junie asked.

Tank winked at Leah and looked over the seat at the girls. "It's a motorcycle club for men. We keep people like your family safe."

"You didn't keep Wiver safe," Junie said.

Leah spun in the seat, gutted. *"Junie, hush!"*

Tank put his hand on hers, looking as grief-stricken as she felt. "It's okay. She's right." He turned his attention back to the girls. "I did everything I could to save River, and I'm sorry I wasn't able to. But that's on me, not the club. The club does different things to keep families safe, like keeping bad guys out of our area and preventing bullying."

"Oh," Junie said solemnly.

"Junie, it wasn't Tank's job to save us." Leah glanced at Tank, her eyes dampening. "But he did, and it wasn't his fault he couldn't save River. He tried his hardest." She lowered her voice to a whisper. "I'm sorry for what I said that night."

"It's okay. And just to clarify, as a volunteer firefighter, it's always my job to help people, but that's not why I went into the water that night. I'd have gone in even if I wasn't a firefighter."

The despair in his voice mirrored the heaviness she felt. He squeezed her hand and began driving slowly down the long driveway, pointing out shelters for sheep and goats and the play area for dogs. He parked in front of the veterinary clinic and pointed out two long buildings, which he said were the main animal shelters.

When they climbed out of the truck, Leah hurried over to him. "*Tank*, I really am sorry for what I said the night of the accident, and I'm sorry for what Junie said just now."

His gaze softened. "It's fine, really. I don't blame you for being upset, and honestly, there's nothing anyone can say that I haven't already said to myself. But I hope you know that I would have given my life to save his if I could have."

From what she'd seen of him, she believed that.

"And as far as Junie goes, she's a smart kid. She wants to understand what happened that night, and I would rather give her the truth than have her come up with the wrong story in her head. It'll take a lot more than one conversation for her to understand it. Hell, Ashley died several years ago, and I'm still asking questions." The girls were calling them, and Tank looked over and said, "One second, chickadees."

The girls giggled and started calling each other *chickadees*.

He stepped closer. "This is going to hurt for a very long

time, and you might hate me again tonight or a week or a month from now. The girls are going to cry. They're going to ask questions and have meltdowns. You will, too, and that's okay. Grief is an unpredictable and vicious motherfucker. But I'm here for whatever you or they need. You can use me as a punching bag seven days a week, and it won't faze me, other than making me feel sad for your grief. There's nothing I can't handle."

She was overwhelmed by his support and thankful for it, even if she didn't fully understand why he was giving it to her. "I won't hit you again—don't worry. But you're right. Grief comes in waves, and when it hits, it's so hard."

"My grandfather Mike is one of the best men I know, and he always says that life is a series of moments. Some chew us up and spit us out, and others put us back together, bringing hope for a better tomorrow. The trick is to stack up the good moments, so when the bad ones hit, you remember *why* you're pushing forward. We can't change what happened, and I know neither of us would ever try to sweep it under the carpet. But we *can* start stacking up good moments and give your girls a great day."

He touched her back on the way to get the girls out of the truck, and she said, "It's like you have a grief handbook."

"No handbook. Just unfortunate experiences and a great family," he said as they lifted the girls out of their carseats.

"Boo!" Rosie reached for her doll.

"I think we'd better leave Boo in the truck so the puppies don't chew on him," Leah said.

"Where are the puppies?" Junie asked, looking around.

"Let's go find out." Tank headed for the shelter, and the girls ran to either side of him, trying to keep up.

Gunner came out of the office wearing a gray T-shirt and jeans. "Hey, bro."

Tank pulled him into a manly embrace. "Thanks for letting us come out."

They greeted each other that way at the Salty Hog, too, but it had never occurred to Leah how special it was until now, as she was struck by a pang of longing for her brother.

"I'm glad you're here." Gunner opened his arms, startling Leah as he embraced her. "I'm so sorry about your brother."

"Thank you." A lump lodged in her throat.

"Gun, these are Leah's kids, Junie and Rosie." Tank ruffled the girls' hair as he said their names. "Girls, this is my *little* brother, Gunner."

"He's not little," Junie said.

"Darn right I'm not." Gunner winked at Junie. "I can see you and I are going to be good friends." He winked at Rosie. "You too, squirt."

Rosie grinned. "Wiver, too? He watchin' us."

Sadness rose inside Leah as Tank put a hand on Rosie's and Junie's shoulders.

"River, too," Gunner reassured her.

"You have *stowies!*" Rosie touched Gunner's tattooed hand.

Gunner looked curiously at Leah, and she explained what had happened earlier that morning. He chuckled. "I see my brother's already a bad influence, huh?"

"Actually, Tank's been great," Leah said.

Tank exchanged a secret look with Gunner that she couldn't read.

"Glad to hear it." Gunner rubbed his hands together and looked at the girls. "I wonder if you can help me out. We rescued a bunch of puppies, and I sure could use a couple of volunteers to do puppy patrol with me. You don't know of anyone who might be interested, do you?"

The girls' eyes widened, and they raised their hands, pleading, "Me! Me!"

He knelt before them. "There are a lot of puppies. Do you think you can handle them climbing on you and licking your face?"

The girls giggled and bounced up and down as they nodded.

"They'll bark a lot, and they might even nip at your fingers with sharp little teeth," Gunner warned. "If they nip at your fingers, you say *no bite*, firm, like you mean it."

Junie furrowed her brow. *"No bite."*

"No bite!" Rosie chirped cheerily.

Leah, Tank, and Gunner laughed.

"Wosie bit me once and I didn't even cwy," Junie said, and the burly men looked like they melted as much as Leah did.

Gunner tickled Rosie's tummy. "You can't bite the puppies, squirt."

She giggled. "Okay."

"We'll be good. I won't let her bite them," Junie promised.

"Well, I guess that settles it. Welcome aboard, puppy patrollers." Gunner held out his hand, and Junie and Rosie took turns shaking it, beaming. "My friend Sidney is with the puppies. Let's head over and meet them."

As they followed Gunner across a field, Tank put a hand on Leah's back and said, "Sid's cool. You'll like her. She's ex-military, like Gunner. She was a dog handler. Now she's a canine physical therapist and trainer. Her dad is also ex-military and a Dark Knight."

"Dark Knights are *everywhere*."

Tank cocked a grin. "You have no idea how true that is.

Teachers, cops, retail shop owners…"

They came to a fenced area where six of the cutest brown, black, and white puppies were playing with Sidney. Sidney was beautiful, about Leah's height, five foot five, with side-parted, shoulder-length wavy brown hair, and she looked to be in her early to midtwenties.

"Puppies!" Junie yelled, and the girls ran over to the fence, causing the puppies to jump and yap.

"Careful," Leah warned. Gunner and Tank beat her to their sides like two giant bodyguards.

"They lick me!" Rosie giggled.

"No bite," Junie said through her giggles.

So much for using a serious tone.

Sidney dropped to her knees, monitoring the puppies from inside the fence. She turned friendly green eyes up to Leah. "Hi. I'm Sidney. You must be Leah. Your girls are adorable."

"Thanks. Junie, Rosie, say hello to Sidney," Leah said.

"Hi," they said in unison between giggles.

"We're puppy patrollers," Junie announced.

"Thank goodness Gunner found us some volunteers." Sidney picked up a puppy and snuggled him. "Why don't you come in here and patrol with me?"

The girls ran toward the gate, and Tank caught up to them in two long strides, his big hands swallowing theirs.

Junie looked up at him. "You're not a puppy patroller."

Tank returned her serious look with one of his own. "I'm a Twitch and Rosie patroller. Where you go, I go."

The girls grinned, and Leah got that gooey feeling inside again as she followed them through the gate. She scooped up a puppy, and it licked her face, wriggling in her arms as the girls ran around with pups yapping at their heels.

Sidney sidled up to her and petted the puppy she was holding. "Gunner told me about the accident. I'm really sorry for your loss."

"Thank you." Had they told everyone they knew? Leah realized it was such a big accident, it was probably on the news.

"I know we only just met and I'm glad Tank is there for you and the girls, but we all know he's not the most talkative guy around. If you need someone else to talk to, I'm a good listener."

"That's really nice. Thank you." Tank might not be warm in a traditional sense, but he was warm toward Leah and her girls. She saw Baz come out of the veterinary clinic and head their way. All the Wicked men were well built, but while Tank was monstrous and Gunner was thickly muscled, Baz was slightly leaner, with longish dirty-blond hair, his father's dimples, and puppy-dog eyes that made the girls in the restaurant swoon.

"I haven't lost a sibling," Sidney said, waving to Baz, "but I lost too many friends in the military. Gunner and I both did, and I'm sure you know they lost their sister."

"Yeah. It's so sad." She looked at Tank sitting on the ground with Rosie on his lap as puppies tried to crawl up her belly while Junie chased puppies around them. His watchful eyes moved between Leah and the girls and held a hint of laughter. That suffocating feeling was lighter now, but she couldn't help wondering if that was wishful thinking. If she was seeing what she needed to lessen her own guilt of soaking in his attention. Were she and the girls really adding to his burden?

Baz sidled up to them outside the fence with a devilish look in his eyes. "What's so sad? The state of Sid's dating life?"

Sidney rolled her eyes. "Not all of us need a harem. Evie was looking for you earlier."

"Most women look for me at one point or another." He turned a warm gaze to Leah. "I heard you were stopping by and I wanted to give you a hug and tell you how sorry I am about your brother."

He reached over the fence, hugging her for a long moment, but it wasn't weird or uncomfortable. It was the embrace of someone who understood grief.

Baz motioned to the girls giggling and playing as Tank and Gunner wrangled nippy puppies. "It looks like the puppies are a big hit."

"The girls needed this." *We all did, and somehow your brother knew that.*

"Mind if I introduce myself?" Baz asked.

"Of course not."

As he came through the gate, Tank said, "Junie, Rosie, this is my other brother, Baz. He's a puppy doctor."

"I wanna play doctor!" Junie cheered.

"Me play!" Rosie hollered.

The guys cracked up.

"Every female around wants to play doctor with Baz," Sidney said quietly to Leah. "They look impenetrable with all those muscles and tattoos, don't they?"

"They're the toughest men I've ever met," Leah said.

"Me too, but don't let them fool you. They've got big, breakable hearts like the rest of us. It's no wonder two of them rescue animals and one rescues people."

Leah wondered if Tank gave everyone he rescued the same attention he gave them. If he did, it was an honorable thing to do. So why did she have a sinking feeling in her stomach?

Because it feels like we're special.

His voice trampled through her mind—*I'm not here out of obligation, darlin'. I don't leave the special people in my life alone. End of story*—leaving her to wonder if their definitions of *obligation* and *special* were different.

LATER THAT NIGHT, as they put the girls to bed, Leah was still picking apart her thoughts. She couldn't remember the last time the girls had laughed so much. After playing with the puppies, they'd picked up lunch and Tank had taken them to a local pond to eat. The girls had played in the sand and put their toes in the water. They were so tuckered out, they'd fallen asleep on the drive home but had woken up the second they'd gotten back home and had been bundles of energy right up to the moment they'd climbed into bed, begging for Tank to tuck them in. The only way the day could have been better was if River had been with them. Leah's grief had ebbed and flowed throughout the day. She'd catch herself laughing with the kids one minute and feeling sad and guilty for being happy the next. Like now, as she watched Tank saying good night to the girls, their memory blankets tucked around them, she pictured River sitting between their beds playing his guitar, and she ached anew.

She worked hard to tuck those memories down deep, focusing on her girls as Rosie hugged Tank.

"I miss Wiver," Junie said, her lower lip quivering.

Leah sat beside her on the bed and hugged her. It was so unfair. They were too little to have lost their father. "I miss him, too, Juju. But he's with Grandpa now."

"He watchin' us," Rosie said.

"Will he ever come back?" Junie asked.

Tears welled in Leah's eyes, and she struggled to keep them at bay. "No, honey."

"But he's always with you," Tank reassured them. "River loved you both and your mother very much, and he left you with something very special."

"What?" Junie asked.

"Memories," Tank said. "When you miss River, all you have to do is think about him and remember all the good times you had together. Then it's like he's right there with you. My sister went up to heaven, too, and when I miss her, I think about the way she'd sneak up on me and jump on my back for piggyback rides and how she'd tease me about being the Jolly Green Giant because I'm so big."

Rosie giggled. "She watchin' you?"

Tank brushed his hand over her golden-brown curls. "She is, all the time. Tell me about River."

Lord, this man…

"He singed," Rosie said.

"He played the guitar and sang our favowite songs," Junie added. "And he told us stowies."

"When we moved here, he got a guitar at the Swap Shop and taught himself to play," Leah explained. "Their favorite songs were 'Idle Town' by Conan Gray and 'Dynamite' by BTS." She could still hear River singing about inventing games, watching the sunrise, and being okay because everyone they loved was right there with them in *their* Idle Town.

Tank nodded with a serious expression. "I don't know those songs, but give me a sec." He pulled out his phone and navigated on it, and then "Idle Town" began playing.

Junie and Rosie exclaimed, "Our Town!"

Leah and the girls sang along, but there was no stopping Leah's tears from falling. Tank reached across the space between the beds and squeezed her hand. Then he focused on his phone again. He held it up, showing her the lyrics, and began singing with them, which caused more tears.

When the song ended, Rosie looked up at the ceiling and said, "G'night, Wiver."

Tank kissed her forehead. "Get some sleep, cheeky girl."

"I love you, baby," Leah said as she kissed Junie good night, and then she and Tank switched places. It was surprising how natural it felt for him to be there with them.

Junie hugged him, and as she lay down, her brow furrowed. "Thank you for saving us."

Leah realized Junie had been thinking about their conversation all day, and her chest tightened. From the look on Tank's face, his had, too.

He moved Junie's ringlets away from her eyes with one thick, tattooed finger and kissed her forehead. "You're welcome."

"Will you be here in the mornin'?"

"Yeah, Twitch, I will. Sweet dreams." He pushed to his feet, taking one last look at the girls, and stopped beside Leah in the doorway, giving her hand another squeeze. "I'll be outside if you need me."

As he walked out, Leah knew she had to talk to him and figure out if she was so grief-stricken, she was misconstruing things, because if she was, then she and the girls needed to wean themselves off him before they got in any deeper.

Chapter Six

TANK PACED BESIDE his truck, feeling all twisted up inside. For the first time since Ashley died, he felt something good amid the grief that weighed down the very air he breathed. That was fucked up, considering the awful circumstances, but he had no idea how to tamp down feelings that were strong enough to burn through years of torment. He should probably put distance between himself and Leah and the girls. But he'd be damned if he'd walk away from them when they needed him most.

He heard the front door open, and Leah stepped onto the porch, cute as hell in skinny jeans and a forest-green sweatshirt. His heart thudded harder as he went to her. "Are the girls okay?"

"Yeah. Thank you for finding that song and helping with them. They fell right to sleep. I just needed some air and thought we could talk. Unless you have to go? I mean, that's okay—"

"Leah, I'm not going anywhere." They sat on the porch steps, and he leaned his forearms on his knees. "Was today too much?"

"No. We needed to get out of the house. The truth is, if it

weren't for the girls, I'd probably hide beneath my covers and never come out. But they deserve more than sitting around watching me try to remember how to breathe. I appreciate that you somehow knew that."

He stared out at the yard, remembering that feeling all too well. "I know about wanting to hide from the rest of the world. After Ashley died, my family tried to get me out of the house, but I wouldn't go. It was a dark time. I said awful things to my brothers when they tried to get through to me, and when Blaine and Maverick tried to tough love me into remembering that I was still alive even if Ash wasn't, I got in a knock-down, drag-out brawl with them. But for the longest time, I felt like if I didn't think of her twenty-four-seven, my memories would slip away."

"That's *exactly* how I feel."

"I figured it was. That's why I'm sharing this with you. It's important to grieve, but it's also important to remember that you're still here, because grief can destroy a person, and I don't want that to happen to you. Especially since the girls rely on you." He cocked his head, meeting her solemn gaze. "It would have been better for everyone if I'd listened to them and gotten out of my own head sooner, but I couldn't. Some days I still struggle. Ashley was six years younger than me. We had a special connection."

"Almost the same age difference as me and River."

"I hate that we have this in common. I wish you'd never experienced this type of pain."

"But I have, and now all I can do is get through it. Talking helps. Tell me about your sister."

"She was…" He sighed, thinking about where to start. "She was a lot like Rosie when she was that age. Ash was always so eager to do everything, happy all the time. She was up with the sun, even as a teenager. I used to tell her she fed off it." He warmed with the memories. "She was thirteen when I moved out of our parents' house. We were so close, she started calling me when she couldn't sleep or when she had something exciting to share. That was our *thing*, you know? She knew I'd drop everything for her. When she went away to school, she still called a lot." His throat thickened. "And then suddenly she was gone, and I had no idea how to move on from there."

"I know how that feels."

"I know you do, but I wish you didn't."

"Do you mind if I ask what happened to Ashley?"

He shook his head. "She was home from college for the weekend and she overdosed. She'd never even touched drugs before that night."

"Oh, *Tank*. I'm so sorry. Do you know why she used drugs that night?"

He nodded. "We found out from her best friend, Bethany, that she'd hooked up with some asshole at school and he ran his mouth about it and was a total dick to her. Ash was tough, but she was sensitive. She'd never hook up with a guy unless she really liked him. Bethany said Ash was so embarrassed, she didn't want to go back to school." He didn't need to tell her that he'd tracked down the fucker and made him pay for what he'd done. "Ash told Bethany that she wanted to forget the stupid prick and she bought ecstasy from someone at school, hoping to do just that. They were going to try it together, but Bethany talked her out of it. I guess Ashley changed her mind when she got home that night." His chest tightened. "She was only nineteen when she died."

"River's age." Tears welled in Leah's eyes, and she put her

hand on his. "I can't imagine what it would feel like if he'd taken his own life."

"That's just it. We don't think Ash was trying to kill herself. If the pills she'd bought had been ecstasy, she probably would have survived. But someone sold her bad shit." He'd tracked down and taken care of that asshole, too. "The autopsy showed lethal levels of PMA, a more toxic drug that takes longer to feel its effects. We think that's why she took so many pills. I was the one who found her."

"Ohmygod. *Tank.*" She leaned against his side. "I'm so sorry."

"I should have pushed her to talk to me earlier that night."

"Did you know she was upset?"

"No, but my family had gotten together for dinner and she'd asked if I could hang out with her the next day. She said she wanted to talk about school. But she didn't seem particularly upset. I tried to get her to tell me what was up, but she was late to meet Bethany. I texted her later that night, and when she didn't respond, I didn't think too much of it. They weren't the kind of girls who went looking for trouble. But when she didn't get back to me by two in the morning, I got worried and went to my parents' house to check on her. She always got back to me, even if it was hours later." Bile rose in his throat, and he closed his eyes for a second to try to pull himself together. He trained his gaze on the concrete between his feet and said, "I tried to revive her, but..." He shook his head.

"That's why I felt that suffocating feeling coming from you," she said, full of wonder.

"What do you mean?"

"It's hard to explain, but you know how I tried to avoid you before the accident?"

"Yeah, I thought maybe I reminded you of someone who had hurt you."

She shook her head. "I'm oddly intuitive. Before the accident, every time our eyes met, I couldn't breathe. I felt like *you* were suffocating, but it affected me and I didn't know why. I didn't know what to make of it. Now I know I was feeling your grief. You're still trying to breathe for Ashley." She put her hand over his. "I'm so sorry that you lost your sister and that I was afraid of what I felt. You must think about that night a lot for me to feel it so strongly."

"I think about it every day."

She touched his right hand, stopping him from rubbing the B-E-N-T tattoos on the fingers of his left hand, and said, "What does that mean? *Bent?*"

"It was one of the last things Ashley said to me. When I tried to get her to talk to me, she said not to worry, she was bent, not broken, and that it could wait until the next day." He gritted his teeth. "If only I'd gone to check on her earlier, I could have saved her."

"But you couldn't have known what she had planned. If I've learned one thing from raising River, it's that you can't blame yourself for other people's choices."

He was pretty damn good at blaming himself, but he didn't need to go there. Especially when the rest of what she'd said was so important. "You raised River?"

"Mm-hm. Our father was an electrician. He worked full time and picked up extra work at night whenever he could. He was working at a factory in the middle of the night when an electrical fire broke out and he was killed. I was eighteen and River was thirteen. You know how I said I was oddly intuitive? The night he died, my father came to me in a dream and told me to take care of River. I woke up in tears, begging him to come back. The police showed up to notify us a little while later."

"Jesus, that's awful. But it says a lot about the connection you had with your father. Have you had other dreams like that?"

"Yeah. When I was little, I had one about River's mom before she left us. I told my dad she was leaving and never coming back. She was gone two days later."

"Damn."

"I've had a lot of those dreams. Stupid things, about school or work, and big things like knowing I was going to have a boy and two girls in my future."

"River and the girls," he said, astonished.

She nodded.

"I can't imagine what it must be like to know things like that before they happen. Did you know about the accident?"

"No, or I never would have let him leave that night."

Now it was his turn to take her hand. "I'm sorry I asked. It must have been rough mourning your father and suddenly raising your brother." *Rough* sounded too mild, but he wasn't great with words. He laced their fingers together and held her hand between both of his.

"We were devastated. We were our father's world, and he was ours. He would have moved heaven and earth for us. He worked a lot to make ends meet, so I'd been pretty much raising River since he was little. I graduated high school early so I could be home when River was out of school, and I worked at a music shop when he was in school. I never minded, though. I loved working, and I'd have done anything for River and my dad. It was just the way our family worked out. But it was hard after our dad died. He had a small life insurance policy, which covered his burial and helped for a little while financially, but we missed him *so* much." Tears slid down her cheeks. "I still miss him, and now I miss them both."

Tank put his arm around her, pulling her closer. "I'd love to hear about them, if you're up to it. What was your father's name?"

She looked at him with a small smile. "You're the first person who has asked me that because you want to know and not for some form or legal reason." Her face brightened. "You know what? Come inside. I have some pictures I can show you while I tell you about him."

He followed her in, and she said, "Have a seat. I'll be right back."

She pulled the girls' bedroom door most of the way closed and went into her bedroom, returning a minute later with a shoebox.

She sat beside him on the couch and opened the box. "These were my dad's pictures. I haven't looked at them in a long time." She withdrew a picture of her sitting on her father's shoulders; her wild mane looked even thicker around her young face. "My dad's name was Leonard, but everyone called him Leo. I always knew he was a great father, but after raising River and the girls, I have a new appreciation for just how amazing he was to have raised us alone. He believed in *all* the right things— family. Hard work. Laughter. Helping others, and he instilled that in us, too."

"How old were you in this picture?"

"Four. Junie's age. We were at a picnic for his work. I remember they had one of those bounce houses for the kids and a clown making ice cream sundaes. Most of the other parents were mingling, but my dad stayed with me the whole time."

"Let me see that." He took a closer look at the picture, noting the light in their eyes, and the similarities he'd noticed in the picture of them in the girls' room. "God you were cute, Lee."

"Thanks." She put the picture back in the box and took out a few more. She was older in them, a skinny little thing, all elbows and knees, standing beside a tiny bicycle. "These were taken when he taught me to ride a bike. One of our neighbors took the ones where my dad is helping me." She pointed to the apartment complex in the background. "And that's our balcony where we lived until I was eight. Then we rented a little house."

They looked through the pictures, which progressed from her father holding the bike as Leah tried to ride, to her falling and scraping her knee, and finally her riding on her own. In that picture, her father stood with his arms up in the air, mouth open, smiling eyes dancing with pride. "He cheered me on like I'd won the Olympics. It was a great feeling."

As they looked through more pictures, she told him stories in a hushed voice to keep from waking the girls, which made each one feel like a secret she was sharing with only him. "He taught me to sew and make memory blankets. This is the first one I made. River was seven in this picture." In the next picture, River was holding a basketball. "This was that same summer. My dad used to play sports with him. It didn't matter how late it was when he got home from work, before going to his evening job, we'd all go outside in the dark so they could play basketball. I'd sit and read, or sew. Sometimes they'd coerce me into playing, but it wasn't my thing."

She went on to show him more pictures of gap-toothed grins taken when she and River had lost their teeth, of River on her hip when she was younger, and of the two of them sleeping on a blanket on the floor by a Christmas tree. There were pictures of them bundled up in winter clothes, making a snowman, and sledding.

"Our father made every day special. He used to wake up the way Rosie does, fully awake the second his eyes opened, and he'd come into our rooms, cheering us on." She lowered her voice. "'Come on, kids, we've got things to do and places to go!' and he was *always* smiling, which was annoying when I was a moody teenager."

Tank chuckled, remembering Ashley in her moodier years, which weren't very moody at all. He imagined Leah's were about the same. "It looks like you had a great childhood."

"We didn't have much, but we had each other and that was enough. It could be pouring down rain outside and leaking through our roof, which happened sometimes at the house we rented. He'd set a bucket down to catch the water and say"— she deepened her voice again—"'Close your eyes and pretend you're in a rain forest.' He'd make up elaborate stories, and when the landlord fixed the leak, I actually missed it. I think that's where River learned to tell stories."

"Your father sounds like a good man. I wish I could have met him."

"He was the best. He just had really bad taste in women." She showed him a picture of a white woman with flame-red hair lying in a hospital bed holding a newborn baby. Leah stood with her father beside the bed. Her father had one hand on Leah's shoulder, the other on the redhead's. "That's River and his mother the day he was born. My dad said my mother looked a lot like her. He had a thing for redheaded women, but he ended up with the ones who didn't stick around. I guess they didn't want to be mothers."

"Maybe not, but they made beautiful children." He held her gaze. Her cheeks pinked up, and she lowered her eyes. "It sounds like your father made up for their absence."

"He did." She put the shoebox on the coffee table. "If I didn't have River to focus on after my dad died, I would have been even more lost. Unfortunately, even though I had a great role model, I was *not* my father, and I didn't do a very good job of keeping River in line."

"What do you mean?"

"A few months after our father died, we had to move out of the house we'd rented and into a cheaper apartment in a not-so-great neighborhood, and I went back to work full time to pay the bills. But River went from being a happy, focused kid to drinking, getting into trouble, and coming home high. He was so angry all the time, and I get that. He was mad at the world because we lost our dad. But he got mixed up with the wrong crowd and with a girl who was two years older than him. She was really bad for him. River inherited my father's attraction to redheads who didn't want to be mothers." She met Tank's gaze with troubled eyes. "He got her pregnant when he was fourteen. She wanted to get an abortion, and he convinced her not to. But he didn't bother to clue me in until she was six months along. When I found out she wanted to give the baby up for adoption, I stepped in. The girl signed over her parental rights, and I adopted Junie—Juniper Lily. My brother loved nature."

He didn't know what he'd expected to hear about the kids, but that wasn't it. "Does Junie know?"

"No. Both of the girls are River's, but in my heart they're mine, too."

"What's Rosie's real name?"

"Don't laugh. It's Primrose Blossom." Leah laughed softly.

"Why would I laugh? That's a great name, and if anyone can pull it off, it's that little cheeky girl. They're great girls, Leah. Will you ever tell them that River was their father?"

"Yes. That was always the plan. I want to tell Junie before she starts school because kids always talk about their parents, and I think it's important that she knows where she came from and how much River adored her."

"You know, Lee, you said your dad was amazing, but the apple sure didn't fall far from the tree. That's a lot of responsibility for a girl who had already taken on more than her fair share."

"I know, but there was a lot at stake. They say mothers fall in love with their babies while they're pregnant, but in River's case, *he* fell in love with the baby during that time. He wanted Junie so badly, he begged me to take her. But the truth is, he didn't need to beg, because once I found out she was his, I wanted her just as bad. We knew what it was like growing up knowing our mothers didn't want us, but we had our father to make up for it. I couldn't imagine letting River's child think he didn't want her."

"Did River clean up his act?"

"Sort of. He watched Junie when I was at work, and he was just as great with her as our dad was with us. But River was only a kid himself, so when I got home, he went out to *play*. I lectured him about birth control and all that, and when he came home and told me he got the same girl pregnant again, we had it out. I didn't know he was still seeing Junie's mother. We had tried to get her to see Junie, but she wanted nothing to do with her. That girl was *toxic*, a partier who had no regard for others. But for whatever reason, River fell for her. Maybe he had mother issues or something. It doesn't matter why. He just did, and I was so in love with Junie, how could I not take the new baby? I wasn't even sure Rosie was his, but that didn't matter. Either way, Junie and Rosie are sisters, and River loved Rosie before she was born just as much as he'd loved Junie." She shifted her eyes away. "We probably sound crazy to you."

"No, you don't." He put his hand on hers, falling harder for the incredible woman before him. "Everything you've said proves how special you are, and how special River was. You never know what you saved the girls from. I have a friend who was adopted as a baby, and her adoptive father abused her until she ran away at sixteen." He was talking about Cait, but he would never betray Cait's confidence by telling Leah who she was without first getting Cait's approval.

"That's horrible."

"I know, but at least she got away and she's been safe for years. I hope River appreciated how much you did for him."

"He did, and he always told me how good I was with the girls and that my dad would be proud." Her eyes teared up. "Even with all the crap he put us through, we were like this." She crossed her fingers. "I could never stay mad at him. I loved him too much. He was a great kid, a great *guy* who just got lost for a while. But once we moved here, everything changed for the better."

"Where are you from?"

"North Carolina."

"I wondered about that sweet Southern accent of yours. How did you end up here?"

"If you didn't think I was crazy before, this might convince you. I dreamed about the area."

"And you just picked up and moved? That takes a lot of

courage."

"The dream was so real, it felt like a sign. I looked up the area the next day, made a few calls about places to live and jobs, and talked to River about it. He knew something had to change, and he was on board with it. Within a week I'd found this place and I had a few interviews set up. I thought it was meant to be, and once we moved here, I was sure it was the right decision. River grew up overnight. He signed up for college courses and was determined to get a degree and show the girls that anything was possible. I was *so* proud of him, and he loved it here, but…" Tears trailed down her cheeks again, slicing him anew. "If we hadn't moved, he'd still be alive."

Tank pulled her into his arms. "You can't know that. With the trouble he was getting into, you don't know where he would have ended up." He drew back so he could see her face, keeping her close with one arm around her. He brushed her curls away from her eyes and wiped her tears with the pad of his thumb. "Do you remember what you said about not blaming myself for Ashley's death?"

She nodded, sniffling.

"That goes for you, too. We live in a fucked-up world where bad shit happens and we'll never know why. All you can do is remember the reasons you moved here. You were looking out for him and the girls, and from what you've told me, it was a good move."

"I thought it was." She swiped at her tears. "This was supposed to be our fresh start, and he was doing so well. The night of the accident, he'd gone out with new friends to play basketball. The guys ended up getting high, but River didn't, and that was huge for him. He called me to come get him. I was so freaking proud of him." She inhaled shakily. "When the car was sinking, instead of saving himself, he spent the little time we had trying to get Junie out of her carseat because the latch was stuck. And now he'll never see the girls grow up, and we'll never see him again." Her voice cracked, and more tears fell.

He pulled her into his arms again, and she cried on his shoulder. "He was a hero, Lee. Never forget that. I wish I could bring him back for you."

LEAH SOAKED IN Tank's comfort as she pulled herself together. They were having such a nice conversation, she didn't want to get lost in sadness again. She sat back and wiped her eyes. "I don't want to remember him in those last panicked moments. I want to remember him sitting by the girls' bed, playing the guitar with Rosie beside him and Junie lying behind him, holding his necklace."

"Then that's what you'll do. Think about that image when you put the girls to bed at night. Do you have a picture of him playing his guitar with the girls like that?"

She shook her head. "Those pictures in the box and the few on the walls are all I have. The rest were on our phones. I meant to get them printed, but our lives were so busy, I never got around to it."

"Did you back them up to the cloud or some other service?"

"No."

"What about social media?"

"*Me?*" she said incredulously. "Who would follow me on social media? I haven't even gone on a date since I got the girls. Are *you* on social media?"

He scoffed. "Hardly. Cait set up social media profiles for the tattoo shop, but she runs them. What about River? Most kids his age are on their phones all the time."

Leah knew Cait superficially from the restaurant, like Tank's other friends. "He was on Instagram and TikTok, but... *Wait.* He uploaded pictures to his laptop."

"Let's check it out."

She pushed to her feet, but when she looked at the staircase, she felt like she might cry again. "I can't go up there yet."

Tank stood beside her. "I'll go, unless you'd rather I didn't."

"No, that's fine. I'm just not ready to see his room yet."

With a nod, he headed for the steps, and she said, "It's probably on his dresser or his bed."

Tank's big body took up the entire staircase, as if he could reach up and pull himself into the room. River's room had a low ceiling that came to a peak in the middle. Tank stood on the stairs looking around, and when he stepped into the room, he had to nearly fold himself in half. He climbed back down with the laptop. "Do you know his passwords?"

"I don't think he used one, but if he did, I can probably guess it."

He sat beside her on the couch, set the laptop on the coffee table, and opened it. The screen lit up to a browser open to River's Instagram account.

Leah's heart skipped. "Ohmygod. *Tank.*" There were dozens of pictures of River, Leah, and the girls. She scrolled through them, aching and happy at once. "Look how many there are."

"He sure loved you guys."

"He really did. He told us all the time." She got another pang of longing as they scrolled through the images. Her eyes were blurry with a mix of happy and sad tears.

"That necklace he has on looks like the one your father had on in the pictures. Was it his?"

"Yeah. River never took it off."

"I get that. Ash gave me mine for Christmas the year before she died, and I never take it off, either." They looked through a few more pictures. "I know you said it's always been just the four of you, but there are no pictures with friends. Have you ever had any girlfriends to lean on?"

"I had friends and a boyfriend before my dad died, but then our lives changed. *I* changed. I grew up real fast. Taking care of River, and the trouble he got into, were more than my boyfriend or my friends wanted to deal with. Then we got Junie and Rosie, and my life has revolved around them ever since."

"The guy should be ashamed of himself, and the girls don't sound like they were real friends. Friends *always* have your back."

The way he said it was visceral, like he didn't have time for what her father used to call fair-weather friends. She liked that about him. "To be honest, I was so busy holding our lives together, I hadn't even given my lack of friends a thought until I started working for your parents, and even then it was only in passing. I thought Gunner and Steph, and Baz and Evie, were couples, but Starr told me they were just best friends. It's not every day you see guys and girls who are that close and not something more."

"Evie and Steph have known us forever. We grew up together, and Evie works for Baz. She's his veterinary assistant, and Steph is Bethany's older sister. After Ash died, Bethany got into drugs, and she's been in and out of Steph's life ever since. It's not easy for Steph. Bethany took off a few years ago, and the club's been trying to track her down."

"Really? You'd think she'd stay far away from drugs after what happened to your sister."

"The night of the accident, when you saw me at the convenience store, I was following up on a lead about her, shaking down a drug dealer for information."

"That sounds dangerous."

Tank shrugged. "I don't want to talk about that, Lee. I want to know about you. Do you miss having friends?"

"Sometimes. But not like I miss River. Let's see what else is on his laptop."

"Careful. At his age, he might have a site or two on there that you don't want to see."

"You mean like porn? I don't care about that." She went through his history, finding his school portal, a few porn sites, music sites, and then she saw TikTok, and she opened to his page, which had short, goofy videos of him and the girls. They watched a few of them, laughing. It was strange to see River having so much fun and knowing he was gone. But she couldn't have been happier to have these memories. She went back to the history and found River's YouTube page with videos of him playing his guitar.

Leah clicked on the first video and got chills as River began playing the guitar and singing "Just the Way You Are" by Bruno Mars. "I've never heard him play this song. It's so pretty."

Tank's jaw was clenched, brows knitted. "That's the song we sing for Ashley every year at the suicide-awareness rally."

"I think I saw flyers for that at work."

"That's the one. Even though we don't believe she was trying to commit suicide, we honor her with the event. This year we also honored Maverick's mother, because she killed herself when he was young."

"Oh, I had no idea. I thought Reba was his mom."

"She and Preacher adopted him when he was a teenager. He's a sculptor, and he made a beautiful piece that we auctioned off at the rally. This song gets me every time I hear it."

Leah took his hand and leaned against him. "Maybe it's a sign that Ashley and River have found each other."

He squeezed her hand. "I'd like to think she's got a friend wherever she is."

They listened to the song again, then made their way through more videos. River had made one for each of the girls' favorite songs. When they found one of him playing "Put Your Records On," Leah teared up, feeling like she might burst with bittersweet happiness. "He used to sing that to me when I had a hard day, and sometimes he'd just tell me to *put my records on*. It was his way of telling me to chill out. Is there a way to save all the videos and pictures so nothing happens to them?"

"Sure. His passwords are all saved. I can get that done for you tomorrow. I'll digitize your father's pictures from the shoebox, too."

"We'll have *all* this *forever*? Thank you!" She threw her arms around him. "I wouldn't have even thought to look for these on his computer."

"I'm glad we found them, darlin'."

She became acutely aware of how good it felt to be in his arms. He smelled deliciously male, of leather and strength, kicking up desires she hadn't felt in years. He pressed his hand flat on her back. Heat radiated outward from his palm, making her body sizzle and her pulse quicken. He wasn't being aggressive, and the longer he embraced her, the more she wanted him to. It felt intimate and natural as he whispered,

"*Lee,*" stirring those fluttery feelings again. Stronger this time. *Inescapable.* She closed her eyes, wanting to memorize the feel of his beard on her cheek, his heart beating against hers. She drew back so she could see his face, and he kept her close. So close, she could smell his minty breath. His dark eyes were penetrating, riveting. *God,* she wanted to kiss him.

"Tank," she whispered. "Are you like this with every girl you rescue?"

His brows slanted. "Fuck no. It's never been like this."

For me, either.

"I've never wanted to do this with any woman I've rescued."

He brushed his lips lightly over hers, flooding her entire being with *want* and *need* as he pressed a kiss to her cheek. His prickly beard sent sparks searing beneath her skin as he whispered, "You're beautiful, Leah, and you have the most exquisite lips."

She had a fleeting thought about how much she'd always hated her lips and how much she loved hearing that he liked them. But it was the longing in his voice that had her clinging to him, barely breathing, anticipation stacking up inside her. He kissed the edge of her mouth, soft as a feather. Sexual tension vibrated around them like live wires. When his lips brushed hers again, she leaned forward, needing more, and felt him smile. *Kiss me.* He was in no hurry, circling her lips with tauntingly tender kisses. Just when she thought she'd combust, his mouth came down over hers, unexpectedly soft and excruciatingly slow, intensifying her need, as if he was giving her room to stop him.

That was the last thing she wanted.

She returned his efforts, every stroke of his tongue drawing her deeper into him. Her body was on fire, her heart hammering against her ribs. He pushed one hand into her hair, kissing her more possessively, as if he couldn't get enough. She hadn't been kissed in years, but she'd *never* experienced anything like this slow seduction, which had her wanting to climb onto his lap and disappear into him. Their kisses went on and on, deep and penetrating, then tender and sweet, until she was dizzy with desire, lost in their connection. When their lips finally parted, she came away breathless, her body trembling, and a whimper fell from her lips. *Come back…*

Tank gazed deeply into her eyes, and as if he'd heard her silent plea, he kissed her again, a light press of his lips, leaving her aching for more. He brushed his thumb over her lower lip, whispering, "Nothing about us is familiar, darlin'."

She blinked several times, trying to clear her lustful haze. "What…*Wait.* Sorry. I can't *think.*"

He pulled her close, burying his face in her hair and laughing softly. "You're so cute."

"I'm not trying to be." But now she was laughing quietly, too. "I've never been kissed like that before. You short-circuited my brain. What did you mean by nothing about us is familiar?"

It took him a second to get his amusement under control, and *wow*, she liked that look on him.

"You asked about women I've rescued, and I want you to know that whatever this is between us, what I feel for you and the girls, is new for me. I haven't ever felt this way before. I was drawn to you when I first saw you at the bar, and my feelings for you grew over the last few months, when I showed up at the restaurant almost every time you were working in an effort to try to understand our connection. But from the moment I saw you and the girls in the water, understanding no longer mattered, because I knew in my heart that I never wanted to leave you. I don't have all the answers, or know what it all means, but I don't want to ignore something that feels so big and right."

He brushed her hair over her shoulder and caressed her cheek. She wanted to lean into his touch, but other than family, she'd never known anyone so forthcoming with his feelings, and she was still making sense of it.

"I know your lives have been turned upside down. Don't worry. I'm not going to pressure you. If you feel the same way, we can take it slow and figure it out together."

He stood, startling her brain into gear. She shot to her feet. "Where are you going?"

"You look a little shell-shocked. I thought I'd give you some space and head out to my truck."

"Tank, you can't keep sleeping in your truck."

He shrugged. "Why not? I want to be close by until I know you and the girls are okay."

"Because it can't be comfortable."

"Don't worry about me, darlin'." He headed for the door.

"You're so stubborn." She knew he wouldn't go home, and she liked that about him, even if she felt guilty for taking up so much of his time.

"You sound like every person who has ever known me."

"Well, if you're not going to go home, then sleep on the couch. I trust you, and at least you'll be more comfortable."

Turning, he cocked a brow. "You sure you can handle that? I'm not going to wake up with you pawing at me, am I?"

She laughed, liking his playful side. It had been forever since she'd been flirted with, and she'd forgotten how fun it was. "I'm pretty sure I can contain myself. It was just a kiss." *A brain-numbing kiss that made my body hum.*

He held her gaze, amusement dancing in his eyes. *"Right."*

"I'll get you bedding and a pillow." She headed for her bedroom to get the extra bedding from her closet. "You might want to wipe that smirk off your face before I change my mind."

When she came out of her bedroom, he was standing by the door. He must have seen the question in her eyes, because he said, "I figured you might have second thoughts and want me to leave."

"Second, third, and fourth thoughts, but I don't want you to go." She put the blanket and pillow on the coffee table.

"You sure? I won't be offended if you change your mind."

"I'm sure." She started spreading the sheet over the couch.

"I can do that." He drew her into his arms, gazing down at her with a serious expression. "I don't do hidden agendas, Lee, and I believe everyone needs to do what's best for them. So if you go into your bedroom and feel even the slightest bit uneasy with me out here, just say the word."

"Okay."

He gave a curt nod and kissed her cheek. "Sweet dreams."

"You too." After using the bathroom and brushing her teeth, she went into her room and closed the door. She changed into her sleeping shirt and shorts and climbed into bed, thinking about him sitting watchfully over them out there. Was she doing the wrong thing by getting close to Tank at such a tumultuous time? She closed her eyes, reliving their kisses and the feel of his arms around her, and *oh*, what a wonderful feeling that was. But in the next moment, she heard River's panicked voice, saw him struggling to get Junie free of her carseat in those last perilous seconds, and heartache moved in.

Chapter Seven

LEAH LAY IN bed staring at the ceiling Sunday morning after a fitful night's sleep, wondering if mornings would ever feel normal again. She used to love getting up with the sun to be showered and ready before the chaos of their day began: River making jokes and flopping on the couch to eat a bowl of cereal with his feet on the coffee table, Rosie's upbeat chatter bouncing off the walls, and Junie sweetly and quietly sitting amid the activity as her body slowly awakened. Since losing River, Leah decided mornings were sneaky and mean, easing in like good intentions, sprinkling sunshine into her bedroom as if to say, *Join me on this beautiful new day*, only to have reality slap her with sadness after she opened her eyes and remembered that River was gone.

She knew mornings would never be the same. How could they? They hadn't remained the same after her father died. She'd just stowed those painful memories so deep, she'd forgotten exactly how cruel mornings had felt. But now she remembered how the need to cry every minute had eventually turned to an ache of despair and, a few weeks later, to sad acceptance, enabling her and River to move on to their *new* normal. She had faith that she and the girls would find their new normal, too, as long as she didn't screw it up.

Her emotions had waffled all night between despair over losing River, comfort in Tank's support, and the warm, tingly feelings being close to him had stirred. On the heels of those tingles came prickles of selfishness and guilt. She more than liked Tank, and the girls adored him. But he was right—their lives had been forever changed, and she was all the girls had left of a family. She couldn't believe she had to bury her brother tomorrow. How was that even possible? They said God never gave a person more than they could handle, but she'd like to slap whoever *they* were. Could God be cruel enough to want to test River's girls like that? To test *her* for a second time?

Her mind reeled with things she needed to take care of and had been avoiding, like giving the insurance company her new number and dealing with the aftermath of the accident. She had medical insurance, but there were hefty deductibles she'd have to cover. She needed to get a car so she could go back to work, but first she had to find childcare for the girls. They'd never been cared for by anyone other than her or River, and the thought of leaving them with a stranger made her sick to her stomach. And then there were River's things to think about. Going through her father's belongings had been torture. How could she do that for her younger brother?

She wasn't supposed to outlive him.

Tears streamed down her temples, and she closed her eyes, telling herself that all of that could wait until after tomorrow. But dealing with Tank couldn't. The girls needed her to do the smart thing, even if it would hurt like hell. She could accept his help, because the truth was, without Tank and his parents, she and the girls would probably *all* be hiding under the covers crying buckets. But she couldn't put the girls' hearts at risk by letting this thing between her and Tank continue. It was better to break her own heart now than theirs later.

She glanced at the time. *7:30.* She was surprised the house was so quiet, but yesterday had been a big day for the girls, and if she was lucky, they were sleeping in. She threw on her sweatshirt, pushed her feet into the fuzzy boot slippers she'd splurged on for the chilly Cape mornings, and quietly opened her bedroom door. She lost her train of thought at the sight of Tank sleeping on the couch with the girls. His right shoulder and hip were angled up against the back cushions, making room for Rosie, who lay tucked against his side, his massive arm belted around her. Junie was fast asleep on his chest, her little body rising and lowering with his every breath and her tiny hand clutching his silver chain. Leah's heart expanded. She wondered what had played out last night and how she hadn't woken up. Had the girls woken up sad and gone looking for her? Had Tank intercepted them? Or had they come out this morning and found him sleeping and snuggled in with him like they did with her sometimes? She wanted to get in on that comfort, to crawl up on top of Tank and drape her arms around all of them.

That was the problem.

For a girl who hadn't even thought about men over the last four years, it sure was easy to fall for Tank. He was kind and gentle with her and the girls. He understood them and accepted them with all their flaws and baggage. It didn't hurt that he was the hottest, toughest man she'd ever met. But there was no guarantee that whatever this was between them would last, and that was a risk the girls couldn't afford.

She went to use the bathroom and brush her teeth, and when she glanced in the mirror, she realized she hadn't really looked at herself since the accident. Her skin was so pale, it made the dark circles under her eyes more prominent. Her hair was a crazy mess, but that wasn't new. She'd given up trying to get it to behave years ago. She stared at her mouth, recalling the hard press of Tank's lips, the feel of his tongue exploring hers, the heat of his hand on her back. Her entire body tingled and burned, greedy for a repeat performance.

And more...

She squeezed her eyes closed, willing those feelings away, but it was like trying to swat a hummingbird that kept darting out of reach and diving back in.

Tank's voice whispered through her mind. *You're beautiful, Leah, and you have the most exquisite lips.* No man other than her father or River had ever told her she was pretty, much less beautiful. She had always felt like she looked nothing short of *odd.* River had looked biracial. But Leah didn't see that in herself. She looked multiracial. She was skinny with a big forehead, a nose that was a bit flat at the bridge like her father's, but narrow and tipped up at the end. Her skin was too pale and freckled for her dark eyebrows and strange mix of dark-brown and red hair. Some strands were almost orange, others like dark chocolate. From what her father had told her, there had been interracial relationships in their family for generations. Her great-grandmother had been Puerto Rican, and somewhere in their past there was American Indian heritage. Leah saw herself as a mix of everyone who had come before her. Interesting to look at, maybe, in the way people stared at funny-looking dogs, but not beautiful. Especially not with puffy, sad eyes and a broken heart.

Maybe Tank needed glasses, or maybe he really found her to be beautiful. She wanted to believe the latter. Not that it mattered, because as she reached for the door with a sinking feeling in her stomach, she knew what she had to do.

"Mama!" Rosie toddled over.

Leah scooped her up and kissed her cheek. "Good morning, Rosie Posey."

"We sleeped with Tank!" Rosie exclaimed.

"I saw that." Leah eyed Tank, sitting on the couch with Junie snuggled against his side, and she melted a little more. His beard shifted with his grin, and he lifted his chin in acknowledgment. She mouthed, *Thank you.*

"Mornin', Mama." Junie slid off the couch and went to her.

Rosie wriggled out of Leah's arms and ran into the bathroom as Leah hugged Junie. "How's my Juju?"

"Good. I gotta pee." She went into the bathroom. "Huwwy, Wosie!"

Leah watched over them and made sure they washed their hands.

"Play puppy patwol!" Rosie darted into her bedroom, and Junie followed her in.

Leah mustered all of her courage and went back to the living room. Tank was on his feet, stretching his arms up and out. The bottom of his shirt inched up, revealing an enticing glimpse of his stomach and part of a tattoo that disappeared beneath the waist of his jeans. Her mind followed that tattoo to darker places, and her body flamed.

No, no, no.

It wasn't like she could delete that image from her memory. How was she supposed to stop thinking about that flash of stomach that her fingers itched to touch, or the ink that had piqued her curiosity?

He reached for her hand, pulling her closer, and kissed her

cheek. "Good morning, beautiful."

She wanted to put her arms around him, go up on her toes, and share more of those toe-curling kisses, but she forced those desires down deep and said, "Did you get any sleep?"

He shrugged one shoulder. "*Enough*. How about you? It sounded like you had a rough night."

"Kinda." She was too nervous about what she had to say to be embarrassed by him having heard her crying. She looked over her shoulder and saw the girls playing in their bedroom. "Can we talk in the kitchen for a second?" He nodded and followed her into the kitchen, every step amping up her anxiousness.

"Is this about last night?"

"Yes." She saw a flash of regret in his eyes.

"I'm sorry if I crossed a line or made you uncomfortable."

"You didn't. I wanted to kiss you." He looked confused. "But our lives *are* in turmoil, and even if *I* want to be with you, I can't put the girls' emotions at risk."

He stepped closer, brow furrowed, and touched her hand. "Leah, I'm not going to hurt them."

"I know you'd never hurt them on purpose. But what if we get closer and then it doesn't work out?"

"I don't have a crystal ball to predict the future. But I was honest with you when I said I've never felt like this before. My life revolves around my family, the club, my tattoo shop, and the firehouse. I spend the little free time I have with the guys, and yeah, I hook up with women. Maybe a lot of women by your standards, but that's *all* it's ever been, and they know the score when we get together. I wouldn't give up a Sunday ride with the Dark Knights for any of the women I've been with, much less every night of the week. But every part of me wants to be with you and the girls."

She'd never had dreams of finding Mr. Right, but if she ever had, she knew he'd more than fit the bill. Except maybe for the number of women he'd been with. She wondered why he'd told her about them, but she had a feeling Tank only knew how to be blatantly honest, which made her realize that he must *really* think of her as beautiful.

This was getting harder by the second.

"Tank, if circumstances were different, I wouldn't need to do this. But they're not, and the girls already rely on you too much." *We all do.*

"I'm sorry about letting them sleep on the couch with me. Junie woke up around three crying for River. I tried to soothe her back to sleep, but she wanted to talk about him. I didn't want to wake you up because, as I said, it sounded like your night was rough. So I brought her out to the living room with me. Rosie woke up right after like it was morning, ready to play."

"I'm sorry," she said softly, pain slicing through her at the thought of Junie crying for River.

"It's okay. I just didn't want to wake you when it sounded like you'd finally fallen asleep. I hope you don't mind, but Junie had a lot of questions about where River is now, *physically*. The other day, after you and I talked about how you should tell the girls, I went online and researched how to speak to kids about death. I was careful with the answers I gave them. We talked about tomorrow, what they can expect and how it's okay to be sad. As difficult as the burial will be, I think it'll help them. It's hard for adults to understand someone being here one day and gone the next, and I imagine it's a hundred times harder for kids. Knowing where River is laid to rest and that they can visit him there might give them comfort."

Tears welled in her eyes. "I can't believe you did all of that for us."

"I think it helped. I also put on one of the videos of River singing. It was a song they liked. Something about shoes and milk. I don't know."

"'Dynamite.'"

"They knew every word. I tried to get them back in their beds, but they clung to me. I just couldn't do it, so we lay on the couch, and we talked about River until they conked out. I didn't have the heart to move them."

Tears burned her eyes, and every iota of her being told her not to say what she'd intended to, but she had to. "That's okay. But, Tank, I think we need some space, for the girls' sake, and if you'd rather not go to the cemetery tomorrow, I understand."

His jaw clenched, but there was no escaping the sadness in his eyes. "If you *need* space, I'll leave. But this doesn't change how I feel, and I can't see my feelings for you and the girls doing anything but getting stronger."

How was it possible that they could feel so much for each other? Especially *now*, when her world was falling apart? A tear slipped down her cheek.

He cupped her cheek, brushing away the tear with his thumb. "You may not be ready for this now, but one day you will be." He paused just long enough for his words to sink in. "I've gotten to know River through you and the girls, and I would like to be there tomorrow to say goodbye to him."

She nodded, trying hard not to cry. How could ending them when they'd only just gotten started hurt so bad?

"I backed up all of River's files on the Wicked Ink server last night, and Baz backed them up to his server, too."

"I don't know what that means." Her head was such a mess,

she'd forgotten about saving River's files.

"It means they're safe. It's like being in a vault. You'll never lose them. Zeke digitized the box of pictures, too." He pushed his hand into his pocket and handed her four flash drives. "Each of these has *all* of River's files and the pictures from the box on it, too. If you lose one, you'll still have more, and even if you lose them all, I can make as many as you want. Do you know how to use flash drives?"

"Yes." She wiped her eyes, feeling like her chest was being crushed. "How did you do this if you were here all night?"

"The backups are done online. Zeke brought me the flash drives when he picked up the box of pictures and brought them back about half an hour before Junie woke up."

"Tank…" She didn't know what to say. Was she making a mistake, or was this really the right thing for the girls? Was the right thing supposed to hurt so much?

Rosie ran out of her bedroom, yelling, "Mouse pincakes!" She barreled into Tank's legs and grinned up at him. "I help!"

Tank ruffled Rosie's hair and crouched before her, sadness welling in his eyes. "I'm sorry, cheeky girl, but I have to go take care of a few things. I heard your mama makes great pancakes, though."

"You're leavin'?" Junie asked as she walked into the kitchen.

"Yeah, Twitch. I have work to do."

Junie stared at him for a minute, brows knitted, and put her hand on his knee. "Can I go with you?"

"I go!" Rosie exclaimed.

Tank's jaw tightened. "Sorry, but not today, babes."

"I *pwomise* to be good," Junie pleaded.

Leah felt her heart shredding.

"Maybe another time, okay?" Tank put his arms around the

girls, looking gutted as he pulled them into a hug and closed his eyes, like he was savoring the moment. He kissed their cheeks and pushed to his feet, meeting Leah's gaze. "Call or text if you need anything. Or if you change your mind."

She nodded, afraid she'd cry if she tried to talk.

He headed for the door, and the girls ran after him. Junie grabbed his hand and said, "Are you comin' back?"

He looked down at the girls, nodding. "Yes. I'll see you tomorrow, okay?"

"Why not today?" Junie asked.

"Because Tank has a life to get back to, honey." *One that doesn't include taking care of us.* She went to them, standing by the front door.

Junie glowered at her, her lower lip trembling.

Leah picked her up. "It's okay, Juju. We're going to make pancakes and have a great day." Tears slid down Junie's cheeks, and it took everything Leah had to hold her tears back. And heck if Tank didn't look like he was ready to break down, too.

Rosie rubbed Junie's foot. "He comin' back!"

"Pwomise?" Junie pleaded. "Wickeds always keep their pwomises."

"I promise, Twitch," he said firmly, and with a single nod, he headed out the front door.

Junie pushed from Leah's arms and ran after him. "Tank!"

Rosie and Leah ran after her, but Tank already had her in his arms, one hand on the back of her head, their foreheads touching, and he was talking quietly. Junie nodded, and Tank hugged her.

Leah's chest constricted as he set Junie on her feet and said, "Go to your mama."

Junie went to Leah and leaned against her side. Rosie went

to Junie and hugged her as Tank climbed into his truck. He started the engine, taking one last long look at her and the girls, his grief coalescing with theirs, as real as the tears filling Leah's eyes as he drove away.

She'd known it was going to hurt, but she'd never imagined it would feel like he was taking pieces of all of them with him.

TANK DROVE HOME with a white-knuckled grip on the steering wheel. He'd experienced all kinds of pain in his lifetime, but being sent away by Leah was a different type of wound, leaving him feeling empty, and he had no fucking idea what to do with that. He showered, guzzled a cup of coffee, threw on his leather vest, and climbed onto his motorcycle. There were only three surefire ways to clear his head—working at the tattoo shop, riding, or fucking. It was too early to meet the guys for their regular Sunday ride, and the only woman he wanted to be buried deep inside had just booted him to the curb. He started up his bike and headed to the tattoo shop.

He'd bought a two-bay auto shop at foreclosure several years ago, and with the help of his uncle and cousins, he'd renovated it. The brick shop was painted gray, with large tinted-glass windows out front and a red door between them. A black sign with WICKED INK in gold lettering spanned almost the full width of the shop above the door and windows. He'd painted the Dark Knights emblem—a skull with sharp brows and a mouth full of jagged fangs—on one side of the building and the club creed on the other side: LOVE, LOYALTY, AND RESPECT FOR ALL.

He parked between Cait's car and Gia's Jeep. The shop wasn't usually open that early on Sundays, but since Cait and Gia were taking over Tank's clients and operational duties while he was helping Leah, they were putting in extra hours. His other employee, tattooist Aria Bad, wouldn't be in until later. He climbed off his bike and headed inside.

Tank didn't like to feel confined, and he'd designed Wicked Ink with an open layout. The lobby was one big open space with a reception counter, two leather couches, three chairs, coffee tables littered with tattoo books and body jewelry displays. It was separated from the work areas by a half wall. There were six separate workstations, three on each side of the shop, separated by half walls, with an aisle in between, and Tank's office and the supply room were in the back.

Gia looked up from behind the reception counter, her thinly manicured brows knitting, bright-red lips pursed. "Hey, boss. You're not supposed to be here." She came around the counter in one of her skintight minidresses and heels, her typical attire. She was all legs and womanly curves, with colorful tattoos decorating her light-brown skin and a short mass of tight curls that stuck out in all directions.

"No shit," he grumbled as Cait came out of the office, looking just as surprised to see him as Gia was.

"What happened?" Gia eyed him curiously. "Are the girls and Leah okay?"

"As well as can be expected." *They'd be better if I were there.*

Cait joined them in her torn jeans and Converse, her sweater hanging loosely over her thin body. Her short black hair was tucked behind one ear as she gave him a scrutinizing look. "You look like hell, which I guess is to be expected, but have you gotten any sleep?"

"I'm fine."

Gia planted a hand on her hip, eyes narrowing, as she and Cait exchanged a disbelieving glance. Cait crossed her arms. They were tough, but while Gia was mouthy, Cait was quiet. Years of abuse did that to a person. When Cait had first come to work for Tank, she'd been alone in the world, unlike Gia, the younger sister of Rubin "Justice" Galant, an attorney and Dark Knight. Gia had been a wild child, getting into trouble and partying too much when Justice had turned to Tank for help. Tank had taken Gia and Cait under his wing. They'd become family, and two of his most trusted friends.

"We know that grumble. You're *not* fine," Gia said as she and Cait circled him like vultures.

"We're worried about you," Cait said firmly. "The accident wasn't just traumatic for Leah and the girls. You couldn't save her brother, Tank. That had to affect you."

He clenched his jaw, not wanting to think about any of it.

Gia took his arm, her gaze softening. "Talk to us. Let us help."

"You're the one who taught us to talk things out," Cait reminded him.

"For Christ's sake," he gritted out. "Yeah, that sucks, and it's tough. I'd have given my life for him, but that's not why I'm here."

"If it's too hard to be with Leah and the girls, that's under-standable," Gia said.

"Yeah, it's like a constant reminder," Cait added.

"I just said it wasn't *that*." He yanked his arm out of Gia's grasp. "I fucked up, okay? I got too close. I kissed her, and she kicked me to the curb."

"Whaat?" Gia dragged out the word. "This I've gotta hear. I

always thought you knew what you were doing with women. What happened? Did you use too much tongue? Not enough?"

Tank scowled. "I fucking know how to kiss a woman."

"If you say so," Gia teased.

"*Gia,*" Cait warned. "This is serious. Leah's been through a lot. Maybe it's just too much."

"You think I don't know that?" He paced. "I don't blame her for needing space. She doesn't want the girls to get too attached in case it doesn't work out. But that doesn't change the fact that every part of me wants to be there with them."

Gia's brows lifted. "Sounds like she knows you aren't a long-term prospect."

Frustration pounded through Tank's veins. He crossed his arms and lowered his chin, holding Gia's gaze. "She can't *know* that."

She and Cait exchanged another glance.

Fuck. "Fine. It's a valid assumption. But I told her that's not what this is."

"And she's supposed to just believe you?" Cait held out her palm, like, *Really?* "That's a lot to ask of anyone, much less a girl who practically ran away from you all summer and just lost her brother."

"Okay, bossman, what do *you* think is going on between you two?" Gia asked.

"Something big," he said firmly, pacing. "Something *real.*"

Gia watched his every step. "I've never seen you like this. Could it be that you just feel a bond with her because you have this tragedy in common and you both lost a sibling?"

"Of course I feel that bond, but that's not all this is. It's *Leah.* It has been since I first saw her, and now it's her and the girls. I can't fucking explain *why* I feel it, especially with all they're going through. But it feels bone deep." He grasped for a way to explain it. "Like when I took my first motorcycle ride and I felt like I'd found a piece of me that I never knew was missing. *That's* what being with them feels like. Like we fucking belong together."

"Damn." Gia shook her head. "Not that I condone you comparing Leah and her girls to a motorcycle, but I get you, Tank. That's *big*."

"The only time I've ever felt like that was when I came here and got to know you guys," Cait said. "So what are you going to do?"

"Give her space," he said sharply. "I'm not an asshole. But I'll be damned if I'll let them go through this alone. I'll be there for them and keep my fucking lips to myself."

"Sounds smart," Cait said.

"If he can do it." Gia waved a finger at him. "Look at the man. He's all tangled up."

Tank swore he had smoke coming out his ears. Holding back his emotions from the only three people he'd ever wanted to share them with sounded like a goddamn nightmare to him. There was no fucking way he could sit still and work today, but maybe he could outrun his feelings. "I'm outta here."

He blew through the doors and climbed onto his bike, heading out to meet the guys.

Twenty minutes later he rolled down Gunner's driveway, passing several groups of guys in the driveway and yard, all wearing vests or jackets with Dark Knights patches. These were the most loyal men Tank knew, and he was proud to be among them. They'd been there for his family when Ashley had passed away, and he knew he could call any one of them, day or night, and they'd have his back. And the night of the accident, a few calls had ensured they'd have Leah's and the girls' backs, too.

He parked by the other bikes. Blaine and Maverick were talking with Justice on the grass, and Baz was on the phone a few feet away. Gunner, Zeke, and Zander were on the porch with Sidney and two of Gunner's dogs. Gunner was holding the fluffy white kitten he'd taken in over the summer. Tank couldn't help thinking about how much the girls would like to see that kitten.

As he took off his helmet, guys called out to greet him. Climbing off his bike, Tank acknowledged them with a nod. He pulled out his phone and sent a text to his mother. *Heading out for a ride. Any chance you can check on Leah later?*

"Hey, Tank," Blaine called over. "I thought you weren't coming."

"Plans changed." Tank's phone vibrated, and he read his mother's response. *Sure. Everything okay?* He thumbed out a response as he headed for the guys. *Yeah. Thanks. Love you.* He pocketed his phone.

"Hey, man." Maverick bumped fists with him. He was a big dude with dark hair, ice-blue eyes, and a close-cropped beard. He looked so much like Blaine and his other siblings, no one could tell he'd been adopted. "How are Leah and her girls holding up?"

"It's a long road. You know how it is." *Every damn one of us does.* "I sent Chloe an email late last night about making something for me. Do you know if she got it?" Chloe Mallery was Maverick's fiancée.

"Yeah, she's got you covered."

"Great." Tank held a hand out to Justice. "How's it going?"

"I can't complain." Justice, a tall Black man with serious eyes and a no-bullshit attitude, had a voice as deep and distinct as James Earl Jones's. He shook Tank's hand and pulled him closer, clapping him on the back. "I got that info you asked for."

Justice handled the club's legal affairs, and Tank had spoken to him about Leah's accident. Tank looked at Blaine and Maverick. "We'll be right back."

As he and Justice walked away, Justice said, "The guy driving the truck that hit Leah is from Connecticut. He was in town to see his girlfriend. They went out for dinner and he left her at the restaurant because they got in a fight. He was *not* over the legal limit for alcohol, but he *was* in a texting argument with his girlfriend, and they think he was going about seventy when he hit Leah's car."

"Jesus Christ. That's a *thirty* zone." Tank hands fisted. "Leah's brother *died* because of fucking *texts*, and that asshole got away with little more than stitches and bruises. I'd like to get my hands on him."

"Tank, you know how this works," Justice said sternly. "He's out on bond, but they're charging him with involuntary manslaughter, which carries up to a twenty-year prison sentence."

"But he's *out* there living his life, and Leah is never going to see her brother again." Anger roiled inside him. "Those two little girls are *River's* children. Now the girls will *never* know him. I want to do right by them, Justice. I'll cover your legal fees, but I want that motherfucker to pay for *everything* the three of them have lost."

"I hear you, Tank. But cases like these can take years to play out. You need to make sure that's what *Leah* wants. Have you talked with her about it yet?"

"No. She's fragile. She's burying her *younger* brother tomorrow." Tank's throat constricted. "She needs some time. I'm just…" *So fucking sad for them.*

"I'm here for you, and I'll do whatever she decides is best. But you know that no amount of money will bring her brother back. Before you go in there with guns blazing, please think about what it will be like for Leah to be dragged through a court case. It's hard to heal when you're trying to put a dollar value on your loved one's life."

"Fuck. I get that, but if you knew her, if you knew the girls…"

"I get it, Tank. I just want you to be aware of the consequences. If she sues, the insurance company pays whatever she's awarded, which is why those types of cases can take years. Insurance companies have the time and resources to fight major claims. There is an alternative, *if* the guy's got money. I can talk with the prosecuting attorney about victim restitution and maybe negotiate it as part of a plea deal."

"A plea deal? That's bullshit."

"None of this is good, Tank. Either Leah and the girls spend years fighting in court, or we go the restitution route, which could give her quick justice but less money. I suggest you find out what Leah wants."

"Right," he said through clenched teeth.

"You're pretty riled up over her." Justice lowered his chin, giving Tank a compassionate, but no-bullshit, stare. "Is there something between you two?"

"I hope there will be one day, but she's worried about the girls getting hurt if it doesn't work out."

"She sounds like a good mother. You know I don't introduce women I hook up with to Patience." Patience was Justice's three-year-old daughter. "Patience comes first, and she always will."

Tank didn't want to just hook up with Leah. "Yeah, I get it," he said as Gunner sauntered over with Zeke and Zander.

Gunner draped an arm around Tank's shoulder and smirked. "Guess Leah got sick of looking at your ugly mug, huh?"

"Guess so." Tank shrugged him off. He didn't have the tolerance for banter today.

"I'm just dickin' with you, bro. How's she doing? The girls are so damn cute, they almost make me want to have one."

"Lord help us all." Zeke laughed. "Can you imagine a little Gunny running around?"

"Hell, yeah. We'd call him *Pistol*," Gunner corrected him. "Or maybe Sig? Moss? Barretta?"

"Winnie for a girl," Zander suggested. "Like Winchester."

"Maybe next you can share hair and makeup tips," Justice joked.

"I don't know about you ladies, but I'm ready to ride." Tank headed for his bike.

"That's not what she said." Zander laughed.

Tank scoffed, and all the guys started razzing him as they rallied the troops and climbed onto their bikes. Tank and Blaine led the pack, and the others fell into line behind them. When they pulled onto the highway, the road opened up, and Tank waited for that feeling of freedom to engulf him. But Junie's voice kept traipsing through his mind. *Can I go with you? I pwomise to be good.*

He sped down the highway, trying like hell to outrun those memories, but Leah's tortured face appeared in his mind, and he heard the cracking of her voice—*Even if I want to be with you, I can't put the girls' emotions at risk*—and Rosie's chipper,

He comin' back!

Tank gritted his teeth. *Damn right I am.*

It had taken thirty-two years for him to feel like this. There was no way in hell he'd let the three best things that had ever happened to him slip through his fingers.

COULD THIS DAY get any worse?

Leah picked up the carton of orange juice she'd dropped and grabbed the roll of paper towels to clean it up. The girls were whiny and cranky, and Junie had been sulking all day. It hadn't helped that Leah had burned the pancakes, causing the girls to melt down, which had made *her* cry. Lunch hadn't turned out any better. She'd hidden in the bathroom to let it all out, only to find out there was no end to her sadness.

"I wish Tank was here," Junie said for the millionth time from the couch, where she was curled up with her memory blanket, clutching Mine's ears. She must have looked out the window a hundred times already.

So do I.

Leah couldn't believe how *much* she missed him. The ache was constant. She closed her eyes for a second, breathing deeply, and then she began sopping up the mess.

Rosie stomped into the kitchen, scowling. "You *bad!* You say Tank *go.*" She turned and stomped away.

Tears spilled from Leah's eyes. The girls had prodded her after Tank had left, and she'd gotten so agitated, she'd made the mistake of telling them that she'd asked him to leave.

There was a knock at the door, and the girls yelled, "Tank!"

They ran to the door, and Leah was right behind them, the spill forgotten. As Junie pulled the door open, Leah's hopes plunged at the sight of Ginger standing on their porch.

"You're not Tank," Junie said sullenly, and skulked back to the couch.

"You no Tank," Rosie parroted, and ran after Junie.

Leah tried to stifle her own jilted hopes. "Sorry, Ginger. It's been a long day. Come in."

"It's okay." Ginger looked compassionately at the girls as she stepped inside. Lowering her voice, she said, "I didn't know you were expecting Tank. He said he was going for a motorcycle ride with the guys and asked if I could stop by and see if you needed anything."

He's still watching out for us, even after I sent him away? That made her miss him even more. "We weren't expecting him. They just miss him."

"Mama told him to leave." Junie pouted.

Ginger looked at Leah curiously.

"I just needed a little space," Leah said, wishing she could disappear.

"I understand. My son can be intense."

"He's great. It's me, not him."

Ginger smiled warmly. "It's okay, honey. You're allowed to want space. I'm sorry for stopping by without calling. I brought the girls a little something to play with." She opened her purse and pulled out two small gift bags. "I'll just leave these with you and be on my way."

Leah felt horrible, but before she could say anything, Rosie yelled, "Pwesents!" and ran over.

Junie slid off the couch, clutching Mine and her blanket in one hand, the blanket dragging behind her.

"What do you say?" Leah asked as Ginger handed them the gifts.

"Thank you," they said in unison, and plopped down beside the coffee table to rummage through the bags, cheering about their new *colowing* books and *cwayons*.

"Thank you so much, Ginger. You didn't have to bring gifts, and you don't need to leave."

"Sweetheart, I have been in your shoes. I understand needing space. Maybe the gifts will make things a little easier and give you some quiet, too. You have my number. Call me if you need anything at all." Ginger embraced her and whispered, "If you'd like me to take the girls for a few hours, I'm happy to."

Leah wanted to be with them, but there was no denying how badly she wanted to crawl into bed and cry herself to sleep. "We're okay, thank you."

"Then I'll see you tomorrow when I pick you up."

As Ginger left, Leah wanted to call after her. To share her worries about the girls and tell her that she and Tank had kissed and how much she'd loved it. *Am I doing the right thing?* She could use advice from a woman she trusted who had been through losing someone, too. But Leah bit her tongue, because Ginger was Tank's mother, and that would be an unfair position to put her in.

Instead, she closed the door and went to sit with the girls.

If only her worries about them were enough to quash her feelings for Tank. But as they colored in their new coloring books and Junie said, "I wish Tank was here," Leah knew she was wishing for an impossibility.

One she didn't really want.

Chapter Eight

LEAH STOOD IN her closet, shoving hangers to the side, with tears running down her cheeks. Ginger was going to be there in twenty minutes to drive them to the cemetery, and she couldn't find the one black dress she owned. The dress she'd worn to her father's burial. She leaned against the doorframe, remembering feeling as gutted then as she did now. She felt sick to her stomach and went to sit on her bed. Her gaze was drawn to the picture on her nightstand of her, River, and their father. *How am I supposed to get through this, Riv?*

She'd never felt so alone.

Her throat thickened painfully, and she looked at the picture of the girls and River that she'd taken the day after they'd moved into the cottage. They were playing in the front yard. River was lying on his back, his curls fanned out around his smiling face. He had one arm around each of the girls, who sat beside him like bookends, Rosie with her hair in pigtails and Junie's red ringlets messy and tangled. They were grinning so hard, Leah remembered thinking that they'd made the best decision *ever* by moving.

Now River was gone, and Leah had made them all even more miserable by sending Tank away. She was mentally and physically exhausted and had no idea how she was still standing. She'd gone to bed when she'd put the girls to bed early last night, but she'd gotten up to look out the window with every noise, hoping it was Tank. She'd spent hours picking apart why she missed him *so* much, wondering if it was just because he'd helped with the girls. There was no denying that it was easier when he was there, but it wasn't because he made pancakes or sang with the girls. It was because even in this tumultuous time that was testing *everything* she had, the four of them fit together in a way that only her family ever had. They were happier when Tank was with them, and after what he'd said to her, she had a feeling he was happier when they were together, too. He'd shown up around one in the morning and parked out front. Her heart had soared, but that happiness had been quickly overridden by guilt and confusion. What kind of a mother would she be if she gave in to her own desires over her girls' well-being—*River's girls*? She'd played the *Should I go out there or shouldn't I* game until she'd fallen asleep, and when she'd gotten up this morning, his truck had been gone.

She couldn't dwell on that now. She *had* to find her dress and get through River's burial. She forced herself to go back into the closet and fished through the hangers again, slower this time. Relief swamped her when she found the simple long-sleeve black dress with lace overlay on a hanger with another dress. She pulled it on, and it tumbled to the middle of her thighs. She zipped the side and buttoned the back of the lace mock turtleneck, then slipped her feet into black pumps. There was no time to try to find tights. She didn't even bother with makeup, knowing she was going to cry and ruin it anyway.

Rosie ran into the bedroom in her long-sleeve cream-colored dress that had pink and green dinosaurs picking flowers all over it. She touched Leah's dress. "Pwetty!"

"Thanks, baby. You look pretty, too." She'd explained where they were going earlier, and Junie had said that Tank had told them, and then she'd asked if he'd be there. Leah had said he would, and she knew Tank wouldn't let her down.

"Look." Rosie pointed to her legs, on which she'd drawn with red marker.

"Oh, Rosie." Leah dropped to her knees to look closer. There were scribbles all over her feet and legs and smudges of marker on the skirt of her dress. "Why did you do this? We don't have time for another bath."

"Stowies for Wiver." She beamed proudly and plopped onto her butt, pointing to the scribbles on her legs. "This Wiver. Guitar. Fwogs…"

Leah listened to River's little girl paying homage to her father, and more tears came. She didn't know how much more her heart could take. She framed Rosie's adorable face between her hands. "I think River would love those stories." She kissed the tip of Rosie's nose. "Now, how about you get Junie and the two of you put on your slippy shoes? The ones with the bows." Junie was wearing the same style dress as Rosie, but hers was green with white polka dots.

Rosie ran out of the room. "Juju! Bow shoes!"

Leah heard a car door close, and her stomach knotted. Leaving the house today would make River's death feel even more final. She grabbed a wad of tissues to wipe her eyes, and then she picked up the whole darn box, knowing they'd need them.

"Ready, girls? Miss Ginger is here. We have to go."

They came out of the bedroom holding Boo and Mine, looking adorable and sweet. Rosie had her shoes on the wrong feet. Leah knelt to fix them, then grabbed their memory blankets just in case. Then she ushered the girls out the door.

"Wiver's picture!" Rosie ran back inside, and Junie ran after her.

Leah sighed. "Sorry, Ginger." She leaned into the house. "Rosie, what pic—"

Rosie was holding the picture of River and the girls that they had on the windowsill, causing another onslaught of emotions. Leah choked out, "Good idea. Where's Junie?"

Junie came out of the bedroom holding two crayon drawings.

"What have you got, honey?"

"A picture for Wiver." As they walked outside, Junie said, "And one for Tank."

Leah stopped in her tracks and looked up at the sky, trying to keep more tears at bay.

Ginger put her arm around her. "How can I help, sweetheart?"

"Please tell me Tank is still coming to the cemetery." She needed him to be there as much as the girls did. She felt stronger when he was around.

"He's beside himself with worry about you and the girls. It would take an act of God to keep him from being there for you today, and even then, I'm pretty sure he'd find a way to show up. Come on, let's get you and the girls in the car."

Leah stared out the window on the drive to the cemetery, hoping Ginger and Tank wouldn't think badly of her for not ordering flowers or having a service, but she hadn't wanted to drive the cost up. As she'd been doing every day since the accident, she tried to remember every little thing about River, and Tank's voice blew through her mind.

He was a hero. Never forget that.

Sadness consumed her, making it hard to breathe as they wound through the narrow lane on the cemetery grounds. Leah fought with everything she had to hold herself together for the girls, but she felt like a sapling in a monsoon—about to be ripped from her roots, blown to pieces.

Ginger parked near a sharply dressed man with olive skin and dark hair, who looked to be in his forties. "That's Lenny Covington, the man you spoke with on the phone."

Lenny opened Leah's door. "Leah? I'm Lenny. I'm so sorry for your loss."

He had kind eyes and a warm voice. As he helped her out of the car, Tank's voice whispered through her mind again. *We call him Saint.*

"Thank you," she said nervously as he opened the back door so she could get Junie out. "Come on, baby girl."

Junie held Mine's ears and her drawings as Leah lifted her out of the car. Ginger and Rosie joined them. Rosie clutched River's picture in one hand, Boo in the other.

"It's nice to see you, Ginger." Lenny kissed her cheek.

"Thank you for helping our special girls," Ginger said.

Ginger's proclamation gave Leah a warm feeling, which was a nice buffer against the sadness swallowing her.

"My pleasure." He looked down at Rosie. "You must be Rosie."

Rosie nodded and held up River's picture. "This Wiver. He dead."

She said it so matter-of-factly, Leah didn't know if she should be sad or glad that Rosie wasn't falling apart. But one thing was certain: She wished she had Rosie's resilience.

Lenny nodded. "Yes, I know. I'm sorry about that."

"He with Gwampa." Rosie pointed to Junie. "That Junie."

Lenny smiled at Junie. "Hello, Junie."

Junie's brows knitted. She put her arm around Leah's leg, leaning against her. Leah put her hand on Junie's back.

Lenny led them toward a beautiful hill by a large tree. A casket with white roses and greenery draped over the middle was surrounded by a green ground covering and several pretty stands holding beautiful bouquets of roses and carnations. There was a large wooden easel facing away from them with what looked like an enormous sign on it. Leah looked around, wondering where River's gravesite was, but as they walked past the easel, she saw the sign wasn't a sign at all, but a poster-size photograph of River's smiling face. RIVER MICHAEL YATES was printed across the top, and FOREVER IN OUR HEARTS was printed beneath the picture.

"Wiver!" Junie and Rosie yelled, and ran to admire the picture.

Thank goodness, because Leah's tears were inescapable as she turned to Ginger and Lenny. *"How...?"*

"Tank," Ginger said softly.

Leah opened her mouth to speak, but all that came out was a sound of disbelief.

Rosie tilted her sweet face up. "Mama sad?"

Leah tried to get her voice to work, but how could she say she was okay when she was anything but?

The rumble and roar of motorcycles cut through the air, and they all turned to see Tank leading a convoy of fifty or more motorcycles, headlights on, with several cars following them. Leah's knees buckled, and she grabbed Ginger's arm, asking, "Who are all those people?" as the girls yelled "Tank!" and started waving and jumping up and down.

"That's your Dark Knights family, sweetheart," Ginger said.

"Behind Tank are Conroy and Preacher, followed by the rest of the members and their families."

"But...they don't even know us," she said through her tears.

"Many know you from the restaurant, and they were all at the hospital the night of the accident, praying for you and your family." Ginger hugged her against her side. "Tank also set up a gathering at his house. A celebration of River's life for you and the girls after you're done here. But if it's too much for you or the girls, there's no pressure to attend."

Emotions clogged Leah's throat. "He did that for us?"

"Yes, sweetheart. He'd do anything for you."

More tears fell as the convoy parked along the road, and Tank climbed off his bike. His eyes locked on Leah and the girls as he strode toward them in his black leather vest over a white dress shirt, jeans, and black boots, followed by a sea of men dressed the same and women wearing jeans, dresses, and everything in between. Junie and Rosie ran toward Tank, carrying their lovies and pictures.

He scooped them up in his strong arms, kissing their cheeks as they hugged him. Relief and something much deeper washed over his handsome face. Junie waved one of her pictures in front of his face, telling him she'd made it for him, and the look in his eyes made Leah's heart turn over in her chest. She wanted to be in his arms, too, but she was overwhelmed, frozen in place, and grateful beyond words.

His eyes never left hers as he closed the distance between them, holding one smiling girl in each arm. Junie rested her head on his shoulder like it was made for her.

"Tank..." Leah's voice cracked.

He stepped forward, bringing her into the fold between the girls. He didn't say a word. After all he'd done, he didn't have to. He pressed a tender kiss to her forehead, and she felt his emotions as deeply as she felt her own, whispering, "Thank you."

"I'll always be here for you, darlin'."

She didn't even try to hold back her tears as they went to stand by River's casket.

Tank stood with Leah and the girls, a pillar of strength when they needed it most, with Ginger and Baz to Leah's right and Conroy and Gunner to Tank's left. The rest of the Dark Knights and their families formed a circle of support around them as Leah and the girls put their pictures on River's casket and said tearful goodbyes to the brother, father, and friend they would miss every day for the rest of their lives.

Chapter Nine

LEAH HAD BEEN dreading today, anticipating nonstop tears and counting down the hours until she could hide under her covers, like the day she'd buried her father. She'd never imagined anything like the celebration Tank had put together, much less how good it would feel to celebrate River's life instead of only wallowing in his death. This was so much better for the girls, and for *her*.

Tank's backyard looked like something out of a dream. Decorative lanterns hung from tree branches, and a string with blue and yellow pennants ran between the deck and a tree at the edge of the woods. Between each pennant was a picture of River, either alone or with Leah, their father, or one of the girls. Zander was playing River's favorite songs on his guitar near three long tables of savory dishes, desserts, and other refreshments. On the other side of the tables was a gorgeous memory board with CELEBRATING THE LIFE OF RIVER YATES written above a collage of pictures of River and their family. Each picture was set in a unique colorful frame made of fabric and ribbons, and there were several cute embellishments interspersed with the pictures: a guitar, a basketball, two sets of pink baby booties, a brother-sister ornament, and a father-son charm.

Across the bottom of the memory board, in fine black letters was

SON – BROTHER – FATHER – FRIEND
– HERO –

Leah glanced at Tank, her anchor in their storm, so handsome in his dress shirt and vest, watching over the girls like they were his. He managed to bring River to life for all the people who came to support them, and he hadn't even known River. All the emotions Leah had been wrestling with since she'd said she needed space rose to the surface. She didn't know what to make of them, but they felt deeply rooted, as if they'd been seeding all summer and were bursting to bloom. She tried to tamp them down and focused on Junie and Rosie, sitting on a blanket with Starr's toddler, Gracie, and Tank's friend Justice's daughter, Patience, the four of them mesmerized by a puppet show put on by Tank's cousin Madigan, a professional puppeteer.

Tank leaned closer. "How are you holding up?"

"I'm okay, thanks to you. I've been dreading today, thinking it would be just like when we buried our father. But *this*…" Tears sprang to her eyes. "You gave River the goodbye he deserved, and look at all these people here to honor him." The yard and two-story deck were packed. "*Everyone* has been so kind to me and the girls, asking about River and about the pictures you hung up. It feels good to share his memory. I think that's the best part of all of this, because after my father died, nobody asked about him, and that made us feel even more alone. Like it was just me and River against the world. I was worried about the girls feeling that way. But look at them."

She motioned to Conroy and Preacher, lowering themselves to the blanket beside the girls. Her heart warmed as Rosie and Gracie scrambled onto Conroy's lap and Preacher gathered Junie and Patience against his sides. "They're anything *but* alone, and *you* did that for them. For all of us. You gave me a chance to celebrate River, to breathe instead of suffocating. I don't even know how to say thank you for something so monumental. I don't know how you knew what we needed again or how you pulled it all together so fast, with the pictures, and the people, and…" She was too choked up to finish.

He drew her into his arms and kissed the top of her head, giving her even more unconditional support. "I'm glad it helped. I worried that I might have overstepped."

She gazed up at him. "I wish you had been there to overstep when my father died."

"You have no idea how much I wish I'd been there for you and River." His brows knitted. "But right now I wish you'd eat something, darlin'. You haven't eaten all day."

"I will soon, I promise." He'd doted on her and the girls as much as his mother and his aunt Reba had.

He glanced over her shoulder with a serious expression. "Looks like the girls are on a mission."

She followed his gaze to Starr, Evie, Steph, Maverick's fiancée, Chloe, and Marly, a gorgeous olive-skinned brunette who hung out with the Wickeds, all heading their way. Leah was comfortable with Starr, but she knew the others only superficially from the restaurant. She secretly called them the Girl Squad. Madigan was usually with them, and they were all very nice to Leah, but they were also a close-knit group of well-put-together women. Leah had been holding her life together with bubble gum for so long, she felt a trickle of insecurity.

"Stand down, bodyguard," Marly said. "We come in peace." She was stunning in a floral wrap dress. "I think Blaine was looking for you."

"That right?" Tank narrowed his eyes, keeping one arm around Leah.

Steph, a curvy brunette with red streaks in her hair, planted a hand on her hip, meeting his stare. "No, but we want to talk to Leah without you hulking over her."

"Come on, Tanky," Evie said sweetly, fluttering her long dark lashes. "We haven't had any girl time with Leah."

He looked at Leah. "You gonna be okay?"

Leah tried not to let her self-consciousness show. "Of course."

His eyes narrowed further and his hand tightened on her hip, as if he wasn't fully buying it.

"It's okay, Tank, really. I'm fine."

He gave her a small smile and a nod, then turned a sterner look on the girls and walked away.

"Whoa, did you guys see that?" Steph asked.

Leah's nerves rattled. "I don't know why he looked at y'all like that. Sorry."

"Oh, *that's* just Tank's way of telling us not to overwhelm you," Steph said. "I was talking about his smile."

"What about it? I think he's got a nice smile."

The girls exchanged a glance, and Evie said, "Tank's smile is spotted less frequently than Big Foot or the Loch Ness Monster. You've touched our gruff giant in a way nobody else has been able to."

Leah knew just how rare those smiles were, and she liked knowing that his friends thought his sharing them with her was as special as she did.

"Leah, I'm so sorry about River." Starr embraced her. "I can't believe I didn't know you had a family."

"I guess our lives are just so busy, I tend to keep to myself," Leah said. "But I sure didn't mean anything by it."

"Listen, as a single mom, I know *all* about being busy," Starr said. "If it weren't for my job at the restaurant and Chloe's book club, I'd speak *toddler* twenty-four-seven."

Leah laughed softly. "I'm pretty sure that's how I sound most of the time. I feel like I haven't had a moment to breathe since we moved, much less make friends outside of work."

"We're going to help you change that." Evie swung her long dark hair over her shoulder and hugged Leah. "Everyone needs girlfriends, and you won't find better friends than us."

"Definitely." Chloe, a tall blonde, looked elegant in her fitted black dress. "We don't know each other very well yet, but I'm sorry for your loss. I can't imagine how hard it is to lose a sibling."

"We're all sorry." Steph hugged Leah.

Marly stepped in to embrace her next. "If you need anything, all you have to do is ask."

"Thank you." They were all so nice, Leah's apprehension faded. "If y'all have any tips for turning off my brain at night so I can sleep, I sure could use them."

"You know what always helps me? When Justin and I turn off all the lights, and—"

"Chloe!" Starr waved her hand. "Action-filled nights are limited for us single moms. How about sharing suggestions that don't include a guy?"

"She can do it alone," Chloe said.

Starr gave her a deadpan look.

Chloe's eyes widened. "Wait, did you think I meant she

should *diddle her fiddle?*"

Everyone laughed, and Leah felt her cheeks burn. It had been so long since she'd had girlfriends, she'd forgotten how uninhibited their conversations could be.

"I was going to say that Justin puts some of the lavender oil that Steph gave me on my feet, wrists, and temples." Chloe's eyes sparked with amusement. "No offense, Steph, but for the record, *Justin* is a much better remedy than dabs of oil. That man wears me out in the *very* best ways."

"No need to brag," Marly teased.

"Chloe, oils are a great idea," Steph said. "Leah, I own an herbal shop, and I'll totally hook you up. I'll put together a basket of all-natural remedies to help you sleep at night. How about some calming teas—and maybe mood-boosting herbs, too? Are you allergic to anything?"

"That all sounds great, thank you. I don't think I'm allergic to anything."

"Great. Let me get your number," Steph said.

Leah gave Steph her number, and Marly said, "I remember those sleepless nights. I lost my older brother to a motorcycle accident several years ago."

"I'm so sorry," Leah said.

"Me too, thanks," Marly said. "He was being reckless. He wasn't wearing a helmet. Now I advocate for helmet safety, and hopefully, save other people's families from going through what we did."

"What a great way to honor your brother's memory." Leah looked around them. "I can't get over how much Tank has done to honor River. I was shocked when everyone showed up at the cemetery, but this celebration? The decorations, the food. How did he get all of this done so fast?"

"He wanted everything to be perfect for you and the girls, and when the Wickeds put their minds to something, they make it happen," Steph said.

"Preacher and Con founded the Bayside chapter of the Dark Knights. The club is all about community and family. They know how to pull together in good times and bad," Evie explained. "Ginger, Reba, Mads, and some of the other wives and daughters of the Dark Knights made the food, and we all helped set up."

"Well, thank y'all for pitching in. I can't get over Zander knowing River's favorite songs."

"Zan's so talented," Steph said. "Tank gave him a list of songs the other night, and he picked them right up."

"I've never known a family like this. You can't imagine how much all of this means to me," Leah said. "Who made those gorgeous memory boards? I swear it feels like River's right here with us."

"That would be me." Chloe waved. "Although Tank picked out all the pictures. He said he knew which ones were your favorites."

Leah felt a tug in her chest. He must have listened to every word she said when they'd looked through the pictures. "They're gorgeous. I can't thank you enough. I was sure the girls were going to have a horrible time at the burial, but they were so happy when they saw the poster of River. You saved them lots of tears, although I cried enough for all of us."

"You're grieving. You're supposed to cry. I'm glad you like them," Chloe said. "Memory boards and albums are my creative outlet."

"Making memory blankets is mine," Leah said.

"Like the ones all over Pinterest with pieces of clothing,

pacifiers, and other things sewn on?" Starr asked.

"Mm-hm. I use the girls' old onesies, Halloween costumes, River's old shirts, all sorts of stuff."

"I'd love to see them," Chloe said, and the others agreed excitedly.

"They're not that great. I mean, they are to *me*. My dad taught me to make them before he passed away, so they're really special."

There was another round of *I'm sorry*s, and Leah told them about raising River, which led to explaining that River was the girls' father and that Leah had adopted them.

"You've definitely had your hands full for a very long time," Evie said. "We meant what we said about if you need anything. We can help babysit, come over to chat, whatever you need."

"We should get the girls together sometime," Starr suggested. "Gracie *loves* being around other kids."

Leah had been so busy holding their lives together, she hadn't even had time to think about the fact that the girls had no friends their age. They'd need friends now more than ever. "I'd like that."

"Great. Give me your number and we'll set something up," Starr said.

"Look at your little Junie cuddled up with Preacher," Marly said as Leah gave Starr her number. "I swear he and Con are everyone's surrogate father or grandfather."

"But check out Tank watching them—and Leah—like a hawk." Steph nodded toward Tank, standing a few feet away from the girls while he talked with Justice, a handsome, sharply dressed Black man.

Tank looked at the girls, then glanced at Leah, sending her pulse into overdrive. He winked and looked at the girls again.

MELISSA FOSTER

Starr nudged Leah. "So…What *other* secrets have you been keeping?"

Leah tore her eyes away from Tank, her cheeks warming.

"Don't worry. We're not here to pressure you for gossip," Evie reassured her.

"Although I am curious about why you avoided Tank all summer," Marly chimed in. "Was it because he was always looking at you? I know it bothered him that he couldn't talk to you. But if you ask me, it was a great way to get his attention."

"Oh my gosh. That's *not* what it was at all," Leah said. "He's so broody, I just…sensed sadness in him, and I didn't know what to make of it. But now that we've gotten to know each other better, I know about his sister, and I get it."

"I am *so* tempted to ask how much better, but I won't," Marly teased. "We all know how enticing those Wicked boys are." Marly glanced at Blaine, talking with Baz and a group of guys. Just beyond them, Gunner fake punched Maverick, who put him in a headlock, the two of them laughing. "They're all so buff and badass."

"Agreed," Starr said, eyeing Blaine.

"And afraid of commitment," Evie added.

"Hey, my Wicked isn't," Chloe said.

Leah wanted to say that Tank wasn't either, but she kept that to herself, as the girls debated the virtues of the Wicked men and some of their bed-hopping ways. They filled Leah in on the players—Zander and Gunner—and the gentlemen—Zeke and Blaine, and came up with the title of *gentleman player* for Baz, which apparently meant that he was really good at being a gentleman but liked playing around.

These women were funny, and they included Leah, asking her opinion on the guys and making jokes. Steph and Evie

142

made them laugh with stories of the Wickeds when they were teenagers, which prompted Leah to share humorous stories of River's younger years.

As Evie relayed a story about Madigan trying to make Tank smile and him growling and baring his teeth, Leah glanced at Tank across the yard. As if he felt the heat of her gaze, he looked over, his dark eyes holding hers, causing flutters in her belly. He mouthed, *Are you okay?* adding deeper emotions to the titillating ones. She smiled and nodded.

"I don't care if they've slept with all of Bayside," Marly said, bringing Leah's attention back to the conversation. "They're hands down some of the best men I've ever known." She leaned closer to Leah. "They haven't slept with everyone. I'm just making a point."

"Where does Tank fit into your player and gentleman classifications?" Leah asked carefully. She had her own idea, since he'd been honest with her about his sexual proclivities, but she was interested in hearing what they thought.

The girls' brows furrowed.

"Women have always thrown themselves at him," Evie said. "But he's private with his personal life."

"I've never seen him look at anyone the way he looks at you, Leah." Steph glanced at Tank, catching him watching Leah again. "Or as openly. He looks like he wants to come over here and steal you away."

Starr linked her arm with Leah's and said, "Not until we check out the dessert table, right?"

Leah couldn't believe she'd been intimidated by these girls who welcomed her into their group so warmly.

Reba and Ginger sidled up to the group. Reba was a little shorter than Leah, with shoulder-length mahogany hair and an outgoing personality. She had a mothering way about her, like Ginger did, and that made Leah want to spend more time around them.

"If you girls haven't had dessert yet, you might want to grab some," Reba said conspiratorially. "We just thwarted Poppy and Zander from raiding the dessert table for the third time."

The other girls laughed.

"Leah, have you met Grandpa Mike—*Poppy*—yet? Con and Preacher's dad? He's not supposed to get all sugared up, but he's a sneaky one." Ginger pointed to an older man with wispy gray hair, a square jaw, and the aura of a tough cookie, like Clint Eastwood.

"Not yet." Leah remembered what Tank had said about Mike being one of the best men he'd ever known, and she was curious about the man whose wisdom Tank had shared with her. "But I'm looking forward to meeting him."

"He and Tank have always been close. They've pulled each other through the toughest times," Ginger said.

"They have a lot in common," Reba added. "They're both ornery as can be, but they say the funniest things, and always with an edge, like the rest of our Wicked men."

"You're in for a treat when you meet him," Chloe said. "I love Grandpa Mike. We have dinner every Wednesday night while the guys are at church."

"Church? Do all the guys go to church together? Does Tank go?" Leah wasn't very religious, and she wondered if that would make a difference to him.

"Yes, but something tells me you're thinking of a religious church," Ginger said.

Leah was confused. "What other kind is there?"

"Church is what the motorcycle club calls their meetings,

and all the members are required to attend."

"Why do they call it church?" Leah asked.

"Honey, that's a question that you'll get too many answers to. Some say it's because the gathering of the club is a religious experience, others say it's all about community, and you'll even hear that they call it church to keep the club under a shadow of mystery." Reba waggled her brows. "But while I can't answer that question, I *can* tell you why we call cupcakes and chocolate cake *delicious*. Who's up for dessert?"

There was a collective *Me!* and they headed for the refreshment tables. Ginger looped her arm through Leah's and said, "Are you doing okay, honey?"

Leah had started the day with dread, and hours later, she was being cared for by Tank and too many others to count, sharing stories about River, watching the girls play with friends their age, and about to have a snack with a group of new girlfriends. She'd probably cry her eyes out later, but right now she could enjoy all of this goodness Tank had brought together for her. "I'm okay. Actually, I'm better than okay."

AS AFTERNOON FADED into evening, the solar lanterns twinkled to life, and the last of the guests left. Everyone had pitched in to help clean up, including Junie and Rosie. The girls walked around the yard with Zeke, Tank, and Leah, picking up trash. Zeke used to be a special education teacher, and he was great with kids. He told the girls stories about nature hikes he'd taken, his favorite subject, and the girls told him about walks they'd taken with River. Tank stuck close by Leah as she teared up one minute and laughed the next. Zeke promised to take the girls on a hike one day, and the girls couldn't stop talking about it. Tank loved seeing his family embracing Leah and the girls.

Now they were all hanging out on the upper deck. Leah sat between Tank and Madigan, talking with his grandfather. Junie was fast asleep on Tank's chest, one little hand wrapped around his necklace, the other holding Mine. Rosie was curled up in Conroy's lap with her memory blanket and Boo. The hum of conversations filled the air, but Tank was listening to his grandfather Mike talking with Leah.

"It's not often that I get to spend time with little ones," Mike said. "Your girls remind me of my daughter, Sonja, when she was just a tiny thing growing up with my three boys, Preacher, Conroy, and Jacob. By the time Sonja was Juju's age, she was bossing her brothers around."

Leah smiled. "You called her Juju. That's what I call her."

"Heck yeah, I did. That's what Smiley calls her." He pointed to Rosie.

That brought a warm glow to Leah, and man, Tank loved that look on her.

Mike waggled his finger. "You've brought them up well, young lady. You should be proud. Raising young ones isn't easy."

"I can't take all the credit. River helped raise them. He was always teaching them right from wrong, but he had a playful way of doing it by telling stories and making them laugh. I remember when he got his guitar at the Swap Shop. It had scratches and broken strings, but he used it to teach the girls about taking care of their things. Funny thing is, while they learned to put their toys away, he always left the darn thing out." She laughed softly. "He acted like there was nothing they couldn't understand. As he taught himself to play the guitar, he taught the girls, too. He'd say the chords and they'd repeat them. He had this way of making us all feel special, like he'd miss us the second he walked out the door. Before he left the house the night of the accident, he bowed dramatically, like he was ending a show, and said, 'Farewell, my beautiful ladies.'" Tears slid down her cheeks.

Tank put his arm around her, hugging her against his side as she dabbed at her tears with tissues.

"He sounds like a very special young man." Mike glanced at the girls. "I think the girls inherited his charm. They had me eating out of the palms of their hands today."

"Don't think we didn't notice you sending them to the cookie tray for you," Reba said. "Your doctors are *not* going to be happy."

Mike scoffed, swatting his hand dismissively. "You saw nothing of the sort."

"Our grandfather is a sucker for little girls and for sweets," Madigan said. "He used to sneak candy bars to me and Ashley when we were little."

"Now he bribes us to sneak them to him," Maverick said, and everyone laughed.

Chloe gave him a stern look, and Maverick leaned in for a kiss, turning the harsh expression to something much warmer. Tank had never been a jealous man, but hell if he didn't wish he could have done that with Leah a hundred times today. It had taken more than a year for Chloe to let go of her preconceived notions about Maverick and see there was something special between them. Tank was confident that his and Leah's time would come.

"A man's got to enjoy himself," Mike grumbled, bringing

Tank's mind back to the moment.

"That's my motto," Gunner said with a smirk.

Mike eyed Gunner. "How about you enjoy yourself into marriage and make me some great-grandchildren?"

Preacher clapped a hand on Gunner's shoulder and said, "Better find *the one* quickly, son, or Mav and Chloe will beat you in the grandchild race."

"Yes, Gunny, how about you do that?" Ginger said.

Gunner pushed to his feet. "I think I hear Undercover calling my name." Undercover was a nightclub in a nearby town. "Who's coming with me?"

"Me!" Madigan popped to her feet, her mahogany hair bouncing around her shoulders. She'd cornered Tank earlier to tell him how much she loved Leah and the girls.

Blaine stood and put an arm around Madigan. "Guess that means I'm going."

Madigan rolled her eyes. "Stop acting like I need a chaperone."

Tank and Blaine exchanged a glance. They worried about Madigan. She'd gone overseas for a semester of college as a starry-eyed girl and had returned focused, driven, and *different*. Within a year she'd started the Mad Truth About Love greeting-card line, which made fun of the more difficult aspects of relationships. Between that and her puppeteering, she rarely dated. She claimed she'd just grown up, but Tank and Blaine had other beliefs about what had gone down when she was too damn far from home.

"We're in." Zander stood and dragged Zeke up by his sleeve.

"Dude, I'm really not into babysitting you tonight," Zeke said.

"*Good,*" Madigan said sharply. "Zeke can keep Blaine busy so I can dance."

"I think it's time we get Mike home, too," Ginger said, and they all decided to call it a night.

As they said their goodbyes, Leah hugged Zander and said, "Thank you for learning River's favorite songs. It meant a lot to me."

"Anytime. If the girls ever want to hear someone play, I'm happy to stop by, or you and Tank can bring them by my place," Zander said. "I'd offer to teach them, the way River was doing, but I don't read music and I suck at teaching. But Mads could teach them. She taught me."

"I sure can." Madigan hugged Leah. "Aunt Ginger told me you and the girls are cooking with her next Sunday. Would you mind if I joined you? I love cooking, and I'll bring my guitar and play for Junie and Rosie."

"That sounds fun," Leah said.

After many hugs, they loaded Tank's truck with leftovers, the memory boards, and the pictures from the pennant string and headed back to Leah's cottage. She was quiet on the drive, gazing out the passenger window. When they arrived, they carried the girls inside, and while Leah changed them into their pajamas and put them to bed, Tank brought the rest of their things inside. He put away the leftovers and set up the easels with the poster and memory board on the far side of the living room.

It had been hell keeping his affections to himself today, and when Leah came out of the girls' room in her bare feet and black dress, looking sweet, beautiful, and exhausted, Tank wanted nothing more than to take her into his arms and hold her. But the ball was in her court, and out of respect for her need for space, he'd take his cues from her.

She closed the girls' door most of the way and came to him.

"I didn't intend for the night to go on so long," he said quietly. "Sorry about that."

"Don't you dare apologize. Everything about today was wonderful. I talked to so many people about River and the girls, and it helped a lot. The girls have never had so much love in their lives."

"I hope you felt that affection, too."

"It would be hard not to. I've never known a family like yours, or people like the ones you introduced me to today." She stepped closer, nibbling on her lower lip, which he was aching to kiss. "I've never known anyone like *you*, Tank." She gazed up at him with trepidation and what looked a hell of a lot like hope in her eyes. "I was wrong about needing space. I missed you last night, and the whole day felt off. *I* felt off. The girls asked for you a million times. I don't know how to protect them, but I don't think staying away from you is the answer." Her brows knitted, and she spoke just above a whisper. "That is, if you haven't changed your mind, because I'd understand if you—"

Her words were silenced by the hard press of his lips. He crushed her to him, pouring all the emotions he'd been holding back into their connection. She tasted sweet and strangely familiar, like their kisses the other night had obliterated everything that came before them. She made lustful noises that burned through him. He lifted her onto the counter, wedging himself between her legs, and buried his hands in her hair, deepening their kisses. He fucking loved the feel of her hair wrapped around his fingers, her sensual mouth devouring his. He wanted to strip her naked and bring her so much pleasure, she would have no space for sadness, but a voice in his head warned him to slow down. He fisted his hands in her curls to keep from running them down her gorgeous body, but he didn't *want* to pull back. He wanted to soak up every kiss she was willing to share, to bury himself deep inside her and stay for fucking *ever*.

But that would make him a dick, so he forced himself to draw back and touched his forehead to hers, careful not to brush her stitches. "I haven't changed my mind," he panted out, and drew back just far enough to look into her eyes. "I *won't* change my mind, Lee, and I'll do my best not to let the girls get hurt. That's a promise."

"I know you will." Tears dampened her eyes.

His chest constricted. "Aw, hell. You're crying. I shouldn't have kissed you so aggressively. I'm sorry. I got carried away."

"It's not that. I love the way you kiss me. It's just that I've been trying to get up the courage to tell you how I felt all day. Now it's like a dam burst, and that's a great feeling, but on the heels of all that goodness are thoughts of today, the cemetery, knowing this was *it*. This was goodbye to River." She buried her face in his chest. "I'm sorry. I don't mean to cry. I promise it's not you."

He held her tight. "It's okay. You *should* cry. It's healing to get it out." He kissed her head, soothing his hand down her back, wanting to bear her pain for her and knowing she needed to experience it.

She tipped her face up. "Will you stay, and just hold me?"

He framed her beautiful face in his hands, kissing her softly. "Baby, I'll do whatever you need, whenever you need it. Why don't you get ready for bed?" He lifted her off the counter and set her on her feet.

She went into the bathroom, and then she went into her

bedroom and closed the door. Tank sat on the couch to take off his boots and pushed to his feet, shrugging off his vest. He laid it over the back of a chair and was taking off his dress shirt when she came out of the bedroom in skimpy white sleeping shorts and a white cotton tank top with a red heart on it. Pain sliced through him at the bruises on her shoulder, arm, and leg. Their eyes collided, and her nipples pebbled against the thin cotton. Her eyes traveled down his bare chest as she closed the gap between them. Her tongue slid across her lower lip; then she trapped that succulent lip between her teeth, her sexy innocence wreaking havoc with his restraint.

Fuuck. He gritted his teeth, telling his throbbing cock to *behave.* He hadn't been with a woman since he'd first set eyes on Leah in early May. This was going to be torture.

He touched his shirt. "Want me to leave this on?"

She shook her head, and with shaky hands, she pushed his shirt over his shoulders, going up on her toes to push it the rest of the way off. It fell to the floor as her fingers trailed over the tattoos on his shoulders and chest as if she were reading braille. She traced Ashley's name over his heart and ran her fingers lightly over one pierced nipple. A low sound of appreciation escaped before he could silence it.

Her brows knitted, and her eyes flicked up to his as she whispered, "Do those hurt?"

"They're for pleasure, not pain."

She seemed to think about that for a second, nibbling on her lower lip and making him ache even more. Her fingers trailed down the tattoos between his pecs, and she traced the ink on his stomach, stopping abruptly, eyes trained on his newest tattoo—RIVER—across the left side of his abs.

Her eyes flicked up to his, and the emotions in them did

him in. She didn't say a word as she pressed a kiss over Ashley's name and another over River's. With a small smile, she took his hand and led him into the bedroom. They left the bedroom door open and climbed onto the bed. He gathered her against him. His thighs pressed against the backs of her legs, her slim body against his chest, her ass nestled within the curve of his hips. She laced her fingers with his, holding them against her chest. He was twice her size, but they fit together as if he were built solely for her. He was still wearing his jeans, and there was nothing sexual about the moment, but he'd never felt so in tune with and connected to another person.

He held her tight, burying his face in her curls and breathing her in, whispering, "Rest, baby. You're safe with me," but she'd already drifted off to sleep.

Chapter Ten

WAKEFULNESS DRIFTED IN slowly, bringing two consecutive thoughts to Leah's groggy mind. River was gone, and she was lying in bed alone. She rolled onto her back, feeling like she'd slept for a month and knowing it was because of Tank. She stared up at the ceiling with a heaviness in her chest for the absence of that split second of thinking River was still alive. She had thought that moment was painful when she'd experienced it these last few days, but waking up with the certainty of knowing he was gone was just as agonizing.

The sounds of giggles sailed in through the closed bedroom door, and Leah bolted up to a sitting position. Had they seen Tank in her bed, shirtless? She thought about his thickly muscled, tattooed body and pierced nipples. She practically salivated over the image blooming before her, but he was a whole lot of man for her, much less for her baby girls to see.

She scrambled out of bed, threw on a sweatshirt, and pulled open her bedroom door. Tank and the girls looked over from where they sat on a blanket in the middle of the living room floor. Junie was wearing Tank's black leather vest over her pajama top, Rosie was sitting on her knees, holding a spoonful of yogurt next to Tank's mouth, and Tank was wearing his dress shirt from last night with a pink bib tied around his neck. He had yogurt in his beard and on his shirt. His raised brows and crooked smile told her he wasn't quite sure how he'd gotten himself into that situation, but his eyes gave away his enjoyment.

"We havin' a tea pawty!" Junie announced. "I'm the papa!"

"I Mama!" Rosie shoved the spoon toward Tank's mouth, dumping more yogurt on his beard. "Feedin' baby!"

Leah snort-laughed, and covered her mouth.

"They found me on the *couch* when they woke up," Tank reassured her.

She had no idea how he knew she needed to know that, but she was relieved not to have to explain why Tank was in her bed.

"Wanna play?" Rosie asked.

"You can be Gwampa and ask Tank to get you cookies," Junie said.

Tank patted the space beside him.

She lowered herself to the blanket and whispered, "You should have woken me up."

"And miss all this? Not a chance."

AFTER A MORNING of yogurt spills and baking cookies— *because Gwampa needs them*—Tank went home to shower and change, while Leah and the girls got ready for the day. As she bathed and dressed them, they chatted about all the people they'd met yesterday at *Wiver's pawty*, which brought a wave of sadness. But the girls didn't miss a beat, begging to see Gracie and Patience again, go on a hike with Zeke, and do about a dozen other things with people they'd met. Leah wished it was as easy for her to move forward as it was for them, but wishing for that brought guilt, so she tried not to think about it and focused on the girls instead. She had exchanged numbers with Starr, Steph, and the rest of the Girl Squad, and although *she* wasn't ready to deal with a playdate just yet, Junie and Rosie were. She texted Starr, and they set one up for next week, which gave Leah time to deal with the aftermath of the accident that she'd been putting off.

The sound of Tank's truck pulling up out front stirred butterflies in Leah's stomach and sent the girls scampering to the window.

"Tank!" Rosie cheered, adorable in her floral leggings and bright pink long-sleeve shirt with a ruffled hem.

"Ginger and Conwoy are he*ah*!" Junie yelled as they ran out the front door.

Leah followed them out, wondering why Tank's parents were there and why they'd brought separate cars. Conroy scooped Junie up and tickled her belly. Junie giggled and squirmed in her black-and-white leggings and a long-sleeve black shirt with SWEET, SASSY, AND SOUTHERN emblazoned down the front. Ginger picked up Rosie, and Rosie smushed a kiss to her lips, but Leah lost her breath at Tank stalking toward her like a lion coming back to the den, confident and hungry. His thick thighs strained against worn denim as his powerful legs ate up the distance between them. Leather bracelets circled one wrist, silver rings glittering in the sunlight. Now that she knew about his piercings, she recognized their outline through the thin cotton shirt hugging his muscular chest, sending fire through her core. *They're for pleasure, not pain.* She didn't even know what kind of pleasure those piercings could bring, but she wanted to find out. There must be some kind of sin wrapped up in wanting a man so badly at a time like this, but as his beard lifted with a smile and he kissed her cheek, it was all she could do to tamp down those desires.

"You look beautiful. Sorry I was gone so long." His brows knitted. "*What* is going through your mind right now, darlin'?"

Embarrassed, she looked away, but he took her chin between his finger and thumb, drawing her eyes back to his. She imagined his question pinging off the sparks between them and managed, "You look nice, too."

A husky laugh fell from his lips, and he lowered his mouth to her ear, whispering, "I'll thank you for that later when little eyes aren't watching."

"Ohmygod, *the girls*. Your *parents!*" she whispered urgently as her brain slammed into gear, and she realized his parents were watching them. They'd seen her ogling their son like a *groupie*. "I'm *so* sorry!"

Conroy laughed. "Don't be. Please continue. We're fine over here."

Mortified, Leah covered her face, and Tank pulled her into his arms, laughing. She looked up at him, but there was no stopping her laughter, which made his parents laugh, too. Rosie and Junie barreled into their legs, giggling.

Leah looked teasingly at Conroy and Ginger. "This is y'all's fault for having such a peach of a son." They chuckled, and she said, "What's going on, anyway? Did I forget we had plans?"

"No. I needed them to help me bring the car over." Tank motioned to a blue sedan. "You are now the proud owner of that sweet ride."

"What do you mean?" Leah looked from Tank to his parents.

He put a set of keys in her hand. "I have to go back to work tomorrow, Lee. I don't want you to be without a car, and my grandfather no longer uses his. He wants you to have it. We all do."

Her jaw dropped. "I can't take your grandfather's *car*. I'm calling the insurance company today. I'm sure they'll give me something for my car." She tried to give him back the keys, but he closed his hand around hers.

"They will, but it won't be enough. This car is ten years old, but my grandfather rarely drove, and we've maintained it well. It's only got thirty-eight thousand miles on it, and more importantly, it's *safe*. Lee, I need to know you're okay when you and the girls are on the road."

"But, Tank—"

"Listen to me, *please*." He said it so seriously, it felt like a command. "You've always had your brother to watch the girls. When you go back to work, you'll need a car and childcare, and at some point you'll want to put the girls in preschool. You'll need the insurance money for those expenses. If it were up to me, I'd take care of all of that so you never had to work again if you didn't want to. But I respect your independence, and I know better than to rush in and take over for a woman who has ruled her kingdom for so long. You need this car, Lee. Please accept it."

She stole a glance at his parents, unable to believe what he'd just said, but they were nodding in agreement.

"He's right, Leah." Conroy stepped closer. "We'll help out as much as we can watching the girls and with whatever else you need, but we all work. You need a safe, reliable car."

"But y'all have done so much already. A car is too much."

Her emotions got the best of her, and her voice cracked.

"Honey, I understand how you feel. I truly do," Ginger said compassionately. "But we're giving you a Honda, not a Maserati, and it would mean a lot to us, and to Mike, to know you and the girls are taken care of."

Leah's eyes teared up. She looked at the blue sedan, her mind reeling.

Conroy held up both hands. "And I do not want to have to tell my father that you refused his gift."

Leah looked at her girls. Rosie smiled up at her. Junie's brows were knitted, her tiny lips pursed. If she accepted the car, what message was she sending them? That life was about getting expensive gifts?

"Lee," Tank said softly, and took her hand. "Cheeky, Twitch, stay with Ginger and Con for a second, okay? I want to talk to your mama."

"About the car?" Junie asked.

"Yeah." He ruffled her hair. "We'll be right back." He led Leah away, speaking quietly. "I didn't mean to blindside you with this. Let's talk about it. Tell me what you're thinking."

"I'm thinking that you've done way too much for us already. What if you regret it tomorrow or next month? What if the girls think this is how life works, that people will just *give* them things?"

"Lee, there are no strings attached to this gift, and if you tell me next week that you never want to see me again, I will *still* feel good about giving you the car. My parents and grandfather will *still* feel good about this decision." He gazed into her eyes and placed his hand on her cheek, caressing it with his thumb. "Baby, you and the girls just lost the most important man in your lives. The girls have learned that people can be taken away from them in an instant. Accepting this car, or anything else, won't undo that harsh lesson or tell them that life will be handed to them on a silver platter. It will show them that we help the people we care about and that when we're down, it's okay to accept that help. You'll be teaching them that paying it forward is the best way to live, and hopefully they'll carry that with them and do the same for others."

Tears welled in her eyes. "How can I say no to *that*?"

"You can't." He gathered her in his arms. "It's the right choice, Lee." He gazed down at her and glanced over her shoulder. He whispered, "The kids aren't looking," and kissed her slow and sweet, righting all the disheveled pieces her worries had caused.

"Thank you," she said as they went to join the others, earning a single nod and a contented smile.

"What do you think?" Ginger asked.

"I think your family is too good to be true." Leah hugged Ginger. "Thank you for everything."

"Our pleasure, sweetheart."

"Are we taking the car?" Junie asked.

"You sure are." Tank picked her up and spun her around.

Junie giggled, and Rosie yelled, "Spin me!"

"I'll spin you, munchkin." Tank put Junie down and lifted Rosie over his head, spinning her around, earning squeals of delight.

"Get in here." Conroy pulled Leah into his arms. "We love you, darlin'. You made the right choice."

"Thank you. I'd like to thank Mike, too. In person, if possible."

Tank put Rosie down. "Absolutely. We can do that today. Grandpa Mike would love to see you."

"Can I see Gwampa Mike?" Junie asked.

Rosie jumped up and down. "I see Gwampa!"

Ginger put her hand over her heart with a warm expression that mirrored the warm, fuzzy feelings Leah felt, but on the heels of those good feelings, Leah wondered if she should correct her girls from calling him *Grandpa*. The trouble was, she knew the window of opportunity to protect their hearts from falling for Tank and his family had already closed, and asking them to call him Mr. Mike would only hurt their feelings.

Tank put a hand on each girl's head. "You bet, chickadees."

"I have to find my driver's license. It was cracked. I'm sure it's ruined." She still hadn't gone through the bag with her purse in it that Tank had retrieved for her.

"We'll get a new one on the way to see Mike," Tank suggested. "I want to register the car in your name anyway."

"Then I need to call the insurance company before we go. I was fixin' to do it today anyway."

"Why don't you go take care of that, and I'll watch the girls," Tank offered.

Conroy put his arm around Tank. "Looks like you've got things covered, son. We need to get over to the restaurant."

Leah thanked them profusely, and after his parents left, Tank sat outside with the girls while they played in the yard and Leah called the insurance company. She'd been putting off making the call to give them her new phone number and handle whatever needed to be handled, but it was painless, and it felt good to do something productive.

She joined Tank on the porch, watching the girls lying in the grass making grass angels, like snow angels without the snow.

"Everything go okay?" Tank asked.

"Yeah. It's about the same rate as my car was. They're still processing the claim for the accident."

"Lee, there's something I wanted to talk with you about. Justice found out that the guy who hit you is being charged with involuntary manslaughter, which carries up to a twenty-year prison sentence."

"Okay," she said softly. "I hate talking about this."

He took her hand. "I know. So do I. I just want to be sure you're taken care of."

"We're *fine*. You've already made more than sure of that."

"But this is part of it. I don't want you to look back in six months or two years and wish you had handled things differently. I need to ask some hard questions, and I apologize ahead of time, but they're important. Have you thought about if you want to sue him?"

"*No*, and I don't want to think about it. I want to forget he exists. I don't want to see his face or hear his voice, and I definitely don't want to spend my energy fighting him for anything."

Tank lifted their joined hands, kissing the back of hers. "I understand and I support your decision, but I wouldn't feel right if I didn't tell you all your options. If you want him to pay for taking away the girls' father and put that money away for their futures without taking the guy to court, Justice can try to negotiate some sort of victim restitution."

He was so good, to think about the things she didn't want to, she mulled it over as she watched the girls chasing each other and giggling. "You mean for college, or a car, or whatever else they need?"

"Yes, or even just so they know the guy paid for what he's done." He turned a pained expression on her. "I can't even begin to imagine how they'll feel years from now, about the accident, or any of it. I hope they'll be okay, but if the guy is out of prison, they could be angry. They're so little right now, there's no way to know."

The pit of her stomach burned thinking about the girls being angry years down the line. "What would you do?"

"This isn't about me, darlin'. It's about doing what you feel is right for you and the girls. If you go the restitution route, it might mean he gets a lighter sentence, but the girls would get something in return."

She leaned against him, whispering, "I hate this."

"Me too." He put his arm around her and kissed her temple. "You don't need to decide now. I just wanted you to think about it."

She thought about what it was like after her father died and whether money would have made a difference. "I know what I want to do. I want to love the girls enough for me *and* River and keep his spirit alive so they know him through me. But I don't want to take dirty money or decide someone else's fate. Money won't bring River back. Let the judge do whatever he's going to do. We did okay after our dad died, and we didn't have much. The girls and I will do fine, too."

"I'll make sure of it." He glanced at the girls, who plopped down in the grass on their stomachs, looking at something, and then he gave her a quick kiss.

She loved that he worried about the girls in the same way she did. As the girls popped up and ran over, she said, "Thank you for caring enough to ask the hard questions."

He nodded as Rosie ran up the porch steps and climbed onto his back, hollering, "Piggyback!"

Tank made a growling noise, sweeping one arm around

Junie and rising to his feet with Rosie hanging on his back and Junie tucked under his arm like a football, both girls giggling. "Who wants to go for a ride in your new car?"

"Me!" Junie and Rosie cheered.

Rosie yelled, "Get Boo!"

As Leah followed them inside, Tank's heavy footsteps clomping into their room and the girls laughing hysterically, she knew she'd made the right choice. There wasn't enough money in the world to inspire love or laughter, much less give the girls a lifetime full of both like they deserved.

LEAH PACKED AN enormous bag of toys and snacks before they left for the Registry of Motor Vehicles. Tank thought she was nuts to pack so much, but after ten minutes of waiting at the registry, he learned about the impatience of little ones and the tricks Leah used to deal with it. They played I Spy, Go Fish, colored, took walks around the waiting room, ate lots of snacks, and drank too many juice boxes. Rosie had a crying fit, and Leah handled it like she was born to be a mother, holding her and talking soothingly. When that didn't work, she gave her a lollipop. *A little sugar goes a long way.*

What felt like eight hours later, but in reality was only two, Leah had a new driver's license and the car was registered in her name. After they put the girls in their carseats, Tank pulled Leah around to the back, where the girls couldn't see them, and drew her into his arms, kissing her smiling lips. "How does it feel?"

Her cheeks pinked up. "I'm not sure. Maybe you should

give me s'more sugar."

He chuckled and lowered his lips to hers, kissing her passionately. She went up on her toes, and it took everything he had not to lift her onto the trunk and kiss her senseless. He forced himself to break their connection but kept her close. "I could kiss you all fucking day."

"Uh-huh," she said breathily, then giggled and buried her face in his chest.

He loved when she did that, so adorably sexy. He palmed her ass, giving it a squeeze. "Let's go before I get us arrested for indecent exposure."

"The things you *say*," she whispered, red cheeked, her hands fisted in his shirt.

He didn't know what the guys she'd been with were like, but he took a chance to see how she would react and brushed his beard over her cheek, speaking gruffly into her ear. "They're not nearly as dirty as the things I want to do with you."

She stared up at him, wide-eyed, and he feared he'd scared her, but in the next second, a slow, sensual, and somehow also bashful smile appeared.

Oh yeah, baby. We'll get there.

"Don't worry, darlin', I'm not in a rush." He leaned closer and said, "But you'd better get behind the wheel before I change my mind."

She laughed softly. "You should drive. I don't know where Mike lives."

Tank tried to cool himself down as he drove to LOCAL, the Lower Cape Assisted Living Facility where Mike lived, but Leah kept stealing glances at him, looking as flirtatious as she did curious, which only made him want to satisfy those curiosities even more. He rolled down his window to cool himself off and stuffed those desires down deep.

"Gwampa has a big house," Junie said when they parked in front of the building.

"This isn't his house," Tank explained. "This is like an apartment complex. Grandpa Mike and lots of other people live here." Mike had only recently moved to LOCAL, and Tank made a point to visit him every Wednesday before church. Mike had lived with Preacher and Reba previously, but he'd wanted his autonomy, and after falling a couple of times and ending up in the hospital, they'd decided to move him there, where he'd have both autonomy and oversight. Tank knew it was the right place for him, but it felt like Mike was one step closer to the end of his life, and Tank fucking hated that.

"Like where we lived before we moved here?" Junie asked.

"That's right," Leah said.

They got the girls out of the car and headed inside. As Tank was signing in, Chloe came down the hall, looking professional in a navy pencil skirt and white blouse. Her eyes lit up when she saw them.

"I didn't expect to see you guys. This isn't Tank's usual visiting day." Chloe hugged Leah.

"I didn't know he had a usual day." Leah eyed him appreciatively, as if she liked knowing he visited Mike regularly.

"Every Wednesday, like clockwork," Chloe said. "Mike will be glad to see you. He was bragging about Leah and the girls to a flock of ladies over breakfast this morning. He's such a flirt." She grabbed a basket of stickers from the counter and knelt in front of the girls.

Rosie beamed at her. Junie put her arm around Tank's leg, and he put his hand on the back of her head.

"Do you remember me from yesterday?" Chloe asked.

Rosie nodded. Junie said, "You kissed Mavwick."

Tank chuckled.

"You're right, I did, because I'm going to *marry* Maverick. How would you two cuties like stickers?" Chloe held out the basket.

"We like *stickuhs*!" Rosie exclaimed, and grabbed a handful of stickers.

"Wosie!" Junie admonished her.

"You can each take *one*," Leah said. "And remember to say thank you."

"Thank you," they said in unison as they fished through the selection of animal and cartoon stickers.

"Can I take one for Gwampa?" Junie asked.

"Yes, of course." Chloe looked at Tank and Leah, mouthing, *They're so cute.*

Tank probably shouldn't get a kick out of Rosie's grabby hands, but he did. Just as much of a kick as he did out of Junie's thoughtfulness.

"I didn't know you worked here," Leah said to Chloe.

"This is my home away from home. I'm the director, and it's serendipitous that you're here because Mads and I were just texting about you. She recently started doing puppetry with our residents, and we were both so impressed with the girls' memory blankets last night, we were wondering if you ever made them for others and sold them. There are lots of grandparents here, and they're always looking for unique gifts to give to family members."

"Oh gosh, *no*. They're not that good," Leah said.

"She's being modest," Tank said. "You saw them. They're incredible."

Leah gave him a disbelieving look.

"I have to agree with Tank," Chloe said. "They're really beautiful. If you're ever interested in branching out, I'd love to talk with you about it."

"Thank you. I appreciate that and I'll keep it in mind, but I don't really have time to do much other than work and take care of the girls."

"I understand," Chloe said.

The girls chose their stickers and thanked Chloe again just as she got pulled away to take a phone call. Junie put on her sticker of a frog, and Rosie ripped off the back of hers, sticking it in the middle of her shirt and exclaiming, "Cheeky bird!"

"Love that," Tank said with a chuckle. "What's your frog's name, Twitch?"

"He doesn't have one," Junie said. "He weminds me of Wiver."

Tank's chest constricted.

"River took them to the creek and they saw frogs. He told the girls a story about eating the frogs and growing a family of them in his belly," Leah explained with a wistful expression.

Hell if he didn't get choked up, too. "Come on, chickadees, let's go see Grandpa Mike."

The girls skipped in front of them singing, "Gwampa Mike! Gwampa Mike!"

Tank reached for Leah's hand. "You okay?"

She nodded. "I want them to remember River as often as they can."

He didn't know much about parenting, but as far as he could tell, Leah was as good a mother as his own, putting the needs of the girls, and previously of River, before herself. For a girl who became the guardian of a grieving teenager when she was just a kid herself, that was pretty fucking impressive.

His grandfather answered the door with his usual furrowed brow, but the minute he saw them, his face brightened. His brown polo shirt was tucked into a pair of tan dress pants, with a brown belt cinched tight, and shoes to match. Tank didn't know why it was, but his grandfather always looked frailer when he was at his apartment than he did when he was away from LOCAL.

"Hi, Gwampa!" Rosie shouted.

Mike grinned. "Hello there, Smiley. What a nice surprise." He shielded the side of his mouth, like he was sharing a secret with only the girls, and said, "Did you girls bring me some candy?"

They giggled and said, "No."

"Cookies?" he asked, eliciting more giggles and a unified "No."

"I bwought you a sticker." Junie held out the sticker of a puppy licking an ice cream cone.

"A sticker? Well, that's about as good as gold in my book." He took the sticker as they followed him into his apartment and put it on his shirt pocket. "This is about the best darn sticker I've ever seen."

The girls touched everything they saw. They sat for a bounce on the couch, climbed giggling into the recliner by the patio doors, and made their way to the shelving unit, intrigued by his grandfather's unsightly old television, which he refused to let Tank replace. There were several collages and pictures of Tank's late grandmother, his uncles and aunts, and the rest of their family, telling his grandfather's history all the way back to when he was a teenager.

The girls touched trinkets and pictures despite Leah following them around, saying, "Don't touch. Be careful."

Mike waved his hand dismissively. "Let 'em be. Things are made to be touched."

"They're good at accidentally breaking things," Leah warned.

"As long as they don't tear up my pictures, we're good."

"Y'all are too much," Leah said sweetly.

"Nonsense. What brings you here today?" Mike asked.

Leah went to him. "I wanted to say thank you for giving us the car. I tried to refuse it, but Tank wouldn't hear of it."

"That's because he's a good man." Mike nodded curtly at Tank.

"Well, I've never been given much of anything, and your family has spoiled us rotten. Thank you for being so generous." She hugged Mike.

"You want to thank me? Keep bringing these little ladies over to visit." He cocked a grin. "And a few cookies wouldn't hurt."

"I'll remember that for our next visit."

"Who dis?" Rosie asked, pointing to a picture of Tank when he was a little boy.

Mike said, "That's my boy Tank when he was just a little older than Juju."

Rosie's eyes bloomed wide. "He little!"

"Once upon a time, he sure was." Mike winked at Leah. "Did you meet Blaine yesterday? He's not as big as Tank, but he has bright blue eyes and he's always looking at pretty ladies."

The girls nodded, and Junie said, "He doesn't have stowies on here." She rubbed Mike's forearm.

Mike cocked a brow at Tank.

"*Tats*, Gramps," Tank explained. "That's right, Twitch. Blaine keeps most of his stories hidden under his clothes."

"Stories, huh? I like that," Mike said. "And I've got some good stories for you. Tank and Blaine were my first ice cream buddies."

"I like ice cweam!" Rosie said.

"Me too!" Junie said.

"Let's see if I've got some for you, then." Mike went into the kitchen, and the girls ran after him.

"You don't have to give them ice cream." Leah started after them.

Tank intercepted her, drawing her into his arms as Mike called out from the kitchen, "Grandpa's house, Grandpa's rules," and the girls giggled.

"Your family spoils us," she said softly.

"You and the girls deserve to be spoiled. You've shouldered a lot for years." He heard his grandfather getting out bowls and talking with the girls, so he lowered his lips to hers.

She looked nervously over her shoulder.

"They're too busy to look for us," he reassured her.

"Sorry," she said softly. "I'm sure you're used to women falling all over you, but I don't want to confuse the girls."

"I get it, but unless you'd rather I didn't, I'm going to take advantage of the few minutes we get when they're busy."

"I'd rather you *did*." She went up on her toes, meeting him halfway in a sweet, slow kiss.

"And now we're going to the *table*," Mike said loudly. He winked at Tank as they came into the room, leading the girls to the dining table. "I think Tank and your mama need some ice cream, too."

"Good idea," Tank said, and Leah blushed as he dragged her into the kitchen, away from little eyes, and kissed her again.

She tore her mouth away, whispering, "Your grandfather is

your *wingman*?"

Tank laughed. "He never has been in the past, but he's doing a hell of a job."

He lowered his lips to hers again, crushing her soft body to his as he deepened the kiss. She came away breathless and flushed.

"We are *not* doing this here," she whispered, and tugged him into the other room, blushing adorably.

"Hey, doll, can you grab that picture off the end table?" Mike pointed to the picture of their last family reunion before Tank's grandmother and Ashley died. "That's it. The one with all the people in it. The girls want to know about Tank's grandmother."

"She dead," Rosie announced.

"Rosie," Leah said exasperatedly as she handed Mike the picture, and she and Tank joined them at the table. "I'm sorry."

"It's okay. She's right." Mike looked thoughtfully at the picture. "This was the last picture with my entire family. See this beautiful woman? That's my Hilda, Tank's grandmother."

"She pwetty," Rosie said.

"Yes, she was, like your mama, and all the rest of these women. We Wickeds know how to pick 'em." Mike winked at Tank.

"And keep their pwomises," Junie said.

Mike gave Tank an approving glance. "That's right, little lady. Let me show you my family." He pointed to each of the people in the picture and told a little story about them as they ate their ice cream.

"Were you sad when Hilda went to heaven?" Junie asked.

"I was. I cried like a baby. When I lost her, I wasn't sure I could go on." Mike patted Tank's forearm. "But this guy came over every night and kept me company. We would get in the car, and some nights we'd drive for hours. Other times we went for ice cream, parked at the beach, and sat in the car eating and watching the sunset, talking about my Hilda."

Leah looked at Tank with so much emotion, he hugged her against his side, memories pummeling him of those difficult times after losing his grandmother. He'd been twenty-three when his grandmother died, and even now, nine years later, he couldn't fathom losing his grandfather, too.

"I fell in love with Hilda the first time I saw her," Mike told the girls. "I was only seventeen, but I'd been on my own for a year, and I knew I'd be with her forever."

"Why were you on your own?" Leah asked.

Mike sat back, his eyes narrowing. "My father ruled with an iron fist, and I'd gotten enough bruises to last a lifetime, so I took off at sixteen, met Hilda a year later, and when I turned eighteen, I put a ring on her finger. I never regretted it. We didn't have much, but we had love, and that was enough."

"I'm sorry you went through that," Leah said.

"It's okay, darlin'. We can't choose our parents, but we can choose how we live our lives." Mike ate a spoonful of ice cream and pointed to Ashley in the picture. "See this beauty? That's our Ashley, Tank's younger sister. She's in heaven, too."

Tank's gut twisted, and Leah put her hand over his.

Junie looked solemnly at Tank and said, "Were you sad when Ashley went to heaven?"

"Yeah, Twitch. Real sad," Tank admitted.

She tilted her head, her ringlets framing her serious face. "How did you get happy?"

He couldn't very well say that he hadn't been happy until Leah and the girls came into his life, so he told her the truth in a way she could handle. "I remembered all the good things about Ashley, and I spent a lot of time with my grandfather and my family."

"Eatin' ice cweam?" Rosie asked.

"Yeah, Cheeky. Eating ice cream, driving around, watching the sunset," Tank said.

"And, some days, watching the sunrise from the front seat of that car, too," Mike reminded him. "Tank would show up at my place at all hours of the night. Sometimes we'd sit on my porch and talk, but usually we went for a drive. Most of the mileage on your mama's car is from those drives. Tank and I could go hours *not* talking, staring out at the water. But the silence was filled with memories of our sweet Ashley. She was smilin' down on us then like she is now, from up in heaven with my Hilda."

"And Wiver and Gwampa Leo," Junie said.

"Probably. What do you think they're doing up there?" Mike asked.

"Havin' a pawty!" Rosie said.

"Watchin' us," Junie answered.

Mike patted their hands. "Maybe you're both right." He eyed Leah. "Do you have plans for the afternoon?"

"No." Leah glanced at Tank. "Do you?"

He shook his head, holding her gaze. "I'm all yours." Her cheeks pinked up, and he squeezed her hand.

"What do you say we finish up our ice cream and go for a ride in that old car?" Mike asked. "I could use a trip to the beach."

The girls cheered and finished their ice cream. As they headed out to the car, the girls holding Mike's hands and Leah tucked beneath Tank's arm, she said, "I *love* your grandfather."

He had an urge to make a joke about taking the old man down if she got too close to him, but honesty won out. "Me too, babe. Me too."

"You didn't tell me the car was so special to you. Are you sure you really want to give it to us?"

"That's *why* I want you to have it."

Chapter Eleven

LEAH SAT WITH Starr on the back porch, nibbling on Goldfish crackers and watching the three girls playing in the yard. Toys were scattered in the grass, and the inside of the house looked like it had been hit by a tornado, but the girls were so excited to play with Gracie, it was worth a little extra cleanup later. Starr had been texting and checking up on them in the week and a half since the funeral, and Leah and Starr had gotten closer. Starr and Gracie had even stopped by last Thursday for a quick visit while Tank was at work. Leah had forgotten how nice it was to have a girlfriend she could trust, and she'd needed a friend that day. She and the girls had missed Tank while he was at work even more than she'd thought they would.

"The girls seem to be doing well," Starr said as she grabbed a few crackers.

"For the most part they are, but it's been up and down. We're still getting used to our new normal. They can be like this one minute and crying for River, or just out of sorts, the next."

"It's got to be hard for them to understand." Starr tucked her long, kinky blond hair behind her ear, gazing at Leah empathetically. "And how about you? How are you *really* doing?"

"Same as them. Sometimes it seems like it's been months since we saw him, and other days I expect him to walk through the door and swing an arm over my shoulder, asking how his favorite sister is. I'm still not ready to go through his stuff."

"I noticed his guitar was still in the living room."

"I like seeing it there. I remember how final it felt when we went through my dad's stuff. I'm just not ready for that yet."

"You don't have to be. You'll know when it's the right time."

"That's true. Grief is so weird. I can be okay all day and think I'm getting my arms around it, but then when I put the girls down or I'm lying in bed, I start to miss him, thinking about how unfair it is that he's gone, and I blubber like a baby."

"I heard that Steph brought you a basket the other day."

"She came by Sunday with teas, oils, and ointments for me and goodies for the girls. I had no idea she was a poet. She wrote me a beautiful poem about the love between siblings."

"Her words are magical, aren't they? Has the stuff she brought helped? Your scar looks good."

"Thanks. I've been using the oils and ointments she gave me on it." She ran her finger over the scar on her forehead. The stitches had dissolved, and the doctor had said the scar would diminish over time. Her bruises had faded to yellowish-brown marks, and Tank lavished them with tender kisses every night. "But I haven't tried her sleep remedies yet." She watched Starr plucking crackers from the bowl, and her pulse quickened as she mustered her courage to tell her why. "Tank has been staying with me at night."

Starr looked at the girls playing with their dolls. "Camping out in his truck, right?"

"Not exactly. He's been staying in my bed, but he gets up before the girls in the morning." She couldn't believe she'd admitted that, but she desperately needed to talk to someone about it.

Starr whipped her head to the side, eyes wide. "*What?* You and Tank?"

"*Sorta? Kinda?*" Leah shrugged, wrinkling her nose in embarrassment and delight.

Starr gave her a deadpan look. "You have that big, delicious man in your bed and you don't *know* if you're together?"

"It's complicated. He's made it clear that he wants to be with me, with *us*, and I love being with him. He's good to us, and he makes *everything* better. I know he doesn't talk a lot to other people, but he does talk with me and the girls, and he *listens* and holds us when we're sad. He even bought me a journal to write down my memories of River so I never forget them." The gift had touched her deeply, and she wrote in it almost daily. It was cathartic, writing down her memories. "I can tell that he truly cares about us, but…"

"But…?"

"Let's just say that I don't think Steph's remedies can fix the things that are keeping me up at night."

"Like his massive pocket rocket?" Starr laughed.

I wish. "That's just it. He flirts with me a *lot*, and I swear, Starr, when he does, my entire body catches fire."

"And that's a problem, why, exactly?"

Leah lowered her voice. "Because he's a perfect gentleman. We kiss all the time, and let me tell you, that man should patent his mouth. I have never felt like I could, *you know*, from a kiss, but with his big body pressed against me, the way he grabs my hair, the things he says, and *the way* he kisses me." She fanned her face, breathing deeply.

"*Girl*, I'd give anything for a little of that."

"Hands off," Leah teased. "Lord have mercy if we do go further, because if he can *plant the field* with as much passion as the way he kisses me, he might need to revive me afterward."

"*Plant the field?*" Starr laughed.

"What do you call it? Knockin' boots? Butterin' the biscuit? Mattress dancin'?" They both laughed. "All I know is, while I'm thankful he's a gentleman, I can't take it. Does that make me a hoochie mama for saying that? Is it wrong to want to be closer to him when I just lost my brother?"

"*No.* Tank adores you, and he obviously adores the girls and knows how to comfort all of you. It makes you a *woman* who wants to be closer to a seriously sexy, good man."

"Thank you for that. I'm out of my league here, and it's really good to have someone to talk to about this stuff. The last time I was with a guy, I was eighteen, and so was he. Tank's a *man*." She whispered, "He's got nipple piercings."

Starr laughed. "You didn't know that?"

"Heck no. Not until I saw him shirtless. How did *you* know?"

"You can see them through his shirt when he doesn't wear his vest. Does that worry you? I don't think he's into BDSM or anything."

"I don't think he is, either. I just really like him, and I don't have as much experience as he does. What if I'm not good enough at all that?"

"I'm sure you're amazing at it, and if you're a little rusty, he seems very take-charge. I'm sure he'll show you the ropes."

"That's the problem," Leah whispered. "Short of grabbin' his *rope*, I'm not sure how to give him the green light without getting all flustered and coming across like a blitherin' fool."

"That's what you're worried about?" Starr patted her hand. "We can fix that. Are you seeing him tonight?"

"Yeah. He stays here every night. He's coming over after his church meeting," she said nervously.

"Perfect. All you've got to do is *show* him you're ready. Landscape your girlie bits, lotion up with something that smells seductive, throw on a super-sexy thong or panties, a shirt that bares *all* your cleavage, and wear a miniskirt or something else that gives him easy access, and then flirt your hot little ass off."

"My sexiest lingerie isn't very sexy."

"With you in it, it'll be scorching, trust me."

Leah was getting more nervous by the second. She looked down at her chest. "My cleavage hasn't seen the light of day in four years."

"Then it's about time for those puppies to come out to play. I'm excited for you. After all those months of him staring at you across the bar, and the way he takes care of you and the girls, when you two come together, it can't help but be perfect."

"Then why do I feel so nervous I could puke?"

Starr bumped her with her shoulder. "Because as you said, he's a lot of man and it's been a long time for you. But what you don't realize is that he's probably nervous, too. Whether you know it or not, *he* knows you're a whole lot of woman, and he's lucky to have you."

THE DARK KNIGHTS' clubhouse was located down the road from the Salty Hog. The old brick building had once been a schoolhouse and had been renovated to include a large meeting area in the main space with pool tables and dartboards off to the side. There was an office, a kitchen, and a few bedrooms upstairs. The Wednesday-night meeting was in full swing. Tank sat with his brothers and cousins, listening to his father and Preacher discuss club finances and prospects—the guys who were trying to become members—and encouraging members to sign up for their upcoming anti-bullying and suicide prevention talks at the local schools. Tank had already signed up for both.

As his father went into detail about dates and times, Tank's mind wandered back to Leah and the girls. Last week the girls had been sad that he wouldn't be there to say good night because he had to go to church. He'd tried to explain to them why the club meetings were important. But they'd wanted to come with him, and after five or six *why nots*, he'd finally told them the meetings were boring rather than try to explain that the club was for men only. Leah seemed to think he'd handled it well, but it was still bothering him. He'd called to check on them and to say good night to the girls before tonight's meeting, and they told him to have fun at his *bowing* meeting. Hearing theirs and Leah's sweet voices had made him long to see them, and it had taken everything he'd had not to tell Leah how much he missed her. But she didn't need that kind of pressure. It was enough that he got to hold her in his arms at night, even if he wanted a hell of a lot more.

Blaine nudged him. "You might want to pay attention. Preacher's talking about Trunk or Treat, and you know the girls would love that."

Every year the club hosted a Halloween event with games and contests. They dressed up in costumes, decorated their cars and trucks, loaded up the trunks and truck beds with candy, and roped off the clubhouse parking lot so children could roam safely under the watchful eyes of the Dark Knights.

"Thanks, man." Tank turned his attention to his uncle, who sat at the head table with the rest of the club officials, his dog Buster lying by his feet. Preacher had a commanding presence. He wore his salt-and-pepper hair slicked back, kept his silver beard trimmed short, and had tattoos down both arms. He was like a second father to Tank. People joked that Tank should have been Preacher's son because they were both broody and serious, while Conroy was playful and easygoing. All Tank knew was that he'd been blessed to be raised by the best men he knew—Conroy, Mike, and Preacher.

"Trunk or Treat is taking place on Halloween this year. That's five weeks from Saturday," Preacher announced. "We've got a sign-up sheet that we'll leave on the table for volunteers to help run games and coordinate parking. If any of the women in your lives want to help Reba and Ginger with baking and other goodies, please sign them up, too. Any and all help is appreciated."

Preacher wrapped up the meeting, and as guys got up to play pool, darts, and grab a beer, Tank pushed to his feet and said, "I'll see you guys Sunday." He planned on joining them for a ride while Leah and the girls were cooking with his mother and Madigan.

"You're taking off?" Zeke asked.

"Yeah. I want to see Leah."

Zeke nodded. "How is she doing?"

"You know. Tough road, but she's strong."

"I meant what I said about taking the girls on a hike when Leah's up to it," Zeke offered. "Or I can just take the girls and give her a break."

"Thanks, man. I appreciate it. Maybe in a couple of weeks."

Zander said, "I meant what I said, too. If it would help the girls to hear me play the guitar, I'm happy to swing by. Anything to make things easier for them."

"I really appreciate it, Zan. We'll set something up."

"You've been spending every night there since the accident," Gunner pointed out.

Tank held his stare. "Yeah, *and?*"

"Nothing man, it's cool." Gunner held his hands up. "I was just wondering if you two were a thing now."

Tank didn't know what they were, but it was a hell of a lot more than a *thing*. "I gotta go."

"Hold on." Gunner got up from his seat and limped toward Tank, dragging one leg behind him.

Tank didn't remember him limping when he'd come in. "What happened to you?"

"Your ball and chain got caught around my ankle." Gunner laughed.

Tank shoved him. "Go ahead, jackass, get all this shit out of your system."

Maverick chuckled. "Hey, man, you all gave me hell for a year about Chloe, remember?"

"That was fun," Tank said. "This is annoying."

Gunner clapped a hand on his shoulder. "I'm just razzin' you, man. Leah's great, and she's lucky to have your ugly mug watching out for her." He held his hand out toward the other guys and wiggled his fingers. "Pay up. Told you he was watching her all summer because he was into her."

"Y'all are idiots." Tank laughed as he headed for the door. He'd heard them placing bets in the weeks after Leah had first started working at the Hog, and truth be known, when he was younger, he'd done the same thing a time or two about them and other women. He waved to his father and Preacher. "See ya Sunday, Pops. G'night, Preach."

Preacher waved.

"Hold on, son. I'll walk out with you," Conroy called from across the room.

Tank waited by the door, watching his burly father close the distance between them. "What's up?"

"I just want to catch up with you. We haven't talked in a few days." They stepped into the brisk evening air, and his father walked with him toward his bike. "How are Leah and the girls?"

"You know, getting there." Tank pulled out his keys.

His father crossed his arms and lowered his chin, scrutinizing Tank. "And you?"

"I'm good." He said it too fast, and his father flinched.

"When you were seven, you'd say you were good and you meant it. After we lost Ash, you didn't even try to pretend you were okay." His father lowered his hands. "I couldn't be prouder of the man you've become, son. You're loyal, compassionate, and successful, but you can't lie worth shit."

They both laughed.

"Want to talk about it?" his father asked.

"It's not any one thing. I said something to the girls that I don't feel good about."

His father's brow furrowed. "Did you lose your temper? That's not like you."

"Nah, nothing like that. They wanted to come to the club, and instead of telling them the truth about why they couldn't, I told them they'd be bored."

"That's not so bad, Tank. They're young, and boredom is

something they can understand."

"That's what Leah said, but it's not sitting right with me. I gave them an easy answer to appease their curiosity, but that's not how I want to be with them, giving them answers that carry the wrong messages. You didn't bring us up like that. There's value in learning the reasons behind things, even if a kid doesn't like hearing it. I want them to understand the importance of the brotherhood and to teach them that life comes with commitments that they might think are boring but that isn't a reason to avoid them. I think I gotta set them straight over breakfast tomorrow."

His father cocked a grin.

"What?"

"I'm just so damn proud of you."

Tank scoffed. "For fucking up? Taking the easy way out?"

"For knowing you fucked up and wanting to fix it." His father held his gaze. "Thinking about the lessons you're teaching is how you know you've turned the corner from a guy who wants to hang out having beers and getting laid to a man who's ready to take care of a family."

His father's words hit him hard, and the truth came easily. "I've never thought about what comes out of my mouth as much as I did around Leah this summer, when she was skittish around me, and even more so around her and the girls these past couple of weeks. Hell, Dad, I've never felt so much, either."

"That accident didn't just change their lives, son. It changed *you*. We were all worried that we'd lose you again when River didn't make it. But those feelings you have for Leah have been growing for a long time, and I think they pulled you through, gave you a bigger purpose. The question is, does Leah feel the same?"

Tank shrugged. "I think so, but this is new territory for me. You know how I am. I usually like my space, and I like it quiet. But everything is different with Leah and the girls. I don't want that space anymore, and I sure as hell don't want quiet. When I'm with Leah, even when we're just texting or talking on the phone, there's this magnetic connection, an *energy*, that draws us together. It's stronger than anything I've ever felt before, and it's not just sexual. We haven't even crossed that line yet. What we have feels deeper and more powerful than *anything* else." He searched for a valid comparison. "Even family and my connection to the club. That's fucked up, right? To feel so much so fast?"

"You're asking the wrong guy. That's how I've felt about your mother since day one. I was walking down the sidewalk with my long hair and my helmet under my arm, wearing my leather jacket and boots, as cocky as Gunny, and she walked out of a café with a suit-and-tie guy. I swear to you, I saw her in slow motion, tossing her long hair over her shoulder and laughing. She was wearing a forest-green sweaterdress that showed off her long legs, and damn, son, I was all kinds of turned on. Our eyes connected for only a split second, but the earth moved."

Tank chuckled, having heard the story before. "For *you*."

"It did for her, too. She was just playing hard to get."

"You *stalked* her."

"No, I *wooed* her. There's a difference."

"Come on, old man. You went to the café every day for two weeks until you saw her again. That's the very definition of stalking."

"That's called determination, son." His father laughed. "And I'd do it all over again, because your mother is one of a kind. She's the leather to my ride, the buckles on my boots, and the other half of my heart, and she always will be."

Tank scrubbed a hand down his face. "So you don't think I'm nuts?"

"Hell no. You're an all-or-nothing guy, always have been. Ever since we lost Ash, you've been going through the motions of living your life. Now you've met a beautiful, smart woman and two very special little girls who have completely stolen your heart and made you want to get back in the game. That's not nuts, son. That's fate."

Chapter Twelve

TANK THOUGHT ABOUT fate all the way to Leah's cottage. Was it fate that had taken Ashley and River away? If so, fate was a nasty bitch. Or were there different types of fate? Good and bad? Any way he cut it, he didn't want the very thing that had brought him and Leah together to be connected to the deaths of their loved ones. But as he climbed the porch steps, he knew separating them was an impossibility. He'd be a different man if he hadn't lost Ashley. Would Leah have given him a second look if she hadn't felt his suffocation? Would they have come together sooner? Spent the summer falling for each other, with their families inclusive of River and Ashley?

He leaned his forearm against the doorframe, taking a second to push those wonders away. He knew better than anyone that there was no changing the past. But when he closed his eyes, he saw Leah front and center, just as he had for the past several months, and he knew in his gut that even if they'd been on two separate continents, they'd eventually have found each other, because soul-deep connections were once in a lifetime.

The door opened before he knocked, and his body ignited at the sight of Leah in a sexy plaid miniskirt and one of his faded Wicked Ink shirts. The short sleeves hung to her elbows, and she'd knotted the shirt just below her waist. Her wild curls billowed around her beautiful face. She tilted her head to the side, rolling her bottom lip between her teeth the way she did when she was nervous, and licked her lips.

Fuuck.

She gazed up at him through her long, dark lashes, blushing, innocent and sexy as hell as she said, "Hi," just above a whisper. "The girls are sleeping."

He lowered his arm from the doorframe, his heart hammering against his ribs as he pulled her close and touched his forehead to hers, breathing her in. He struggled to gain control of his raging desires, but it was like holding back a bike with an open throttle, and the truth growled out. "How am I supposed to keep my hands off you when you're dressed like that?"

HE SMELLED LIKE leather and lust, and the desire in his voice sent what felt like *years* of spine-tingling anticipation slamming into Leah. Her well-thought-out words were lost to the need pounding between them, and *"Tank"* came out with a nervous laugh.

"What, sexy girl?" He kissed her neck.

"You're crazy. I wanted to dress sexy for you, but it's been so long since I've dressed that way, it felt weird, so I threw on your shirt."

His eyes bored into her. "Baby, don't you know how I feel about you? You don't have to *try* to be sexy. It's innate. It's in your eyes, your smile, the way you roll your lower lip into your mouth. It's how you mother the girls and weather storms for them." He brushed his lips over her cheek, spreading heat like wildfire through her core. "You could wear a hazmat suit and I'd still be walking around half-cocked, because you're *you*, and I'm me, and we're fucking combustible."

"Tank," she panted out.

He tightened his hold on her and slicked his tongue around the shell of her ear. "Nothing is hotter than seeing you in my shirt."

He nipped her earlobe, sending lightning to her very lonely lady parts. It was a good thing he was holding her up, because her knees gave out.

He tightened his hold on her and said, "So tell me, beautiful, how am I supposed to keep my hands off you?"

He grazed his teeth on the sensitive skin just below her ear and sealed his mouth over her neck, drawing out her lustful response. *"You're not."*

He pulled back just enough for his dark eyes to pin her in place, searching for answers to silent questions, every passing second making her heart beat faster, her body flame hotter. She managed a nod, hoping he got the message, and his lips came down over hers, kissing her *once, twice.* Every press of his lips sparked little fires within her, until her entire body pulsed with them. He continued the titillating temptations, kissing her longer, deeper, and slower, making her pulse pound faster, her chest flutter with anticipation. How was it possible a man that big and strong could kiss like a gust of hot, glorious wind, sweeping her up in them until they felt like one being?

His arm tightened around her as he stepped into the house without breaking their kisses. In one swift move, he closed the door and pinned her against it with his hard body. His arousal pressed into her stomach, and a needy sound escaped her lips, drawing a hungry growl in return. He intensified his efforts, taking the kiss deeper and rocking against her, sending her body into a frenzy of passion and need. His beard abraded her skin, but she didn't care. She wanted to feel *all* of him, his lips, tongue, teeth, fingers, hands, and all his other fiercest parts. Just when she was sure she'd melt into a pool of lava, he framed her face between his rough hands, gazing into her eyes with so much emotion and desire it brought a lump to her throat.

"God, Lee," he said huskily. "You're *everything...*"

She pulled his mouth back to hers, unable to wait. He lavished her with more intoxicating kisses. *"I missed you,"* he whispered, his warm breath trailing over her flesh between urgent kisses. *"I want you."* His affection was addicting, his greediness contagious. He devoured her, and when he tore his mouth away, gritting out, "I need to feel you beneath me," "Yes" rushed from her lips.

He crushed himself to her from mouth to knees and every delicious point in between. He lifted his foot, trying to work his boot laces free without breaking their kisses, but they both ended up laughing, and he left her a panting, dizzy mess of desire and quickly removed them. She pushed at his vest, and he shrugged it off and tugged his shirt over his head, dropping it to the floor. His hands dove into her hair and fisted as he angled her mouth beneath his, taking her in a penetrating kiss that sang through her veins, drawing her deeper into them. She felt his piercings through her clothes, bringing a thrill of the unknown. But it was the fullness in her heart, the rampant crying out for the man whose emotions were as real as the moon, who treasured her girls and felt her grief as his own, that had her bowing off the door, winding her arms around his neck and whispering, "Bedroom."

Their mouths fused together as he lifted her into his arms. Her legs wound around his waist, and he carried her into the bedroom and closed the door. He pulled the blanket back and lowered them to the mattress. Their eyes collided for a hot second, and she swore time stood still. Was she even breathing? His mouth came coaxingly down over hers in a kiss so sweet and sensual, her thoughts fractured. They kissed and groped, hips rocking, gyrating, *grinding*, their needy moans filling the air. He trapped her lower lip between his teeth, tugging just hard enough to send heat searing down her body. Her eyes flew open, and his wolfish grin sent shivers of desire racing through her.

He trailed openmouthed kisses down her neck, slowing to suck and nip, his every touch taking her higher. He pushed up her shirt, and she rose off the mattress, allowing him to take it off. Her bra went next, and his eyes roamed over her bare breasts. She thought she'd be even more nervous when he saw her pale, freckled body, but he licked his lips, wickedness pooling in his eyes.

"Jesus, baby. You're a fucking goddess. *My* goddess." He kissed her again, slow and tender. "I'm going to take away all your pain and make you feel so good, you'll never want to leave this bed." He brushed his lips over hers. "That's a promise."

Wickeds always keep their promises. Her body shuddered in anticipation.

He lowered his mouth to hers, taking her in another toe-curling kiss. She couldn't think, could barely breathe, as he moved lower, exploring with his hands and mouth, kissing, sucking, licking, groping, caressing, until she was shaking and whimpering with need. He dragged his tongue around her nipple as his hand slid up her thigh and beneath her skirt. He teased her through her panties and she lifted her hips, needing more. His eyes drilled into hers, stringing her nerves tighter. But he didn't strip off her panties. He moved his thumb over them, expertly working that bundle of nerves through the thin material.

Her breath hitched as mind-numbing sensations slithered down her core, radiating outward to her fingers and toes. A slow smile curved his lips, as if he felt her pleasure as his own. He lowered his mouth over her nipple, sucking it to the roof of his mouth. She gasped, her eyes slamming shut at the scintillating pleasures consuming her. She fisted her hands in the sheets as he sucked and stroked until she was gasping for air, hanging on to her sanity by a fast-fraying thread. When he grazed his teeth over her nipple, pinpricks skittered over her flesh, and she thrashed beneath him.

He tore his mouth away. "Too much?"

"Heavens *no*."

She grabbed his head, guiding his mouth to her breast again, and he worked her into a blithering mess, sucking her nipple so hard she lost all control. Her hips bucked, a stream of greedy sounds flying from her lungs. He captured those sounds in a punishingly intense kiss, stroking between her legs so perfectly, her climax ravaged her. When she finally came down from the high, he eased their kisses to a new realm of pleasure, one that pulsed through her, drawing out moans and mewls and leaving her light-headed. Her heart hammered against her ribs as her eyes fluttered open, but her body was still electrified, and they closed again.

He brushed his beard over her cheek, reigniting the fire within her, and kissed her cheek, speaking huskily into her ear. "I cannot wait to taste you."

Lord, he had a wicked mouth.

And she freaking loved it.

She lay trying to catch her breath as he kissed a path between her breasts, down her stomach, and licked circles around her belly button. His tongue lapped over it and delved inside. He sealed his mouth over it like it was her mouth, or her promised land, and holy moly, what that did to her! She was going to pass out from pleasure, she just knew it. Her body vibrated with anticipation as he curled his fingers into the waist of her panties and skirt, his eyes flicking up to hers.

Her nerves came alive as she lifted her hips, giving him the approval he sought. He slowly stripped off her bottoms, kissing the skin he bared all the way down to her ankles. His jaw tightened and his eyes drifted slowly up the length of her, hovering over her sex, then lingering on her breasts. His chest heaved with his every breath as he crawled over her body, perching above her, and kissed her softly.

He brushed his nose along her cheek, whispering, "I'm so lucky to be yours."

She melted like butter in the sun. It was such an intimate comment, it made their connection feel even more special. He kissed her again, light as a feather, and stepped from the bed to strip off his jeans and socks, his eyes never leaving her. She was lost in her own visual devouring, drinking in the tattoos snaking down his abs, over the broad head of his cock breaching the waist of his black boxer briefs. If desire were a drug, she'd be wasted. Her eyes trailed down the rigid outline of his shaft, over the tattoos decorating his muscular thighs as he crawled onto the bed, settling on his knees between her legs.

Their eyes locked as he ran his hot hands down her hips, trailing kisses in their wake. He kissed his way up her inner thigh, and her nerves caught fire. Her eyes closed, and he nipped at her sensitive skin, bringing them open again.

"I want to see the pleasure in your eyes. Keep them open."

*Lord have mercy...*She met his hungry gaze, trying to ignore the heated blush crawling up her chest and neck as he splayed his hands over her inner thighs and opened her to him. He dragged his tongue along the very heart of her, and she nearly jumped out of her skin, earning an appreciative guttural sound from him. He lowered his mouth over her sex, and holy mother of...Her eyes closed, her hips moving with him, as she ground against his mouth, whimpering and moaning. Every slick of his tongue brought a jolt of pleasure, a rock of her hips. When he pushed his fingers inside her, finding that secret spot with laser precision, and used his mouth on her other sensitive bundle of nerves, she bowed off the bed. Scintillating sensations built up inside her with every stroke and glide of his tongue, every graze of his teeth. He quickened his efforts, and she nearly shot through the roof, crying out his name. She covered her mouth, clamping it closed to keep from waking the girls, and he didn't relent. He continued his masterful ministrations as she surrendered to the ecstasy consuming her, until she collapsed to the mattress, limp as a rag doll, her body jerking with aftershocks.

He kissed his way up her body, slowing to suck one of her nipples, sending her overly sensitive body into another frenzy of explosions. Then he gathered her trembling body in his arms, raining kisses over her cheeks as she tried to get her brain to function.

"How's my girl?"

"I can't...move," she panted out.

He laughed softly and kissed her. "You don't have to."

She snuggled closer, loving the feel of his body against hers.

He nuzzled against her neck, pressing a kiss there, and whispered, "I just found my new favorite pastime."

She buried her face in his chest, unable to stop grinning, and said, "And I thought sewing was fun," earning a rare, rumbly laugh.

TANK AWOKE TO the sound of Junie whimpering at three in the morning. Leah was fast asleep beside him, her beautiful mane spread across the pillow, his T-shirt billowing around her body, one butt cheek covered in blue panties peeking out. He slipped quietly out of bed, pulled on his jeans, and went into the girls' room.

Junie was curled up around Mine, whimpering in her sleep. Tank sat beside her and brushed her springy curls away from her face. He caressed her forehead, soothing her back to sleep, and glanced at Rosie, sleeping with Boo on her pillow. His thoughts turned to River, and the accident came roaring back, bringing with it the agonizing terror that had gripped him as he'd seen the truck slam into their car and the *"No!"* that had torn from his chest as the car had careened into the water. The rush of relief that had swamped him when he'd dragged Leah and the girls up to the surface returned. He could still feel the burning in his lungs as he'd fought to save River.

He leaned forward, elbows on his knees, and lowered his face to his hands, gritting his teeth, wishing he could bring the girls' father back.

Their *father.*

It was hard to believe that young boy he'd tried to save had already been through so much and had brought these precious girls into the world. He looked at the girls, damn thankful they were safe, and his father's words came back to him. Was *fate* a thing? Had the universe known Leah would need the girls as much as they needed her? Or that Tank hadn't just saved the three of them but that *they* had rescued him? Was there a universal plan that they didn't have knowledge of? Was that fate?

He'd thought his need to protect his family had been the strongest emotion he'd ever feel, but man was he wrong. His need to protect Leah and the girls was brutal, and the other, softer emotions that had been pooling inside him and now filled him to the brim were even more visceral. With that realization, something else came into focus. The loss he felt from Ashley's death couldn't be half as devastating as what his parents felt for their loss. How had they managed to put the well-being of the rest of their children ahead of their own despair?

He pushed to his feet, and he didn't have to look far, because the amazingly strong woman watching him from the doorway had done the very same thing for those two little sleeping beauties. His feelings for Leah bubbled over as he put his arm around her and kissed her cheek, whispering as they went back to her room. "Junie was making noises in her sleep, but she's okay."

"You should have woken me up."

"You needed to sleep." He sat on the edge of the bed, knowing he needed to go out to the couch, and not wanting to.

She stepped between his legs, and he wrapped his arms around her, feeling her heart beating against his cheek as she kissed the top of his head. She ran her fingers through his hair, and damn that felt good. She felt so fucking right in his arms, stirring all those emotions he'd been trying to tamp down. He ached to be closer, but he knew she was tired and forced himself to stand. "I'd better go out to the couch."

She slid a finger into one of his belt loops, holding his gaze as she pressed her sexy lips to his chest. She continued kissing his chest, her shaky hands moving up his torso as she slicked her tongue over his nipple, teasing the piercing. Heat streaked to his balls.

"*Christ*, Lee." He grabbed her ass, holding her against his erection so she could feel what she was doing to him. She teased one nipple with her mouth, the other with her fingers, driving him out of his fucking mind. He reached over with one hand and closed the door, bringing her eyes to his. Her tongue darted out and circled his nipple. He gritted his teeth. "*Fuck*, baby, don't stop."

She lowered her mouth over his piercing as he pulled her panties down, and they puddled at her feet. He grabbed her ass with one hand, working her clit with the other. She moaned around his nipple, and he quickened his efforts. Her eyes closed, and her head fell back.

"I need your mouth on me," he growled, and she dragged her tongue over and around his piercing. "Tug it with your teeth." She tugged his piercing, and he groaned. "Fuck yeah. *Again*."

He pushed his fingers inside her, using his thumb on her clit as they drove each other wild. She gasped several quick inhalations, her legs flexing. He grabbed her hair, taking her in a punishingly intense kiss as he worked her faster, sending her over the edge. She cried out into their kisses, her hips thrusting, inner muscles clenching tight around his fingers as he swallowed her sinful sounds. As she came down from the clouds, he tore his mouth away, guiding hers back to his nipple, but her trembling hands moved lower, working the button on his jeans open and pushing them down. As he stepped out of them, she palmed him through his briefs.

He grabbed her wrist. "Baby, you're playing with fire. I haven't been with anyone since I set eyes on you."

"You…" She swallowed hard. *"Really?"*

The emotions in her voice brought his lips to hers in a passionate, promissory kiss. "There's only you, darlin'."

All the emotions he'd heard coalesced with a seductive look that reached all the way up to her eyes, and she kissed a trail down his stomach, every touch of her lips making his cock jerk with anticipation. She yanked down his briefs, and his erection sprang free, slapping against his stomach. Her eyes widened, brimming with desire as she wrapped her delicate fingers around his shaft and dragged her tongue across the broad head, sending heat blazing through him. His hips rocked forward. Her gaze darted up to his for only a second, as if she were checking in with him, and then she licked him from base to tip. His beard hit his chest with a *hiss*, and she glanced up again. Curious innocence looked back at him, and he realized this was new for her. His emotions reeled, and two thoughts moved to the forefront of his mind. He was the luckiest motherfucker on the planet to be with Leah, and if he continued standing while she had her mouth on him, he was likely to thrust his dick so far down her throat she'd choke.

He took her hand and lifted her to her feet. "You don't have to do this."

"I want to," she said, pink cheeked.

Her trust felt like a gift. "God, Lee. You *slay* me." He kissed her deeply and sat on the edge of the bed, bringing her between his legs. "Get on your knees, baby. You'll be more comfortable."

She knelt before him, trapping her lower lip between her teeth. He leaned forward and kissed her lip free.

"Lift up on your knees." When she did, he took her hand, licking it from fingertip to palm, and wrapped it around his cock. "Work me tight and suck me hard."

She lowered her mouth over his cock, moving slowly, her hand following her lips along his shaft. Watching her pleasuring him was the hottest thing he'd ever seen, but her careful movements had him grinding his teeth, needing more. He covered her hand with his, squeezing tighter. "Hold it like you *need* it, baby." She tightened her grip. "That's it. Suck harder." He pushed his hands into her hair as she sucked harder and stroked tighter. It took all his restraint to let her set her pace. *"So good,"* he gritted out between clenched teeth.

Her efforts intensified as her confidence grew. She reached for his nipple ring, and he pressed her hand against his chest.

"You do that and I'll come hard and fast." He kissed her palm. "I'm not done with your mouth yet, sweetheart."

She smiled around his cock and worked him faster, tighter, and so damn perfect, it took everything he had to keep from coming. He reached between her legs, his fingers gliding through her wetness. She inhaled sharply, her beautiful eyes flicking up to his as she loved him with her mouth.

"You didn't think I wasn't going to take care of my special girl, did you?"

Appreciation glittered in her eyes. He pressed on her clit, and she moaned, her eyes closing. They pleasured each other right up to the edge of madness. "I want to come in your mouth," he growled. "If you don't want that, tell me now."

She sucked harder, worked him faster.

"My fucking goddess. Don't stop sucking while you come, baby. It'll make it even better for both of us."

He quickened his efforts between her legs, and her eyes squeezed closed. She sucked harder. Heat skated down his spine, and just as her climax gripped her, he gave in to his own powerful release. He gritted out her name as their bodies rocked and jerked. She rode his fingers, loving him with her mouth and taking everything he had to give, until they both went limp. He leaned over her, threading his fingers into her hair, and gently tugged her head back. Her cheeks were flushed, her lips swollen and red, her eyes dazed.

He brushed his lips over hers. "Nothing has ever felt as good as being close to you." He punctuated his words with a passionate kiss and lifted her into his lap. He gathered her hair in one hand, caressing her jaw with the other. "Did I hurt you?"

She shook her head with a small, sated smile and rested her head on his shoulder. He held her for a long time, reveling in their closeness, the new level of intimacy binding them together. Eventually they put clothes on. Then he gathered her in his arms and gazed into her sleepy eyes, wanting nothing more than to sleep beside her and knowing she needed him to be strong enough not to. "I'll be on the couch, darlin'."

"Can you hold me first?"

So much for his strength. "Of course."

She climbed into bed and he lay behind her, as he had every night for the last week. Only this time she turned in his arms, kissing him, and whispered, "Thank you."

"For what?"

She was quiet for the longest time before saying, "For being you."

Unsure how to respond, he kissed her forehead, thinking

about what she meant as she drifted off to sleep. He was still thinking about it when he headed into the living room. He lay on the couch and closed his eyes, resting his forearm over them. His thoughts were so full of Leah, he knew without a shadow of a doubt that the parts of himself he gave to her and the girls couldn't exist for anyone else. He lowered his arm, realizing how he should have responded to her.

I'm only me because you're you.

Maybe they were fated to be after all.

Chapter Thirteen

GINGER HADN'T BEEN kidding about making a day out of cooking while Tank and the guys went for their Sunday ride. Leah and the girls had arrived after lunch, and Ginger and Madigan had shuttled them straight to the grocery store. Growing up with a busy single father, Leah had learned that errands should be handled swiftly, with no dallying. She carried that lesson forward the way she did everything he'd taught her and had always tried to have River watch the girls while she shopped, because it took twice as long with them in tow. But Ginger doled out lessons like she did hugs, as if she had a never-ending supply, suggesting that kids took pride in learning responsibility and would enjoy cooking more and develop a better appreciation for it if they were included in every step of the process. That seemed a heavy load for such little girls, but as the girls collected ingredients, picked out pears and vegetables and put them in baggies, she saw pride on their little faces at their jobs well done.

Now Ginger's kitchen was filled with laughter, chatter, and the sounds of Ginger and Madigan singing to music playing on an old-fashioned radio on the counter. The girls had been as intrigued by the radio as they had been by Mike's old television set. Madigan danced as she made pie crust, taking the girls' hands and spinning them around the room, which looked like it had been hit by a hurricane. The countertops were covered with dozens of ingredients and dishes in various stages of preparation. There was flour everywhere, and Junie and Rosie were sticky messes, but they were having the best time. They'd helped make two loaves of corn bread and two trays of sliced zucchini fries with Parmesan cheese, which were ready for the oven, and an enormous pot of homemade marinara sauce loaded with vegetables and Grandma Hilda's famous meatballs, which was simmering on the stove. The girls had made the oddly shaped meatballs, some as small as peas, others the size of baseballs, because Junie had insisted that *Tank needs big ones*, to which Rosie had added, *He a pig!*

"Like this, *Gingy*?" Junie asked.

Leah loved the nickname her girls had coined for Ginger. She looked up from the pears she was cubing for Tank's and Conroy's favorite dessert, pear and cranberry crumble, and warmed at the sight of her girls standing on stools on either side of Ginger. They were using rolling pins on mounds of dough for buttermilk biscuits. The three of them wore bibbed aprons and chef hats that were frayed and stained. They were the same aprons and hats that Ginger had used with her own children, which made the wonderful day feel even more special.

"Yes. That's perfect." Ginger patted Junie's hand.

"I perfect!" Rosie exclaimed as she pushed her rolling pin over the dough.

Ginger tapped Rosie's nose. "Yes, you are, Rosie Posey. Maybe you and Junie will grow up to be cooks."

Rosie beamed.

"I'm going to draw stowies on people when I get bigger,"

Junie said.

Ginger put her hand over her heart with a dreamy expression. "I think that's a lovely idea." She got that dreamy look in her eyes a lot around the kids.

"Juju, why do you want to draw stories?" Madigan asked as she made the topping for the crumble.

"So people never forget them." Junie rolled the dough. "I'm gonna get Wiver on me like Tank has."

"Me too!" Rosie patted her stomach. "Wight he*ah*."

Ginger and Madigan looked curiously at Leah.

"He tattooed River's name on the left side of his stomach. I didn't know he'd done it until afterward," Leah explained.

"I'm not surprised," Ginger said. "All of his tattoos are meaningful."

Leah had recently found that out. They'd spent the last few nights exploring each other's bodies. Between steamy kisses and mind-numbing orgasms, she'd traced many of his tattoos, and he'd shared the stories behind them. They hadn't gone all the way yet, but there was an intimacy, a closeness between them, that she'd never imagined possible. Tank was gentle when he needed to be and more aggressive when they both wanted it. He was patient, helping her discover how she liked to be touched, bringing her such intense pleasure, she was sure everyone felt the earth move just as she did. She could only imagine what it would be like when they finally made love.

"Sunshine and Whiskey" came on the radio, and Madigan squealed, pulling Leah from her thoughts. "I love this song!" She danced around the island, pulling Leah out to dance with her. "Come on, girl, swing those hips."

Leah laughed. "I haven't danced since I was eighteen and worked at a music store." She used to walk to work with her earbuds in, dancing along the way.

"All the more reason to do it now." Madigan put her hands up, swinging her hips as she danced around Leah.

The girls laughed, and Ginger said, "Come on, girls. Let's show Mama how it's done."

The four of them danced and giggled, and Leah couldn't help but join in. She was embarrassed at first, but it was so fun, she let herself go, and soon she felt the music in her veins, just as she used to.

"Go, Leah!" Madigan cheered.

They laughed and danced until they were all out of breath. Leah couldn't remember the last time she'd had so much fun.

The girls finished preparing the biscuits and began making trail-mix cookies. Ginger was brilliant when it came to cooking with kids. She gave them each a bowl, so they could make their own batches of cookie dough without fighting.

Madigan and Leah finished getting the crumble ready to bake and began cleaning up. Madigan pulled Leah over to the sink as she washed a bowl and said, "Now that little ears are distracted, is something going on with you and Tank?"

Leah's nerves tingled. She wondered if Starr had said something. "Why do you ask?"

"Oh, I don't know," she said sarcastically. "Maybe because the sparks between you two could ignite an ocean."

Leah could hardly suppress her smile.

Madigan whispered, "This makes me *so* happy."

"I didn't *say* anything."

"You didn't have to."

Junie and Rosie giggled and told on each other as they gobbled down chocolate chips and pretzels.

"Save some for the cookies," Leah said as she collected more dishes.

"It's okay, honey," Ginger reassured her. "I learned a long time ago to let kids enjoy the prep time. Otherwise you end up with a Gunner catastrophe."

"What's a Gunner catastrophe?" Leah asked.

"Just one of the many times my boys nearly gave me a heart attack," Ginger said. "The kids and I were making cookies the week before Christmas when Gunny was six. He kept eating handfuls of chocolate chips, and Tank got on him about it. The next thing we knew, Gunny was gone. We searched high and low for him. Ashley got teary, Baz put together a search plan, and Tank was just so angry with himself, he could barely see straight. I called Con, and twenty minutes later the neighborhood was full of Dark Knights searching for our boy. They found him asleep in a cabinet in the garage, clutching the empty bag of chocolate chips. From then on, I learned to buy extra everything and decided snacking was permissible when cooking."

"You must have been terrified," Leah said.

"I was, but Tank was even more so. After we found Gunny, Tank didn't let him out of his sight for a month."

"I can see him doing that. He's so protective, even of me and the girls," Leah said.

Ginger helped Junie and Rosie mix their ingredients. "He's quite taken with you and your little ladies."

Leah felt her cheeks warm. "We are of him, too." *Of all of you, really.* They'd taken the girls to visit Grandpa Mike again a few days ago, and they'd had such a good time, she hoped to be able to take them to see him more often.

"If you ever need a babysitter, you know who to call," Madigan interjected. "I'd love to spend more time with the girls."

"Thanks, but we don't really go out without them."

"You should," Ginger said softly. "I know you've got a lot on your plate, and I remember how being happy brought guilt and other hard feelings after we lost Ashley. But *you-know-who* are learning from you, and having gone through something similar, I wish I'd done things a little differently. It's important that they see you grieve, but it's equally important to show them it's okay to keep living. We only have one turn at this amazing life we're given, and we need to make the most of it." She pushed her glasses to the bridge of her nose. "And here I go spouting off like I'm your mother. I'm sorry."

"Actually, Tank said something like that to me a couple of weeks ago. I needed to hear it again. Thank you."

"Any time you want to talk," Ginger said compassionately. "I'm here."

"Okay, enough mush," Madigan teased. "Let's get these cookies done and go through the pictures before I have to leave to meet Zander." She and Zander were writing a song together.

"Pictures?" Leah asked.

"I thought you and the girls might get a kick out of seeing pictures of Tank and the boys when they were younger," Ginger said as Rosie shoved a handful of chocolate chips into her mouth, and Junie admonished her.

"They're so stinking cute." Madigan took out her phone to take a picture of Rosie with her cheeks full of chips and Junie scowling, but the second she held up her phone, Rosie grinned and chips fell from her mouth.

"Ew! Wosie!" Junie hollered.

Rosie laughed, sending chips flying in all directions. Junie ran away, giggling, which made Rosie laugh harder, spewing spittle and causing the rest of them to erupt into laughter.

They cleaned the kitchen *again* and scrubbed the girls' hands and faces.

"I'm sorry about the cookies," Leah said.

"We have plenty of other food, and the fun was worth it." Ginger put her arm around Leah as they headed into the living room. "You know what I always say? A house full of laughter is a home full of love."

"I couldn't agree more, even if it's not always easy." Leah's father might not have said those words, but it described how they'd lived, and in turn, how she and River had lived.

Ginger hugged her against her side. "You'll get there again. I promise."

The living room was warm and inviting, with deep-cushioned couches, oversized chairs, and French doors that led to a large patio and a beautiful yard. Ginger opened a chest that was against the wall and pulled out a photo album. "Let's sit on the couch."

Junie sat on Leah's lap, and Rosie sat on Madigan's, with Ginger between them as Ginger showed them pictures of her and Conroy on their wedding day.

"Pwetty," Rosie said.

"That's me and Conroy on our wedding day," Ginger said.

"That's not Conwoy," Junie said. "His hair is the *wong* color."

"That's him, sweetie. When he was younger, he had black hair like Tank. We were *so* young. I was only twenty-two when we got married."

"Can you imagine being married that young?" Madigan shook her head.

"I was parenting River at eighteen, and Junie came along

when I was twenty, and then Rosie. Twenty-two doesn't seem too young to be married. Was it love at first sight for you, Ginger?"

"Yes. I knew the *second* I saw him swaggering toward me in his leather jacket and black boots, with that arrogant grin plastered on his face, that he was *the one*. That grin *still* gives me goose bumps. But he was *so* full of himself. Imagine Zander and Gunny put together. That was Con." Ginger laughed softly. "God, he was something."

"And you've been together from that moment on?" Leah asked.

"Oh, no, sweetheart. I played hard to get. But I never stood a chance. The Wicked men are a special breed. Ask Reba—she'll tell you. It's like they have a homing device to their one true love, and when Conroy's and Preacher's hearts spoke, ours had to listen."

"Hear that, Leah?" Madigan teased. "It's you and Tank forever."

Leah opened her mouth to dispute that she and Tank were getting that serious, but she'd never felt so connected, understood, and protected, and she couldn't bring herself to say otherwise.

"Don't scare her away, Mads," Ginger said.

"You're the one touting true love," Madigan said. "I know better. The Dark Knights might be loyal as all get out, but other guys aren't. One broken heart is enough for me."

"Your heart bwoken?" Rosie kissed Madigan's shoulder. "Better?"

"Much." Madigan nuzzled against Rosie's cheek.

"What happened?" Leah asked.

"That's a story for another time and a pitcher of margaritas," Madigan said. "But I'm fine. My life is way too busy for romance."

"Honey, if we all waited for the right time, we'd be single forever. I know you're not big on love right now, Mads, but when it hits, you won't be able to walk away." Ginger lowered her voice. "By the way, I've never admitted to Con that he had me at *that* grin, so keep that to yourselves. What's said among us girls stays among us girls."

She showed them baby pictures of Tank, with big dark eyes and pudgy cheeks, and pictures of him through the years. The girls couldn't believe Tank had ever been so little. There were pictures of Tank and his siblings and cousins sledding and playing at the beach. A few stood out to Leah, like one of Tank at seven years old, sitting on a couch holding one-year-old Ashley so tight, he looked like he wasn't going to let anyone take her away.

The girls got fidgety and went to play with the toys Leah had brought, while Leah continued looking at pictures with Madigan and Ginger. They came to one of Tank and his siblings standing in a field in the rain. Tank was tall and thick waisted and looked to be about fifteen, his dark hair hanging into his eyes, his boyish, handsome face free from stubble and piercings. He had his arms around Baz and Blaine, and Ashley and Madigan were sitting on the wet ground by their feet, looking up with their mouths open, catching raindrops.

"Remember that festival, Mads?" Ginger didn't wait for an answer. "We go to a music festival in Barnstable every year. We got rained out that time, but it was still fun."

"We should take Leah and the girls next time," Madigan said.

"We'd love that," Leah said, imagining how fun it would be.

Her thoughts tiptoed back to River and how much he'd have enjoyed going to a music festival. That brought a pang of longing, but it didn't bring tears this time, only a realization that he'd want them to go and enjoy it. It was a bittersweet feeling.

They looked through holiday photos and school pictures with goofy grins, pictures of Baz with all sorts of animals he'd brought home over the years, and several pictures of all the siblings helping a humanity group get beached whales back into the water. There were pictures of the kids on their parents' motorcycles. They came to a picture of Tank sitting on a motorcycle with a glimmer of pride in his eyes. Ashley sat behind him with her arms folded on his back, her cheek resting on them, and the happiest expression lighting up her eyes.

"That was Tank's first bike. He bought it right after his eighteenth birthday." Ginger ran her finger over the picture. "He'd worked at the restaurant and got an online job illustrating graphic novels through high school and saved all his money to buy that bike. That was the first time he took it out. I'll never forget the way Ashley had bounced on her toes, trying to keep from begging him to take her with him. She always wanted to go wherever Tank did, and we'd told her she couldn't beg him for his first ride. But he'd taken one look at her and said, 'Get up here.'" She paused with a thoughtful expression. "Ashley was on that bike in three seconds flat."

"I love that about him," Leah said.

"Me too," Ginger agreed.

"Look, Mama!" Rosie ran over with a sparkly blue-and-white skirt.

"That's Ashley's middle school cheerleading skirt. You girls must have gotten into my treasure chest." Ginger took the skirt from Rosie and held it up.

"Sorry," Leah said.

"Don't be. They're just curious." Ginger ran her hand down the sparkly skirt. "Ashley loved cheering in middle school, but her brothers drove her batty, standing over her like bodyguards. Needless to say, she didn't cheer in high school."

"That's not why she quit. She secretly loved the way they protected her," Madigan said. "She stopped cheering because she didn't like being leered at. It made her feel self-conscious."

"Really?" Ginger asked. "That's good to know, Mads."

"What's his name?" Junie popped up behind the other couch holding a stuffed bear with matted fur. It was missing one eye and had stitches along one ear.

"That's Rory." Ginger went around the couch and knelt by the chest with Junie. "Grandpa Mike gave him to Tank when Tank was two. He slept with it every night until he was about six, when Baz made fun of him."

"I can't wait to tease Tanky about that," Madigan said as she and Leah joined Ginger and the girls.

Rosie pulled a tiny knit hat out of the chest. "This Wowy's?"

Ginger put the skirt and bear in her lap and took the hat. "That's about the right size, but Ashley wore that home from the hospital the day she was born. I have a lot of the kids' baby stuff in here."

Junie peered into the chest and plucked out a faded black T-shirt with the Red Hot Chili Peppers logo on the front. "Whose is this?"

"That was Ashley's. It's one of Tank's old shirts." Ginger took the shirt and rubbed it against her cheek. "She loved sleeping in her brothers' shirts. Way back when, the Red Hot

Chili Peppers was one of Tank's favorite bands, and he had two shirts like that. Ashley stole both of them. There's another one in there somewhere."

"Mama sleeps in Tank's shirts," Junie said.

Leah's cheeks burned. "He sleeps on the *couch*."

Madigan stifled a laugh. "Mm-hm. I'm *sure* he does."

"He has booby wings," Junie said loudly.

"Me want booby wings!" Rosie exclaimed.

And I want to crawl into a hole and disappear. Leah covered her face.

"Cat's out of the bag now," Madigan said quietly. "What else does he have pierced?"

"Madigan!" Ginger snapped.

"Nothing." As the word left Leah's lips, she realized she'd just admitted to seeing Tank *naked* and quickly added, "I mean, probably nothing. How would I know?" She shoved her hand into the chest and pulled out a football jersey. "Look! Whose is this? Tank's? Baz's? Gunner's? How about this?" She pulled out a rattle, and Rosie grabbed it from her and started shaking it.

Ginger put her arm around Leah. "You don't have to be embarrassed about following your heart, especially when you make my son so happy."

"Thanks, but I think I'll just shrivel up and disappear now."

"There will be no disappearing." Ginger patted her shoulder. "How about if we just pretend that part of our conversation never happened?"

"Deal."

Leah was beyond thankful that Ginger kept that promise as they went through the chest, and she shared more of her treasured memories. Madigan sat on the couch playing her guitar for the girls and teaching them songs, and Ginger had a pile of memorabilia in her lap and more scattered on the floor around her and Leah.

"You have so many of Ashley's things. Would you like me to make you and Con a memory blanket with some of them?"

"You would do that for us?" Ginger asked.

"Your family has done so much for me and the girls—I would be honored to make you one."

"I love the blankets you made for the girls, and I would love to have one for Ashley." Ginger hugged her. "Thank you."

"Actually, I want to thank *you* for today. I never knew my mother, and I didn't think I'd missed out on anything because I had such a great father. But today has been really special, and I think I did miss out on some things my dad just didn't have time for. I'd like to make River proud by being the best mom I can for the girls, and today you helped show me ways to do that. I really appreciate you inviting us over and spending the day with us."

"Honey, you are very welcome, and I look forward to spending more time together. Your father must have been an amazing man, because he raised an incredible daughter. Don't sell yourself short, sweetheart. You have done an excellent job of raising two happy, well-adjusted girls. And you taught me something today, too."

"What could I have possibly taught you?"

"That I've raised a gentleman and that I need to steer clear of conversations about my son's piercings. And if it ever comes up again, I do *not* want to know if he has anything else pierced."

Chapter Fourteen

TANK TOOK OFF his helmet in his parents' driveway as his brothers and father climbed off their bikes. Seeing his grandfather's car parked out front with the girls' carseats in it and knowing Leah was waiting for him inside brought a rush of emotions.

"Great ride, huh?" his father said, clapping him on the back.

"Yeah." They'd ridden out to Cape Ann. Tank hadn't been there in years, and all he could think about was taking Leah and the girls there.

"You ready for a nap, old man?" Gunner teased their father as they headed inside.

Their father scoffed. "You'd better hope not, considering you have my genes."

Tank held the door open for them and called over to Baz, who was on his phone in the driveway. "You coming?"

"I'm talking to Evie. I'll be there in a minute."

The house smelled delicious. Tank followed the sounds of the girls into the kitchen and made a beeline for Leah, a sight for sore eyes in a clingy black sweater and skinny jeans.

"Tank!" Junie yelled, and she and Rosie ran to him.

He scooped them up, one in each arm, without breaking his

stride, and kissed their cheeks. They giggled about his beard tickling as he leaned down and kissed Leah on the lips, feeling like he hadn't seen them for a month.

Leah blushed.

"They might as well get used to seeing me kiss you, darlin'. I couldn't have waited until we were alone any more than I could have waited to hold them." He looked at his family watching them with approving smiles and said, "That goes for you, too. Get used to it, 'cause it's not going to change."

"Well, okay then," Ginger said. "Who's hungry?"

Everyone except Tank and Leah yelled, "Me!"

Tank put the girls down and pulled Leah into his arms as the girls helped Ginger carry baskets of biscuits and corn bread to the table. "On a scale of one to ten, how much did I just screw up?"

Her eyes filled with wonder. "You didn't. After the day we've had, it was going to be hard for me to hold back, too."

"Now, that's what I like to hear."

As he lowered his lips to hers, Baz said, "Are we eating or making out?"

Leah buried her face in Tank's shirt, and he scowled at Baz.

"Don't look at me like that. I wasn't the one kissing her." Baz chuckled. "For the record, Leah, I'm Team Tank and Leah all the way."

As everyone settled around the dining room table, Tank sat between Leah and Junie, and Rosie pleaded to sit between *Conwoy* and *Gingy*. Hell if that nickname didn't make him feel good all over. They devoured spaghetti and meatballs and all the delicious sides the girls had made. Junie and Rosie talked excitedly about their day, getting sauce and spaghetti everywhere, which was the cutest damn thing Tank had ever seen.

Everyone raved about the food, and his family took the mess in stride. He leaned closer to Leah and whispered, "Did you have as much fun as they did?"

"I loved every minute of it."

"I'm glad." He kissed her cheek.

Rosie reached over and patted Conroy's chest. "No wings?"

Conroy looked at Leah with a question in his eyes, and she turned beet red. Gunner and Baz burst into hysterics.

"Piercings, Pop," Tank clarified. "No, Cheeky. I'm the only one cool enough to have those." He put his arm around Leah and kissed her temple. "Sorry."

Rosie pulled her shirt up and announced, "I get wings!"

Everyone tried to stifle their laughter.

"*Rosie*, put your shirt down," Leah said sharply. "We don't show our bodies at the dinner table." She looked at Tank's parents. "I'm so sorry."

"Ah, that's nothing," his father said. "We were at a Dark Knights picnic when your boyfriend over there was about three or four, and he climbed onto the picnic table and peed into the punch bowl."

Everyone laughed.

"Don't give them any ideas, *Conwoy*," Ginger teased. "Why don't you guys tell us about where you rode today."

"We had a great ride," Gunner said. "We went out to Cape Ann and had lunch by the water."

"Where is that?" Leah asked.

Baz stabbed a meatball and said, "It's about two hours from here."

"I'd like to take you and the girls there sometime," Tank said. "I think you'd like it."

"Have you taken the girls to see the Woods Hole Aquarium

yet?" Ginger asked.

"No. We haven't explored the area at all since we moved here," Leah said.

Tank finished eating and put his arms around Junie and Leah. "We're going to fix that. We'll take Twitch and Cheeky girl over there to see all the cool stuff."

His parents rattled off fun things to do with the kids, and the girls chattered excitedly.

"Don't forget about Trunk or Treat on Halloween," Baz added. "Everyone dresses up, and the girls can collect candy and play games. They'll have a blast."

"Candy!" the girls yelled, talking over each other about costumes.

"Tank told us all about it the other night," Leah said. "We're going to take the girls costume shopping soon. Last year we trick-or-treated in the apartment complex where we lived. It sounds like this will be a lot more fun."

"Tank mentioned that you moved from North Carolina. What brought you to the Cape?" Gunner asked.

"I had a dream about the area, and when I looked it up, I loved what I saw. I thought it would be a good place for us."

"I'm sure there was a good-looking biker in that dream, right?" Tank waggled his brows.

She laughed.

"Don't be shy. You can tell us," he urged.

"You were *not* in my dream." She bumped him with her shoulder.

"That's a shame, baby, because you've been in mine for months."

"Aw, come on." Gunner threw his napkin at Tank. "Could you be any cheesier?"

They all laughed, and the rest of dinner passed with small talk, fun banter, and laughter. When they finished eating, the girls went to play with their toys, and the rest of them cleaned up.

"That was a phenomenal dinner," his father said as they cleared the table. "The perfect end to a great day. It's been ages since I've been on a ride with you guys. Ging, let's make arrangements so you can come next time."

"Sounds great." Ginger looked at Leah. "How about you, honey? We could ask Mads to babysit and you could join us."

"Me?" Her eyes widened. "I've never even sat on a motorcycle."

Tank put his arms around her from behind and kissed her cheek. "It's time to change that."

"Hell yeah it is," Baz said. "Why don't you take her for a spin?"

"Good idea." Tank was dying to be alone with her. "Mom, can you watch the girls?"

"Absolutely. Leah, there's nothing like being out on the open road. It's freeing," Ginger said. "You can borrow one of my helmets."

"Wait. You mean we should go *now*?" Leah asked.

"*Yes,*" she urged. "You can ride out to the beach and watch the sunset. The girls are happy here, and we have no plans."

"I'll stick around and hang out with them so they can see what cool Uncle Baz is like." Baz headed into the living room where the girls were playing.

"I've never left them with anyone but River."

"All the more reason you should go," Ginger said. "You mentioned earlier that you're talking with Corinne Langley about watching the girls when you go back to work."

Corinne was the daughter of a Dark Knight, and Tank had met her several times. She'd gone through a messy divorce in Colorado and had moved back to the Cape four years ago with her then three-year-old daughter to be near her parents. She babysat Patience and Gracie, and Tank trusted her with Leah's girls.

"Yes, Starr gave me her number. We've spoken a few times, and I really liked her. I'm meeting her in a couple of weeks. If it goes well, then I'll take the girls to meet her."

"This will be good practice for them," Ginger said. "And you know they're safe here, so you can relax and have fun."

His father said, "When's the last time you got to do anything other than go to work or be a parent?"

"Before my father died. When I was eighteen."

"And how old are you now?" he asked.

The girls' giggles floated into the room as she said, "Twenty-four."

His father took her by the shoulders, just as he had Tank many times, and said, "Sweetheart, you've had a lifetime of responsibility. Go out for an hour or two and be a twenty-four-year-old girl out with her beau. Be loud and silly, or whatever you want to be, without the worry of the girls watching."

Leah looked hopefully, and a little nervously, up at Tank. "What do you think?"

"Baby, I will *never* turn down time alone with you, and the idea of you on the back of my bike. *Mm-mm.*" He cocked a grin. "There's nothing hotter than that."

"Riding on the back of his motorcycle is how a biker tells the world you're his woman and he's your man," his father explained.

Leah met Tank's gaze, a new intensity rising in her eyes.

"Okay. But I need to talk to the girls first."

They went into the living room and found Gunner and Baz on all fours, giving Rosie and Junie rides on their backs.

"Stallion wides, Mama!" Junie giggled.

"I cowgirl!" Rosie exclaimed.

Leah laughed. "Are you having fun?"

"Yes!" They giggled.

"Tank and I are going to go out for a little while," Leah said. "Gingy and Con will watch you, okay?"

"Okay!" they yelled.

"And Baz and Gunny?" Junie asked.

"You bet," Baz said, and winked at Tank and Leah.

"Want to give me a kiss goodbye?" Leah asked.

The girls kissed the air and shouted, "Bye!"

Tank draped an arm around her shoulder. "Still worried?"

"No." As they walked out of the living room, she said, "Now I'm getting excited. Does that make me a bad mom?"

"Hell no." He drew her into his arms. "But I'm having fantasies about you being a *naughty* mom."

"THOSE AREN'T FANTASIES. They're memories of the last four nights," Leah whispered as they went into the kitchen.

"Don't fool yourself, darlin'." He flashed a wolfish grin that made her stomach flip-flop. "I've got lots of dark fantasies, and you star in every one of them."

"*Hush.* You'll get me all revved up," she whispered, but it was too late. She'd spend the whole ride wondering about those naughty fantasies.

She tried to tamp down her curiosity as she borrowed one of Ginger's helmets and thanked her and Conroy again for watching the girls. Tank gave her a lesson in motorcycle safety, and by the time she climbed onto the back of his bike, she felt fully prepared, and a little nervous. But as they cruised out of his parents' driveway and onto the main drag, the brisk wind whipping through her sweater sleeves and the world racing by clearer than anything she'd ever seen through car windows, Leah realized how wrong she'd been. Nothing could have prepared her for the thrill of the ride or the heat pooling between her legs at being pressed against Tank's thick body, riddled by the titillating vibrations of the engine.

The longer they drove, the more her nerves gave way to exhilaration. She'd thought Tank had gone on long rides as a way to bond with the guys, but now she understood that the camaraderie was only part of the experience.

She clung to him as he turned off the main road and drove down one road after another until the ocean appeared in the distance. He cruised into the nearly empty parking lot and parked near the beach. The sun had just started its slow descent, leaving gorgeous trails of oranges, pinks, blues, and yellows in its wake.

Tank cut the engine, but her body continued vibrating. He climbed off the bike and took off his helmet, pushing a hand through his dark hair. Leah had always thought he was hot, but now that they were together, now that she knew how caring he was, how it felt to be held, touched, and kissed by him, she saw him much more clearly. She saw the lonely places that Ashley had left behind—the places she wanted to heal—his loving heart that was so big she had no idea how it fit in his chest, and the honesty he gave her and the girls, all of which made him even more beautiful.

He helped her take off her helmet, and the scent of the sea swirled around them as he put their helmets on the pavement and straddled the bike, facing her. His arm circled her, and he hauled her closer. "You were too far away."

His eyes took on a familiar sensual hunger that made her want to straddle *him*. He used the backs of his fingers to brush her hair away from her face and closed his hand around her thick mass of curls, using it to bring her in for a kiss. *Oh*, how she loved that! He kissed her deep and slow, the way he *knew* made her come untethered, and he did it so thoroughly, when their lips parted, she was leaning forward, clinging to his thighs with both hands.

"How did you like it?" His voice was low, drenched with desire.

"The ride?" she asked breathily. "Or the kiss?"

His eyes narrowed, and his fist tightened in her hair. "You know what you do to me when you talk innocent and sweet like that."

She knew exactly what she was doing to him. He'd told her two nights ago that when she spoke like that, it made him want to do dirty things to her, which was precisely why she'd done it. She swallowed hard, her pulse quickening, and licked her lips, knowing what that did to him, too, and was rewarded with another heat-thrumming kiss that drew her emotions like water from a faucet.

"The ride was so much more than I thought it would be, but I know it wasn't just the motorcycle that made me feel free and safe at once, or made the world look brighter and more inviting. It's *you*, Tank. I can't believe I was ever scared of what I felt in you." He was holding her so close their noses touched, and she felt a shift in his energy, knots unfurling. "You're the most compassionate, strong, loving man I've ever met. And I don't mean just because you're built like a beast." He smiled, and she touched his cheek, wanting to feel his emotions. He turned slightly, kissing her palm, then rested his cheek there. "You share your strength with me, and it makes me feel whole. You give me space without disappearing, and you understand when I feel like my heart is being torn to shreds over thoughts of my brother. The way you hold me, the way you look at me and the girls, the way you're there for us…"

"*Lee,*" he practically growled, full of emotion and restraint.

Feeling and seeing all those delicious muscles fighting his urge to devour her emboldened her. It was like he'd become one big aphrodisiac, body, mind, and soul, and she wanted to swallow him up. She threw caution to the wind and crushed her mouth to his. He held her there, kissing her harder, belting his arm around her so tightly, their chests touched as they feasted on each other. "Skip the sunset," she said between kisses. "Take me home."

She didn't have to ask twice. Only they didn't go to her cottage. He drove to his house.

"It was closer," he gritted out as he lifted her off the bike and into his arms. Her legs circled his waist as their mouths came together, and he carried her up to the door. He fumbled with the lock. She sealed her mouth over his neck, sucking and kissing, earning one sexy growl after another, amping up her arousal. He threw the door open and kicked it closed behind them, taking her in another ferocious kiss on the way to the bedroom.

He lowered her feet to the floor, and they tore at each other's clothes. Their shirts flew through the air between urgent kisses. "I should feel guilty about this," she panted out as she stripped off the last of her clothes.

"Like hell you should." He picked her up and tossed her on the bed, making her laugh as he came down over her. "The girls are in good hands, and so are *you*."

He dipped his head, sucking her nipple into his mouth. She arched off the bed, digging her fingernails into his back, trying to stifle her moans.

He lifted his face with a wicked grin. "You don't have to be quiet, darlin'. Nobody's going to hear us." He pinned her wrists on either side of her head and continued driving her out of her mind, rubbing his cock against her center, grinding it against her clit as he trailed tantalizing kisses down her arm, lingering in the crook of her elbow. They'd discovered that surprising erotic zone two nights ago. She panted and whimpered, and he recaptured her mouth, hands groping, bodies grinding. She felt like she was going to crawl out of her skin if she didn't get *more*.

"I want you," she said between fervent kisses.

"I'm all yours, baby." He nipped at her lower lip. "Only yours."

"*Tank,*" she whispered, catching his full attention. "I want *all* of you."

His eyes flamed. "Are you sure? I can wait."

"I'm more than sure. Do you have protection?"

"Yes." His lips covered hers slow and sweet, like he was making love to her mouth, which made her want to make love to him even more. "Baby…"

She could tell by the strain in his voice that he was struggling with something. She ran her hand down his side. "What is it?"

"*You,*" he said softly. "I've never felt like this before, and once we do this, once I know how it feels to be inside you, I'm not sure I'll ever be the same again."

Her heart swelled. "Then that makes two of us, because I haven't been the same since our very first kiss."

When he kissed her again, it felt different, more meaningful, more *solid*, sealing their confessions with a golden ribbon. He reached into his nightstand, fishing out a condom, and rose up on his knees. She ran her hands up his thighs, feeling his muscles flex as he tore the package open with his teeth. His hand circled his cock, giving it one slow stroke. She shuddered, as she did every time she saw him touch himself. It felt *taboo*, like their dirty little secret. She sat up and teased the broad crown of his cock with her tongue, earning a guttural moan, and ran her fingers over his balls as she lay back down.

His eyes narrowed. "You fucking destroy me."

"That's your fault," she teased. "You showed me how you like to be touched, and I just happen to be an excellent student." She dragged a finger down her body to her sex, the way she knew he liked to see, and said, "Sorry if I destroy you, but I'm pretty sure we're about to put you back together again."

"Jesus, baby. I'm crazy about you."

He watched her watching *him* as he rolled on the condom. He was so well endowed, she should probably have been nervous, but she wasn't. She knew he would be careful with her.

As he came down over her, she said, "I haven't done this since before Junie was born."

"I assumed that, baby." He skimmed his hand down her thigh. "We'll go slow."

The head of his shaft nudged at her entrance as he lowered his mouth to hers. Their bodies came together with the gentleness of the wind and the unrelenting pressure of a mounting wave, until he was buried so deep, she felt him in every pore of her body. She wanted to freeze the moment, to memorize the feel of his heart thundering against hers, the weight of him bearing down on her, the warmth of his mouth loving hers.

He held her tighter. *"Jesus…"* he said. *"Lee."*

She couldn't speak, but she *knew* what he felt because she felt it, too, the pulse of need throbbing between them. She pressed her fingers into the back of his hips, and he slanted his mouth over hers in a merciless kiss. They began moving slow and careful, as her body adjusted and they found their rhythm. His every thrust brought a gasp of pleasure, a rock of her hips. Her mind was void of worry. There was no room for it when she was so full of *them*. He cradled her beneath him, her anchor in this stormy world, and took her harder, driving her deeper into the mattress, stroking over the secret spot that had her toes curling under and fire searing over her skin. Lust coiled hot and tight inside her. She tried to hook her heels behind his legs, but he was too big, and they slipped off. He grabbed her just below her knees, pushing her legs up and out, running his hands down her hips, then clinging tight as he thrust deeper, sending heat like wildfire up her chest and down her limbs. He was totally in control, loving her sensually and passionately, touching her like she was precious and just rough enough to heighten their every move.

Her head fell back. Delirious with desire, she clawed at his skin as he pumped and gyrated, grinding so exquisitely, desperate pleas fell from her lips. *"More. Don't stop."* Her emotions whirled and skidded as he catapulted her into a world of unrelenting pleasure.

When she finally floated down from the peak, he whispered

sweet sentiments against her skin between tender kisses. His every word brought another rush of emotions as he loved her excruciatingly slowly and impossibly deep. Their bodies moved in perfect sync. He pushed his hands beneath her, angling her hips and moving in circles deep inside her, bringing gusts of pleasure as he hit that magical spot, then circled away, coming back time and time again until she anticipated it, *cried out* for it, needed it more than the air she breathed. An orgasm built, swelled, *taunted* just out of reach. Tank tightened his hold on her bottom as he thrust, sending a bolt of lightning through her.

"*Again!*" she pleaded.

He continued his masterful pursuit of her pleasure, taking her right up to the edge of a cliff, and held her there. Her body tingled from head to toe, his every thrust *almost* sending her over the edge, like a taunt of the very best kind. Just when she was sure she'd pass out from need, he sank his teeth into her shoulder, and torrents of pleasure tore through her, sending her body into a wild frenzy of thrusts and moans. Tank reared up, and with his next thrust, he abandoned all restraint, burying his face in her neck and gritting out her name as they spiraled into oblivion.

When they melted into the mattress, spent and sated, he gathered her in his arms, holding her tight as their slick bodies shuddered with aftershocks. He pressed his lips to hers, and everything felt different, lighter and heavier at once, as if he carried her burdens and her joy and she carried his, giving *becoming one* a whole new meaning.

Chapter Fifteen

"NO!" ROSIE CLUTCHED three plastic Halloween costume packages to her chest. Tears streaked her cheeks, and her lower lip protruded in a heart-wrenching pout. There were four other costume packages at her feet, and she wanted them *all*.

Leah didn't remember costume shopping being this hard. They'd been at the store for more than an hour. Rosie wanted to be everything under the sun, and Junie didn't like anything she saw. After showing Junie dozens of costumes, Leah asked her again what she wanted to be for Halloween, and Junie said *Tank*. Leah had found a little biker outfit with a fake leather vest, but Junie had refused that, too. At least she wasn't crying.

Leah crouched in front of her frustrated littlest girl. "Rosie, you cannot be everything for Halloween."

"I can!" she yelled so loud two other mothers looked over.

Great. Just what she needed. Pitying looks. She was glad Tank wasn't witnessing this fiasco. He'd seen enough meltdowns to last a lifetime, although he never appeared overwhelmed by the girls' moods. He'd planned to shop for costumes with them, but he'd gotten called into the firehouse last night when they were shorthanded. Leah had slept fitfully without him and had woken up with a weird feeling. Even though she hadn't remembered having any bad dreams or premonitions, she'd texted Tank and asked him to be extra careful today, just in case. Now she was pretty sure that weird feeling had been a warning about Rosie's meltdown and not something worse.

She took a deep breath and tried one more time. "I have an idea, Rosie Posey. How about if we let Junie wear one of the costumes you like? If you wear one and she wears one, that's *two* of your favorites." Assuming Junie was willing.

"No. *Mine!*" Rosie whined.

Ohmygod. Leah rubbed her temples.

"I don't wanna be what she likes," Junie said, sullen faced, holding her bunny's ears.

Leah was at a loss, and she'd had enough. She began gathering the packages from the floor. "You know what? You're both having off days, so we're going home. We'll find costumes another time."

"No!" Rosie and Junie wailed.

Leah silently prayed for strength and began hanging up the costumes.

"No!" Rosie dropped the packages she was holding and began ripping down the ones Leah hung up.

"*Rosie.* Stop that." She glared at Rosie, who let out a loud wail. Leah looked up at the ceiling and closed her eyes. *Forget strength. Just give me patience before I lose my mind.* She breathed deeply and knelt by Rosie, putting her arm around her and pulling her closer. "Sweetie, we can't afford that many costumes, but maybe I can make you one costume that has *everything* you want on it."

Rosie shook her head and buried her teary face in Leah's shoulder. Leah rubbed her back and huffed out a breath.

"Is this *our* mess?"

Her head whipped around as Rosie and Junie yelled, "Tank!" and ran to him.

He scooped them up, handsome as could be in a black Henley and jeans. "Hard day?"

Leah pushed to her feet, and he leaned in for a kiss. "You could say that." She began picking up the packages again. "Rosie wants everything, and I have no idea what Junie wants. She said she wanted to be you, but she refused the biker costume I found. What're you doing here? I thought you had to work."

"Sean made it in about an hour ago. I showered and came straight over." He cocked a grin. "*Put your records on*, baby. I've got your back."

Her heart turned over in her chest at his use of River's words.

He looked at the girls, Rosie's tears subsiding, Junie's head resting on his shoulder. "What're the tears for, Cheeky?"

"Mama say no *'tumes*," she whined, and the waterworks started again.

"That's not true, Rosie. I said you could have *one* costume," Leah corrected her.

He gave Rosie a serious look. "Do you know what it's called when you don't tell the truth?"

"A fib," Junie answered.

"I *no* fib." Rosie whimpered, shaking her head.

"Yes, you did," Junie said.

"No, I didn't!" Rosie hollered.

"Enough," Tank said sharply, and both girls quieted. "Maybe you didn't mean to fib. That happens sometimes. But I don't like fibs. I gotta be able to trust you, and that only happens when you tell the truth. Got it?"

Rosie nodded, but then more tears came. "*Mama* fib. *No 'tumes.* We *leavin'.*"

"Ohmygosh," Leah said incredulously. "She's right. I did say that. I told her she could have one costume, but it was like I'd started a war, so I said we were leaving."

Rosie grinned. "Mama *bad.*"

Tank tried to stifle a grin. "You have a great mother, and I don't ever want to hear you say otherwise. But she *did* forget what she'd said, which can be misconstrued as a fib. I'll be sure to punish her properly later." He winked at Leah.

"Will Mama get a time-out?" Junie asked.

I sure hope so. Leah locked eyes with Tank, the space between them vibrating. It had been a week since they'd first made love. The next night they'd fallen asleep together in her bed, and the girls had come running in the next morning and jumped on them, asking for *pincakes.* Leah had been shocked and relieved that they'd had no reaction to finding Tank in her bed, other than wanting to snuggle between them, which they'd done the very next morning and every morning he'd been there since.

"Something like that," Tank answered. "Now, let's talk about this mess."

He set them down, and Rosie pleaded her case in broken sentences about wanting to be a dozen different characters. Tank gave her his full attention, arms crossed, brows knitted, until she'd said all she needed to. Then he turned to Junie. "And what's going on with you, Twitch?"

"I wanna be you for Halloween."

"Your mama said she found you a biker costume."

"I don't wanna be a biker," she said solemnly. "I wanna be a stowy dwawer."

"*Oh*, Juju," Leah said as understanding dawned on her.

"You want to be a tattooist." Tank crouched in front of her. "I wear regular clothes when I do tattoos, baby, not a costume."

Junie's brow knitted.

"I think I know how to fix this." Tank rose to his feet and pointed at the girls. "Don't move." He draped his arm over Leah's shoulder, turning their backs to the girls.

"I'm sorry. I know you didn't sign up for this."

"Knock it off, Lee. I knew *exactly* what I was getting into with the three of you. If you think a few tears are going to scare me away, you're wrong." He glanced over his shoulder at the girls. "I think Rosie's having a hard time because it's like costume overload in here. Of course she wants everything. Zan used to do the same thing. Give me a few minutes with her, and we'll get it sorted out. Then, if you're cool with the idea, I think we should take the girls to my tattoo shop so Junie can see what it's all about. She's obviously curious. It'd be good for her to see what I do for a living."

"I'm okay with that. The girls met Gia, Cait, and Aria at the celebration for River, so they'll probably be excited to see them again." Leah was excited to see them again, too. When she'd been introduced to them at the celebration, she'd recognized them from the Salty Hog, although she hadn't seen Aria there very often. "But it might be easier if you just take Junie. Rosie's not exactly having a great day. I can stay home with her."

"No way. They're kids. They're going to have bad days. Hell, *we* have bad days. What kind of message would we be giving her? That she gets punished for having a hard time? I know she needs ramifications for bad behavior and all that, but the girls have gone through a lot of changes lately, and it's got to take a toll. Besides, how can she learn to behave if she's sheltered from situations where she needs to? I'll help you keep her in line."

Could he even begin to know how much his thoughtfulness meant to her? "Okay. But what's your plan with Rosie and the costumes?"

"I'll do what Preacher used to do with Zan. Tell her she can take as many costumes as she can carry into the dressing room, and then when we're in there, I'll explain that she can't have them all because other kids need them. She'll choose. It's easier when there aren't a hundred other sparkly costumes everywhere."

"I should have thought about that."

Tank scoffed. "I don't know how you could think at all with Rosie pitching a fit like she was."

"How do you know what she was doing before you got here?" She glanced at the girls, who were under some sort of good-behavior spell he'd cast on them.

"Because I saw her following you and ripping those damn costumes off the hooks when I came in the front door. When I reached the aisle, I saw you holding her, offering to make one fantastic costume with everything she wanted. You're a kick-ass mom, Lee. Don't you doubt that for a second. And don't doubt my feelings for you and those meltdown munchkins, either. Got it?"

She gazed up at him with a full heart. "Yeah, I've got it."

"And how about that weird feeling you had? What're you thinking about that?"

She shrugged. "I'm hoping it was just because Rosie's having an off day."

"Good. Now let's hope she doesn't prove too strong-willed

for Preacher's tricks."

Junie was so excited to see Tank's tattoo shop, she was bouncing up and down as she and Leah waited outside the dressing room for Tank and Rosie. Leah heard the low rumble of Tank's voice. She couldn't make out what he was saying, but over the next ten minutes, one by one the plastic packages were pushed out from beneath the curtain, and Leah quickly put them away. When they finally emerged, Rosie was clutching a single costume against her chest, and Tank wore a crooked smile like he was stuck between being victorious and uncomfortable.

"Do we have a winner?" Leah asked.

Rosie grinned, holding up her choice. "Tinky Bell!"

"That's wonderful!" Leah hugged her. "You'll be the cutest Tinky Bell ever."

"Tank Petey Pan!" Rosie exclaimed.

Leah laughed, imagining him dressed up as Peter Pan. "You'll look great in green tights."

"Whoa." He eyed Rosie. "You never said anything about green tights."

Rosie grinned. "Petey gween."

Tank's eyes narrowed. "Let's see what they've got."

They went to the adult section, and Tank found a Peter Pan costume that came with a green shirt, hat, a brown belt, green wrist cuffs, and green tights.

"It has bwacelets," Junie said cheerily, touching one of the thick leather bands around Tank's wrist. "You like bwacelets."

"Yeah, I do." He looked down at Rosie. "We need to renegotiate our deal. I'll wear the shirt and everything else, but I can't wear green tights."

Rosie's pouty lip came out, and she whined, "We dealed. *You fib!*"

Tank uttered something under his breath. *"Fine.* I'll wear the friggin' tights."

Leah tried to stifle her laughter as they headed to the register, falling even harder for the burly softy.

THEY DROPPED TANK'S motorcycle at Leah's house and took her car to Wicked Ink. Before heading inside, Tank picked up the girls and sat them on the hood, which they thought was the coolest thing ever and made them giggle their little heads off. He was surprised at how excited he was about introducing Leah and the girls to more of his world.

"A'right, munchkins, listen up. This is where I work, which means it's not a playground. Got it?"

They nodded, Rosie beaming, Junie's face serious.

"Real tattoos are made using sharp instruments. It's important that Gia, Cait, and Aria are not distracted while they're working."

Junie and Rosie gasped excitedly. Rosie said, *"Giacaitawia!"* and clapped.

Tank chuckled. "Let's not skip the *no distractions* part. That means no yelling and no running."

"We won't," Junie said. "We pwomise."

Rosie nodded, clapping again. "Pwomise!"

He lifted the girls off the hood and set their feet on the ground. Leah gave him a hopeful smile, holding up crossed fingers on both hands. He hooked his arm around her neck, pulling her in for a quick kiss, and whispered, "I give Rosie ten seconds before she breaks the rules or bursts from trying not to."

Rock music blared from the speakers as they headed inside, and the girls' faces lit up. Tank saw Cait with a customer in her piercing station and Aria setting up for her next appointment. Gia came out of the back room, and Rosie jumped up and down, yelling, *"Giagiagia!"*

"Rosie." Leah shushed her.

Rosie slapped her hand over her mouth and stared up at Tank, wide-eyed. He did his best to school his expression and patted her head while shaking his, wondering how the hell parents kept straight faces when kids were so fucking cute.

"Baby girls are in the house!" Gia announced as she strutted toward them in a tight white shirt tied above her belly button, leopard-print bell-bottoms, and sky-high heels. There was a graphic on her shirt of a giant leopard-print mouth with teeth biting the lower lip.

Aria looked over with a silent greeting in her eyes. At twenty-four, she was petite and shy with long dirty-blond hair, several tattoos, and a nostril piercing. She had issues with social anxiety, but her confidence came out in her art, which was stellar.

Cait glanced over her shoulder, nodded a greeting, and turned back to her customer.

"How're my favorite little ladies? Are you here for tattoos?" Gia bent at the waist and tickled their bellies, earning giggles.

Junie petted Gia's leg. "I like your pwetty pants."

"Why, thank you." Gia went to Leah. "And how's Mama holding up?"

"I'm doing pretty well, thanks," Leah said as Gia hugged her. "How are you?"

"Fanfriggingtastic, thanks to you." Gia eyed Tank. "The boss hasn't been so tightly wound since you and the girls came into his life."

"*Gia,*" Tank warned.

Gia planted her hand on her hip. "What? I can't compliment your woman? Get over yourself." She glanced at the girls. "He's quite bossy, isn't he?"

Leah laughed softly, and the girls giggled.

Gia took Leah's hand and ran her fingers down her arm. "You have the prettiest skin. Are you here to get inked? I would *love* to put some art on your gorgeous body."

Tank glowered. "She's perfect without ink, and if anyone's going to give her a tattoo, it's *me.*"

"I see boss man is possessive of his lady," Gia teased. "That's a new look on you. It's kind of hot. If you're not here to ink your girl, what're you doing here on your day off?"

"Junie wants to be a tattoo artist," Tank explained. "I thought I'd show her what it's like."

"Junie, you want to be like Auntie Gia!" Gia clapped her hands together.

Junie nodded. "I wanna dwaw stowies."

"Stories? That is the perfect way to describe them." Gia reached for her hand as Aria came out of her workstation and headed up the aisle. "Come on, sugar. I'll show you around. We'll be back, boss."

As she and Junie walked away, Rosie shouted, "Awia!" and ran to her.

"Inside voice, Rosie," Tank reminded her.

Rosie whispered, *"Awia!"*

Aria picked her up and carried her around the lobby, talking quietly as she showed her the pictures on the walls.

"Gia is hilarious," Leah said.

"She used to be major trouble. She's Justice's younger sister, and she drove him batshit crazy with her wild ways," Tank explained. "Justice needed someone to help him get her under control, and that's when she started working here."

Leah ran her finger down the center of his chest. "And you came to their rescue. Why doesn't that surprise me?"

Aria walked over with Rosie. "Hi, Leah. It's nice to see you again." Her voice was as soft as a feather.

"You too," Leah said. "Sorry to barge in like this."

"Don't be. I love seeing you and the girls," Aria said as Rosie petted her long hair. "I'm just waiting for Zeke to get here."

"What's he coming in for?" Tank knew damn well why his cousin was coming in for the fourth time in as many weeks. Aria was several years younger than Zeke. He'd tutored her when she was in high school, and he'd been protective of her ever since. Before Aria had come to work for Tank, Zeke had taken it upon himself to help Tank and their families and friends understand her anxieties and had schooled them in ways to help her feel more comfortable around them.

"I'm working on his forearm," Aria said.

"Mind if we watch?" Tank asked. "Junie wants to see how it's done."

Aria shrugged one shoulder. "Fine by me."

"Zeke!" Rosie pointed to the front door as Zeke pulled it open. She wriggled out of Aria's arms and ran to him.

"Hey, Rosie Posey." Zeke's eyes locked on Aria as he picked up Rosie, his broad shoulders straining against his T-shirt. He was tall and fit from years of hiking, biking, running, and working construction with his father and Zander, and he turned heads everywhere he went. But Zeke wasn't just good-looking. He was smart and supremely thoughtful, thinking of ramifications to others before taking action in any part of his life.

The way he was looking at Aria as he sauntered over confirmed Tank's suspicion that his protectiveness toward her was turning into something else.

"How's it going?" Zeke said, looking from Tank and Leah to Aria.

"I'm almost ready." Aria held up one finger. "I just need one sec."

Zeke watched her walk away and gave Leah a one-armed hug. "I didn't expect to see you guys here. Where's your other mini-me?"

"Getting a tour from Gia." Leah pointed to Junie sitting in Gia's tattoo chair.

"You don't mind if we watch Aria do a few minutes of your tat, do you?" Tank asked. "Junie wants to be a tattoo artist for Halloween, and I want to show her how it's done."

"Sounds good to me. I just came from helping Grandpa Mike find his Dracula cape." Mike wore his Dracula cape to Trunk or Treat every year. Zeke tickled Rosie's belly. "I hear Grandpa has a fan club."

Rosie giggled.

"The girls love visiting him," Leah said. "We've stopped by a few times."

"He enjoys your visits." Zeke bounced Rosie. "What are you going to be for Halloween?"

"Tinky Bell!" Rosie pointed to Tank. "He Petey Pan!"

Zeke eyed Tank with amusement. "Do they make Peter Pan costumes big enough for him?"

Rosie nodded. "He buyed tights!"

"Tights?" Zeke laughed. "Dude, this might be the best Halloween ever."

Tank smirked. "Rosie, tell Zeke what you want *him* to be

for Halloween."

Rosie tilted her head from one side to the other, looking at Zeke. "Boo!"

"Your doll with the skirt?" Zeke's brow furrowed.

Rosie nodded, wide-eyed. *"Please."*

Zeke looked pleadingly at Tank.

Tank chuckled. "You can't get that two-letter word out of your mouth, can you?"

Leah covered her mouth, but her apple cheeks gave away her stifled laughter.

"I'm secure in my manhood. Sure, Rosie," Zeke said. "I'll be your *favorite* doll."

"Yay!" Rosie hugged him.

"What're you going to be, Leah? Wendy?" Zeke asked.

She eyed Tank with a mischievous glimmer in her eyes. "I have a costume in mind, but it's a surprise."

"Zeke!" Junie ran up the aisle and plowed into his legs.

"Hey, Junie bug." Zeke ruffled her hair.

"Did you thank Gia?" Leah asked. She was always reminding the girls to use their manners.

"Yes." Junie looked up at Zeke. "Are we going on a hike?"

Rosie said, "I hike!"

"I would love to go on a hike." Zeke set Rosie down as Aria waved him over. "But right now I have to get a tattoo. We'll have to figure out a time that works with your mom."

The girls badgered Leah about going on a hike as they followed Zeke to Aria's work area. Tank grabbed two more chairs and stopped in Gia's work area to thank her for showing Junie around.

"No problem. She's a great kid, and I wasn't kidding, Tank. They're good for you."

"Yeah, they are." It felt good to say it aloud. He brought the chairs into Aria's work area and set them down.

"*When*, Mama?" Junie asked. "Awia, we're going on a hike!"

Rosie cheered, "Hike! Hike!"

"*Shh*. Inside voices," Tank urged, though he had a feeling it was a losing battle when they were that excited.

Cait walked out of her work area, heading up front with her client, and Rosie yelled, "Cait!"

Cait waved. "I'll see *you* in a minute."

Rosie wiggled in delight. "She comin' back!"

"Zeke, are you sure you don't mind taking the time to hike with us?" Leah asked.

"Absolutely. I promised the girls," he said, watching Aria set out her ink.

"*Mama,*" Junie said exasperatedly. "Wickeds *always* keep their pwomises."

Tank loved that she knew the value in that statement, and by the approving look Zeke was giving him, his cousin did, too. "Lee." He motioned to a chair, and as she sat down, he lowered himself into the other one and patted his lap. "Come here, girls." The girls climbed onto his lap.

"What day works best for you, Zeke?" Leah asked. "I'm not back to work yet, so we're pretty open, but mornings are easier for the girls than later in the day."

"We're finishing up a job this week. I could go Saturday around ten if that works for you," Zeke suggested. "We can pack a lunch and eat on the trail."

"Saturday?" Junie asked hopefully. "Can we, Mama?"

"*Please,*" Rosie pleaded.

"Yeah, that sounds good. I'll make lunch," Leah said.

Tank knew the perfect place to take them. "Zeke, remember

the half-miler?"

A smile stretched across Zeke's face. "Hell yeah. That'd be a great first hike."

"What's the half-miler?" Leah asked.

Tank leaned in and kissed her cheek. "If I told you, it wouldn't be a surprise, would it?"

"Tank, I'll park at the end and meet you at the trailhead," Zeke offered.

Leah looked excitedly at Tank. "You're coming? What about work?"

"I wouldn't miss this for the world. I'll make it happen." He hugged the girls. "Someone's got to carry these little-legged munchkins when they get tired."

"*You* cawwy us," Rosie said.

He liked that she wasn't asking but knew she could count on him.

"I won't get tired," Junie said. "We went on lots of hikes with Wiver."

"Then maybe you'll carry me," Tank teased.

Junie and Rosie giggled, and Leah looked at him like he was the best thing she'd ever seen, and damn, he liked that a hell of a lot.

Zeke touched the back of Aria's hand as she put ink into her tattoo gun. "You want to join us for the hike?"

Aria looked at Tank and Leah, and with a small smile, she shook her head.

"Okay," Zeke said softly, holding her gaze and running his fingers over her hand for only a second before moving them. "Maybe another time."

They made plans for their hike, and as Aria began cleaning Zeke's arm, Tank quieted the girls and explained what she was doing. Junie watched Aria's every move, while Rosie bounced on Tank's lap.

"Aria, how did you get into tattooing?" Leah asked.

Aria glanced up. "I've always been into art. Painting, drawing. I went to art school for a little while, but it wasn't for me, and then Zeke introduced me to Tank."

"Do you enjoy the work?" Leah asked.

Aria nodded as she got ready to start on Zeke's tattoo.

Zeke cocked a grin. "She gets to put her hands on me. Of course she likes it."

Aria rolled her eyes, her cheeks blushing.

"Let's keep this PG, Zeke," Tank warned.

"What's PG?" Junie asked.

Zeke chuckled. "Yeah, Tank. What's PG?"

Tank wasn't about to go there. "How about we get started on that tattoo?" He explained to the girls how the tattoo gun worked and answered a handful of questions, which prompted him to give them a warning. "I never want to catch either of you trying to use anything sharp on yourselves or anyone else. Got it?"

The girls nodded.

"I'm serious. Junie, Rosie, look at me." They met his gaze. "I want you to make a *promise* to me and your mother that you will never use anything sharp on yourself or anyone else."

"I pwomise," Junie said.

Rosie bounced on his leg. "Pwomise!"

Zeke gave him an approving nod, and Leah, the person who mattered most, leaned closer and said, "Thank you."

When Aria started tattooing Zeke's arm, Junie whispered, "Does it hurt?"

"Sometimes," Tank said quietly. "But Zeke's tough, and

Aria is an excellent tattooist. She's super careful."

Junie watched intently, mesmerized by the process, while Rosie made buzzing sounds.

Leah put her hand on Tank's back and whispered, "I don't think I could ever get one."

"Baby, you don't ever need to. I'll be the canvas for your stories." Their eyes connected, the emotions humming between them obliterating the sound of the tattoo gun.

Tank had hated staying at the firehouse last night. He had barely slept, like all the years before he and Leah had come together. Only it wasn't the ghosts of his past keeping him awake at night. It was thoughts of Leah and the girls. Making love with Leah had changed him, shattering everything he'd thought he knew about sex and himself. Mornings had become special, sharing secrets with Leah and snuggling with the girls. He'd never thought he'd need anyone, but he'd never known that taking care of the three of them, hearing them laugh, holding them when they cried, and knowing they were safe could fill him with such happiness. And now that Leah was making a memory blanket for his parents, seeing her meticulously and thoughtfully piecing together his family's keepsakes drove those feelings deeper.

Leah leaned against him, drawing him from his thoughts. "Look at them. They're loving this. Thanks for bringing us here."

"Anything for you and the girls."

Cait came down the aisle, and Junie whispered loudly to her, "We need to be quiet while she makes his stowy."

"Good idea." Cait touched Leah's arm, whispering, "I'm so happy to see you and the girls again. Tank's been keeping us up to date on how you all are holding up, and all the cute things they do."

Leah eyed him curiously. "I'm glad I got to see you again, too."

Didn't she know how proud he was to be in their lives?

Junie touched the tattoos on Cait's arm. "You have lots of pwetty stowies."

Tank looked at Cait apologetically. Even though it had been years since she'd been abused, he knew it was moments like this that brought it all rushing back. Cait patted his shoulder, letting him know it was okay.

"Some are prettier than others." Cait leaned down, speaking closer to his ear. "I never thought I'd see the day. This looks good on you."

Pride swelled inside him.

"Leah," Cait said quietly, "Gia told me that Junie wants to be Tank when she grows up."

"I wanna be Gia," Junie said.

"What?" Tank said more harshly than he meant to.

Everyone else chuckled.

"I wanna wear her clothes for Halloween," Junie said.

"Oh boy." Zeke chuckled. "This ought to go over well."

"We'll get you all fixed up for Halloween, sugar." Gia strutted over from her workstation and leaned on the half wall. "You'll be the cutest tattoo artist for miles around."

Junie beamed.

Tank glared at Gia. "There will be *no* mouths on her shirt."

"Yes, Papa Tank." Gia rolled her eyes.

"Papa Tank! Papa Tank!" Rosie threw her arms around his neck, and Junie joined in the Papa-Tank mantra.

Everyone laughed except Leah, the surprise on her face rivaling the warmth in his heart.

Chapter Sixteen

THE REST OF the week passed with more ups than downs, more bedtime stories than Conan Gray songs, and more laughter than tears. It wasn't *easy*, but they were finding their footing. Leah's crying jags came and went the way they had for the previous couple of weeks, with no rhyme or reason, but they hit less frequently. It was hard to believe that River had been gone for a little more than a month. Leah had been forced to move his guitar so the girls didn't break it, but she'd felt like she was moving *River* out of the living room, which had swamped her with sadness. When Tank came over after work that evening, he'd taken one look around the living room and had known the missing guitar was the cause of her tears. He'd relegated her to a hot bath and had taken the girls and gone straight to the music store, where he'd bought a guitar wall mount. That evening he and the girls hung River's guitar on the living room wall. When she'd said people would think she was nuts, or making a shrine to River, he'd said, *Fuck them. River's part of your lives and he always will be. If you want to see his guitar every day, then you're damn well going to.* After the girls had gone to bed, he'd led her into the bedroom and held her. They'd lain in the darkness wrapped up in each other, talking about River, her father, and Ashley. They'd laughed and they'd cried. It was moments like those that allowed them to soothe and heal their deepest wounds.

If only he'd been as accommodating when she'd asked about where they were going hiking today. But he couldn't have been more secretive. This morning when she'd packed a backpack for the outing, he'd said, *Bring extra clothes. The girls are going to get dirty.* He'd looked at her lasciviously and added, *So are we.* That look had led her to believe there was no way he'd meant with real dirt. But when she'd come out of the bedroom wearing one of her nicer pairs of jeans and a peach sweater, he'd sent her back to change into something that could *literally* get dirty. Then he'd followed her into the bedroom, hauled her into his arms, and kissed her senseless. After which, he'd said, *You won't be wearing clothes when we get dirty*, and smacked her ass on the way back out to the living room, leaving her stunned and reeling for more.

On the way to meet Zeke, the girls chattered endlessly about their upcoming hike. They were adorable in their leggings and animal-eared hoodies. Leah had pinned the girls' hair up in pigtails, and French braided the two sides of her own and braided them into one thick plait in the back. She loved their affinity for nature, and she knew they'd gotten it from River. She wanted to do everything she could to keep that love alive and was glad that when Tank had schooled Leah and the girls about deer ticks, snakes, and poison ivy, the girls hadn't batted an eye. Rosie had said, *You 'tect us*, which had earned a hearty *Damn right.*

They parked at the end of a gravel road surrounded by sparse woods, and as they helped the girls out of the truck, Leah looked for a trailhead. "Are you sure we're in the right place?"

Tank shouldered the backpack, closing the distance between them like a hungry panther on the prowl. He looked like that more often than not these days. Her stomach flip-flopped as he dipped his head to kiss her neck, his beard tickling her skin.

"Yes, and I dig your hair up like that. How am I supposed to think about hiking when all I want to do is kiss your neck?"

"Papa Tank!" Rosie tugged on his jeans. The nickname had stuck, and Tank ate it up.

Leah laughed. "I think you'll have enough distractions."

He looked down at Rosie. "What's up, Cheeky?"

She held up a tiny pinecone.

"That one's just your size."

"Pocket?" Rosie reached for his pocket.

"I got it." He pocketed the pinecone. "Just don't bring me a snake."

"Zeke!" Junie pointed to Zeke, walking down the gravel road toward them in cargo shorts, hiking boots, and an open navy zip-up sweatshirt over a gray shirt. He carried a backpack over his shoulder, and his dark hair poked out from beneath a black knit hat.

The girls ran after him with Tank on their heels. Their great 'tector.

Zeke had always been kind to Leah at the Salty Hog, and women flocked to him, like they did with all the Wickeds. But she'd noticed that he wasn't overly flirtatious, like Zander and Gunner. He was smoother, charming, sort of like Blaine. The Girl Squad had pegged them as gentlemen, and Leah had to agree. Although most of the time she got the feeling Zeke had someplace better to be than the Salty Hog, unless it was one of the rare occasions when Aria was with them. When she was there, he was as protective of her as Tank was of Leah.

"Mornin'," Zeke called out as he knelt to catch Junie and Rosie in a hug.

"Morning," Leah said, and Tank gave his usual chin-lift greeting.

Rosie told Zeke about her pinecone, and Junie said, "Papa Tank told us about poison ivy and snakes and ticks. Leaves of thwee, let them be!"

"Let be!" Rosie exclaimed.

"Sounds to me like Papa Tank did a good job of preparing you for our hike." He shrugged off his backpack and unzipped it. "All good explorers need tools of the trade." He pulled out two lightweight children's backpacks, one purple and one pink.

The girls gasped, and Rosie cheered, "Pwesents!"

"I love purple!" Junie exclaimed.

"Then purple you shall have." Zeke handed her the purple backpack and gave Rosie the pink one. "Let's see what's inside them."

Leah's heart melted. "What do you say to Zeke?"

"Thank you!" they said in unison.

As Zeke showed them how to use their binoculars, flashlights, compasses, magnifying glasses, and other toys, Leah leaned against Tank's side and said, "He's great with them."

"He was a special ed teacher before he started working with Preacher and Zan."

"Why did he stop teaching?"

"He was fired because some prick made demeaning comments about the kids in the program at an event, and Zeke went after him."

She looked at Zeke, putting the girls' whistles around their necks, explaining that if they get lost, they should blow them, and reassuring the girls that they shouldn't worry, because he wouldn't let them out of his sight, but that it was good to be prepared. "It's a shame that he can no longer teach."

"Yeah, but he did the right thing. You can't let bullies get away with that shit, and Zeke still works with kids. He tutors and volunteers at the community center."

She was glad to hear that.

The girls ran over to show them their new goodies, and Leah hugged Zeke. "You can't imagine how much this means to me."

"Probably about as much as it means for me to see my broody cousin living life again." Zeke motioned in Tank's direction. He was helping the girls put on their backpacks. "Thank you for that."

She carried that compliment with her as they headed into the woods.

The guys kept eagle eyes on all three of them. The girls stopped every few seconds to check out leaves or bugs or point to birds flying overhead. It was fascinating to watch Zeke and Tank with them. Zeke was a born teacher and a serious nature lover, relaying fun facts about everything from trees and animals to the history of the area. Tank was their preemptive protector, scooping Rosie into the air before she tripped over a log and crouching behind Junie with one thick arm around her middle, pointing out a fox den and explaining why she should give it a wide berth. Leah swore Tank checked in with her as often as he did the girls.

River would have loved seeing the girls with them. She felt him around them in a way she hadn't the first few weeks after the accident. Sometimes she wondered why she hadn't dreamed about losing him before it had happened, but she was glad she hadn't. That would have been too much for her to handle.

She pushed those thoughts away and focused on the here and now. Junie's tiny hand was wrapped around Tank's index finger. She was smiling up at him, red ringlets hanging just above her eyes as she stopped to pick a flower and gave it to him.

"Thanks, Twitch." He reached over and tucked the flower behind Leah's ear.

"Pwetty." Junie plucked another flower and tried to put it behind her ear.

"I've got you, baby girl." Tank did it for her.

"Me!" Rosie shouted.

Junie plucked another flower, and Tank put it behind Rosie's ear. Leah went behind him, pushing the stems into their braids so they'd stay in place.

"When you're older, I'll take you girls camping," Zeke suggested. "We'll set up a tent and have a campfire."

"Can we camp now?" Junie asked. "I'm big enough."

"Me camp!" Rosie chimed in. "Me big."

Zeke winced. "Uh-oh. Sorry, but I can't go tonight, girls. I meant another day."

"*Okay,*" Junie said sadly. Then she turned pleading eyes on Leah. "Can *we* camp tonight?"

"It's too cold to camp outside, but we can go when it's warmer," Leah said.

"I'll wear a coat," Junie begged.

"*Please*, Papa Tank?" Rosie pleaded.

Tank arched a brow at Rosie's attempt to circumvent Leah's decision. "That's up to your mama, baby girl."

"How about if we set up a blanket fort in our living room?" Leah suggested.

"That's not a tent," Junie said sullenly.

Tank leaned closer to Leah and whispered, "I can pitch a tent in my living room and build a campfire in the fireplace."

Her heart skipped. "I love that idea. Are you sure?"

"Hell yeah. It'll be a blast."

"Let's do it," she whispered.

He gave her a quick kiss. "You tell them so Rosie doesn't think she found a way around the boss."

She chuckled. "Hey, girls, how about a slumber party at Tank's house?"

The girls cheered and clapped.

Zeke sidled up to Leah. "They've got him wrapped around their little fingers."

Almost as much as he's got us wrapped around his.

Happy about their camping victory, the girls went back to exploring. Leah took loads of pictures, and the guys bantered back and forth, sharing stories about hikes they'd taken with their families. The girls were as fascinated by their stories as they were by their surroundings, reminding Leah of how they'd loved to listen to River's stories.

Tank put his arm around Leah. "Hey, darlin'. Are you having fun?"

"I'm loving every second of this. Zeke knows so much about the outdoors."

"Yeah, he's a bit of a nature whisperer." He kissed her neck. "We're going to have to do more of this. The girls are really enjoying it."

She put her arm around him, inching closer as they followed the girls. "That sounds great, but I go back to work in a couple of weeks, and your mom said she'll give me daytime hours so I can be home when the girls go to bed. It might be tough finding time to take them on hikes when we're both off work."

"I'll make it happen. This kind of stuff is important for their development."

"You do realize those words are like mama porn, right?"

He laughed, and Zeke looked over with a grin.

"I didn't think you'd hear that," she said to Zeke.

"You've got to watch him," Tank said. "He hears everything."

"Speaking of mommy P-O-R-N," Zeke said, eyeing the girls. "Be forewarned that ever since my mom heard that you're making a memory blanket for Ginger and Con, she's been gathering a bunch of stuff from when we were little. I think she's going to hit you up for one."

"Really? I'd be happy to make her one."

"That's because you're a sweetheart." Tank kissed her.

The woods gave way to grass, and up ahead to their right was a breathtaking view of a cranberry bog. Inky water surrounded a sea of cranberries, contained in a perfect circle.

"Papa Tank, *look*! The water's bleeding!" Junie shouted.

"Surprise," Tank whispered in Leah's ear, and pressed a kiss beside it. "Those are cranberries, Twitch, and that's a cranberry bog."

"Yummy!" Rosie exclaimed. "Make pie!"

Zeke laughed. "Leah, how do you stand it? They're so cute."

"My dad used to say that kids were cute twice as often as they misbehaved, so one outweighed the other." She had nearly forgotten about that until now.

The girls ran along the grass, and as they rounded a bend, music floated in the air, and a sea of white canopies and crowds of people milling about came into view.

"*Zeke!*" Tank nodded to Rosie as he swept Junie up in the air, plopping her onto his shoulders.

Zeke did the same to Rosie, and the girls giggled hysterically, shouting, "We high!" and "Look at me!" Rosie banged on Zeke's head like a drum, and Junie hugged Tank's head, pressing a kiss to it.

"Grandpa Leo used to carry me and River on his shoulders." Happiness bubbled up inside Leah with the memories as she took pictures of them, the bog, and tents. "What is all this?"

"Cranfest. We used to come with our families every year. There are arts and crafts and games for the kids. Sack races, that sort of thing." Tank pointed to the water. "See the people going in the water? We're going to do that."

Leah was touched that Tank had thought to bring them there.

"Me?" Rosie shouted.

"Yeah, you," Zeke answered. "Even your mama is going in. That is, if you're not afraid of spiders. There are spiders in bogs."

"I no 'fwaid," Rosie said.

Junie leaned over Tank's head, peering down at him. "Can I stay on your shoulders?"

"Sure can." Tank took her hand and pressed a kiss to it. "I think your sister will have to go in on Zeke's shoulders, too."

Rosie shook her head. "No, me not!"

"We'll see, cheeky girl," Tank said. "Maybe it won't be too deep and you won't mind the spiders."

"Me no mind," Rosie said emphatically.

Leah laughed softly. She had a feeling her little one would mind very much, but she kept that to herself. "This is amazing. I've never seen a cranberry bog up close."

"They're harvesting the cranberries. See the equipment by the water?" Zeke pointed to the trucks on the far side of the canopies.

"I see it!" Junie shouted. "What's hawvestin'?"

Zeke went into an explanation about how cranberries grow. "When the cranberries are ripe, the bog is flooded, and that big machine reaches into the water and shakes the cranberries loose from the vines. Cranberries are empty inside, so they float up to the top."

"They gwow in a circle?" Junie asked.

"It would be cool if they did, but they don't," Zeke said. "See the black thing around the berries? That's called a rubber boon, and it keeps them in a circle. They'll use a big hose to suck them out of the water and onto a conveyer belt, where they'll be rinsed and loaded into a truck."

"Then what?" Junie asked.

Zeke smiled at Leah, obviously not minding Junie's questions. "Then they're packed and sold in stores so you can make pies, sauces, preserves, muffins, and about a thousand other things."

"I wanna make muffins!" Junie looked at Leah. "Can we? Please?"

Zeke chuckled. "Sorry, Leah."

"Are you kidding?" Leah exclaimed. "*I* want to make muffins, too."

They ate lunch by the bog and spent the rest of the afternoon checking out all the arts and crafts and tasting cranberry cookies, muffins, and candies. The bandstand was surrounded by hay bales, pumpkins, mums, and other fall decorations. They danced as a group, taking turns picking up the girls to dance with them. They took loads of pictures, and Zeke pulled both girls into his arms, allowing Tank to dance with Leah. The music was fast, but Tank held her close, and they danced slowly as they gazed into each other's eyes.

He whispered about how beautiful she was and how happy he was to be in their lives. "We're going to be dancing at this festival when the girls are old enough to make fun of us and tell us it's gross when we kiss. I'm falling hard for you, darlin', and every day those feelings get bigger."

Leah felt like she might cry, but he stole her thoughts with a tender kiss. For a spine-tingling moment, the rest of the world fell away, and there was only the two of them, dancing at a festival, without shadows of lost loved ones or responsibilities. And then two giggling girls barreled into their legs, and they scooped them up, the four of them dancing together as Zeke took their pictures, and that moment was even better than the first.

When they were done dancing, the girls got their faces painted, and they made their way to the bog. They rented waders, and Rosie ended up wanting to ride on Zeke's shoulders after all. As they stood in the sea of berries close together so Leah could take a selfie of them, a frog leaped at her, landing right in front of them. The girls squealed with delight. Leah moved, but the frog followed, and when she stepped away again, it stayed with her, sending the girls into fits of giggles. She couldn't help but feel like it was a sign from River, as if he really *was* with them. But she knew that was silly and quickly dismissed the idea. A nearby couple offered to take their picture, and as Leah moved between Tank and Zeke, the frog jumped again, landing on the bib of her waders, sending everyone into hysterics and warming her to her core. Sign or not, this was a day to be remembered, and Leah couldn't wait to get the pictures printed out.

After doing everything there was to do and promising Tank

and Zeke she'd forward *all* the pictures to them, Leah and Tank picked up the tuckered-out tykes and got ready to leave. Leah shifted Rosie in her arms as Tank started following Zeke toward the parking lot. "Tank, don't we need to go back the way we came?"

"No. Zeke parked here and walked over to meet us so he could drive us back to the truck. I figured the girls would be tired."

"Our dads used to do it with us," Zeke added.

"But the girls need carseats," she reminded them.

"I've got them," Zeke said. "I was going to borrow them from Tank's parents, but I decided to buy my own. That way if anyone else needs to pick up the girls, both families have carseats."

"I…" She didn't know what to say to that other than "Thank you."

As they carried the girls across the parking lot, a man and woman began arguing at the far side of the lot. Tank slowed his pace, confusing Leah, because she wanted to speed up so the girls weren't exposed to the angry shouts. The guy shoved the woman against the car, and she cried out. Leah flinched.

"Get them in the Jeep." Tank shoved Junie into Zeke's arms and shrugged off the three backpacks, blazing a path toward the arguing couple, arms out, hands fisted.

"What's he doing?" Leah asked as panic trickled in.

Zeke picked up the backpacks. "He's fine. Let's get the girls in the vehicle." He hurried them toward a four-door Jeep Wrangler.

"Where's Papa Tank going?" Junie asked.

"He's just taking care of something, Junie bug," Zeke said. "Climb into your seat."

As Leah put Rosie in her carseat, she looked through the windshield at Tank arguing with the man. The other guy was shouting, but as Tank's chest expanded, he stepped closer, his deep voice nothing more than a rumble in the distance. The guy reached for the woman again, and Tank grabbed his arm, wrenching it behind his back, and slammed him face-first into the hood of the car. Leah gasped.

"What's Papa Tank doing to that man?" Junie asked, on the verge of tears.

"He fightin'?" Rosie asked.

"No, he's...he's okay, honey." At a loss, Leah looked imploringly at Zeke.

"Tank's got this. There's nothing to worry about." Zeke leaned into the Jeep in front of the girls, drawing their attention. "Papa Tank is just having a talk with that guy, okay? Leah, do you have their stuffed animals?"

"In the backpack," she said quickly. She should have thought about their lovies, but she was in shock. "I'll get them."

As she dug out their lovies, she saw Tank sending the woman over to the Jeep. The woman looked scared but not panicked, like Leah felt. Zeke went to meet her, and Tank leaned over the man he was holding against the hood. She didn't need to hear his words to know he was seething through gritted teeth. His body looked coiled tight, ready to strike. He yanked the guy up and threw him into the front seat, planting himself between the car and where Zeke and the woman stood. The guy sped away, and Tank pulled out his phone, making a call as he headed their way.

"Papa Tank okay!" Rosie exclaimed.

"Yeah, he's okay," Leah said, trying not to sound like her heart wasn't hammering against her chest. "I'll be right back."

"I called Cuffs. He'll be here in ten," Tank said to Zeke as Leah waited a few feet away.

"I'll wait with her," Zeke offered. "The keys are on the driver's seat. Go get your truck."

Tank nodded and went to Leah.

"What the heck just happened?" Leah asked frantically. "Is she okay? Are you okay?"

"She's fine, but she's got old bruises. This isn't the first time he's roughed her up. Cuffs is a cop, another Dark Knight. He's on his way. Zeke will take care of her and make sure she files a report and gets a restraining order or presses charges. Let's get the girls out of here." He turned to get in the Jeep.

"Wait." She grabbed his arm. "Tank, what if that guy had a gun or a knife?"

He seemed unfazed. "Then better he use it on me than her."

"You could've been hurt—or *worse*—and the girls would have seen the whole thing."

"*Shit.*" He scrubbed a hand down his face. "You're right. Sorry. Get in the Jeep. Let's get outta here."

They climbed into the Jeep, and Tank started it up. When he turned to look at the girls, Junie said, "What were you doing?"

"Just having a chat with a bad man. Remember how I told you that the Dark Knights keep people safe?"

The girls nodded.

"But no Wiver," Rosie said, and Leah's heart cracked. "You twied."

"That's right, baby. I did try my very hardest." The muscles in his jaw tensed. "But I *was* able to help that lady out there that's talking to Zeke. That man was going to hurt her, so I stepped in to make sure he didn't. Now the police will come and they'll keep her safe."

"Did he hurt you?" Junie asked.

"No, sweetheart. There's not a man alive who can hurt Papa Tank."

"You stwong!" Rosie exclaimed.

Tank nodded, but Junie remained silent, her little brows knitted. Tank reached over the seat and put his hand on hers, giving it a reassuring squeeze. "I'm sorry if that scared you, but I had to do the right thing, and the right thing is to help when I can. Okay?"

Junie and Rosie nodded.

He took Leah's hand and lowered his voice. "I'm sorry you and the girls saw that, but they've got to know it's not okay for a man to hurt a woman."

As he drove out of the parking lot, Leah looked at the woman he'd helped and knew he was right. He'd done the right thing. But that didn't stop a worry from burrowing deep inside her, that one day he might go up against the wrong person, and he may not be as lucky as he was today.

AFTER PICKING UP clothes for Leah and the girls, they went to Tank's house for their indoor camping adventure. Baths were taken, a tent was erected in the living room, and hot dogs were roasted over a fireplace *campfire*. The girls were exhausted and had barely made it through ten minutes of a story before falling asleep cuddled up with Boo, Mine, and their memory blankets inside the tent. Tank and Leah zipped two sleeping bags together across the room from the tent, in front of the glowing embers in the fireplace. Tank lay in a pair of shorts with Leah in his arms, her head on his shoulder, her leg over his, and her fingers playing over his chest. He couldn't stop thinking about how different his house felt with her and the girls in it and worrying about how quiet Leah had been since they'd left the festival. He'd noticed her watching him and the girls more closely than usual, too, and wondered what was on her mind.

He kissed her forehead, bringing her eyes up to his. "You okay?"

"I was just thinking about how great today was. I felt River around us the whole time we were hiking and at the festival."

"You did?" That could explain her quietness. "Was that okay? How did it make you feel?"

"It was a good feeling. I remember it happening after we lost our dad. I don't feel River around us now, but this afternoon it was like he was spending the day with his girls."

"And you, babe. You were his world, too."

"Yeah," she agreed.

"You and the girls have become mine, too, Lee." He caressed her leg. "My house has never felt like this before. It's always just been a place to rest my head. A shelter from the elements."

"What does it feel like now?"

As he searched for words to describe the changes he felt, he laid her head on the pillow and leaned on his elbow beside her so he could see her better. Her thick curls fanned out around the beautiful face he knew by heart, the face he saw when he closed his eyes and conjured when they were apart. It was the face of the woman he wanted to wake up to every day for the rest of his life.

"It feels *right*, like we do. I realized today that I've tried to keep my memories of Ash alive for so long, I never gave any thought to creating memories of my own. I want that with you and the girls, Lee. Days like today. Nights like tonight." He brushed his lips over hers, whispering, "The good, bad, happy, and sad. *Everything.*"

Her breathing quickened.

"But part of that is learning to know you so well that I hear the things you're not telling me, like now." He held her gaze, wanting his words to sink in. "You're looking at me with as much desire as careful curiosity."

"Tank..." she whispered.

"What is it, Lee? You've got to be able to talk to me about anything. Why have you been watching us so closely tonight? Was it because of what happened in the parking lot?"

She lowered her eyes, trailing her fingertips along his stomach. "Yes."

"Talk to me, Lee."

She met his gaze, emotions brimming in her eyes. "You know how I had wanted to keep my distance from you at first to protect the girls from another heartbreak, and I couldn't stay away?"

His muscles tensed, his mind going to the worst possible place. "Yes. Do you regret that now?"

"No," she said quickly. "Today just made me realize how much you mean to us. I can't stop thinking about the worst possible outcome of something like what happened today. What if he pulled a gun? What if he stabbed you or ran you over with his car?" Tears dampened her eyes. "We would have lost you, and we've only just found you."

He dipped his head beside hers. "You're not going to lose me, darlin'."

"You can't promise us that. From what I saw today, you'll jump into any situation to help people regardless of the risks."

He lifted his face, fearing the truth might be too much for her to accept and knowing he had to be honest. "You're right. I can't promise you that. But this is who I am, Lee. This is how I was raised. It's the way of the Dark Knights. It's in my blood, baby. I can't change that part of myself."

She touched his cheek, and he leaned into her palm, needing the connection. "That's just it. I don't want you to change. You stand for all the right things, and you don't just talk the talk. You step in. Not just like today, but you go into schools and teach kids about hard, important aspects of life. If you weren't the brave, caring man you are, you wouldn't have gone into the water and saved us. I could have lost River *and* Junie."

"Don't say that. I don't even want to think about that."

"Neither do I, but it's true. Today you saved someone else, and we don't know what tomorrow will bring. But I know this much is true, *Benson Wicked*—"

"Say that again." It came out as a demand, but he couldn't have stopped it if he'd wanted to. Hearing his real name roll off her lips, full of desire and confidence, brought a new rush of emotions.

"I know this—"

"My real name, baby. Say it again."

Her eyes glittered devilishly. "*Benson* Wicked," she said seductively.

"How can a name I've heard hundreds of times sound so different coming from you?"

She shrugged adorably.

He couldn't keep from kissing her deeply, *passionately*, reveling in the emotions coursing through him. As their lips parted, he said, "Sorry, go on. What were you saying?"

"You can't kiss me like that and expect my brain to jump back to reality that fast." She laughed softly. "Not that I'm complaining." She rose up and touched her lips to his in a quick kiss. "I was saying that the girls and I want you in our lives, and I know I can't protect them or myself from what you've already become to us, which means I need to figure out how to deal with the fear that we could lose you at any time."

"But nobody knows when their days are going to end, Lee."

"That's true, but the risks you take are bigger than most people, and it seems like you take them often. Like I said, this is *not* about you changing. It's about *me* figuring out how to live with that reality. In a perfect world, I could prepare the girls and myself for the worst. But I'd never do that. If I had known we'd lose River, it wouldn't have hurt any less, and I would have lived every minute in fear, just waiting for it to happen. That's not *living*."

He moved over her, aching to be closer. "How can I make it less scary?"

"I don't think you can. But I am glad I told you how I felt, because even though it won't change anything, it's better than keeping it inside."

"I'm sorry, darlin'."

"Don't be sorry for being who you are. You're the bravest man I know, and I thank God you were too bullheaded to walk away from us."

He laughed softly. "Who are you calling bullheaded?"

"You're like mine and the girls' curls. I can brush them, use special rinses and conditioners, and try a hundred ways to tame them. They might behave for ten minutes, but they're going to do exactly what they were made to do and turn into unruly masses of springy curls, and there's not a darn thing I can do about it."

He threaded his fingers through her hair and held on tight. "You have no idea how much I adore your hair."

"Yes, I do," she whispered. "You like it as much as I love when you grab it like that. And as much as I like doing *this*." She pushed her hands into the back of his shorts, grabbing his bare ass.

Heat seared through him, and a hungry growl escaped. He rocked against her center. "I just figured out how to deal with your worries." He kissed her lips. "I need to make sure that every day is better than your last." He trailed kisses down her neck, whispering as he lifted her shirt over her breasts. "That you're pleasured so thoroughly, there's no room for worries."

As he lowered his mouth over her breast, she said, "And my hands on your butt gave you that answer?"

"Your touch always gives me the *best* ideas. You should touch me every time you need answers." He glanced at the tent. "What about the girls?"

"They're down for the count. We'll hear them if they wake up."

He kissed the warm crevice between her breasts. "Then try not to make too much noise while I research my theory."

He loved his way down her body and took off her shorts, lifting her hips as he lowered his mouth to her sex, feasting mercilessly. She ground against his mouth, fisting her hands in his hair so tight, pleasure and pain seared straight to his cock. He used teeth and tongue to take her to the edge of release, holding her there, unwilling to relent until he'd taken his fill. She was so fucking sexy, he was going to lose his mind with her writhing against him, greedy noises sneaking out as he homed in on all her neediest spots.

"I can't take it," she whispered urgently.

Her pleas tugged at all his best parts, and he gave her what she needed. Her hips shot up as she shattered against his mouth. She tasted sweet and hot and so damn good, he made her come again—*hard*. He pushed off his shorts, taking them with him as he climbed up her body, dragging his tongue along her heated flesh. He rubbed his cock against her wetness, taking her in a long, slow kiss, sparking another surge of desire.

He rose up and lowered his nipple to her mouth. "Use your teeth."

Holy hell, she reached between them, stroking his cock as she used her teeth and tongue on his nipple, driving him insane. He thrust his hips, fucking her fist as she tugged on his piercing, sending fire blazing through him. He reclaimed her mouth, kissing her deeply and possessively, wanting to brand her from the inside out.

"I want to watch you fuck me." He rolled them over so he was on his back and she was straddling him.

Her eyes flamed as he fished a condom out of the pocket of his shorts. As he tore it open, she slid her wetness along his rigid length. He groaned at the feel of her. Even with her luscious body covered by his shirt, she was sexy as sin. She ground her wetness against him, and he gritted out a curse. She bit her lower lip, trapping a grin.

"Jesus, baby. Everything you do makes me want you even more."

He grabbed the base of his cock to roll the condom on, but she took the latex from him. Watching her sheathe his length was another turn-on. He grabbed her hips as she rose up and sank down, her body swallowing every inch of him, drawing another hungry growl that he fought hard to stifle. She ran her fingers down the center of his abs, her eyes darkening as her smile widened. She toyed with him, riding him slow and gyrating when he was buried to the hilt. She played with his nipples, sending beats of pleasure pulsing up his limbs, pounding in his core, and burning through his chest, until he felt like his entire body was going to explode. He clutched her hips tighter, moving her up and down along his length, faster, harder, and then held her tight against him as he ground up into her. He clenched his teeth against the erotic pleasures consuming him. Her eyes closed, and her head fell back as he did it again, and again, in a mind-numbing rhythm. He pushed a hand into her hair, pulling her down over him as he pushed up her shirt and sealed his mouth over her breast. She moaned loudly.

"*Shh*, baby."

He grabbed her ass with both hands, sucking her breast as he thrust into her. He slid his fingers to her entrance, feeling his cock moving in and out of her tight heat, earning more moans. He wanted to turn her over onto all fours and take her from behind, but it wasn't the time or place to get that wild. He tucked that urge away, sucking harder, thrusting faster, until she lost all control. He released her breast, and she arched back, riding him fast, hard, and so fucking perfectly, he *nearly* came. But he fought the urge, letting her ride out her climax. As she came down from the peak, he wrapped his arms around her and rolled them over. She gazed up at him, looking as drunk on him as he was on her.

"Baby," he whispered against her lips, lacing their fingers together. "I could make love to you twenty-four hours a day and it wouldn't be enough."

He lowered his mouth to hers, loving her slower and more tenderly than he ever imagined possible, reveling in all that they were and all that he hoped they'd become. Their bodies moved in exquisite harmony, bringing a world of new sensations crashing down over him as they found their mutual release and sailed into ecstasy.

Chapter Seventeen

WEDNESDAY MORNING LEAH was a nervous wreck about meeting the sitter. Tank had tried to calm her nerves last night and again this morning, but she was *wired*. He'd left earlier than usual to run an errand before heading into the tattoo shop for an early appointment, because he had church tonight. He'd offered to cancel his clients so he could go with her to meet Corinne, but he'd already done so much for them, and it wasn't like she couldn't handle interviewing a babysitter. She'd written down all of her questions so she wouldn't forget them, and she already knew that Corinne had taught first grade in Colorado and had opened her in-home daycare to make the transition easier for her then-three-year-old daughter when she'd moved back home to the Cape. She'd enjoyed it so much, she'd never gone back to teaching and had assured Leah that after four years of running her daycare, she had no intention of stopping. Leah knew the girls would be safe with her, but that didn't change the fact that she was taking another step toward moving on. A step that put River further behind them.

She hadn't sensed him around since their hike last weekend. She felt like she was holding her breath, waiting to feel him again, and she knew that wasn't healthy. She'd tried to go through his things to get a sense of closure, but she just couldn't do it. She'd gone through this after losing her father, and she knew she *needed* to make it happen or she'd always have one foot in the past.

Just like I need to make this visit with Corinne happen.

But that didn't soothe the worry that she might be making a decision that could have a negative impact on the girls. Starr was coming over to stay with them while Leah went to meet Corinne, and they were excited to see Starr and Gracie. But how would they adjust to being in daycare every time Leah went to work? Would it set them back in their healing over losing River? Make them miss him even more? Would they be angry with Leah for leaving them all day? Could *she* handle leaving them with someone other than River?

She knew she had to, and that one way or another they'd get through this, just like she and River had after they'd lost their father. She wore a path in the living room floor as the girls finished eating. Rosie started following her as she paced.

Rosie giggled. "This fun!"

"I wanna play." Junie climbed down from her seat and fell into line behind Rosie.

"We ma-chin'," Rosie said.

The girls lifted their knees high like they were in a marching band. Leah knew better than to try to get them to stop following her. Thinking it was a game was a heck of a lot better than thinking Mommy was losing her mind.

The front door opened, and Tank walked in. Leah stopped pacing, and the girls ran into her butt, reeling with giggles.

Tank arched a brow. "Playing Pied Piper?"

Leah couldn't believe her eyes as the kids yelled, "Papa Tank's home!" and ran to him. She didn't know how their lives had blended together so seamlessly and come to the point where River's girls called him Papa Tank, how he had burrowed so deep into their hearts so fast, or how he'd become her *rock*. It had happened too naturally to have seen it coming, too powerfully to be disregarded, and she'd never been more thankful for anything in her life. Tank centered her. He didn't even need to say a word for her to feel stronger, safer, *better*.

"Did you forget something?"

"Yeah." He finished hugging the girls, and patted their heads. "Go play so I can talk to Mama, chickadees."

"Come on, Wosie. Let's play explower." Junie ran into their bedroom, and Rosie followed.

"What'd you forget?" Leah asked.

The girls ran out of their bedroom with their explorer backpacks and sat on the living room floor to empty them.

Tank took Leah's hand, leading her away from them. "I know you can handle today, but I thought this might help." He pulled a black velvet bag out of his pocket and put it in her hand.

Her pulse quickened. "What is this?"

"Open it and see."

She opened the bag and lost her breath as she withdrew a gold locket with the tree of life etched into it, surrounded by a circle of diamonds. *"Ohmygod"* came out just above a whisper. *"Tank...?"*

"I bought it for you last week and hid it at my house so the munchkins wouldn't find it. I was just waiting for the right time to give it to you. Open the locket, sweetheart."

She opened it with trembling hands as the kids ran around the room looking through their magnifying glasses. Her heart stumbled at the photographs of her father and River inside.

FOREVER IN MY HEART was inscribed above her father's picture, and ALWAYS BY MY SIDE was inscribed above River's. Tears spilled from her eyes as she felt something on the back of the locket and turned it over, reading the inscription through the blur of tears. TO LEE, WITH ALL MY LOVE, BENSON.

She could barely breathe past the emotions clogging her throat and threw her arms around him. "I love it. I've never owned anything so beautiful. Thank you."

He held her tight, kissing the top of her head. "The tree of life represents the connection between earth and heaven. I thought it might help to have them with you today."

She looked up, in awe of the man who had stolen—and was healing—her heart one painfully beautiful moment at a time. "It already has."

LATER THAT MORNING, Leah pulled up in front of Corinne Langley's modest Cape-style home, and her nerves prickled again. She sat back, taking in the gardens and the white picket fence surrounding the house. Ivy snaked up the cedar shingles between the windows and the front door. This was it. This would change everything. She touched the locket and closed her eyes, seeing River's and her father's supportive faces. And then Tank's and the girls' faces moved into the forefront, filling her with strength and determination.

With a deep breath, she grabbed her bag and headed up the walk.

Corinne opened the door with a welcoming smile and a little towheaded boy in her arms. Her light-brown hair was flecked with blond and cascaded just past her shoulders with a few wispy layers. Little voices rang out from within the house. "Leah?"

"Yes, hi. It's nice to meet you."

The little boy waved. "I Twevor."

"Hi, Trevor. I'm Leah."

"Come in." Corinne stepped aside. "Trevor is almost three and he loves to meet new people. I was just telling him about Rosie and Junie." Corinne tickled Trevor's belly. "Do you want to show Leah the playroom?"

Trevor giggled and wriggled as she set him down. He ran ahead of them into the main living area, which looked exactly like what Leah had hoped to see. Cubbies filled with toys lined the area beneath the windows, and dolls, plastic vehicles, stuffed animals, and other toys littered the floor. An alphabet banner hung on the wall above two plastic tables and chairs, where another little boy was coloring. Two little girls were playing with a plastic storefront and kitchen. Trevor plopped onto his bottom and began playing with cars on a rug printed with roads and stores. A brightly colored play area with a spongy mat was set up across the room from the couch, which had kids' blankets strewn across it.

"Wow, this looks great."

Corinne looked at her like she was crazy. "You don't have to be kind. It looks like the room exploded, but as I said on the phone, I would rather play with the kids, read to them, teach them what I can so they're ready for preschool, and let them *be* kids than worry about the mess. There's plenty of time for that after everyone goes home. Why don't you take off your jacket and we can sit on the couch and chat."

She was so warm and easygoing, Leah's nerves calmed as she

shrugged off her jacket, and they sat down.

"That's a beautiful necklace."

"Thank you." She touched the locket. "I was a little nervous about coming here, and my boyfriend surprised me with it this morning. It has a picture of my brother and father inside it." She was surprised *boyfriend* came out so easily, but it felt good to say it. She'd already told Corinne about her relationship with Tank and about losing River and her father.

"That's a really thoughtful gift." Corinne touched her arm. "Don't worry, Leah. I understand being nervous, especially after all you and your girls have been through. I'm looking forward to getting to know you, and I want to hear all about them."

Nearly two hours later, Leah climbed back into her car with her questions answered and plans to bring the girls by tomorrow to meet Corinne. Corinne was even more wonderful than Starr had said. Leah had a good feeling, like something inside her had shifted, stepping from the depths of grief into acceptance. It had been happening in baby steps for weeks, and at the same time, some of those steps felt like long strides.

She texted Starr to say thank you for referring her to Corinne and to check on the girls, and then she texted Tank to say the meeting went great and she'd tell him about it tonight. Starr sent her a picture of the girls playing dress-up. Gracie wore a tiara and a princess dress. Rosie wore a tutu and several of her beaded necklaces, and Junie had on one of Tank's T-shirts he'd let her sleep in, tied in a giant knot at her waist above her paw-print leggings, and yellow rain boots.

Another message bubble popped up from Starr. *Guess what Junie is.*

Leah thumbed out, *Gia?*

Starr's response came immediately. *Yup! I think your little girl has a wild side.*

Leah sent a laughing emoji and headed home. For the first time since losing River, she took the route that led to the sight of the accident. Her chest constricted as she passed the convenience store where they'd seen Tank, and River's voice whispered through her mind. *I can defend you, you know. I'm not a little kid anymore.* She swallowed hard. If only she'd let him talk to Tank, they might have missed that truck.

The road that crossed the water came into view. Her heart raced, and her hands began to shake and sweat. She pulled onto the shoulder of the road and threw the car into park, the split seconds of the accident playing out in her head like a horror movie—*River's scream as the truck impaled them, being hurled into the water, and the soul-crushing panic that followed.* She threw open her door, the brisk October air stinging her lungs. Tears soaked her cheeks as she stumbled toward the grass, still torn up from the emergency vehicles. She was surprised to see a wooden cross with River's name on it sticking out of the ground where Tank had tried to revive him, surrounded by remnants of dozens of bouquets, and a number of cards and candles. She clutched her locket as images of Tank trying to revive River assaulted her. She closed her eyes against memories of Baz and a fireman trying to pull Tank away and Tank breaking free, refusing to give up on her brother.

She turned her face up to the opaque sky, tears swamping her. *Are you up there watching me, Riv? I miss you every single minute of the day. I miss your stupid jokes, the way you always made us all laugh. I miss seeing you with the girls and hearing you sing and play the guitar. I listen to your videos a lot. I've turned into your biggest groupie.* She laughed softly, knowing he would laugh, too.

"If you're watching us, then you know about Tank. You'd like him, Riv. He's…" She searched for the right words, but there were too many. "He's like us, and he loves the girls so much. He doesn't use those words, but I feel his love in my bones, and they're crazy about him." She swiped at her tears. "I am, too."

She rubbed her thumb over the locket, gazing up at the clouds. "I need your help, Riv. Do you remember when I had to let go of Dad enough to move on?" Sobs tumbled out, and she crumpled to her knees in the grass. "I *hate* this," she choked out. "I won't ever let you go, and I'll never let the girls forget you. You *know* that. But we have all these changes coming. The girls have to go to a sitter when I go back to work, and I know you'd spin that to something positive and talk about friendships and the fun they'll have." She rocked forward and back, tears pouring down her cheeks. "But I feel like I'm standing on the corner of *our* old life and mine and the girls' futures." She craned her neck, eyes closed, her throat and chest swelling painfully. "I know you trust me, but I wish"—*you were here*—"you could send me a sign letting me know it's okay to move forward, because I have to."

She sat there among the remnants of a lifetime lost forever as the brisk air stung her cheeks and tears tore from the depths of her being, listening, hoping, *praying* for a sign that never came.

"YOU HEADING HOME?" Gunner asked after church.

"To Leah's. You?" Tank straddled his bike. He'd hung

around for a game of pool after the meeting, and he wanted to get home to her. He'd picked up the pictures from the weekend, and he knew she'd go crazy over them.

"Steph asked me to stop by her parents' house. She's getting shit out of their attic."

"Tell her folks I said hello. I'll see you 'round." Tank put on his helmet, cranked the engine, and cruised out of the lot.

The lights were out in Leah's cottage, save for the kitchen and the one in River's bedroom. *Shit.* Tank gritted his teeth and grabbed the pictures from the saddlebag on his bike, heading up the walk. After the toll putting away the guitar had taken on Leah, he'd wanted to be with her when she went through the rest of River's things.

He heard her crying as he opened the door and headed for the stairs, passing the memorabilia for his mother's memory blanket spread out on the couch and coffee table. He took the stairs two at a time, wishing he hadn't stayed for that game of pool. When he reached the attic, his gaze swept over open drawers, an empty cardboard box, a trash bag, papers, CDs, and other shit. Leah looked up from where she sat in the middle of River's bed, tears streaming down her face, the clear plastic bag of River's belongings from the hospital in her lap.

Fuck.

He went to her, dropping the pictures on the bed, and gathered her in his arms. "I've got you, babe. I'm here."

"It's all my fault," she cried against his chest. "I never should have let him go out that night."

"Don't do that to yourself, baby."

"It's *true.*" She pushed from his arms. "The last few times River went out, I had this strange feeling, like I missed him even before he'd left. I thought it was because he was growing up and getting a life. But I had it wrong. It was because the accident was coming."

"Lee, you couldn't have known that."

She swiped at her tears. "I've had enough dreams and weird feelings come true that I *should* have thought harder about it."

"I won't let you put that guilt on yourself. River wouldn't want that. For all we know, those feelings really *were* because he was growing up, and you missed the times when you and the girls were his *whole* world. We can't rewrite the past, babe, and picking it apart isn't going to change it. Take it from a guy who spent years trying."

She lowered her eyes, tears sliding down her cheeks. "My head knows you're right, but my heart doesn't."

"Look at me, sweetheart." He cradled her face in his hands, wiping her tears with the pads of his thumbs, her pouty lower lip gutting him. "I know you're hurting, but you're not alone anymore. You don't have to tackle the hard stuff by yourself. I told you I'd go through River's things with you."

"I was going to wait until you got home, but then I got the *mail.*" Her voice cracked. "There was a letter from River's school saying he was losing credit because he'd missed too many classes. I just…" Tears flooded down her cheeks, and she buried her face in his chest, racked with sobs.

Damn it. "I'm sorry, Lee. I didn't think about that. I should have notified his school."

"No. *I* should have."

He held her tighter. "Either way, I still don't understand why you didn't wait for me to come up here."

She turned sad eyes up to him. "Because I stopped by the site of the accident today after seeing Corinne."

"You went there *alone?* Jesus, baby. I would have gone with you."

"I know you would, but I wasn't *thinking*," she said sharply. "I just ended up there. I'm setting up babysitting and going back to work soon, and you and I are getting closer. I *needed* to talk to my brother, to get...I don't know. *Closure*." She wiped her eyes. "I asked him to send me a sign that I was doing okay in this life without him so I could go through his stuff and move forward. I thought the letter was the sign, that he was telling me to tie up loose ends."

Tank embraced her again, furious with himself for not taking the day off. "I should have been with you today. I'm sorry."

"You've done enough. You're always here for me."

"Obviously not always." He leaned back so he could see her face. "I don't know if that letter was a sign or not, but I think these are." He handed her the pictures.

"I'm too upset to look at pictures."

"Trust me, Lee. You want to see them."

Her brow furrowed, but she opened the envelope and pulled out the pictures. The picture of the frog on the pocket of her waders when they were standing in the bog was on top. It brought a smile that didn't quite reach her eyes. She looked at the next picture and the next, her eyes flicking up to his in disbelief, fresh tears spilling down her cheeks. "The *frog*..." She began lining up the pictures on the bed. "It's in almost every picture."

"I know. I've hiked that area dozens of times with my family, and I don't remember ever seeing frogs. I called Zeke, and he said he's never seen one there, either."

"This is River's sign!" She swiped at her tears. "I *told* you I felt him around us that day. He *was* with us every step of the way." She leaned over the pictures, pointing to the frog in each of them—just behind Junie's right foot and beside Rosie as she crouched to pick a leaf up off the ground. On Junie's backpack as she leaned over to look at something through her magnifying glass. "How did I miss *that* one?" Leah laughed softly and pointed to another picture. "Look. He's on a branch behind you in this one."

"I've been thinking about it all day. I can't figure out how none of us noticed it." He touched her hand. "Lee, promise me that the next time you're having a rough day, you'll call me."

Her expression warmed. "You can't just drop everything for me all the time. You've done way too much already."

"I absolutely *can*, and there's no such thing as too much."

"*Tank...*" She shook her head. "I got the hospital bill today, and it had already been paid in full. I called their billing department, and I *know* you paid it. As much as I appreciate your help, I don't want you to feel like you have to take care of us. We'll manage. We always do."

"I didn't pay the bill because I had to. I did it because you and those baby girls of yours, of *River's*, had already lost enough. I made those arrangements right after the accident, *before* you and those little darlin's became the very air that I breathe. And I'd do it all over again because I know how hard it is to pick up the pieces after losing someone you love."

"But it was a lot of money."

"Who gives a damn? Money is just dirty paper that allows us to have a roof over our heads and food in our bellies." He lifted her onto his lap and gathered her hair over her shoulder. "Don't you see, Lee? The ways I've helped just allow you to focus on more important things."

"But—"

He silenced her with a kiss. "No buts. You and the girls are what matter most. You're everything that's good and right in this world, and it's about time you got a break."

"You're too good to me. You *have* to stop paying for things."

"And you, my sexy girl, need to accept the fact that that's not going to happen."

"Oh, *Benson*." She put her arms around him and rested her forehead against his. "What am I going to do with you?"

"I can think of a few dozen things." He cocked a grin.

She laughed softly, pressing her lips to his. "I don't know what I did to deserve you."

"It's the other way around, darlin'." He kissed her again, wiped her tears, and looked around the room. "How far did you get in here?"

"The bag from the hospital." She picked up the bag and withdrew a silver necklace. "I saw River's necklace and thought about how Junie used to hold it as she fell asleep and play with it when he carried her, like she does with yours. I was thinking of saving it for her, but I don't want Rosie to feel left out."

"We could have it made into two bracelets and give it to them when they're older."

"That's a great idea." She teared up again and rested her head on his shoulder with a tired sigh. "Can we do this another night? I know I can get through it with you by my side, but right now all I want is to be in your arms...and maybe revisit what you said about us being the very air you breathe." She lifted her head with a sweet smile. "What would your biker friends say if they knew you were so romantic?"

"Who gives a fuck? I'm not romancing them."

As he lowered his mouth toward hers, she whispered, "I feel the same about you, Benson Wicked."

Chapter Eighteen

AFTER NEARLY THREE weeks of brisk fall days and chilly nights, the Cape was blessed with an unseasonably warm weekend for Trunk or Treat. Leah hadn't minded the cooler weather. Her burly man kept her toasty warm with steamy kisses, cozy cuddles, and endless nights of luxurious lovemaking. But a warmer evening was perfect for the costume she had in mind for tonight. Although, it wasn't really a costume. She was surprising Tank and dressing up as a biker chick. Madigan was helping her get ready, and she'd come armed with a slew of outfits from the Leather and Lace clothing line, which was designed by her cousin Dixie's husband, Jace Stone. The bed was littered with the sexiest clothes Leah had ever seen. Nearly every piece was black, silver, gray, or red and made of leather and lace, with silver zippers, buckles, and leather straps or ties that revealed far too much skin for Leah's comfort zone.

Leah turned to the side in front of the bedroom mirror, admiring herself in a pair of Madigan's skintight black leather leggings and one of her black-and-red bustiers. She had never worn anything like it before, but she had to admit, even though it was too revealing, she felt sexy in it. She hardly ever wore much makeup, but Madigan had helped her do her face, using a desert taupe lipstick that added just a touch of color and eyeliner that made the green flecks in her eyes look even brighter.

Tank would eat her up in that outfit. He was at the club helping set up for Trunk or Treat while Leah and the girls got ready. Leah probably shouldn't have waited so long to pick out an outfit, but life had been busy the last few weeks. She and Tank had finally finished cleaning out River's room. They'd donated most of his things, but Leah couldn't part with some of his favorite shirts and hoodies, and she'd saved keepsakes for her and the girls. It had been even more difficult and had taken longer than she'd thought it would, but she was glad they'd done it. It definitely helped her take another step forward, which she'd needed in order to return to work. The first day back at the Salty Hog had been the worst, worrying about the girls at Corinne's and trying to get back into the swing of things. Coming home with the girls after work the first day had also been difficult. Leah had been inundated with memories of River greeting her after work, and it had felt like all those baby steps forward had created a vast emptiness between her and River. She had cried a lot that night, but Tank had known just what to do. He'd run her a hot bath, and as he'd done so many times before, he'd put on the videos of River playing his guitar, held her, and talked with her about how she felt. That was the best part. She didn't have to hold anything in with Tank.

Thankfully, it had gotten a little easier every day.

She pulled the bustier higher on her boobs and then lower to cover her stomach, but it was like playing tug-of-war with skintight leather. A cacophony of giggles erupted in the living room, and she peeked out.

Madigan was sitting on the couch with Junie on her lap,

pulling the paper off one of the temporary tattoos she had brought for the girls and Leah to use. Junie couldn't wait to show Gia her leopard-print bell-bottoms, black sweatshirt with a leopard-print heart on it, and the special black boots with a silver buckle that Tank had surprised her with last week. She'd worn the boots from morning until bedtime every day. Rosie stood behind the couch in her green and yellow Tinker Bell outfit with a yellow turtleneck underneath, tapping Madigan's shoulders with the sparkling light-up fairy wand Tank had gone to great lengths to find for her. Leah had made Rosie a jacket/cape with holes for her wings to wear over her costume tonight so as not to *wuin her wings*.

"Leah, your gossip girls are telling me how much they love sleeping in their big bed at Papa Tank's house."

They'd had so much fun at his house during the living-room camping trip, they'd stayed at his place a few more times, and the girls slept in one of the double beds in his extra bedrooms.

"We eat s'mea*ah*s!" Rosie shouted.

"S'm*owahs*," Junie corrected her.

Rosie grinned, nodding. "S'mea*ah*s!"

"I bet Mama and Papa Tank saved some of that gooey chocolate for a midnight snack." Madigan waggled her brows at Leah.

"Mawshmallows, too," Junie exclaimed.

Madigan gave Leah a knowing look and laughed.

Leah felt her cheeks burn. She and the girls had been spending more time with Tank's extended family, which included their closest friends. Leah had gotten close with Madigan and the rest of the Girl Squad. She loved having girlfriends again. Not just for herself, but for the girls, too. Junie and Rosie ate up the attention everyone gave them, and they especially enjoyed their visits with Grandpa Mike. They were all so happy, sometimes Leah fell into a well of guilt, because River had missed out on this wonderful circle of friends, but Tank was always there to catch her and to remind her that River was still with them, even on days when he felt really far away.

"Thank you for the ink, Tattoo Girl." Madigan patted Junie's bottom. "Now, hop off so I can help your mama get ready before Papa Tank gets here."

The girls ran for their toys, and Madigan strutted into the bedroom looking hotter than Scarlett Johansson in her *Black Widow* outfit. She ran her eyes up and down Leah. "Holy shitake mushrooms, woman. My cousin is going to lose his freaking mind over you."

Leah wrinkled her nose and picked up another top. "I'm not wearing this one."

"Why *not*? You're smokin' in that bustier."

"I feel like a banana, and you know he'll just want to *peel* me."

They both laughed.

"Isn't that the point?" Madigan plopped onto the bed, leaning back on her palms, and crossed her legs, watching Leah.

"The *point* is to show him that I like everything about him and his world, not to show his world all my naughty bits."

"Oh, please, girl. Guys like showing off their women. They're like cavemen." She lowered her voice and spoke in a deep voice. *"Me man. Fuck woman. You no touch."*

Leah laughed. "Let's hope Tank doesn't say that."

"He's crazy about you, and after what he did at the Salty Hog the other day, he doesn't need to *say* a word. Gossip spreads faster than mono at a teenage party around here.

Everyone knows you guys are together."

"There weren't *that* many people there." Tank had plowed into the restaurant Wednesday afternoon like a man on a mission. He'd carried an enormous vase of red roses in one arm and hauled Leah against him with his other, kissing her breathless. He'd flashed one of his wolfish grins, handed her the gorgeous flowers, and said, *I hope today is better than yesterday for you, darlin'.* Then he'd taken a seat at the bar, like he hadn't left her weak-kneed and light-headed. Ginger had looked over and said, *Guess that takes care of that.* Leah had never been given flowers before, and she sure as heck had never been claimed by a man like that. She didn't care if what he'd done was a little Neanderthalish, because it was so very *Tank*, and Madigan was right. She was head-over-heels crazy about him.

Madigan sat up and said, "Aunt Ginger had lunch with my mom and their friends, and they burned up the gossip lines like wildfire. And of course my mom called her sister-in-law, Red Whiskey, Dixie's mom, in Maryland, and Red told Dixie, who called Maverick to see if it was true. By now I'm sure even our relatives in Colorado have heard the news."

Leah could do little more than gape at her. "Okay. *Wow.* That's a lot."

"Is it time to go see Connie and Gingy yet?" Junie yelled from the other room.

"Not yet. Soon." Leah glanced into the living room. Junie was lying on the floor coloring, and Rosie was tapping Junie's butt with her wand.

"Connie," Madigan said with a laugh. "I love that so much."

"I tried to get them to call him Conroy, and they'd do it for like a minute; then it's all *Connie* this and *Connie* that. The girls even tried to get me to put *Connie* and *Gingy* on the memory blanket I'm making for Tank's parents."

"You know they're so in love with your girls, they could call them Tweedledee and Tweedledum and they'd be fine with it." Madigan fished through the clothes and held up a button-down lace blouse with three-quarter sleeves and a plunging scalloped neckline. "This is you. It's classy and super sexy. It even has built-in flesh-colored cups so your nips don't show. Try it on."

Leah slipped off the bustier and put on the shirt, tucking it into the low-waisted leather leggings. It clung to her, but it felt soft, not itchy and not tight like the leather tops did.

"Oh *yeah*, baby. That's it. That's the one." Madigan jumped to her feet and pulled Leah over to the mirror. "Look at how gorgeous you are."

Leah felt feminine and pretty in it. The low neckline some-how made her bushy hair look not quite so overpowering, and the way the shirt and leggings hugged her body, she actually looked like she *had* curves. "I've never worn anything with such a low neckline. Will yours or Tank's parents think it's inappro-priate?"

Madigan rolled her eyes. "They're bikers. They believe women should be confident and sexy, and you look *classy*, not slutty. Tank is going to lose his mind. But we'd better hurry and get the finishing touches done."

"Finishing touches?" She looked at her curiously.

Madigan reached into her bag and waved something in the air. "I had special temporary tattoos made just for you. Let's put them on in the bathroom."

"Would you mind if I let Junie put one on me?" Leah asked. "She's so excited about being a tattooist."

"She can put the rose tattoo on your arm." Madigan took Leah's hand and dragged her out of the bedroom. "But the others are going where nobody but *Tanky* will see them."

Junie loved putting the tattoo on Leah's arm, and both girls helped Madigan put T-A-N-K'S on the fingers of Leah's right hand and G-I-R-L on the left. Madigan put a heart with TANK + LEAH inside it on the swell of Leah's right breast. As Madigan finished applying the last tattoo, Leah heard Tank come through the front door and the girls running to him. Leah's pulse sprinted.

Madigan raised her brows. "Ready?"

"What if he doesn't like me dressed like this?"

Madigan snort-laughed. "Yeah, *right*. C'mon, hottie. Go strut your stuff."

As Leah walked into the living room, Tank's eyes locked on her. His jaw tightened as he put the girls down and dragged a hungry gaze slowly down the length of her, leaving an inferno in its wake. He closed the distance between them as the girls jumped up and down around them, and his chest hit Leah's, backing her up toward the bedroom. He gritted out, "Girls, go play. I want to talk to your mama in private."

His voice was so thick with desire Leah could swim in it. "*Mads* is here." She couldn't contain her breathlessness at the intensity of his stare. She'd never seen him look so greedy for her, and oh, how she loved it!

"I'm leaving," Madigan said with a giggle. "I'm taking the girls to see Connie and Gingy!"

The girls squealed with delight as Madigan collected their jackets and said, "I'm leaving my keys on the counter and taking your car."

"Just *go*," Tank commanded, his eyes drilling into Leah.

Anticipation stacked up inside Leah as Madigan hurried the girls out the door. The second they were gone, Tank's mouth claimed hers, pushing her backward into the bedroom. He feasted on her, fumbling with the buttons on her shirt. He cursed against her lips, grabbed her shirt with both hands and tore it right down the center.

"That was Madigan's!" she said as he tossed it aside.

"I'll buy her seventeen new ones." He recaptured her mouth as he stripped her bare. His eyes blazed down her body, lingering on the PROPERTY OF TANK WICKED tattoo just above her sex. *"Damn right you are."* He took her in another punishingly intense kiss, so demanding and confident, she wanted *more*—more of his heat, more of his greed, more of *him*. She palmed him through his jeans, earning a guttural groan, and he lifted her onto the dresser, leaving her panting as he grabbed a condom from the box in the nightstand drawer, quickly stripped naked, and sheathed himself. He wedged his big body between her legs, tugged her to the edge of the dresser, and drove into her in one hard thrust. He cursed, and she cried out with sheer pleasure, clawing at his back. He palmed her ass with one rough hand, holding tight as he pounded into her, his every thrust setting off turbulent explosions. There were no sweet words, no finesse, just raw passion drawing greedy sounds and hungry gasps. He tore his mouth away, lifted her legs, and held them open wider as their heated bodies slammed together. Prickling sensations climbed up her limbs, simmering, burning, *boiling* in her inner thighs. *"Dontstop,"* she pleaded as she grabbed the edges of the dresser for leverage.

His hips pistoned harder, taking her deeper, bringing a hurricane of sensations as overpowering and magnificent as the emotions they brought. His body flexed, hard and delicious, and with his next thrust, her head fell back and they both cried out. He released her legs, hauling her against him, and sealed his teeth over her neck, sending fiery heat blazing over her flesh as they careened into a world of rapture all their own.

When they finally, blissfully collapsed into each other's arms, she panted out, "I guess it's safe to say you like my costume."

He laughed against her neck, and then he took her face in his hands the way she'd come to love, his dark eyes moving slowly over her face. "It's not the clothes." He kissed her softly. "It's you, Lee. I spent today talking about you with family and friends, *missing* you. I'm so in love with you, when I saw you walk into the room, I just couldn't hold back."

Happiness bubbled up inside her as he lowered his lips to hers, breathing air into her lungs and even more love into her heart. But when their lips parted, the truth came out. "I love you, too, Benson," she whispered. "I love you so much it scares me. I lost the last two men I loved."

"Don't be scared, baby." He kissed her again. "Nothing is going to take me away from you." He embraced her, whispering, "I promise."

She clung to that promise as he stepped back to take off the condom, believing like the girls did that his promise could never be broken.

He hooked one arm around her, lifting her off the dresser. "Shower time, sexy girl. I got you dirty, and I'm going to have fun cleaning you up."

She loved showering together when they could sneak one in before the girls got up in the morning, or after they were asleep. She headed for the bathroom, and he slapped her ass. She let out a surprised gasp and spun around. "What the heck, *Tank*?"

Confusion rose in his eyes. "I thought you wanted that."

"Why on earth would you think I *wanted* to be spanked?"

she snapped, although she wasn't altogether sure she didn't.

"The tattoo above your ass that says TANK'S TO SPANK."

"What?" She stalked into the bathroom. "Madigan told me she was putting hearts there!"

He threw out the condom and pulled her into his arms, nuzzling against her neck. "Does that mean no spanking?"

"Yes. No. I don't *know."*

His eyes flamed. "Then I look forward to finding out."

A little thrill shot through her. She turned around and looked in the bathroom mirror at the tattoo above her ass. "I'm going to kick your cousin's butt."

"I'm going to thank her." He turned on the shower. "Let's go, hot stuff."

"Wait. I have to pin my hair up."

"No you don't." He took her hand, leading her into the shower. "I'll be the only one on their knees."

"WE'RE BEYOND LATE, and Madigan will never lend me clothes again." Leah wiggled into the sexiest leather bustier Tank had ever seen. "I can't believe you ripped her shirt, which was a major turn-on, by the way. I like seeing you go all Hulk like that."

"Want to see me do it again? Because if you wear that leather fuck-me top you've got on, it's going to look like Peter Pan is hiding Pinocchio under the bottom of his shirt." He pulled his tights away from his balls. "Between these ball huggers and this tight fucking shirt, I can barely breathe."

"You could have told Rosie no."

"No, I couldn't. You saw her little face."

"Thank you for loving them." She went up on her toes and kissed him, then pushed her feet into a pair of Madigan's boots and grabbed Madigan's leather jacket.

"You look great, Lee. If you like Mad's clothes, why don't we go shopping and get you some of your own."

"These clothes are just for tonight, for *you*. I'm more comfortable in my normal clothes. I might not be a real biker girl, but I'm *your* girl, and I wanted you to know that I love that part of your life, too."

He swept her into his arms and kissed her. "I love you in your normal clothes almost as much as I love you naked. How about the boots and jacket? Do you want some of your own?"

"I love both, but I can buy those for myself at some point."

He made a mental note to call Dixie tomorrow and order Leah the cutest damn jacket and boots they had.

She waggled her finger. "Get that look off your face. You are *not* buying me anything. We need to hurry. Are you ready?"

"Yeah, this shirt is fucking uncomfortable." He rolled his shoulders back, expanding his chest with a deep inhalation, and the front of the costume ripped down to his sternum.

Leah gasped.

He blew out a breath. "That's *so* much better."

"Now you really are my Hulk. Let's go."

BY THE TIME they arrived at the clubhouse, Trunk or Treat was in full swing. Halloween music competed with the sounds of children making their way around the perimeter of the roped-off parking lot, collecting candy from the decked-out vehicles and taking part in sack races, coloring contests, and other fun activities and adults mingling. A few of the Dark Knights had dressed up as clowns and were making animal balloons for the kids in the grass. As Tank and Leah climbed off Madigan's Vespa, he spotted Gunner and Steph dressed up as Woody and Jessie from *Toy Story* and scanned the grounds for the girls.

"Do you see them?" Leah asked.

He took her hand and pointed across the lawn to his parents talking with his grandfather, Preacher, and Reba while watching the girls trying to keep balloons up in the air with a group of kids. His parents and aunt and uncle were dressed up as Fred, Daphne, Shaggy, and Velma from *Scooby-Doo*, and Grandpa Mike was wearing his Dracula cape. He probably had his fangs in, too. Rosie ran to Grandpa Mike and grabbed his hand, pulling him into the group of kids. He tapped a balloon, and Rosie jumped up and down.

"Oh, Tank. Look how happy they are," Leah said.

"Dude," Gunner said loudly as he and Steph headed over. "You're driving Madigan's pink Vespa?" He laughed. "Wearing tights? I can't even...It's too easy." He cracked up. "But *whoa*, Leah. Look at you channeling your inner biker babe. I'm lovin' it."

"Thanks." Leah leaned into Tank's side the way she did when she was nervous, and he put his arm around her.

"You look incredible," Steph said. "Whatever you do, *don't* ask Gunner what he's dressed up as."

"He's Woody, isn't he?" Leah asked, and Tank knew what was coming.

"That I am." Gunner draped an arm around Steph. "You

know you love my wood."

"In your dreams." Steph shrugged out from under his arm and touched the front of Tank's shirt. "What happened here? Did Leah get handsy with you?"

He hugged Leah against his side. "Something like that."

"He's my Incredible Hulk." She quickly added, "But don't tell Rosie."

As they walked toward the grass, Gunner said, "Rosie and Junie are having a blast. They walked around checking out everyone's costumes, and the guys made a big deal out of Junie giving them tattoos and Rosie casting spells on them with her wand."

"Gia raved about Junie's outfit, and Rosie was thrilled to see Zeke dressed up as Boo." Steph pointed to Zeke talking with Baz and Evie, dressed up as the Joker and Harley Quinn, and Maverick and Chloe, who were the Mad Hatter and Alice from *Alice in Wonderland.* "Zeke has great legs, doesn't he?"

"They're nothing compared to mine." Gunner smirked.

"I've seen your legs, and you don't see me writing home about them," Steph teased.

"Look out, world! Leah *Biker Chick* Yates is in the house!" Marly shouted from across the field. She and Madigan strutted toward them, whistling and making catcalls. Blaine was right behind them, dressed as Captain Jack Sparrow, checking out Marly's ass in her red-and-black flamenco dancer costume.

"Ohmygod." Leah melted into Tank's side.

"Better get used to it, babe," Tank said. "You look hot."

She tipped her beautiful face up. "I love your friends. It's worth the embarrassment."

"We're your friends, too," Steph said.

"That's right, babe." Tank lowered his lips to Leah's.

"Get a room!" Madigan hollered.

"I think they already did." Blaine motioned to Tank's shirt.

"Wait...?" Madigan opened the leather jacket Leah had borrowed from her. "What happened to the lace shirt you were wearing?"

"About that..." Leah wrinkled her nose, her cheeks pinking up.

Tank took Leah's hand. "I'll buy you a new one, Mads."

Madigan burst into laughter. "Oh, *Tanky*, you are *so* far gone for our girl." She patted Tank's face, and he snarled at her. "I couldn't be happier for both of you."

"Good, then tell me you'll babysit next weekend so I can take my gorgeous girl out on a proper date and wine and dine her."

"What?" Surprise rose in Leah's eyes.

He winked, earning one of her radiant smiles.

"Absolutely! We'll figure out a time. But right now we're stealing Leah." Madigan took Leah's other hand, tugging her away.

"Wait," Leah said. "I need to check on the girls."

"I've got 'em, babe." As her fingers slipped from Tank's, he said, "Go have fun. Love you."

Happiness glittered in Leah's eyes. Madigan, Marly, and Steph gave him approving looks as Evie and Chloe joined them, and they all huddled together, giggling as they walked away.

Gunner sidled up to Tank. "Bro, you just said you *love* her."

Tank slid a knowing gaze to Blaine, who was nodding supportively, and set a serious stare on Gunner. "I drove here on a pink Vespa, wearing tights and a fucking Peter Pan outfit. That should answer any questions you might have."

"Actually, it raised more questions," Gunner teased. "I'm

happy for you, man. I was just surprised to hear it, you know? Your heart's been locked up tighter than a virgin in a chastity belt for so long, I wasn't sure you'd ever let anyone get close."

"Life's short, Gun. You need to live it *now*, because who the fuck knows what tomorrow will bring."

He headed over to check on Junie and Rosie with Blaine and Gunner by his side. Baz and their cousins caught up with them, giving each other a hard time. His parents waved, and the girls ran toward him, yelling, "Papa Tank!" As he swept Junie and Rosie into his arms and they rattled on about everything they'd done so far and everything they wanted to do, a future Tank had never imagined bloomed before his eyes. He could see it all so clearly, Leah walking down an aisle, the girls tossing rose petals, more babies, more laughter, more hikes and Halloweens, barbecues and bike rides.

The girls were still rattling on about their candy, their little faces bright as the sun.

"Hey," he said firmly, and they quieted. "I love you guys."

"Love you, Papa Tank!" they said in unison, and went right back to talking about their night.

His parents exchanged knowing glances with Reba and Preacher.

His grandfather clapped a hand on his shoulder, baring his Dracula fangs as he said, "How're you doing, son?"

This was what Tank wanted for Leah and the girls. To be surrounded by so many people who loved them—women to mother them and men to protect them—that there was no beginning or end to their family, so they never felt alone again.

"I've never been better."

Chapter Nineteen

LEAH RELAYED THE lunch specials to the older couple sitting by the windows at the Salty Hog and took their order, trying to shake the feeling of dread that had been with her since early that morning. "I'll be back with your drinks."

She made her way to the computer to input the order, which would be relayed to the kitchen. The bar was packed for a Saturday afternoon outside of tourist season. Being that busy was usually enough to sidetrack Leah from just about anything, but that heavy feeling still clung to her like a second skin. She didn't understand it, but she'd driven extra slowly on the way to Corinne's to drop off the girls, and to work, and she'd asked Tank to be careful, too. But it wasn't like he had anything dangerous going on. He was working at the tattoo shop, not the firehouse. Today of all days she should be on cloud nine, not fretting about who knew what.

Tonight Tank was taking her out to dinner and a movie on their *proper date*, a term she still found funny. Life with two toddlers was anything but proper. It was loud and chaotic. Even their love life took some creativity. Getting dressed after sex wasn't optional. It was necessary. Leah longed to spend one entire night naked in Tank's arms and wake up to a lazy morning in bed, loving each other until they were so tired, they fell asleep in each other's arms, instead of speeding through a morning to-do list for herself and the girls, or rushing out the door with a backpack full of anything the girls might need while she was at work and worrying she'd forgotten something. Tonight she'd get that chance. She and Tank were staying at his place tonight, and Madigan was staying overnight with the girls at the cottage.

Starr sidled up to her. "Did you find out where Tank's taking you to dinner?"

"No. All he'll tell me is that it's not in Harwich. Do you think the green dress I showed you is okay? What if he's taking me someplace fancy?"

"You'll look gorgeous in anything. Besides, Tank loves you in jeans and no makeup. Stop worrying about clothes and think about being on a real date with your man."

"That's *all* I've thought about for the last week, and Tank is as ridiculously excited as I am. Every time he walks past me, he whispers something like, *Only three more nights*, or, *I can't wait to get my girl alone.*"

"You're so lucky."

"Is it bad that I don't feel guilty about leaving the girls tonight? They adore Madigan, and they're as excited for a slumber party with her as she is with them."

"Guilty? *Please.* I'd pay a zillion dollars to have a guy like Tank love me enough to set that up," Starr said. "It's really romantic. I'm beyond jealous, and I want all the details of your kid-free night!"

"Dinner? *Yes.* Movie? *Sure.* Sexy times? *Still off-limits.*" Leah hadn't shared any of the intimate details of her and Tank's sex life with anyone. They were their secrets, and she liked it that way.

Starr rolled her eyes and switched places with Leah so she could input an order into the computer. "I'll make you a deal. You can keep your sexy secrets if you'll read the December book club selection and go to the meeting with me. It'll be fun. I promise."

"I don't need a deal to keep my secrets, but I would *love* to do the book club with you." She'd been so busy working on the memory blanket for Tank's parents, she hadn't picked up a book in weeks. But it was worth it. She loved piecing together Ashley's life. It made her feel even closer to Tank's family.

Starr wiggled her shoulders. "Well, look at you, all confident with your sexy secrets."

They both laughed.

"Drinks up, Leah," Ginger called from behind the bar.

"Gotta run." Leah went to pick up the drinks.

As Ginger slid the drinks across the bar, Conroy came out of the office and said, "Leah, you're just the person I was looking for. I'm working on the rest of this month's schedule. I was going to give you Thanksgiving eve off, but I've learned my lesson about assuming where women are concerned."

"I taught you well." Ginger leaned over the bar to kiss Conroy.

Tank's family was celebrating Thanksgiving with Reba and Preacher's family, and Ginger had invited Leah and the girls to join her and Reba, Chloe, and Madigan the day before to make pies.

"If it's not a problem, I would like to have that day off. Tank's taking a shift at the firehouse, and I already mentioned baking with Ginger to the girls. But if you need me, I'll make it work."

"It's not a problem at all. The girls need their *Gingy* time," Conroy reassured her. "It's going to be a great holiday this year."

"I hope Tank doesn't miss it. He said he doesn't know what time he'll get off on Thanksgiving, but he hoped no later than four or five."

"He's taken that shift every year since he started volunteering and he's never missed Thanksgiving yet," Ginger said. "He usually rolls in around three or four."

"It's good to be young. I couldn't stay up all night and make it through a rowdy Thanksgiving without a nap." Conroy put his hand on Leah's back. "I'm glad you won't be alone this holiday. Your first Thanksgiving without River might be tougher on you and the girls than you think."

"Tank and I have been talking about that. I know it'll be hard, but I couldn't ask for more supportive people to spend the holiday with." Leah put the drinks on the tray and felt her phone vibrate in her pocket. She pulled it out, and Corinne's name flashed on the screen. The pit of Leah's stomach sank. "Ginger, it's Corinne. She wouldn't call unless it was important. Do you mind if I take it quickly?"

"It's fine. Take it in the office." Ginger reached for the tray. "I'll bring the drinks to your customers."

"Thanks, sorry." Leah hurried to the office and answered as she slipped through the door. "Hi, Corinne. What's wrong?"

"It's Junie. She's got a fever of one hundred point five."

"Oh no. She seemed fine this morning. How's Rosie?"

"She's not sick, but she's worried about Junie. She's such a little caregiver, rubbing Junie's head and singing to her about making up games and watching the sunrise."

"Idle Town." She felt a tug in her chest, remembering how

River would do exactly what Rosie was doing for them when they were sick. She touched her locket. "I'll be there as quickly as I can."

Leah ended the call, worried about Junie but breathing a sigh of relief. Junie's fever explained the heaviness Leah had felt all day. She went to talk with Conroy and Ginger, whose only concern was for Junie. On the way to pick up the girls, Leah stopped to get Pedialyte and Pedialyte freezer pops.

When they got home, she gave Junie medicine and set her up on the couch with her blanket, Mine, and a sippy cup of Pedialyte to watch a movie. Rosie gathered their stuffed animals and put them all around Junie so she could be close to her *fwends*. Once everyone was settled, Leah texted Tank to let him know that Junie had a fever. She hated the idea of canceling their date, but she knew he'd understand.

Her phone rang seconds later. "How bad is her fever? Did you call the doctor?" he asked without saying hello.

"Her fever isn't bad. It's one hundred point five. I called the doctor before I picked up the girls in case he wanted me to bring her in, but he didn't think I needed to. He said to give her Motrin and keep her hydrated. If her fever doesn't go down, then I'll bring her in."

"Okay. What about Rosie?"

"She's fine."

"And you, babe? Are you doing okay? This must be why you had that funny feeling this morning."

"I think it is. I'm sorry about canceling our date, and I feel bad for the girls. They were looking forward to playing with Mads tonight. Do you want to call Mads, or should I?"

"I'll call her. You have enough on your plate. Can I talk to Twitch?"

Her heart warmed. "Of course. Hold on." She sat on the couch between the girls. "Junie, Tank would like to say hi."

"Me?" Rosie asked.

"You can talk to him, too, if he has time. He's at work." Leah handed Junie the phone.

"Hi, Papa Tank," Junie said groggily. Her brows knitted as she listened. "Okay." She paused. "I will." She went quiet again. "Pwomise." She was quiet again. "Love you, too. Can you talk to Wosie?" She handed the phone to Rosie.

"Hi, Papa Tank!" Rosie listened and nodded.

"You have to use your words, Rosie," Leah reminded her. "He can't hear you nod."

"He *talkin'*." Rosie listened, nodded, nodded some more, before exclaiming, "Love you!" and tossing the phone on Leah's lap as she scooted off the couch to go play.

Leah picked up the phone. "Are you still there?"

"Yeah. Poor Twitch. She promised she'd drink as much as she could. I'm booked until six, but I can try to cancel the last two appointments."

"You don't have to do that. We're fine. We've been through fevers before."

"Okay, but call me if she gets worse. I love you."

"I will. I love you, too." When she ended the call, she cuddled up with Junie.

"Can Maddie still come for a slumber pawty?" Junie asked.

"No, baby. We don't want to get her sick. But you can have a slumber party with her another night."

A little while later, Madigan called to speak to the girls, promising to find another time for their slumber party, Ginger called to see how Junie was doing, and a little while later, Tank called to check in. Leah sat on the couch with Junie's head in her lap, thinking about how lucky they were. Her father and River would have done anything to be loved as wholly and completely as Tank and his family loved her and the girls.

TANK PULLED UP to the cottage feeling like he'd been gone for a year. He'd texted Leah throughout the day for updates and knew Junie had napped, and the medicine was keeping her fever down, which was a relief. He grabbed the stuffed animals he'd bought for the girls and the bouquet of roses for Leah and headed up the walk. Rosie waved through the window, and he saw Junie lying on the couch, bundled up under her memory blanket with Mine tucked beneath her arm. His heart ached for his little munchkin.

He pushed open the door and heard music playing softly. Leah was lighting candles on the bar, and the coffee table was set for four with plates, cups, and utensils. In the middle of each plate was a paper with MENU written across it and the girls' crayon scribbles and drawings.

"Datin'datin'datin'!" Rosie cheered, jumping up and down in front of him.

"Hey, Cheeky." He wasn't sure what she was saying, but he was sure glad to see her little smile. "Did you take good care of your sister today?"

Rosie nodded, wide-eyed.

"Good girl. Then this is for you." He handed her the stuffed bird, and she hugged it and thanked him. He winked at Leah as he went to Junie, and she lifted her arms, clutching Mine in one hand. He picked her up, and she rested her head on his shoulder, wrapping her little hand around his necklace. "I'm sorry you don't feel well, baby. I thought this might help." He handed her the stuffed frog he'd gotten for her, and she tucked it under her arm.

"Thank you," she said sleepily.

He went to Leah, the candles reflecting in her beautiful eyes. "I missed you, darlin'." He kissed her, and as he handed her the roses, he saw plates of pancakes, eggs, and bacon in the kitchen. "What's all this?"

Rosie jumped around them. "We datin'! We datin'!"

An adorable smile crawled across Leah's face. "I know it's not a proper date, but it's about as proper as we're going to get. The girls made menus, and Rosie and I made dinner. I thought we could all eat at the coffee table, so Junie could lie down on the couch."

His heart swelled. He slid his arm around her, pulling her close. "The hell with proper. A date with my three beautiful girls is the best date of all."

Chapter Twenty

NOVEMBER PAINTED THE Cape with silver skies and lingering bursts of fall colors in the shrubs and trees. It was much colder than North Carolina, but that didn't keep Leah and Tank from enjoying the great outdoors with the girls. They'd bundled up and taken the girls out for walks at the creek and along the shore, and last week they'd gotten together with Tank's family and his cousins for a big family breakfast before taking the girls to Woods Hole for the day with Ginger and Conroy. Leah had loved the aquarium as much as the girls had. They'd strolled through the town, enjoyed lunch at a café, and had found even more common ground when Leah had mentioned how much River would have loved that area and Conroy had said it was one of Ashley's favorite places.

Leah parked among a long line of cars, trucks, and motorcycles in front of Ginger and Conroy's house early afternoon on Thanksgiving Day. She filled with the same warm feelings she had when she'd come home to her father's house and to River and the girls. Her father's house and her little rented cottage couldn't be more different from Conroy and Ginger's rambling two-story, with its wide front porch, enormous yard, and two-car garage, but that feeling of coming home to family was the same. She cut the engine and touched her locket, missing her father and brother.

"There's Connie and Preachy!" Junie yelled, jerking Leah from her thoughts.

Conroy and Preacher were coming around the side of the house. Conroy waved as Leah went to help the girls out of their carseats. She waved to the two men who looked as different as Tank and his brothers did. Conroy with his silver hair brushing the collar of his gray sweater, playful smile, and easygoing stride, and Preacher's slicked-back salt-and-pepper hair and beard, serious eyes, black leather jacket, and tough-guy swagger. But like with Tank and his brothers, the ways in which they were similar were hard to miss. Conroy and Preacher were warm, loving, and protective, and it was no wonder they'd raised such wonderful sons and daughters. Leah didn't need to have known Ashley to include her in that thought. She'd learned so much about Tank's sister over the past few months, she had no doubt she'd missed out by not knowing her.

"*Out!*" Rosie rocked in her carseat as Leah helped Junie out.

"I'm coming." Leah set Junie on her feet, and Junie sprinted toward Conroy and Preacher. Even though Tank's family didn't dress up for Thanksgiving, the girls had wanted to wear their favorite fall-colored jumper dresses, Junie with her black boots and Rosie with her ballet flats. After Halloween, Junie had wanted more fake tattoos, and Tank had drawn a number of them for her and had them made so she could put them on whenever she wanted. Beneath her dress, RIVER was stenciled across her rib cage, just like Papa Tank, and Rosie had a tattoo of a frog on her hand.

The second Rosie's feet hit the ground, she ran after Junie, who'd been scooped up by Preacher. Conroy lifted Rosie over his head the way Tank often did, and she giggled up a storm. Leah grabbed the gift bag with Ginger and Conroy's memory blanket in it and closed the car door. She'd been itching to give it to Ginger last night when she and the girls had come over to bake, but Conroy had been at church, and she'd wanted him to be there when she gave it to them.

"Happy Thanksgiving, darlin'." Conroy kissed Leah's cheek. "You look as beautiful as ever."

"Thank you." She'd worn skinny jeans, Tank's favorite green sweater of hers, which he said brought out the green in her eyes, and the leather boots from Jace's Leather and Lace line that Tank had surprised her with after Halloween. She couldn't afford to buy him gifts, but she knew how much he loved the little things they did. He'd hung up drawings the girls had made for him and pictures of all of them at his house and in his tattoo shop for all the world to see, and he was always raving to Ginger and Con about her and the girls. But nothing spoke louder than the way he lit up when he walked in the door after work and swept them into his arms.

"Get on in here." Preacher pulled Leah in for a one-armed hug. "How're you doing, sweetheart?"

She knew he was really asking how she was doing without River, and she appreciated that. She'd been afraid of forgetting River and being the only one who had concrete memories of him, but Tank had changed that. He'd helped her bring so much of River—his pictures, personality, likes, dislikes, strengths, jokes, and so much more—to their lives, she felt like his entire family had known him, too.

"I'm doing well. Thanks for asking."

Rosie patted Conroy's cheek and said, "That your blanky!"

"*Wosie*, it was supposed to be a *supwise*," Junie reminded her, and the guys laughed.

"Is that the memory blanket my wife is jealous over?" Preacher asked as they headed inside.

"It *is*." Leah loved that Reba wanted one, too. What Preacher didn't know was that Tank and Ginger were helping her gather keepsakes so she could make Reba and Preacher one for Christmas.

The kitchen door opened, and Maverick ran out with Blaine and Gunner on his heels, the three of them laughing and shouting as they chased each other around the yard. Zander came flying around the side of the house and tackled Blaine at the same time Zeke sauntered out the front door. He gave Leah and the girls a casual wave and took off running, jumping on Gunner's back. Then all of them were rolling around on the ground, laughing hysterically and shouting funny remarks.

"I play?" Rosie asked.

"Sorry, baby girl," Preacher said. "Not when they're playing this rough."

"They're not going to hurt each other, are they?" Leah asked.

Conroy laughed. "If they do, they do."

"Too bad Papa Tank isn't here," Preacher said. "You haven't seen anything until you've seen him pick up one of them in each hand like rag dolls."

Leah loved that image. "He'll be here soon, I hope."

"Baz and Grandpa Mike should be here soon, too," Conroy said. "Baz had an emergency at the clinic. He's picking up Mike on his way over."

Preacher looked at Conroy and arched a brow, nodding toward the guys wrestling in the yard.

"Seriously?" Conroy chuckled.

Preacher shrugged. "If not now, when?"

"Good point." They put the girls down, and Conroy said, "Girls, stay with your mama and watch how real men win a wrestling match."

As the men strode onto the lawn, they straightened their spines, their chests expanding, arms arcing out from their bodies, ready to conquer anything. Their sons exchanged challenging glances, and then chaos erupted, and they became a tangle of burly bodies, laughing and wrestling. One would jump to their feet, and the others would take him down. Leah and the girls cracked up. She took pictures and texted them to Tank.

Madigan and Chloe came out onto the porch. As Leah and the girls went to join them, Madigan yelled, "I'm not taking anyone to the emergency room!"

Reba and Ginger came out the front door, shaking their heads.

"Again?" Ginger said.

Reba shouted, "*Robert Wicked!* You're supposed to be an adult."

The guys stopped wrestling, and all eyes turned toward the porch.

"Oh *crap*," Madigan said under her breath.

The guys charged toward them, hollering, "Get 'em!"

Leah and the girls shrieked as Blaine threw Leah over his shoulder, Zeke picked up Junie, and Gunner grabbed Rosie. Conroy and Preacher grabbed their wives, who threatened them as they did it, and Maverick hoisted Chloe over his shoulder like a sack of potatoes. Zander did the same to Madigan. Everyone cracked up as the guys ran around the yard with them.

When they finally put them down, Leah was laughing so hard her stomach hurt. The girls jumped and cheered, wanting to play more, and Zeke and Zander were happy to comply with piggyback rides. Maverick pulled Chloe into his arms and kissed her, Conroy reached for Ginger's hand, and Preacher and Reba were hugging. There was so much love in that front yard, Leah knew their loved ones could feel it in the heavens above.

Blaine put his arm around her and held up his phone, taking a selfie of them. "I'm sending that smile to Tank. Welcome to the family, sweetheart."

He and the guys took Junie and Rosie out back to play, and Leah went inside with the others. The house smelled like roasting turkey and family.

Leah gave Conroy and Ginger their gift before they got busy and watched them open it. "If it's not what you had in mind, I can change it. Tank told me that Ashley's favorite colors were purple and yellow, so I used it where I could."

"Oh, Leah," Ginger said as she and Conroy admired the blanket. "This is gorgeous."

Leah had included as many keepsakes as she could, like Ashley's cheerleading skirt, the knit hat she'd worn home from the hospital as an infant, a pink bib with an *A* embroidered on it, Ginger's favorite onesie, and part of Tank's Red Hot Chili Peppers shirt that Ashley had slept in. She'd also sewn in one of Ashley's frilly toddler dresses, her Christmas stocking, a key chain with her name on it that she'd been given when she'd learned to drive, part of her baby blanket, and Ashley's lucky socks with a hole in the toe that she'd refused to throw out.

"A nest," Conroy said softly, running his fingers over the nest Leah had made out of one of Ashley's tiny corduroy jumpers from when she was young. Leah had embroidered Ginger's and Conroy's names onto two large purple hearts and sewn them into the nest with four smaller yellow hearts in front of them, with their children's names on them. The larger hearts looked like they were embracing the smaller ones.

"Ashley would have loved that," Madigan said.

Tears spilled from Ginger's eyes as she touched the photos of Ashley that had been printed onto the fabric: Ashley with all three of her brothers, Ashley with Conroy and Ginger, Ashley and Grandpa Mike, and a few others with Reba and Preacher's family. Conroy put his arm around Ginger, his own eyes dampening. Reba and Madigan leaned against Preacher, as emotional as Ginger and Conroy. Even Chloe and Leah got teary-eyed.

"These pictures," Ginger said. "How did you get this done?"

"Zeke found a company that makes pictures into fabric," Leah explained. "I have the information if you want to get more."

"What *more* could we want?" Conroy said. "You've given us a way to celebrate our little girl. How can we ever thank you?"

Tears slid down Leah's cheeks. "You just did."

After several teary embraces, too much gushing, a little laughter, and a lot of love, Conroy draped the blanket over the back of the couch in the living room, and he and Preacher went to put the leaves in the dining room table, while Leah and the ladies went into the kitchen to finish getting dinner ready.

Ginger turned on the radio and got everyone started on making the sides. Madigan and Ginger sang to the music, and the rest of them hummed along. Leah peeled potatoes on the counter next to the sink and peeked outside at the girls playing while the guys horsed around.

"Leah, would you make a wedding blanket for me and Justin?" Chloe asked.

"I would love to."

"How about a *baby* blanket?" Reba urged.

"Way to pressure her, Mom," Madigan teased. "They don't even have a wedding date yet."

"Actually, we do." Chloe placed another marshmallow on the sweet potato casserole, grinning like a peacock. "Justin got a call yesterday about a cancellation at Ocean Edge Resort, and he booked the second weekend in January. Now all we have to do is pull it all together."

They all talked at once, congratulating Chloe and offering to help plan the wedding.

"It'll be fun to plan with everyone," Chloe said. "I meant what I said before, Leah. If you'll make us a wedding blanket, I'll make you a memory book with your pictures."

"Sure. That sounds great," Leah said.

Reba whispered, *"Baby blanket."*

"Mom." Madigan shook her head.

Reba looked up from the vegetables she was cutting. "I'm just inquiring about blankets. I'm not saying they need to have babies right away."

"Yeah, right," Ginger said sarcastically.

"You can borrow Juju and Rosie anytime you'd like, Reba," Leah offered.

Reba winked. "I will take you up on that offer, sweetheart. Your girls have got everyone wrapped around their little fingers. Junie reminds me so much of Preacher, and of Tank when he was young."

"Doesn't she?" Ginger said. "I swear Leah and Tank were meant to be."

Leah tucked away that happy thought.

Over the next hour, sides went into the oven and simmered on the stove, the guys came in and out of the kitchen, stealing tastes and being shooed out the door. Everyone told stories of past holidays, and Leah loved sharing stories about her dad and River.

"Leah, can you pull the green bean casserole out of the lower oven, please?" Ginger asked from across the kitchen.

"Sure. Everything smells so good." Leah grabbed potholders, and as she pulled the casserole out of the oven, heat spread over her face, and all at once she felt a crushing sensation in her chest and back. The air rushed from her lungs, and Tank's desperate voice slammed into her—*Lee*—echoing in her head. The dish fell from her shaking hands, shattering at her feet as she stumbled backward, clutching at her chest, gasping for air that wouldn't come, choking out, *"Tank"* with every ragged inhalation. Someone put an arm around her, shouting about calling for help as she struggled for breath. Leah eked out another *"Tank"* with a painful inhalation. Tears flooded down her cheeks as his anguished face appeared before her eyes, and a pained, *I'm sorry, Lee*, hit her with the impact of a freight train, and she finally gulped air into her lungs and shouted, *"Nooo!"* She fought against whoever was holding her. *"Tank.* I need to get to Tank!"

The kitchen door flew open, and Baz charged in with Grandpa Mike on his heels, their faces sheet-white. Leah broke free and ran to them, grabbing Baz's shirt and pleading through her sobs. "Where is he? What happened?"

"Sean called. They were checking out a gas leak and they cleared the building, but some kid said his sister was still inside. Tank ran back in. He got the girl, but there was an explosion as he carried her out. They were thrown across the parking lot, and he used his body to shield her from the impact. His head hit the pavement. It's bad. He was unresponsive when they rushed him to the hospital."

"No!" Leah screamed as Tank's voice pummeled her—*I'm sorry, Lee. I love you*—and she collapsed into darkness.

Chapter Twenty-One

LEAH SAT ON a chair in the waiting room between Ginger and Madigan, eyes closed, pressing her forehead to her clasped hands, throwing out silent prayers as she rocked forward and back. Grandpa Mike, Chloe, and Zeke had stayed with the girls, but everyone else, and it looked like half the town, was at the hospital waiting for news about Tank. He'd been knocked unconscious and suffered a subdural hematoma and broken ribs. The doctor had said terrifying things Leah wished she hadn't heard—*deadliest of head injuries, compressed brain tissue, possibility of brain injury.* He'd been in surgery for hours, and every minute felt like a lifetime.

She hadn't heard Tank's voice since she'd passed out, and that petrified her. She clutched her locket. *River, Dad, if you can hear me, please don't let Tank join you. Send him back to us. We need him.* Tears flowed down her cheeks, and she whispered to Tank as she rocked, "Come back to me. You have to be okay. *Please.*"

Conroy knelt before her. "Are you okay, sweetheart?"

Leah looked at him through the blur of tears. "I didn't want to get close to him because I wanted to protect the girls."

"Protect them from Tank? I don't understand."

"Protect them from *this*. From *loving* him. We might *lose* him. He *promised* he'd never leave us." It wasn't a rational thing to say. She knew that, and Conroy was the last person she should be crying to, because his pain was surely equal to hers, but she could no sooner hold it in than she could have kept from falling in love with Tank in the first place.

Conroy took her hands in his. "He's going to be okay. He made you a promise, and Wickeds *always* keep their promises."

Sobs burst from Leah's lungs, and she fell into his arms, clinging to him as she cried. She felt Ginger's hand on her back, and then Conroy said, "Tank has *never* had more of a reason to fight for anything in his life. He's going to pull through this."

Leah nodded, wanting—needing—to believe it.

Conroy's face was a mask of strength, like almost everyone else's in there. The room was bursting with love and support from family and friends consoling them, but she saw the underlying fear in their eyes. It was hard to escape that kind of terror, especially when she had it in her heart. She could barely breathe. She kept hearing Tank's desperate voice in her head, telling her he was sorry and he loved her. And she couldn't stop thinking about the last time she'd been at that hospital when she'd lost River.

She couldn't survive losing Tank.

Preacher came over and put a hand on Conroy's shoulder. "I just talked to Zeke. The girls are doing fine. They ate, and they're watching a movie with Grandpa Mike."

"Thank you." Leah didn't remember passing out, but when she'd come to, Ginger had said the girls hadn't seen or heard anything. Conroy told them that Tank had a boo-boo and they were going to check on him and would be back a little later. He'd said Junie had asked questions, but Leah had been too anxious to process the details. She knew the girls were safe, and that's what mattered.

"Can I get you anything, sweetheart?" Preacher asked.

Tank, please was on the tip of Leah's tongue, but she kept that to herself and said, "No, thank you."

Time moved in slow motion, every second more painful than the last. When the doctor finally came through the doors, Leah rushed to her feet, wanting to run to him, but she hung back, allowing Ginger and Conroy the space they needed.

"You're with us, baby girl." Ginger reached for Leah's hand.

More tears fell as they crossed the room to speak with the doctor, whose expression gave nothing away. *Please let him be okay. Please. I'll do anything.*

Ginger hugged her against her side. "Whatever he says, we'll deal with it together."

Leah nodded, unable to respond.

The doctor said, "The surgery went well."

A sob escaped before Leah could stop it, and she covered her mouth. Tears streamed down Ginger's face, and Conroy's eyes were damp as he put his arms around both of them.

"The next few hours will be critical," the doctor explained. "It was a small bleed and he's responding well, but we'll watch him closely to make sure there are no further issues—"

"Further issues?" Conroy asked.

Leah held her breath.

"There's a possibility of seizures, memory loss, dizziness, numbness. As I said, we'll watch him closely," the doctor explained.

Every word hit Leah like a knife to the heart, but any of that was better than losing Tank forever.

"Can we see him?" Ginger asked.

"Yes, soon," the doctor answered. "He's going to be a bit out of it from the anesthesia, and he was asking for *Lee*."

Another sob escaped, and Conroy hugged Leah against his side.

The doctor looked at Leah. "I take it that's you?"

She nodded, swiping at her tears. "Yes."

"He'll be happy to see you. The nurse will be out to get you soon."

As the doctor walked away, Conroy pulled Ginger and Leah into his arms. "He's going to be okay." The relief in his voice was as strong as his embrace. "Our boy's going to be okay."

The wait to see Tank was excruciating. Conroy relayed the good news to everyone, and the room erupted in a cacophony of hugs, tears, and joyous comments. Preacher called Zeke to give him and the others the good news, and when the nurse came to get Conroy and Ginger, they invited Leah to go with them to see Tank.

As they followed the nurse down the hall, Conroy said, "Leah, people look different in hospital beds. You should prepare yourself. I know you can't imagine this, but he might look frailer and vulnerable."

"I don't care what he looks like. I *need* to see him."

"We know, honey, and you will." Ginger stopped at the entrance to the recovery room. "But Con's right. You're used to seeing the Tank who can conquer anything, and it might be a shock to see him hooked up to IVs and machines."

"I appreciate you trying to prepare me, but it's a *gift* that he's alive and that we get to see him at all." Tears spilled down her cheeks. "I would have given anything to see my father or River looking vulnerable in a hospital bed instead of burying them six feet under."

"Oh, honey. You're absolutely right." Ginger embraced her.

Leah followed them into the room, her heart aching as she stood back, giving Conroy and Ginger a moment with Tank. His eyes were closed, his head bandaged. His right cheek was scraped up, and there was another bandage on his cheekbone, which must have been from the stitches the nurse had mentioned. The sheet rose and fell with his even breaths, each one making her heart beat steadier, and her tears fall harder.

Ginger leaned in to kiss his face, and his eyes fluttered open. Leah put her hand over her mouth to silence her sobs as Ginger said, "You gave us quite a scare, honey. But you're going to be okay."

"Lee?" Tank said groggily.

"She's right here." Conroy motioned for Leah to join them.

Leah went to the other side of the bed and put her hand over Tank's. He curled his fingers around hers, sadness rising in his eyes. She opened her mouth to say so many things—*Thank God you're alive. I love you. I was terrified we'd lose you. I can't handle you risking your life for everyone else when we need you so badly*—but emotions stole her voice, and instead, she leaned in to give him a gentle hug, just needing to be closer. His arm circled her, and she felt his heart beating against hers and was hit with the memory of him leaning over River, refusing to give up on the young man he'd never met. Her breath caught, and she knew she was wrong about not being able to handle his risking his life for others. There was *nothing* she couldn't handle for the man she loved.

Tank held her there against his chest, whispering, "I'm so sorry."

"No," she choked out, and gazed into his heavy-lidded eyes. "Don't apologize. You saved someone's little girl. I was terrified

we'd lose you, but I'm so proud of you for saving another mom from that devastating loss. That outweighs everything else."

"I need to stop volunteering," he said sleepily. "I have you and the girls to think about now."

"And you always *do* think about us. We both know you can't stop being you. You're always going to be the guy who wants to save everyone, and I'm always going to be the girl who worries about losing you."

"Lee—"

"*Shh.* I have a plan."

His lips tipped up. "Please tell me there's a gnarly biker in that plan."

God, she loved him. Fresh tears welled in her eyes. "There is, but you don't have to change to keep us together. The girls and I love you just as you are, Benson, and we're going to spend every free minute showing you just how much."

He ran his hand down her back. "You already do that."

"I mean for the rest of our lives."

"I'm groggy, so bear with me." A new light shimmered in his eyes. "Are you asking me to marry you?"

"*What?* No. I…*Ohmygosh.*" Her cheeks burned, and she looked at his parents' hopeful expressions. "I didn't mean—"

"Lee." He touched her face, bringing her eyes back to him. "I was joking, but I have a plan, too. You're right. I'll always be the guy who helps others. It's in my blood." He paused, as if it took all his strength to speak. "But I'm not a career firefighter. I'm a biker and a tattoo artist. And more importantly, I'm your man and Papa Tank to the girls." He quieted again, swallowing hard, his words tugging at her. "You and the girls are everything to me, and now I know the truth." He glanced at his parents and then back to Leah. "I could save the world and it won't bring Ashley back, but it could take me away from the people I love most." He pulled her closer. "I can help people without leaving you frantic with worry every month while I'm at the firehouse. I'm done volunteering."

"But—"

He pulled her lips to his, silencing her with a kiss. "Let me finish." He breathed heavier. "Baby, if we get a hundred years together, it won't be enough, and I don't want to waste a second of it." He cradled her face between his hands, gazing into her eyes. "Marry me, Lee. Let me be Papa Tank for real. We'll have more babies with wild hair who ask too many questions and ruin dates, only to make them twice as good as they would have been."

Emotions whirled between them, bringing more tears as his love wrapped around her as powerfully and all-consuming as the man himself.

He whispered against her lips, "Please say yes before I fall back to sleep and miss it."

She was vaguely aware of his mother sniffling and his father whispering as all of the emotions she'd been trying to hold back rushed out. "Nothing would make me happier than marrying you." She pressed her lips to his, her salty tears slipping between them. "I love you, Benson Wicked. I love you so much I can no longer picture my life with the girls without seeing you right there by our sides."

He whispered, "And now you'll never have to," and sealed his promise with a kiss.

Chapter Twenty-Two

CHRISTMAS MORNING ARRIVED with two excited little girls bounding into Tank and Leah's bed at six o'clock in the morning. The last month had brought a whirlwind of changes beyond the end to Tank volunteering at the firehouse, which he didn't regret one bit. He wanted to be around for every noisy Christmas, every school graduation, the girls' first dates, their weddings, Leah's first gray hair, and every other moment of their hopefully very long lives. When they'd told the girls they were getting married, they had been over the moon. Tank had offered to buy the cottage that Leah had rented so she'd never lose the memories she had there and he'd never forget how she'd responded. *It's not the four walls that keep memories alive. It's us. We celebrated River's life at your house. It makes sense that we celebrate our love there, too.*

His brothers and cousins had moved the girls and Leah in while Tank was still in the hospital, and there was no greater feeling than coming back to *their* home. They hung up River's guitar and Leah's family photos in the living room, and the refrigerator was constantly covered with the girls' drawings. The house had never felt so much like a *home*. They'd had a revolving front door for weeks as family and friends visited. Gia had threatened to kick Tank's ass if he even thought about coming back to work before the doctor cleared him, but she'd have to get in line behind Leah and the rest of his family.

His recovery had forced him to slow down and let Leah take care of him. That had taken some getting used to, but he was finally starting to feel like himself again. Only *better*. He was happier, more complete, and utterly in love with his three girls.

For the last hour, Junie and Rosie had ripped through their presents, hollering "Look!" every three seconds, while he and Leah cut open plastic packages that he swore were sealed to survive nuclear wars. He'd never seen so many twist ties on dolls and toys. The floor was littered with toys, crayons, wrapping paper, and coloring books.

Rosie was setting up plastic food in the toy kitchen that Santa had brought her, while Junie put tattoos on her dolls in the toy tattoo shop Santa had left under the tree. Leah sat beside Tank on the couch, adorable in flannel pajama pants and a T-shirt, taking pictures. Her gorgeous curls were still tangled from his hands in her hair last night when they'd made love.

He pulled her closer and kissed her cheek. "What's going through your mind, beautiful?"

"How happy we are. How special yesterday was."

He'd had the foundation for River's headstone put in a few weeks before the ground had frozen, and yesterday he'd taken Leah to the cemetery and surprised her with the headstone he'd had Maverick make. Maverick had etched into the headstone an image of River sitting by the girls' bed playing the guitar, with Rosie beside him, and Junie lying behind him, holding his necklace, with SON – BROTHER – FATHER – FRIEND – HERO beneath it.

Leah took a selfie of the two of them and set down the

phone, snuggling closer. "The only thing that would make this morning more perfect is if it snowed and we had a white Christmas."

"It's gonna snow," Junie said as she played.

"You think so, Twitch?" Tank asked.

Junie nodded, her springy curls bouncing around her face. "Wiver told me."

"He did?" Leah asked, running her fingers along Tank's arm.

"Uh-huh," Junie said absently.

"Well, I hope he's right," Leah said.

Junie had been making up stories about talking with River lately. He and Leah had talked about having her meet with a therapist, and they'd decided to give it some time and see where it went.

Rosie snatched Leah's gift from under the tree and toddled over in her red-and-green footed pajamas. "This mine?"

"No, Cheeky. That one's Mama's."

Leah's brow wrinkled. "I thought yesterday was my gift."

"I guess you thought wrong."

"Open!" Rosie climbed onto Tank's lap.

"What have you done, Mr. Spoiler?" Leah looked at him with that sweet, bashful, and excited expression he adored as she unwrapped the gift, revealing the black ring box.

Rosie bounced on Tank's leg. "Openopenopen!"

Leah opened the box, and tears sprang to her beautiful eyes, her mouth falling open. Tank took the box from her and withdrew the white-gold ring with diamonds snaking up one side of the thin band and curling around a white South Sea pearl.

"A *wing*!" Rosie exclaimed, and Junie came to check it out.

"Pwetty! Is that your mawwied wing?" Junie asked.

"This is called an engagement ring. I'll buy Mama another ring that she'll wear with this one when we get married." Tank took Leah's left hand in his and slid the ring onto her finger. "I'm sorry it took so long, but I wanted to get you a ring that was as unique and beautiful as you are. You and the girls changed my life, darlin'. I look forward to teaching the girls to ride bikes and climb trees, teaching Junie to tattoo and Rosie to do whatever she's into. But most of all, I look forward to a lifetime of loving you."

"Oh, *Tank*. I look forward to all of that, too." She threw her arms around him. "I love you, and I love the ring."

"We mawwied!" Rosie cheered.

Tank pulled them all into a group hug, laughing. "Maybe now we can start thinking about a wedding date."

"I think that's a good idea." Leah reached under the couch and pulled out a gift-wrapped box.

"More pwesents!" Rosie climbed off Tank's lap, and she and Junie dropped to their bellies, looking under the couch.

"There's no more presents. Just this one for Papa Tank." Leah handed the gift to him. "You changed our lives, too, in so many incredible ways."

Rosie jumped up and down. "Openopenopen!"

Junie patted Tank's leg as he unwrapped the gift.

He opened the box and choked up at the sight of a gorgeous memory blanket. He looked at Leah in disbelief as he took it out of the box and held it up. Rosie ran away giggling, and Junie ran after her. Tank couldn't believe his eyes. Across the top of the blanket were the words WE LOVE YOU, PAPA TANK, and beneath that, Leah had made a tree with leaves from his family's memorabilia, including one of his shirts Ashley used to sleep in, part of the skirt from Rosie's Halloween costume, and the heart from the sweatshirt Junie had worn on Halloween. The tree trunk was decorated with a quilted heart with BENSON + LEAH FOREVER inside, pancakes with PINCAKES written across them, earrings with EARHOLES embroidered beneath them, and the words BOOBY WINGS along the edge. His heart bubbled over at pictures the girls had drawn for him that she'd had made into fabric and fabric photographs of the four of them. She'd embroidered their names and the names of each of his family members on leaves, including River. Along the bottom of the blanket were THE DARK KNIGHTS AT BAYSIDE, a motorcycle, and LOVE, LOYALTY, AND RESPECT FOR ALL.

He looked at the woman who had brought him back to the world of the living and had a hard time speaking past the lump in his throat. "Lee, this is amazing. When did you have time to do this without me seeing it?"

"If I told you that, I'd never be able to surprise you again. I plan to make a lot more of them for the family and friends, so it's good to know my stealth sewing skills aren't lacking."

He pulled her into a kiss. "I love you so damn much. This is the best present I've ever been given."

"I think you might want to reserve judgment on that until you open the other gift in the box."

He moved the blanket and peered into the empty box. "There's nothing in there."

Rosie looked up from where she was hunched over a coloring book. "This pen bwoken."

Leah's eyes widened, and laughter burst from her lungs. "Rosie, that's Tank's gift! Can you give it to him, please?"

"You got me a broken pen?"

Leah wrinkled her nose. "Not exactly."

Rosie ran over and tossed it in his lap. "Bwoken!" She ran off to play with Junie.

Tank turned over the plastic thing Rosie had given him, and his jaw dropped at the word PREGNANT in the little clear window. "Preg...We're...A *baby*?"

Leah was nodding, grinning from ear to ear.

"Baby! We're having a *baby*!" He hauled her into his lap and kissed her. "A baby. How?"

She giggled, whispering, "Remember the shower the morning after Junie was sick, when you said you'd be careful and then we got carried away?"

His body flamed with the memory of that incredible morning. "Best shower ever." He pressed his lips to hers and put his hand over her belly. "Should I say I'm sorry?"

"No, Benson. Just say you'll marry me before I get a big belly."

"Darlin', I'd marry you today if I could. I'm so fucking happy." He lowered his lips to hers, whispering, "We're having a baby."

Rosie yelled, "It snowin'!"

"Wiver was wight!" Junie cheered, and the girls ran around the room, yelling, *"Wiver was wight! Wiver was wight!"*

"I told you River would always be with us no matter where we lived." Leah wound her arms around him and said, "What do you think, Mr. Wicked? Can you handle sleepless nights and messy diapers on top of this craziness?"

He pushed his hands into her hair and kissed her. "Haven't you learned yet? There's nothing Papa Tank can't handle."

Are you ready for Dwayne Wicked?

He's the ultimate player. She wants him to teach her the game in hopes of scoring his cousin. Practices heat up as roommates become teammates and rules are broken. Let the wicked fun begin…

Have you met the Dark Knights at Peaceful Harbor?

The Dark Knights at Peaceful Harbor novels are waiting for you at all book retailers, starting with TRU BLUE.

There's nothing Truman Gritt won't do to protect his family—including spending years in jail for a crime he didn't commit. When he's finally released, the life he knew is turned upside down by his mother's overdose, and Truman steps in to raise the children she's left behind. Truman's hard, he's secretive, and he's trying to save a brother who's even more broken than he is. He's never needed help in his life, and when beautiful Gemma Wright tries to step in, he's less than accepting. But Gemma has a way of slithering into people's lives, and eventually she pierces through his ironclad heart. When Truman's dark past collides with his future, his loyalties will be tested, and he'll be faced with his toughest decision yet.

Fall in love on the sandy shores of Cape Cod Bay

Follow Chloe's sister, Serena, and each of their friends to their happily ever afters in the Bayside Summers series, starting with Bayside Desires.

Desiree Cleary is tricked into spending the summer with her badass half sister and a misbehaving dog. What could go wrong? Did I mention the sparks flying every time she sees her hunky, pushy neighbor, Rick Savage? Yeah, there's that...

Fall in love with the Steeles on Silver Island

Settle in on the sandy shores of Silver Island, home to coffee shops, boat races, midnight rendezvous, and the sexy, sharp-witted Steeles.

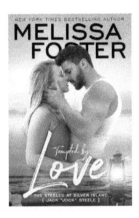

Enjoy a heart-meltingly beautiful and toe-curlingly sexy romance in *Tempted by Love*, an emotionally riveting story about a man who has lost it all and carries a torturous secret, a divorced single mother who has everything to lose, and the little girl who helps them heal.

Love Melissa's Writing?

Discover more of the magic behind *New York Times* bestselling and award-winning author Melissa Foster. The Wickeds are just one of the many family series in the Love in Bloom big-family romance collection, featuring fiercely loyal heroes, sassy, sexy heroines, and stories that go above and beyond your expectations! See the collection here:

www.MelissaFoster.com/love-bloom-series

Free first-in-series ebooks, downloadable series checklists, reading orders, and more can be found on Melissa's Reader Goodies page:

www.MelissaFoster.com/Reader-Goodies

More Books By Melissa Foster

LOVE IN BLOOM SERIES

SNOW SISTERS
Sisters in Love
Sisters in Bloom
Sisters in White

THE BRADENS at Weston
Lovers at Heart, Reimagined
Destined for Love
Friendship on Fire
Sea of Love
Bursting with Love
Hearts at Play

THE BRADENS at Trusty
Taken by Love
Fated for Love
Romancing My Love
Flirting with Love
Dreaming of Love
Crashing into Love

THE BRADENS at Peaceful Harbor
Healed by Love
Surrender My Love
River of Love
Crushing on Love
Whisper of Love
Thrill of Love

THE BRADENS & MONTGOMERYS at Pleasant Hill – Oak Falls
Embracing Her Heart
Anything for Love
Trails of Love

Wild, Crazy Hearts
Making You Mine
Searching for Love
Hot for Love
Sweet, Sexy Heart

THE BRADEN NOVELLAS
Promise My Love
Our New Love
Daring Her Love
Story of Love
Love at Last
A Very Braden Christmas

THE REMINGTONS
Game of Love
Stroke of Love
Flames of Love
Slope of Love
Read, Write, Love
Touched by Love

SEASIDE SUMMERS
Seaside Dreams
Seaside Hearts
Seaside Sunsets
Seaside Secrets
Seaside Nights
Seaside Embrace
Seaside Lovers
Seaside Whispers
Seaside Serenade

BAYSIDE SUMMERS
Bayside Desires
Bayside Passions
Bayside Heat

Bayside Escape
Bayside Romance
Bayside Fantasies

THE STEELES AT SILVER ISLAND

Tempted by Love
My True Love
Always Her Love
Enticing Her Love
Caught by Love
Wild Island Love

THE RYDERS

Seized by Love
Claimed by Love
Chased by Love
Rescued by Love
Swept Into Love

THE WHISKEYS: DARK KNIGHTS AT PEACEFUL HARBOR

Tru Blue
Truly, Madly, Whiskey
Driving Whiskey Wild
Wicked Whiskey Love
Mad About Moon
Taming My Whiskey
The Gritty Truth
In for a Penny
Running on Diesel

SUGAR LAKE

The Real Thing
Only for You
Love Like Ours
Finding My Girl

HARMONY POINTE
Call Her Mine
This is Love
She Loves Me

THE WICKEDS: DARK KNIGHTS AT BAYSIDE
A Little Bit Wicked
The Wicked Aftermath

SILVER HARBOR
Maybe We Will

WILD BOYS AFTER DARK
Logan
Heath
Jackson
Cooper

BAD BOYS AFTER DARK
Mick
Dylan
Carson
Brett

<u>HARBORSIDE NIGHTS SERIES</u>
Includes characters from the Love in Bloom series
Catching Cassidy
Discovering Delilah
Tempting Tristan

More Books by Melissa
Chasing Amanda (mystery/suspense)
Come Back to Me (mystery/suspense)
Have No Shame (historical fiction/romance)
Love, Lies & Mystery (3-book bundle)
Megan's Way (literary fiction)
Traces of Kara (psychological thriller)
Where Petals Fall (suspense)

Acknowledgments

I hope you loved Tank, Leah, and their families as much as I do. When I was writing this story, I adored River so much, I came very close to putting him in a coma and letting him live in the end. But Leah's story came to me as it is written, and after years of waiting to give it a voice, I couldn't bring myself to change it, just as we cannot change real life. Heaps of gratitude go out to Lisa Filipe for agreeing with me and pushing me to stay true to my heart when so many others were trying to sway me in a different, easier direction.

I'm looking forward to writing love stories for all of our Wicked world family and friends. In the meantime, if you want to know more about Justin and Chloe, pick up A LITTLE BIT WICK-ED, the first book in this series. My original Dark Knights series, The Whiskeys: Dark Knights at Peaceful Harbor, is also available for your binge-reading pleasure.

If this is your first introduction to my work, please note that all of my books can be read as stand-alone novels, without cliffhangers. Characters appear in other family series, so you never miss out on an engagement, wedding, or birth. You can find information about the Love in Bloom series and my books here: www.MelissaFoster.com/melissas-books

I offer several free first-in-series ebooks. You can find them here: www.MelissaFoster.com/LIBFree

I chat with fans often in my fan club on Facebook. If you haven't joined my fan club yet, please do! www.Facebook.com/groups/MelissaFosterFans

Follow my author page on Facebook for fun giveaways and updates of what's going on in our fictional boyfriends' worlds. www.Facebook.com/MelissaFosterAuthor

If you prefer sweet romance, with no explicit scenes or graphic language, please try the Sweet with Heat series written under my pen name, Addison Cole. You'll find the same great love stories with toned-down heat levels.

Many thanks to my incredible editorial team, Kristen Weber and Penina Lopez, my meticulous proofreaders, Elaini Caruso, Juliette Hill, Lynn Mullan, and Justinn Harrison, and my last set of eyes, Lee Fisher. My work would not shine without all of your help.

Lastly, I'd like to thank my son Jake, musician name, Blue Foster, for introducing me to Conan Gray's music and for always having my back. Continue shining bright, my boy. I love you and look forward to watching you make your mark in this wild and wonderful world.

Meet Melissa

www.MelissaFoster.com

Melissa Foster is a *New York Times, Wall Street Journal,* and *USA Today* bestselling and award-winning author. Her books have been recommended by *USA Today's* book blog, *Hagerstown* magazine, *The Patriot,* and several other print venues. Melissa has painted and donated several murals to the Hospital for Sick Children in Washington, DC.

Visit Melissa on her website or chat with her on social media. Melissa enjoys discussing her books with book clubs and reader groups and welcomes an invitation to your event. Melissa's books are available through most online retailers in paperback and digital formats.

Melissa also writes sweet romance under the pen name Addison Cole.

Free family trees and more:
www.MelissaFoster.com/Reader-Goodies

CPSIA information can be obtained
at www.ICGtesting.com
Printed in the USA
LVHW040248240222
711841LV00005B/108